THE MISSISSIPPI BUBBLE

How the Star of Good Fortune Rose and Set and Rose Again,
by a Woman's Grace, for One John Law of Lauriston

A Novel by

EMERSON HOUGH

1ˢᵗ WORLD
LIBRARY
Literary Society

The Mississippi Bubble

Emerson Hough

© 1st World Library, 2007
PO Box 2211
Fairfield, IA 52556
www.1stworldlibrary.com
First Edition

LCCN: 2007927776

Softcover ISBN: 978-1-4218-4531-9
Hardcover ISBN: 978-1-4218-4447-3
eBook ISBN: 978-1-4218-4615-6

Purchase *"The Mississippi Bubble"*
as a traditional bound book at:
www.1stWorldLibrary.com/purchase.asp?ISBN=978-1-4218-4531-9

1st World Library is a literary, educational organization
dedicated to:

- Creating a free internet library of downloadable ebooks

- Hosting writing competitions and offering book publishing
scholarships.

Interested in more 1st World Library books? contact:
literacy@1stworldlibrary.com
Check us out at: www.1stworldlibrary.com

1ˢᵗ World Library Literary Society

Giving Back to the World

"If you want to work on the core problem, it's early school literacy."

- James Barksdale, former CEO of Netscape

"No skill is more crucial to the future of a child, or to a democratic and prosperous society, than literacy."

- Los Angeles Times

"Literacy... means far more than learning how to read and write... The aim is to transmit... knowledge and promote social participation."

- UNESCO

"Literacy is not a luxury, it is a right and a responsibility. If our world is to meet the challenges of the twenty-first century we must harness the energy and creativity of all our citizens."

- President Bill Clinton

"Parents should be encouraged to read to their children, and teachers should be equipped with all available techniques for teaching literacy, so the varying needs and capacities of individual kids can be taken into account."

- Hugh Mackay

TO

L.C.H.

CONTENTS

BOOK I

BOOK II

BOOK III

BOOK I

ENGLAND

CHAPTER I

THE RETURNED TRAVELER

"Gentlemen, this is America!"

The speaker cast upon the cloth-covered table a singular object, whose like none of those present had ever seen. They gathered about and bent over it curiously.

"This is that America," the speaker repeated. "Here you have it, barbaric, wonderful, abounding!"

With sudden gesture he swept his hand among the gold coin that lay on the gaming table. He thrust into the mouth of the object before him a handful of louis d'or and English sovereigns. "There is your America," said he. "It runs over with gold. No man may tell its richness. Its beauty you can not imagine."

"Faith," said Sir Arthur Pembroke, bending over the table with glass in eye, "if the ladies of that land have feet for this sort of shoon, methinks we might well emigrate. Take you the money of it. For me, I would see the dame could wear such shoe as this."

One after another this company of young Englishmen, hard

players, hard drinkers, gathered about the table and bent over to examine the little shoe. It was an Indian moccasin, cut after the fashion of the Abenakis, from the skin of the wild buck, fashioned large and full for the spread of the foot, covered deep with the stained quills of the porcupine, and dotted here and there with the precious beads which, to the maker, had more worth than any gold. A little flap came up for cover to the ankle, and a thong fell from its upper edge. It was the ancient foot-covering of the red race of America, made for the slight but effectual protection of the foot, while giving perfect freedom to the tread of the wearer. Light, dainty and graceful, its size was much less than that of the average woman's shoe of that time and place.

"Bah! Pembroke," said Castleton, pushing up the shade above his eyes till it rested on his forehead, "'tis a child's shoe."

"Not so," said the first speaker. "I give you my word 'tis the moccasin of my sweetheart, a princess in her own right, who waits my coming on the Ottawa. And so far from the shoe being too small, I say as a gentleman that she not only wore it so, but in addition used somewhat of grass therein in place of hose."

The earnestness of this speech in no wise prevented the peal of laughter that followed.

"There you have it, Pembroke," cried Castleton. "Would you move to a land where princesses use hay for hosiery?"

"'Tis curious done," said Pembroke, musingly, "none the less."

"And done by her own hand," said the owner of the shoe, with a certain proprietary pride.

Again the laughter broke out. "Do your princesses engage in shoemaking?" asked a third gamester as he pushed into the ring. "Sure it must be a rare land. Prithee, what doth the king in handicraft? Doth he take to saddlery, or, perhaps, smithing?"

"Have done thy jests, Wilson," cried Pembroke. "Mayhap there is somewhat to be learned here of this New World and of our dear cousins, the French. Go on, tell us, Monsieur du Mesne—as I think you call yourself, sir?—tell us more of your new country of ice and snow, of princesses and little shoes."

The original speaker went a bit sullen, what with his wine and the jests of his companions. "I'll tell ye naught," said he. "Go see for yourselves, by leave of Louis."

"Come now," said Pembroke, conciliatingly. "We'll all admit our ignorance. 'Tis little we know of our own province of Virginia, save that Virginia is a land of poverty and tobacco. Wealth—faith, if ye have wealth in your end of the continent, 'tis time we English fought ye for it."

"Methinks you English are having enough to do here close at home," sneered Du Mesne. "I have heard somewhat of Steinkirk, and how ye ran from the half-dressed gentlemen of France."

Dark looks followed this bold speech, which cut but too closely to the quick of English pride. Pembroke quelled the incipient outcry with calmer speech.

"Peace, friends," said he. "'Tis not arms we argue here, after all. We are but students at the feet of Monsieur du Mesne, who hath returned from foreign parts. Prithee, sir, tell us more."

"Tell ye more—and if I did, would ye believe it? What if I tell ye of great rivers far to the west of the Ottawa; of races as strange to my princess's people as we are to them; of streams whose sands run in gold, where diamonds and sapphires are to be picked up as ye like? If I told ye, would ye believe?"

The martial hearts and adventurous souls of the circle about him began to show in the heightened color and closer crowding of the young men to the table. Silence fell upon the group.

"Ye know nothing, in this old rotten world, of what there is yet to be found in America," cried Du Mesne. "For myself, I have been no farther than the great falls of the Ontoneagrea—a mere trifle of a cataract, gentlemen, into which ye might pitch your tallest English cathedral and sink it beyond its pinnacle with ease. Yet I have spoke with the holy fathers who have journeyed far to the westward, even to the vast Messasebe, which is well known to run into the China sea upon some far-off coast not yet well charted. I have also read the story of Sagean, who was far to the west of that mighty river. Did not the latter see and pursue and kill in fair fight the giant unicorn, fabled of Scripture? Is not that animal known to be a creature of the East, and may we not, therefore, be advised that this new country takes hold upon the storied lands of the East? Why, this holy friar with whom I spoke, fresh back from his voyaging to the cold upper ways of the Northern tribes, who live beyond the far-off channel at Michilimackinac—did he not tell of a river of the name of the Blue Earth, and did he not himself see turquoises and diamonds and emeralds taken in handfuls from this same blue earth? Ah, bah! gentlemen, Europe for you if ye like, but for me, back I go, so soon as I may get proper passage and a connection which will warrant me the voyage. Back I go to Canada, to America, to the woods and streams. I would see again my ancient Du L'hut, and my comrade Pierre Noir, and Tete Gris, the trapper from the Mistasing—free traders all. Life is there for the living, my comrades. This Old World, small and outworn, no more of it for me."

"And why came you back to this little Old World of ours, an you loved the New World so much?" asked the cynical voice of him who had been called Wilson.

"By the body of God!" cried Du Mesne, "think ye I came of my own free will? Look here, and find your reason." He stripped back the opening of his doublet and under waistcoat, and showed upon his broad shoulder the scar of a red tri-point, deep and livid upon his flesh. "Look! There is the fleur-de-lis of France. That is why I came. I have rowed in the galleys, me—me a free man, a man of the woods of New France!"

Murmurs of concern passed among the little group. Castleton rose from his chair and leaned with his hands upon the table, gazing now at the face and now at the bared shoulder of this stranger, who had by chance become a member of their nightly party.

"I have not been in London a fortnight since my escape," said the man with the brand. "I was none the less once a good servant of Louis in New France, for that I found many a new tribe and many a bale of furs that else had never come to the Mountain for the robbery of the lying officers who claim the robe of Louis. I was a soldier for the king as well as a traveler of the forest. Was I not with the Le Moynes and the band that crossed the icy North and destroyed your robbing English fur posts on the Bay of Hudson? I fought there and helped blow down your barriers. I packed my own robe on my back, and walked for the king, till the *raquette* thongs cut my ankles to the bone. For what? When I came back to the settlements at Quebec I was seized for a *coureur de bois*, a free trader. I was herded like a criminal into a French ship, sent over seas to a French prison, branded with a French iron, and set like a brute to pull without reason at a bar of wood in the king's galleys—the king's hell!"

"And yet you are a Frenchman," sneered Wilson.

"Yet am I not a Frenchman," cried the other. "Nor am I an Englishman. I am no man of a world of galleys and brands. I am a man of America!"

"'Tis true what he says," spoke Pembroke. "'Tis said the minister of Louis was feared to keep these men in the galleys, lest their fellows in New France should become too bitter, and should join the savages in their inroads on the starving settlements of Quebec and Montreal."

"True," exclaimed Du Mesne. "The *coureurs* care naught for the law and little for the king. As for a ruler, we have discovered that a man makes a most excellent sovereign for himself."

"And excellent said," cried Castleton.

"None of ye know the West," went on the *coureur*. "Your Virginia, we know well of it—a collection of beggars, prostitutes and thieves. Your New England—a lot of cod-fishing, starving snivelers, who are most concerned how to keep life in their bodies from year to year. New France herself, sitting ever on the edge of an icy death, with naught but bickerings at Quebec and naught but reluctant compliance from Paris—what hath she to hope? I tell ye, gentlemen, 'tis beyond, in the land of the Messasebe, where I shall for my part seek out my home; and no man shall set iron on my soul again."

He spoke bitterly. The group about him, half amused, half cynical and all ignorant, as were their kind at this time of the reign of William, were none the less impressed and thoughtful. Yet once more the sneering voice of Wilson broke in.

"A strange land, my friend," said he, "monstrous strange. Your unicorns are great, and your women are little. Methinks to give thy tale proportion thou shouldst have shown shoon somewhat larger."

"Peace! Beau," said Castleton, quickly. "As for the size of the human foot—gad! I'll lay a roll of louis d'or that there's one dame here in London town can wear this slipper of New France."

"Done!" cried Wilson. "Name the one."

"None other than the pretty Lawrence whom thou hast had under thine ancient wing for the past two seasons."

The face of Wilson gathered into a sudden frown at this speech. "What doth it matter"—he began.

"Have done, fellows!" cried Pembroke with some asperity. "Lay wagers more fit at best, and let us have no more of this thumb-biting. Gad! the first we know, we'll be up for fighting among ourselves, and we all know how the new court doth look on that."

"Come away," laughed Castleton, gaily. "I'm for a pint of ale and an apple; and then beware! 'Tis always my fortune, when I come to this country drink, to win like a very countryman. I need revenge upon Lady Betty and her lap-dog. I've lost since ever I saw them last."

CHAPTER II

AT SADLER'S WELLS

Sadler's Wells, on this mild and cheery spring morning, was a scene of fashion and of folly. Hither came the elite of London, after the custom of the day, to seek remedy in the reputed qualities of the springs for the weariness and lassitude resultant upon the long season of polite dissipations which society demanded of her votaries. Bewigged dandies, their long coats of colors well displayed as they strutted about in the open, paid court there, as they did within the city gates, to the powdered and painted beauties who sat in their couches waiting for their servants to bring out to them the draft of which they craved healing for crow's-feet and hollow eyes. Here and there traveling merchants called their wares, jugglers spread their carpets, bear dancers gave their little spectacles, and jockeys conferred as to the merits of horse or hound. Hawk-nosed Jews passed among the vehicles, cursed or kicked by the young gallants who stood about, hat in hand, at the steps of their idols' carriages.

"Buy my silks, pretty lady, buy my silks! Fresh from the Turkey walk on the Exchange, and cheaper than you can buy their like in all the city—buy my silks, lady!" Thus the peddler with his little pack of finery.

Emerson Hough

"My philter, lady," cried the gipsy woman, who had left her donkey cart outside the line. "My philter! 'Twill keep-a your eyes bright and your cheeks red for ay. Secret of the Pharaohs, lady; and but a shilling!"

"Have ye a parrot, ma'am? Have ye never a parrot to keep ye free and give ye laughter every hour? Buy my parrot, lady. Just from the Gold Coast. He'll talk ye Spanish, Flemish or good city tongue. Buy my parrot at ten crowns, and so cheap, lady!" So spoke the ear-ringed sailor, who might never have seen a salter water than the Thames.

"Powder-puffs for the face, lady," whispered a lean and weazen-faced hawker, slipping among the crowd with secrecy. "See my puff, made from the foot of English hares. Rubs out all wrinkles, lady, and keeps ye young as when ye were a lass. But a shilling, a shilling. See!" And with the pretense of secrecy the seller would sidle up to a carriage of some dame, slip to her the hare's foot and take the shilling with an air as though no one could see what none could fail to notice.

Above these mingled cries of the hangers-on of this crowd of nobility and gentles rose the blare of crude music, and cries far off and confused. Above it all shone the May sun, brighter here than lower toward the Thames. In the edge of London town it was, all this little pageant, and from the residence squares below and far to the westward came the carriages and the riders, gathering at the spot which for the hour was the designated rendezvous of capricious fashion. No matter if the tower at the drinking curb was crowded, so that inmates of the coaches could not find way among the others. There was at least magic in the morning, even if one might not drink at the chalybeate spring. Cheeks did indeed grow rosy, and eyes brightened under the challenge not only of the dawn but of the ardent eyes that gazed impertinently bold or reproachfully imploring.

Far-reaching was the line of the gentility, to whose flanks clung the rabble of trade. Back upon the white road came yet other carriages, saluted by those departing. Low hedges of English green reached out into the distance, blending ultimately at the edge of the pleasant sky. Merry enough it was, and gladsome, this spring day; for be sure the really ill did not brave the long morning ride to test the virtue of the waters of Sadler's Wells. It was for the most part the young, the lively, the full-blooded, perhaps the wearied, but none the less the vital and stirring natures which met in the decreed assemblage.

Back of Sadler's little court the country came creeping close up to the town. There were fields not so far away on these long highways. Wandering and rambling roads ran off to the westward and to the north, leading toward the straight old Roman road which once upon a time ran down to London town. Ill-kept enough were some of the lanes, with their hedges and shrubs overhanging the highways, if such the paths could be called which came braiding down toward the south. One needed not to go far outward beyond Sadler's Wells of a night-time to find adventure, or to lose a purse.

It was on one of these less crowded highways that there was this morning enacted a curious little drama. The sun was still young and not too strong for comfort, and as it rose back of the square of Sadler's it cast a shadow from a hedge which ran angling toward the southeast. Its rays, therefore, did not disturb the slumbers of two young men who were lying beneath the shelter of the hedge. Strange enough must have been the conclusions of the sun could it have looked over the barrier and peered into the faces of these youths. Evidently they were of good breeding and some station, albeit their garb was not of the latest fashion. The gray hose and the clumsy shoes plainly bespoke some northern residence. The wig of each lacked the latest turn, perhaps the collar of the coat was not all it should have been. There was but one coat visible, for the other, rolled up as a pillow, served to support the heads of both. The elder of the two was the one who had sacrificed his covering. The other was more restless in his attitude, and though thus the warmer for a coat, was more in need of comfort. A white bandage covered his wrist, and the linen was stained red. Yet the two slept on, well into the morn, well into the rout of Sadler's Wells. Evidently they were weary.

The elder man was the taller of the two; as he lay on the bank beneath the hedge, he might even in that posture have been seen to own a figure of great strength and beauty. His face, bold of outline, with well curved, wide jaw and strong cheek bones, was shaded by the tangled mat of his wig, tousled in his sleep. His hands, long and graceful, lay idly at his side, though one rested lightly on the hilt of the sword which lay near him. The ruffles of his shirt were torn, and, indeed, had almost disappeared. By study one might have recognized them in the bandage about the hand of the other. Somewhat disheveled was this youth, yet his young, strong body, slender and shapely, seemed even in its rest strangely full of power and confidence.

The younger man was in some fashion an epitome of the other, and it had needed little argument to show the two were brothers. But why should two brothers, well-clad and apparently well-to-do, probably brothers from a country far to the north, be thus lying like common vagabonds beneath an English hedge?

Far down the roadway there rose a cloud of dust, which came steadily nearer, following the only vehicle in sight, probably the only one which had passed that morning. As this little dust-cloud came slowly nearer it might have been seen to rise from the wheels of a richly-built and well-appointed coach. Four dark horses obeyed the reins handled by a solemn-visaged lackey on the box, and there was a goodly footman at the back. Within the coach were two passengers such as might have set Sadler's Wells by the ears. They sat on the same seat, as equals, and their heads lay close together, as confidantes. The tongues of both ran fast and free. Long gloves covered the arms of these beauties, and their costumes showed them to be of station. The crinoline of the two filled all the body of the ample coach from seat to seat, and the folds of their figured muslins, flowing out over this ample outline, gave to the face of each a daintiness of contour and feature which was not ill relieved by the high head-dress of ribbons and bepowdered hair. Of the two ladies, one, even in despite of her crinoline, might have been seen to be of noble and queenly figure; the towering head-dress did not fully disguise the wealth of red-bronze hair. Tall and well-rounded, vigorous and young, not yet twenty, adored by many suitors, the Lady Catharine Knollys had rarely looked better than she did this morning as she drove out to Sadler's, for Providence alone knew what fault of a superb vital energy. Her eyes sparkled as she spoke, and every gesture betokened rather the grand young creature that she was than the valetudinarian going forth for healing. Her cheek, turned now and again, showed a clear-cut and untouched soundness that meant naught but health. It showed also the one blemish upon a beauty which was toasted in the court as faultless. Upon the left cheek there was a *mouche*, excessive in its size. Strangers might have commented on it. Really it covered a deep-stained birth-mark, the one blur upon a peerless beauty. Yet even this might be forgotten, as it was now.

The companion of the Lady Catharine in her coach was a young woman, scarce so tall and more slender. The heavy hoop concealed much of the grace of figure which was her portion, but the poise of the upper body, free from the seat-back and erect with youthful strength as yet unspared, showed easily that here, too, was but an indifferent subject for Sadler's. Dark, where her companion was fair, and with the glossy texture of her own somber locks showing in the individual roll which ran back into the absurd *fontange* of false hair and falser powder, Mary Connynge made good foil for her bosom friend; though honesty must admit that neither had yet much concern for foils, since both had their full meed of gallants. Much seen together, they were commonly known, as the Morning and Eve, sometimes as Aurora and Eve. Never did daughter of the original Eve have deeper feminine guile than Mary Connynge. Soft of speech—as her friend, the Lady Catharine, was impulsive,—slow, suave, amber-eyed and innocent of visage, this young English woman, with no dower save that of beauty and of wit, had not failed of a sensation at the capital whither she had come as guest of the Lady Catharine. Three captains and a squire, to say nothing of a gouty colonel, had already fallen victims, and had heard their fate in her low, soft tones, which could whisper a fashionable oath in the accent of a hymn, and say "no" so sweetly that one could only beg to hear the word again. It was perhaps of some such incident that these two young maids of old London conversed as they trundled slowly out toward the suburb of the city.

"'Twould have killed you, Lady Kitty; sure 'twould have been your end to hear him speak! He walked the floor upon his knees, and clasped his hands, and followed me about like a dog in a spectacle. Lord! but I feared he would have thrown over the tabouret with his great feet. And help me, if I think not he had tears in his eyes!"

"My friend," said Lady Kitty, solemnly, "you must have better care of your conduct. I'll not have my father's old friend abused in his own house." At which they both burst into laughter. Youth, the blithely cruel, had its own way in this old coach upon the ancient dusty road, as it has ever had.

But now serious affairs gained the attention of these two fairs. "Tell me, sweetheart," said Lady Catharine, "what think you of the fancy of my new dresser? He insists ever that the mode in Paris favors a deep bow, placed high upon the left side of the 'tower.' Montespan, of the French court, is said to have given the fashion. She hurried at her toilet, and placed the bow there for fault of better care. Hence, so must we if we are to live in town. So says my new hair-dresser from Paris. 'Tis to Paris we must go for the modes."

"I am not so sure," began Mary Connynge, "as to this arrangement. Now I am much disposed to believe—" but what she was disposed to believe at that time was not said, then or ever afterward, for at that moment there happened matters which ended their little talk; matters which divided their two lives, and which, in the end, drove them as far apart as two continents could carry them.

"O Gemini!" called out Mary Connynge, as the coachman for a moment slackened his pace. "Look! We shall be robbed!"

The driver irresolutely pulled up his horses. From under the shade of the hedge there arose two men, of whom the taller now stood erect and came toward the carriage.

"'Tis no robber," said Lady Catharine Knollys, her eyes fastened on the tall figure which came forward.

"Save us," said Mary Connynge, "what a pretty man!"

CHAPTER III

JOHN LAW OF LAURISTON

Unconsciously the coachman obeyed the unvoiced command of this man, who stepped out from the shelter of the hedge. Travel-stained, just awakened from sleep, disheveled, with dress disordered, there was none the less abundant boldness in his mien as he came forward, yet withal the grace and deference of the courtier. It was a good figure he made as he stepped down from the bank and came forward, hat in hand, the sun, now rising to the top of the hedge, lighting up his face and showing his bold profile, his open and straight blue eye.

"Ladies," he said, as he reached the road, "I crave your pardon humbly. This, I think, is the coach of my Lord, the Earl of Banbury. Mayhap this is the Lady Catharine Knollys to whom I speak?"

The lady addressed still gazed at him, though she drew up with dignity.

"You have quite the advantage of us," said she. She glanced uneasily at the coachman, but the order to go forward did not quite leave her lips.

"I am not aware—I do not know—," she began, afraid of her adventure now it had come, after the way of all dreaming maids who prate of men and conquests.

"I should be dull of eye did I not see the Knollys arms," said the stranger, smiling and bowing low. "And I should be ill advised of the families of England did I not know that the daughter of Knollys, the sister of the Earl of Banbury, is the Lady Catharine, and most charming also. This I might say, though 'tis true I never was in London or in England until now."

The speech, given with all respectfulness, did not fail of flattery. Again the order to drive on remained unspoken. This speaker, whose foot was now close to the carriage step, and whose head, gravely bowed as he saluted the occupants of the vehicle, presented so striking a type of manly attractiveness, even that first moment cast some spell upon the woman whom he sought to interest. The eyes of the Lady Catharine Knollys did not turn from him. As though it were another person, she heard herself murmur, "And you, sir?"

"I am John Law of Lauriston, Scotland, Madam, and entirely at your service. That is my brother Will, yonder by the bank." He smiled, and the younger man came forward, hesitatingly, and not with the address of his brother, though yet with the breeding of a gentleman.

The eyes of Mary Connynge took in both men with the same look, but her eyes, as did those of the Lady Catharine, became most concerned with the first speaker.

"My brother and I are on our first journey to London," continued he, with a gay laugh which did not consort fully with the plight in which he showed. "We started by coach, as gentlemen; and now we come on foot, like laborers or thieves. 'Twas my own fault. Yesterday I must needs quit the Edinboro' stage. Last night our chaise was stopped, and we were asked to hand our money to a pair of evil fellows who had made prey of us. In short—you see—we fared ill enough. Lost in the dark, we made what shift we could along this road, where we both are strangers. At last, not able to pay for better quarters even had we found them, we lay down to sleep. I have slept far worse. And 'tis a lovely morning. Madam, I thank you for this happy beginning of the day."

Mary Connynge pointed to the bandage on the younger man's arm, speaking a low word to her companion.

"True," said the Lady Catharine, "you are injured, sir; you did not come off whole."

"Oh, we would hardly suffer the fellows to rob us without making some argument over it," said the first speaker. "Indeed, I think we are the better off hereabouts for a brace of footpads gone to their account. I made them my duties as we came away. Will, here, was pricked a trifle, but you see we have done very well."

The face of Will Law hardly offered complete proof of this assertion. He had slept ill enough, and in the morning light his face showed gaunt and pale. Here, then, was a situation most inopportune; the coach of two ladies, unattended, stopped by two strangers, who certainly could not claim introduction by either friend or reputation.

"I did but wish to ask some advice of the roads hereabout," said the elder brother, turning his eyes full upon those of the Lady Catharine. "As you see, we are in ill plight to get forward to the city. If you will be so good as to tell me which way to take, I shall remember it most gratefully. Once in the city, we should do better, for the rascals have not taken certain papers, letters which I bear to gentlemen in the city—Sir Arthur Pembroke I may name as one—a friend of my father's, who hath had some dealings with him in the handling of moneys. I have also word for others, and make sure that, once we have got into town, we shall soon mend our fortune."

Lady Catharine looked at Mary Connynge and the latter in turn gazed at her. "There could be no harm," said each to the other with her eyes. "Surely it is our duty to take them in with us; at least the one who is wounded."

Will Law had said nothing, though he had come forward to the road, and, bowing, stood uncovered. Now he leaned against the flank of one of the horses, in a tremor of vertigo which seized him as he stood. It was perhaps the paleness of his face that gave determination to the issue.

"William," called the Lady Catharine Knollys, "open the door for Mr. Law of Lauriston!"

The footman sprang to the ground and held open the door. Therefore, into the coach stepped John Law and his brother, late of Edinboro', sometime robbed and afoot, but now to come into London in circumstances which surely might have been far worse.

John Law entered the coach with the dignity and grace of a gentleman born. He bowed gravely as he took his seat beside his brother, facing the ladies. Will Law sank back into the corner, not averse to rest. The eyes of the two young women did not linger more upon the wounded man than upon his brother. He, in turn, looked straight into their eyes, courteously, respectfully, gravely, yet fearlessly and calmly, as though he knew what power and possibilities were his. Enigma and autocrat alike, Beau Law of Edinboro', one of the handsomest and properest men ever bred on any soil, was surely a picture of vigorous young manhood, as he rode toward Sadler's Wells, with two of the beauties of the hour, and in a coach and four which might have been his own.

Now all the sweet spring morning came on apace, and from the fields and little gardens came the breath of flowers. The sky was blue. The languor of springtime pulsed through the veins of those young creatures, those engines of life, of passion and desire. Neither of the two women saw the torn garb of the man before them. They saw but the curve of the strong chest beneath. They heard, and the one heard and felt as keenly as the other, the voice of the young man, musical and rich, touching some deep-seated and vibrating heart-string. So in the merry month of May, with the birds singing in the trees, and the scent of the flowers wafted coolly to their senses, they came on apace to the throng at Sadler's Wells. There it was that John Law, finding in a pocket a coin that had been overlooked, reached out to a vender and bought a rose. He offered his flower with a deep inclination of the body to the Lady Catharine.

It was at this moment that Mary Connynge first began to hate her friend, the Lady Catharine Knollys.

CHAPTER IV

THE POINT OF HONOR

"Tell me, friend Castleton," said Pembroke, banteringly, "art still adhering to thy country drink of lamb's-wool? Methinks burnt ale and toasted apple might better be replaced in thy case by a beaker of stronger waters. You lose, and still you lose."

"May a plague take it!" cried Castleton. "I've had no luck these four days. 'Tis that cursed lap-dog of the duchess. Ugh! I saw it in my dreams last night."

"Gad! your own fortune in love must be ill enough, Sir Arthur," said Beau Wilson, as he pushed back his chair during this little lull in the play of the evening.

"And tell me why, Beau?"

"Because of us all who have met here at the Green Lion these last months, not one hath ever had so steady a run of luck. Sure some fairy hath befriended thee. *Sept et le va, sept et le va*—I'll hear it in my ears to-night, even as Castleton sees the lap-dog. Man, you play as though you read the pack quite through."

Emerson Hough

"Ah, then, you admit that there is some such thing as a talisman. I'll not deny that I have had one these last three evenings, but I feared to tell ye all, lest I might be waylaid and robbed of my good-luck charm."

"Tell us, tell us, man, what it is!" cried Castleton. "*Sept et le va* has not been made in this room before for many a month, yet here thou comest with the run of *sept et le va* thrice in as many hours."

"Well, then," continued Pembroke, still smiling, "I'll make a small confession. Here is my charm. Salute it!"

He cast on the table the Indian moccasin which had been shown the same party at the Green Lion a few evenings before. Eager hands reached for it.

"Treachery!" cried Castleton. "I bid Du Mesne four pounds for the shoe myself."

"Oh ho!" said Pembroke, "so you too were after it. Well, the long purse won, as it doth ever. I secretly gave our wandering wood ranger, ex-galley slave of France, the neat sum of twenty-five pounds for this little shoe. Poor fellow, he liked ill enough to part with it; but he said, very sensibly, that the twenty-five pounds would take him back to Canada, and once there, he could not only get many such shoes, but see the maid who made this one for him, or, rather, made it for herself. As for me, the price was cheap. You could not replace it in all the Exchange for any money. Moreover, to show my canniness, I've won back its cost a score of times this very night."

He laughingly extended his hand for the moccasin, which Wilson was examining closely.

"'Tis clever made," said the latter. "And what a tale the owner of it carried. If half he says be true, we do ill to bide here in old England. Let us take ship and follow Monsieur du Mesne."

"'Twould be a long chase, mayhap," said Pembroke, reflectively. Yet each of the men at that little table in the gaming room of the Green Lion coffee-house ceased in his fingering the cards, and gazed upon this product of another world.

Pembroke was first to break the silence, and as he heard a footfall at the door, he called out:

"Ho, fellow! Go fetch me another bottle of Spanish, and do not forget this time the brandy and water which I told thee to bring half an hour ago."

The step came nearer, and as it did not retreat, but entered the room, Pembroke called out again: "Make haste, man, and go on!"

The footsteps paused, and Pembroke looked up, as one does when a strange presence comes into the room. He saw, standing near the door, a tall and comely young man, whose carriage betokened him not ill-born. The stranger advanced and bowed gravely. "Pardon me, sir," he said, "but I fear I am awkward in thus intruding. The man showed me up the stair and bade me enter. He said that I should find here Sir Arthur Pembroke, upon whom I bear letters from friends of his in the North."

"Sir," said Pembroke, rising and advancing, "you are very welcome, and I ask pardon for my unwitting speech."

"I come at this hour and at this place," said the newcomer, "for reasons which may seem good a little later. My name is

John Law, of Edinboro', sir."

All those present arose.

"Sir," responded Pembroke, "I am delighted to have your name. I know of the acquaintance between your father and my own. These are friends of mine, and I am delighted to name ye to each other. Mr. Charles Castleton; Mr. Edward Wilson. We are all here to kill the ancient enemy, Time. 'Tis an hour of night when one gains an appetite for one thing or another, cards or cold joint. I know not why we should not have a bit of both?"

"With your permission, I shall be glad to join ye at either," said John Law. "I have still the appetite of a traveler—in faith, rather a better appetite than most travelers may claim, for I swear I've had no more to eat the last day and night than could be purchased for a pair of shillings."

Pembroke raised his eyebrows, scarce knowing whether to be amused at this speech or nettled by its cool assurance.

"Some ill fortune?"—he began politely.

"There is no such thing as ill fortune," quoth John Law. "We fail always of our own fault. Forsooth I must explore Roman roads by night. England hath builded better, and the footpads have the Roman ways. My brother Will—he waiteth below, if ye please, good friends, and is quite as hungry as myself, besides having a pricked finger to boot—and I lost what little we had about us, and we came through with scarce a good shirt between the two."

A peal of laughter greeted him as he pulled apart the lapels of his coat and showed ruffles torn and disfigured. The speaker smiled gravely.

"To-morrow," said he, "I must seek me out a goldsmith and a haberdasher, if you will be so good as to name such to me."

"Sir," said Sir Arthur Pembroke, "in this plight you must allow me." He extended a purse which he drew from his pocket. "I beg you, help yourself."

"Thank you, no," replied John Law. "I shall ask you only to show me the goldsmith in the morning, him upon whom I hold certain credits. I make no doubt that then I shall be quite fit again. I have never in my life borrowed a coin. Besides, I should feel that I had offended my good angel did I ask it to help me out of mine own folly. If we have but a bit of this cold joint, and a place for my brother Will to sit in comfort as we play, I shall beg to hope, my friends, that I shall be allowed to stake this trifle against a little of the money that I see here; which, I take it, is subject to the fortunes of war."

He tossed on the board a ring, which carried in its setting a diamond of size and brilliance.

"This fellow hath a cool assurance enough," muttered Beau Wilson to his neighbor as he leaned toward him at the table.

Pembroke, always good-natured, laughed at the effrontery of the newcomer.

"You say very well; it is there for the fortune of war," said he. "It is all yours, if you can win it; but I warn you, beware, for I shall have your jewel and your letters of credit too, if ye keep not sharp watch."

"Yes," said Castleton, "Pembroke hath warrant for such speech. The man who can make *sept et le va* thrice in one evening is hard company for his friends."

John Law leaned back comfortably in his chair.

"I make no doubt," said he, "that I shall make *trente et le va*, here at this table, this very evening."

Smiles and good-natured sneerings met this calm speech.

"*Trente et le va*—it hath not come out in the history of London play for the past four seasons!" cried Wilson. "I'll lay you any odds that you're not within eye-sight of *trente et le va* these next five evenings, if you favor us with your company."

"Be easy with me, good friends," said John. Law, calmly. "I am not yet in condition for individual wagers, as my jewel is my fortune, till to-morrow at least. But if ye choose to make the play at Lands-knecht, I will plunge at the bank to the best of my capital. Then, if I win, I shall be blithe to lay ye what ye like."

The young Englishmen sat looking at their guest with some curiosity. His strange assurance daunted them.

"Surely this is a week of wonders," said Beau Wilson, with scarce covered sarcasm in his tone. "First we have a wild man from Canada, with his fairy stories of gold and gems, and now we have another gentleman who apparently hath fathomed as well how to gain sudden wealth at will, and yet keep closer home."

Law took snuff calmly. "I am not romancing, gentlemen," said he. "With me play is not a hazard, but a science. I ought really not to lay on even terms with you. As I have said, there is no such thing as chance. There are such things as recurrences, such things as laws that govern all happenings."

Laughter arose again at this, though it did not disturb the newcomer, nor did the cries of derision which followed his announcement of his system.

"Many a man hath come to London town with a system of play," cried Pembroke. "Tell us, Mr. Law, what and where shall we send thee when we have won thy last sixpence?"

"Good sir," said Law, "let us first of all have the joint."

"I humbly crave a pardon, sir," said Pembroke. "In this new sort of discourse I had forgot thine appetite. We shall mend that at once. Here, Simon! Go fetch up Mr. Law's brother, who waits below, and fetch two covers and a bit to eat. Some of thy new Java berry, too, and make haste! We have much yet to do."

"That have ye, if ye are to see the bottom of my purse more than once," said Law gaily. "See! 'tis quite empty now. I make ye all my solemn promise that 'twill not be empty again for twenty years. After that—well, the old Highland soothsayer, who dreamed for me, always told me to forswear play after I was forty, and never to go too near running water. Of the latter I was born with a horror. For play, I was born with a gift. Thus I foresee that this little feat which you mention is sure to be mine this very night. You all say that *trente* has not come up for many months. Well, 'tis due, and due to-night. The cards never fail me when I need."

"By my faith," cried Wilson, "ye have a pretty way about you up in Scotland!"

John Law saw the veiled ill feeling, and replied at once:

"True, we have a pretty way. We had it at Killiecrankie not so long ago; and when the clans fight among themselves, we need still prettier ways."

"Now, gentlemen," said Pembroke, "none of this talk, by your leave. The odds are fairer here than they were at Killiecrankie's battle, and 'tis all of us against the Scotch again. We English stand together, but we stand to-night only against this threat of the ultimate fortune of the cards. Moreover, here comes the supper, and if I mistake not, also the brother of our friend."

Will bowed to one and the other gentlemen, unconsciously drifting toward his brother's chair.

"Now we must to business," cried Castleton, as the dishes were at last cleared away. "Show him thy talisman, Pem, and let him kiss his jewel good by."

Pembroke threw upon the table once more the moccasin of the Indian girl. John Law picked it up and examined it long and curiously, asking again and again searching questions regarding its origin.

"I have read of this new land of America," said he. "Some day it will be more prominent in all plans."

He laid down the slipper and mused for a moment, apparently forgetful of the scene about him.

"Perhaps," cried Castleton, the zeal of the gambler now showing in his eye. "But let us make play here to-night. Let Pembroke bank. His luck is best to win this vaunter's stake."

Pembroke dealt the cards about for the first round. The queen fell. John Law won. "*Deux*," he said calmly, and turned away as though it were a matter of course. The cards went round again. "*Trois*," he said, as he glanced at his stakes, now doubled again.

Wilson murmured. "Luck's with him for a start," said he, "but 'tis a long road." He himself had lost at the second turn. "*Quint*!" "*Seix*!" "*Sept et le va*!" in turn called Law, still coolly, still regarding with little interest the growing heap of coin upon the board opposite the glittering ring which he had left lying on the table.

"*Vingt-un, et le va*!"

"Good God!" cried Castleton, the sweat breaking out upon his forehead. "See the fellow's luck!—Pembroke, sure he hath stole thy slipper. Such a run of cards was never seen in this room since Rigby, of the Tenth, made his great game four years ago."

"*Vingt-cinq; et le va*!" said John Law, calmly.

Will touched his sleeve. The stake had now grown till the money on the hoard meant a matter of hundreds of pounds, which might he removed at any turn the winner chose. It was there but for the stretching out of the hand. Yet this strange genius sat there, scarce deigning to smile at the excited faces of those about him.

"I'll lay thee fifty to one that the next turn sees thee lose!" cried Castleton.

"Done," said John Law.

The iciness in the air seemed now an actual thing. There was, in the nature of this play, something which no man at that board, hardened gamesters as they all were, had ever met before. It was indeed as though Fate were there, with her hand upon the shoulder of a favored son.

"You lose, Mr. Castleton," said Law, calmly, as the cards came again his way. He swept his winnings from the coin pushed out to him.

"Now we have thee, Mr. Law!" cried Pembroke. "One more turn, and I hope your very good nerve will leave the stake on the board, for so we'll see it all come back to the bank, even as the sheep come home at eventide. Here your lane turns. And 'tis at the last stage, for the next is the limit of the rules of the game. But you'll not win it."

"Anything you like for a little personal wager," said the other, with no excitement in his voice.

"Why, then, anything you like yourself, sir," said Pembroke.

"Your little slipper against fifty pounds?" asked John Law.

"Why—yes—," hesitated Pembroke, for the moment feeling a doubt of the luck that had favored him so long that evening. "I'd rather make it sovereigns, but since you name the slipper, I even make it so, for I know there is but one chance in hundreds that you win."

The players leaned over the table as the deal went on. Once, twice, thrice, the cards went round. A sigh, a groan, a long breath broke from those who looked at the deal. Neither groan nor sigh came from John Law. He gazed indifferently at the heap of coin and paper that lay on the table, and which, by the law of play, was now his own.

"*Trente et le va*," he said. "I knew that it would come. Sir Arthur, I half regret to rob thee thus, but I shall ask my slipper in hand paid. Pardon me, too, if I chide thee for risking it in play. Gentlemen, there is much in this little shoe, empty as it is."

He dandled it upon his finger, hardly looking at the winnings that lay before him. "'Tis monstrous pretty, this little shoe," he said, rousing himself from his half reverie.

"Confound thee, man!" cried Castleton, "that is the only thing we grudge. Of sovereigns there are plenty at the coinage—but of a shoe like this, there is not the equal this day in England!"

"So?" laughed Law. "Well, consider, 'tis none too easy to make the run of *trente*. Risk hath its gains, you know, by all the original laws of earth and nature."

"But heard you not the wager which was proposed over the little shoe?" broke in Castleton. "Wilson, here, was angered when I laid him odds that there was but one woman in London could wear this shoe. I offered him odds that his good friend, Kittie Lawrence—"

"Nor had ye the right to offer such bet!" cried Wilson, ruffled by the doings of the evening.

"I'll lay you myself there's no woman in England whom you know with foot small enough to wear it," cried Castleton.

"Meaning to me?" asked Law, politely.

"To any one," cried Castleton, quickly, "but most to thee, I fancy, since 'tis now thy shoe!"

"I'll lay you forty crowns, then, that I know a smaller foot than that of Madam Lawrence," said Law, suavely. "I'll lay you another forty crowns that I'll try it on for the test, though I first saw the lady this very morning. I'll lay you another forty crowns that Madam Lawrence can not wear this shoe, though her I have never seen."

These words rankled, though they were said offhand and with the license of coffee-house talk at so late an hour. Beau Wilson rose, in a somewhat unsteady attitude, and, turning towards Law, addressed him with a tone which left small option as to its meaning.

"Sirrah!" cried he, "I know not who you are, but I would have a word or two of good advice for you!"

"Sir, I thank you," said John Law, "but perhaps I do not need advice." He did not rise from his seat.

"Have it then at any rate, and be civil!" cried the older man. "You seem a swaggering sort, with your talk of love and luck, and such are sure to get their combs cut early enough here among Englishmen. I'll not tolerate your allusion to a lady you have never met, and one I honor deeply, sir, deeply!"

"I am but a young man started out to seek his fortune," said John Law, his eye kindling now for the first time, "and I should do very ill if I evaded that fortune, whatsoever it may be."

"Then you'll take back that talk of Mrs. Lawrence!"

"I have made no talk of Mrs. Lawrence, sir," said Law, "and even had I, I should take back nothing for a demand like yours. 'Tis not meet, sir, where no offense was meant, to crowd in an offensive remark."

Pembroke said nothing. The situation was ominous enough at this point. A sudden gravity and dignity fell upon the young men who sat there, schooled in an etiquette whose first lesson was that of personal courage.

"Sirrah!" cried Beau Wilson, "I perceive your purpose. If you prove good enough to name lodgings where you may he found by my friends, I shall ask leave to bid you a very good night."

So speaking, Wilson flung out of the room. A silence fell upon those left within.

"Sirs," said Law, a moment later, "I beg you to bear witness that this is no matter of my seeking or accepting. This gentleman is a stranger to me. I hardly got his name fair."

"Wilson is his name, sir," said Pembroke, "a very good friend of us all. He is of good family, and doth keep his coach-and-four like any gentleman. For him we may vouch very well."

"Wilson!" cried Law, springing now to his feet. "'Tis not him known as Beau Wilson? Why, my dear sirs, his father was friend to many of my kin long ago. Why, sir, this is one of those to whom my mother bade me look to get my first ways of London well laid out."

"These are some of the ways of London," said Pembroke, grimly.

"But is there no fashion in which this matter can be accommodated?"

Pembroke and Castleton looked at each other, rose and passed him, each raising his hat and bowing courteously.

"Your servant, sir," said the one; and, "Your servant, sir," said the other.

CHAPTER V

DIVERS EMPLOYMENTS OF JOHN LAW

"And when shall I send these garments to your Lordship?" asked the haberdasher, with whom Law was having speech on the morning following the first night in London.

"Two weeks from to-day," said Law, "in the afternoon, and not later than four o'clock. I shall have need for them."

"Impossible!" said the tradesman, hitherto obsequious, but now smitten with the conviction regarding the limits of human possibilities.

"At that hour, or not at all," said John Law, calmly. "At that time I shall perhaps be at my lodgings, 59 Bradwell Street, West. As I have said to you, I am not clad as I could wish. It is not a matter of your convenience, but of mine own."

"But, sir," expostulated the other, "you order of the best. Nothing, I am sure, save the utmost of good workmanship would please you. I should like a month of time upon these garments, in order to make them worthy of yourself. Moreover, there are orders of the nobility already in our hands will occupy us more than past the time you name. Make it three weeks, sir, and I promise—"

His customer only shook his head and reiterated, "You heard me well."

The tailor, sore puzzled, not wishing to lose a customer who came so well recommended, and yet hesitating at the exactions of that customer, sat with perplexity written upon his brow.

"So!" exclaimed Law. "Sir Arthur Pembroke told me that you were a clever fellow and could execute exact any order I might give you. Now it appears to me you are like everybody else. You prate only of hardships and of impossibilities."

The perspiration fairly stood out on the forehead of the man of trade.

"Sir," said he, "I should be glad to please not only a friend of Sir Arthur Pembroke, but also a gentleman of such parts as yourself. I hesitate to promise—"

"But you must promise," said John Law.

"Well, then, I do promise! I will have this apparel at your place on the day which you name. 'Tis most extraordinary, but the order shall be executed."

"As I thought," said John Law.

"But I must thank you besides," resumed the tradesman. "In good truth I must say that of all the young gentlemen who come hither—and I may show the names of the best nobility of London and of some ports beyond seas—there hath never stepped within these doors a better figure than yourself—nay, not so good. And I am a judge of men."

Law looked at him carelessly.

"You shall make me none the easier, nor yourself the easier, by soft speech," said he, "if you have not these garments ready by the time appointed. Send them, and you shall have back the fifty sovereigns by the messenger, with perhaps a coin or so in addition if all be well."

"The air of this nobility!" said the tailor, but smiling with pleasure none the less. "This is, perhaps, some affair with a lady?" he added.

"'Tis an affair with a lady, and also with certain gentlemen."

"Oh, so," said the tailor. "If it he, forsooth, an enterprise with a lady, methinks I know the outcome now." He gazed with professional pride upon the symmetrical figure before him. "You shall be all the better armed when well fitted in my garments. Not all London shall furnish a properer figure of a man, nor one better clad, when I shall have done with you, sir."

Law but half heard him, for he was already turning toward the door, where he beckoned again for his waiting chair.

"To the offices of the Bank of England," he directed. And forthwith he was again jogging through the crowded streets of London.

The offices of the Bank of England, to which this young adventurer now so nonchalantly directed his course, were then not housed in any such stately edifice as that which now covers the heart of the financial world, nor did the location of the young and struggling institution, in a by-street of the great city, tend to give dignity to a concern which still lacked importance and assuredness. Thither, then, might have gone almost any young traveler who needed a letter of credit cashed, or a bill changed after the fashion of the passing goldsmiths.

Yet it was not as mere transient customer of a money-changer that young Law now sought the Bank of England, nor was it as a commercial house that the bank then commanded attention. That bank, young as it was, had already become a pillar of the throne of England. William, distracted by wars abroad and factions at home, found his demands for funds ever in excess of the supply. More than that, the people of England discovered themselves in possession of a currency fluctuating, mutilated, and unstable, so that no man knew what was his actual fortune. The shrewd young financier, Montague, chancellor of the exchequer, who either by wisdom or good fortune had sanctioned the founding of the Bank of England, was at this very time addressing himself to the question of a recoinage of the specie of the realm of England. He needed help, he demanded ideas; nor was he too particular whence he obtained either the one or the other.

John Law was in London on no such blind quest as he had himself declared. He was here by the invitation, secret yet none the less obligatory, of Montague, controller of the financial policy of England. And he was to meet, here upon this fair morning, none less than my Lord Somers, keeper of the seals; none less than Sir Isaac Newton, the greatest mathematician of his time; none less than John Locke, the most learned philosopher of the day. Strong company this, for a young and unknown man, yet in the belief of Montague, himself a young man and a gambler by instinct, not too strong for this young Scotchman who had startled the Parliament of his own land by some of the most remarkable theories of finance which had ever been proposed in any country or to any government. As Law had himself arrogantly announced, he was indeed a philosopher and a mathematician, young as he was; and these things Montague was himself keen enough to know.

It promised, then, to be a strange and interesting council, this which was to meet to-day at the Bank of England, to adjust the value of England's coinage; two philosophers, one pompous trimmer, and two gamblers; the younger and more daring of whom was now calmly threading the streets of London on his way to a meeting which might mean much to him.

To John Law, adventurer, mathematician, philosopher, gambler, it seemed a natural enough thing that he should be asked to sit at the council table with the ablest minds of the day and pass upon questions the most important. This was not what gave him trouble. This matter of the coinage, these questions of finance—they were easy. But how to win the interest of the tall and gracious English girl whom he had met by chance that other morn, who had left no way open for a further meeting; how to gain access to the presence of that fair one—these were the questions which to John Law seemed of greater importance, and of greater difficulty in the answering.

The chair drew up at the somber quarters where the meeting had been set. Law knew the place by instinct, even without seeing the double row of heavy-visaged London constabulary which guarded the entrance. Here and there along the street were carriages and chairs, and multiplied conveyances of persons of consequence. Upon the narrow pavement, and within the little entrance-way that led to the inner room, there bustled about important-looking men, some with hooked noses, most with florid faces and well-fed bodies, but all with a certain dignity and sobriety of expression.

Montague himself, young, smooth-faced, dark-eyed, of active frame, of mobile and pleasing features, sat at the head of a long table. The high-strung quality of his nervous system was evidenced in his restless hands, his attitude frequently changed.

At the left of Montague sat Somers, lord keeper; older, of more steady demeanor, of fuller figure, of bold face and full light eye, a politician, not a ponderer. At the right of Montague, grave, silent, impassive, now and again turning a contemplative eye about him, sat that great man. Sir Isaac Newton, known then to every nobleman, and now to every schoolboy, of the world. A gem-like mind, keen, clear, hard and brilliant, exact in every facet, and forsooth held in the setting of an iron body. Gentle, unmoved, self-assured, Sir Issac Newton was calm as morn itself as he sat in readiness to give England the benefit of his wisdom.

Beyond sat John Locke, abstruse philosopher, a man thinner and darker than his *confrere*, with large full orb, with the brow of the student and the man of thought. In dignity he shared with the learned gentleman sitting near him.

All those at the board looked with some intentness at the figure of the young man from the North, who came as the guest of Montague. With small formality, the latter rose and advanced to meet Law with an eager grasp of the hand. He made him known to the others present promptly, but with a half apology.

"Gentlemen," said he, "I have made bold to ask the presence with us of a young man who has much concerned himself with problems such as those which we have now in hand. Sir Isaac Newton, this is Mr. Law of Edinboro'. Mr. Law, the fame of John Locke I need not lay before you, and of my Lord Somers you need no advice. Mr. Law, I shall pray you to be seated.

"I shall but serve as your mouthpiece to the Court, gentlemen," resumed Montague, seating himself and turning at once to the business of the day. "We are all agreed as to the urgency of the case. The king needs behind him in these times a contented people. You have already seen the imminence of a popular discontent which may shake the throne of England, none too safe in these days of change. That we must reorganize the coinage is understood and agreed. The question is, how best to do this without further unsettling the times. My Lord Keeper, I must beg you for your suggestions."

"Sir," said Somers, shifting and coughing, "it is as you say. The question is of great moment. I should suggest a decree that the old coin shall pass by weight alone and not by its face value. Call in all the coin and have it weighed, the government to make future payment to the owner of the coin of the difference between its nominal and its real value. The coin itself should be restored forthwith to its owner. Hence the trade and the credit of the realm would not suffer. The money of the country would be withdrawn from the use of the country only that short time wherein it was in process of counting. This, it occurs to me, would surely be a practical method, and could work harm to none." My Lord Somers sat back, pulling out his chest complacently.

"Sir Isaac," said Montague, "and Mr. Locke, we must beg you to find such fault as you may with this plan which my Lord Keeper hath suggested."

Sir Isaac made no immediate reply. John Locke stirred gently in his chair. "There seemeth much to commend in this plan of my Lord Keeper," said he, leaning slightly forward, "but in pondering my Lord Keeper's suggestion for the bringing in of this older coin, I must ask you if this plan can escape that selfish impulse of the human mind which seeketh for personal gain? For, look you, short as would be the time proposed, it taketh but still shorter time to mutilate a coin; and it doth seem to me that, under the plan of my Lord Keeper, we should see the old currency of England mutilated in a night. Sir, I should opine in the contrary of this plan, and would base my decision upon certain principles which I believe to be ever present in the human soul."

Montague cast down his eye for a moment. "Sir Isaac," at length he began, "we are relying very much upon you. Is there no suggestion which you can offer on this ticklish theme?"

The large, full face of the great man was turned calmly and slowly upon the speaker. His deep and serene eye apparently saw not so much the man before him as the problem which lay on that man's mind.

"Sir," said Sir Isaac, "as John Locke hath said, this is after all much a matter of clear reasoning. There come into this problem two chief questions: First, who shall pay the expense of the recoinage? Shall the Government pay the expense, or shall the owner of the coin, who is to obtain good coin for evil?

"Again, this matter applieth not to one man but to many men. Now if one half the tradesmen of England rush to us with their coin for reminting, surely the trade of the country will have left not sufficient medium with which to prosper. This I take to be the second part of this problem.

"There be certain persons of the realm who claim that we may keep our present money as it is, but mark from its face a certain amount of value. Look you, now, this were a small thing; yet, in my mind, it clearly seemeth dishonesty. For, if I owe my neighbor a debt, let us say for an hundred sovereigns, shall I not be committing injustice upon my neighbor if I pay him an hundred sovereigns less that deduction which the realm may see fit thus to impose upon the face of my sovereign? This, in justice, sirs, I hold it to be not the part of science, nor the part of honesty, neither of statesmanship, to endorse."

"Sir Isaac," cried Montague, striking his nervous hands upon the table, "recoin we must. But how, and, as you say, at whose expense? We are as far now from a plan as when we started. We but multiply difficulties. What we need now is not so much negative measures as positive ones. We must do this thing, and we must do it promptly. The question is still of how it may best be done. Mr. Law, by your leave and by the leave of these gentlemen here present, I shall take the liberty of asking you if there doth occur to your mind any plan by which we may be relieved of certain of these difficulties. I am aware, sir, that you are much a student in these matters."

A grave silence fell upon all. John Law, young, confident and arrogant in many ways as he was, none the less possessed sobriety and depth of thought, just as he possessed the external dignity to give it fitting vehicle. He gazed now at the men before him, not with timorousness or trepidation. His face was grave, and he returned their glances calmly as he rose and made the speech which, unknown to himself, was presently to prove so important in his life.

"My Lords," said he, "and gentlemen of this council, I am ill-fitted to be present here, and ill-fitted to add my advice to that which has been given. It is not for me to go beyond the purpose of this meeting, or to lay before you certain plans of my own regarding the credit of nations. I may start, as does our learned friend, simply from established principles of human nature.

"It is true that the coinage is a creature of the government. Yet I believe it to be true that the government lives purely upon credit; which is to say, the confidence of the people in that government.

"Now, we may reason in this matter perhaps from the lesser relations of our daily life. What manner of man do we most trust among those whom we meet? Surely, the honest man, the plain man, the one whose directness and integrity we do not doubt. Truly you may witness the nature of such a man in the manner of his speech, in his mien, in his conduct. Therefore, my Lords and gentlemen, it seems to me plain that we shall best gain confidence for ourselves if we act in the most simple fashion.

"Let us take up this matter directly with Parliament, not seeking to evade the knowledge of Parliament in any fashion; for, as we know, the Parliament and the king are not the best bed-fellows these days, and the one is ready enough to suspect the other. Let us have a bill framed for Parliament—such bill made upon the decisions of these learned gentlemen present. Above all things, let us act with perfect openness.

"As to the plan itself, it seems that a few things may be held safe and sure. Since we can not use the old coin, then surely we must have new coin, milled coin, which Charles, the earlier king of England, has decreed. Surely, too, as our learned friend has wisely stated, the loss in any recoinage ought, in full justice and honesty, to fall not upon the people of England, but upon the government of England. It seems equally plain to me there must be a day set after which the old coin may no longer be used. Set it some months ahead, not, as my Lord Keeper suggests, but a few days; so that full notice may be given to all. Make your campaign free and plain, and place it so that it may be known, not only of

Parliament, but of all the world. Thus you establish yourselves in the confidence of Parliament and in the good graces of this people, from whom the taxes must ultimately come."

Montague's hands smote again upon the table with a gesture of conviction. John Locke shifted again in his chair. Sir Isaac and the lord keeper gazed steadfastly at this young man who stood before them, calmly, assuredly, and yet with no assumption in his mien.

"Moreover," went on John Law, calmly, "there is this further benefit to be gained, as I am sure my countryman, Mr. Paterson, has long ago made plain. It is not a question of the wealth of England, but a question of the confidence of the people in the throne. There is money in abundance in England. It is the province of my Lord Chancellor to wheedle it out of those coffers where it is concealed and place it before the uses of the king. Gentlemen, it is confidence that we need. There will be no trouble to secure loans of money in this rich land, but the taxes must be the pledge to your bankers. This new Bank of England will furnish you what moneys you may need. Secure them only by the pledge of such taxes as you feel the people may not resent; give the people, free of cost, a coinage which they can trust; and then, it seems to me, my Lords and gentlemen, the problem of the revenue may be thought solved simply and easily—solved, too, without irritating either the people or the Parliament, or endangering the relations of Parliament and the throne."

The conviction which fell upon all found its best expression in the face of Montague. The youth and nervousness of the man passed away upon the instant. He sat there sober and thoughtful, quiet and resolved.

"Gentlemen," said he at last, slowly, "my course is plain from this instant. I shall draw the bill and it shall go to Parliament. The expense of this recoinage I am sure we can find maintained by the stockholders of the Bank of England, and for their pay we shall propose a new tax upon the people of England. We shall tax the windows of the houses of England, and hence tax not only the poor but the rich of England, and that proportionately with their wealth. As for the coin of England, it shall be honest coin, made honest and kept honest, at no cost to the people of old England. Sirs, my heart is lighter than it has been for many days."

The last trace of formality in the meeting having at length vanished, Montague made his way rapidly to the foot of the table. He caught Law by both his hands.

"Sir," said he, "you helped us at the last stage of our ascent. A mistake here had been ruinous, not only to myself and friends, but to the safety of the whole Government. You spoke wisely and practically. Sir, if I can ever in all my life serve you, command me, and at whatever price you name. I am not yet done with you, sir," resumed Montague, casting his arm boyishly about the other's shoulder as they walked out. "We must meet again to discuss certain problems of the currency which, I bethink me, you have studied deeply. Keep you here in London, for I shall have need of you. Within the month, perhaps within the week, I shall require you. England needs men who can do more than dawdle. Pray you, keep me advised where you may be found."

There was ill omen in the light reply. "Why, as to that, my Lord," said Law, "if you should think my poor service useful, your servants might get trace of me at the Green Lion—unless I should be in prison! No man knoweth what may come."

Montague laughed lightly. "At the Green Lion, or in Newgate itself," said he. "Be ready, for I have not yet done with you."

CHAPTER VI

THE RESOLUTION OF MR. LAW

The problems of England's troubled finances, the questions of the coinage, the gossip of the king's embroilments with the Parliament—these things, it may again be said, occupied Law's mind far less than the question of gaining audience with his fair rescuer of the morn at Sadler's Wells. This was the puzzle which, revolve it as he might, not even his audacious wit was able to provide with plausible solution. He pondered the matter in a hundred different pleasing phases as he passed from the Bank of England through the crowded streets of London, and so at length found himself at the shabby little lodgings in Bradwell Street, where he and his brother had, for the time, taken up their quarters.

"It starteth well, my boy," cried he, gaily, to his brother, when at length he had found his way up the narrow stair into the little room, and discovered Will patiently awaiting his return. "Already two of my errands are well acquit."

"You have, then, sent the letters to our goldsmith here?" said Will.

"Now, to say truth, I had not thought of that. But letters of credit—why need we trouble over such matters? These

English are but babes. Give me a night or so in the week at the Green Lion, and we'll need no letters of credit, Will. Look at your purse, boy—since you are the thrifty cashier of our firm!"

"I like not this sort of gold," said Will Law, setting his lips judicially.

"Yet it seems to purchase well as any," said the other, indifferently. "At least, such is my hope, for I have made debt against our purse of some fifty sovereigns—some little apparel which I have ordered. For, look you, Will, I must be clothed proper. In these days, as I may tell you, I am to meet such men as Montague, chancellor of the exchequer—my Lord Keeper Somers—Sir Isaac Newton—Mr. John Locke— gentry of that sort. It is fitting I should have better garb than this which we have brought with us."

"You are ever free with some mad jest or other, Jack; but what is this new madness of which you speak?"

"No madness at all, my dear boy; for in fact I have but come from the council chamber, where I have met these very gentlemen whom I have named to you. But pray you note, my dear brother, there are those who hold John Law, and his studies, not so light as doth his own brother. For myself, the matter furnishes no surprise at all. As for you, you had never confidence in me, nor in yourself. Gad! Will, hadst but the courage of a flea, what days we two might have together here in this old town!"

"I want none of such days, Jack," said Will Law, soberly. "I care most to see you settled in some decent way of living. What will your mother say, if we but go on gaming and roistering, with dangers of some sudden quarrel—as this which has already sprung up—with no given aim in life, with nothing certain for an ambition—"

"Now, Will," began his brother, yet with no petulance in his tone, "pray go not too hard with me at the start. I thought I had done fairly well, to sit at the table of the council of coinage on my first day in London. 'Tis not every young man gets so far as that. Come, now, Will!"

"But after all, there must be serious purpose."

"Know then," cried the elder man, suddenly, "that I have found such serious purpose!"

The speaker stood looking out of the window, his eye fixed out across the roofs of London. There had now fallen from his face all trace of levity, and into his eye and mouth there came reflex of the decision of his speech. Will stirred in his chair, and at length the two faced each other.

"And pray, what is this sudden resolution, Jack?" said Will Law.

"If I must tell you, it is simply this: I am resolved to marry the girl we met at Sadler's Wells."

"How—what—?"

"Yes, how—what—?" repeated his brother, mockingly.

"But I would ask, which?"

"There was but one," said John Law. "The tall one, with the brassy-brown, copper-red hair, the bright blue eye, and the figure of a queen. Her like is not in all the world!"

"Methought 'twas more like to be the other," replied Will.

"Yet you—how dare you think thus of that lady? Why, Jack, 'twas the Lady Catharine Knollys, sister to the Earl of Banbury!"

Law did not at once make any answer. He turned to the dressing-table and began making such shift as he could to better his appearance.

"Will," said he, at length, "you are, as ever, a babe and a suckling. I quite despair of you. 'Twould serve no purpose to explain anything to so faint a heart as yours. But you may come with me."

"And whither?"

"Whither? Where else, than to the residence of this same lady! Look you, I have learned this. She is, as you say, the sister of the Earl of Banbury, and is for the time at the town house in Knightwell Terrace. Moreover, if that news be worth while to so white-feathered a swain as yourself, the other, damsel, the dark one—the one with the mighty pretty little foot—lives there for the time as the guest of Lady Catharine. They are rated thick as peas in a pod. True, we are strangers, yet I venture we have made a beginning, and if we venture more we may better that beginning. Should I falter, when luck gave me the run of *trente et le va* but yesterday? Nay, ever follow fortune hard, and she waits for you."

"Yes," said Will, scornfully. "You would get the name of gambler, and add to it the name of fortune-hunting, heiress-seeking adventurer."

"Not so," replied John Law, taking snuff calmly and still keeping the evenness of his temper. "My own fortune, as I admit, I keep safe at the Green Lion. For the rest, I seek at the start only respectful footing with this maid herself. When first I saw her, I knew well enough how the end would be. We were made for each other. This whole world was made for us both. Will, boy, I could not live without the Lady Catharine Knollys!"

"Oh, cease such talk, Jack! 'Tis ill-mannered, such presumption regarding a lady, even had you known her long. Besides, 'tis but another of your fancies, Jack," said Will. "Wilt never make an end of such follies?"

"Yes, my boy," said his brother, gravely. "I have made an end. Indeed, I made it the other morning at Sadler's Wells."

"Methinks," said Will, dryly, "that it might be well first to be sure that you can win past the front door of the house of Knollys."

John Law still kept both his temper and his confidence.

"Come with me," said he, blithely, "and I will show you how that thing may be done."

CHAPTER VII

TWO MAIDS A-BROIDERING

"Now a plague take all created things, Lady Kitty!" cried Mary Connynge, petulantly flinging down a silken pattern over which she had pretended to be engaged. "There are devils in the skeins to-day. I'll try no more with't."

"Fie! For shame, Mary Connynge," replied Lady Catharine Knollys, reprovingly. "So far from better temperance of speech, didst ever hear of the virtue of perseverance? Now, for my own part—"

"And what, for your own part? Have I no eyes to see that thou'rt puttering over the same corner this last half hour? What is it thou art making to-day?"

The Lady Catharine paused for a moment and held her embroidery frame away from her at arm's length, looking at it with brow puckering into a perplexed frown.

"I was working a knight," said she. "A tall one—"

"Yes, a tall one, with yellow hair, I warrant."

"Why, so it was. I was but seeking floss of the right hue, and found it difficult."

"And with blue eyes?"

"True; or perhaps gray. I could not state which. I had naught in my box would serve to suit me for the eyes. But how know you this, Mary Connynge?" asked the Lady Catharine.

"Because I was making some such knight for myself," replied the other. "See! He was to have been tall, of good figure, wearing a wide hat and plume withal. But lest I spoil him, my knight—now a plague take me indeed if I do not ruin him complete!" So saying, she drew with vengeful fingers at the intricately woven silks until she had indeed undone all that had gone before.

"Nay, nay! Mary Connynge! Do not so!" replied Lady Catharine in expostulation. "The poor knight, how could he help himself? Why, as for mine, though I find him not all I could wish, I'll e'en be patient as I may, and seek if I may not mend him. These knights, you know, are most difficult. 'Tis hard to make them perfect."

Mary Connynge sat with her hands in her lap, looking idly out of the window and scarce heeding the despoiled fabric which lay on her lap. "Come, confess, Lady Kitty," said she at length, turning toward her friend. "Wert not trying to copy a knight of a hedge-row after all? Did not a certain tall young knight, with eyes of blue, or gray, or the like, give pattern for your sampler while you were broidering to-day?"

"Fie! For shame!" again replied Lady Catharine, flushing none the less. "Rather ask, does not such a thought come over thine own broidering? But as to the hedge-row, surely the gentleman explained it all proper enough; and I am sure—yes, I am very sure—that my brother Charles had quite approved of my giving the injured young man the lift in the coach—"

"Provided that your Brother Charles had ever heard of such a thing!"

"Well, of that, to be sure, why trouble my brother over such a trifle, when 'twas so obviously proper?" argued Lady Catharine, bravely. "And certainly, if we come to knights and the like, good chivalry has ever demanded succor for those in distress; and if, forsooth, it was two damsels in a comfortable coach, who rescued two knights from underneath a hedge-row, why, such is but the way of these modern days, when knights go seeking no more for adventures and ladies fair; as you very well know."

"As I do not know, Lady Catharine," replied Mary Connynge. "To the contrary, 'twould not surprise me to learn that he would not shrink from any adventure which might offer."

"You mean—that is—you mean the tall one, him who said he was Mr. Law of Lauriston?"

"Well, perhaps. Though I must say," replied Mary Connynge, with indirection, "that I fancy the other far more, he being not so forward, nor so full of pure conceit. I like not a man so confident." This with an eye cast down, as much as though there were present in the room some man subject to her coquetry.

"Why, I had not found him offering such an air," replied Lady Catharine, judicially. "I had but thought him frank enough, and truly most courteous."

"Why, truly," replied Mary Connynge. "But saw you naught

in his eye?"

"Why, but that it was blue, or gray," replied Lady Catharine.

"Oh, ho! then my lady did look a bit, after all! And so this is why the knight flourisheth so bravely in silks to-day—Fie! but a mere adventurer, Lady Kitty. He says he is Law of Lauriston; but what proof doth he offer? And did he find such proof, it is proof of what? For my part, I did never hear of Lauriston nor its owner."

"Ah, but that I have, to the contrary," said Lady Catharine. "John Law's father was a goldsmith, and it was he who bought the properties of Lauriston and Randleston. And so far from John Law being ill-born, why, his mother was Jean Campbell, kinswoman of the Campbell, Duke of Argyll; and a mighty important man is the Duke of Argyll these days, I may tell you, as the king's army hath discovered before this. You see, I have not talked with my brother about these things for naught."

"So you make excuse for this Mr. Law of Lauriston," said Mary Connynge. "Well, I like better a knight who comes on his own horse, or in his own chariot, and who rescues me when I am in trouble, rather than asks me to give him aid. But, as to that, what matter? We set those highway travelers down, and there was an end of it. We shall never see either of them again."

"Of course not," said Lady Catharine.

"It were impossible."

"Oh, quite impossible!"

Both the young women sighed, and both looked out of

the window.

"Because," said Mary Connynge, "they are but strangers. That talk of having letters may be but deceit. They themselves may be coiners. I have heard it said that coiners are monstrous bold."

"To be sure, he mentioned Sir Arthur Pembroke," ventured Lady Catharine.

"Oh! And be sure Sir Arthur Pembroke will take pains enough that no tall young man, who offers roses to ladies on first acquaintance, shall ever have opportunity to present himself to Lady Catharine Knollys. Nay, nay! There will be no introduction from that source, of that be sure. Sir Arthur is jealous as a wolf of thee already, Lady Kitty. See! He hath followed thee about like a dog for three years. And after all, why not reward him, Lady Kitty? Indeed, but the other day thou wert upon the very point of giving him his answer, for thou saidst to me that he sure had the prettiest eyes of any man in London. Pray, are Sir Arthur's eyes blue, or gray—or what? And can you match his eyes among the color of your flosses?"

"It might be," said Lady Catharine, musingly, "that he would some day find means to send us word."

"Who? Sir Arthur?"

"No. The young man, Mr. Law of Lauriston."

"Yes; or he might come himself," replied Mary Connynge.

"Fie! He dare not!"

"Oh, but be not too sure. Now suppose he did come—'twill

do no harm for us to suppose so much as that. Suppose he stood there at your very door, Lady Kitty. Then what would you do?"

"Do! Why, tell James that we were not in, and never should be, and request the young man to leave at once."

"And never let him pass the door again."

"Certainly not! 'Twould be presumption. But then"—this with a gentle sigh—"we need not trouble ourselves with this. I doubt not he hath forgot us long ago, just as indeed we have forgotten him—though I would say—. But I half believe he hit thee, girl, with his boldness and his bow, and his fearlessness withal."

"Who, I? Why, heavens! Lady Kitty! The idea never came to my mind. Indeed no, not for an instant. Of course, as you say, 'twas but a passing occurrence, and 'twas all forgot. But, by the way, Lady Kitty, go we to Sadler's Wells to-morrow morn?"

"I see no reason for not going," replied Lady Catharine. "And we may drive about, the same way we took the other morn. I will show you the same spot where he stood and bowed so handsomely, and made so little of the fight with the robbers the night before, as though 'twere trifling enough; and made so little of his poverty, as though he were owner of the king's coin."

"But we shall never see him more," said Mary Connynge.

"To be sure not. But just to show you—see! He stood thus, his hat off, his eye laughing, I pledge you, as though for some good jest he had. And 'twas 'your pardon, ladies!' he said, as though he were indeed nobleman himself. See!

'Twas thus."

What pantomime might have followed did not appear, for at that moment the butler appeared at the door with an admonitory cough. "If you please, your Ladyship," said he, "there are two persons waiting. They—that is to say, he—one of them, asks for admission to your Ladyship."

"What name does he offer, James?"

"Mr. John Law of Lauriston, your Ladyship, is the name he sends. He says, if your Ladyship please, that he has brought with him something which your Ladyship left behind, if your Ladyship please."

Lady Catharine and Mary Connynge had both arisen and drawn together, and they now turned each a swift half glance upon the other.

"Are these gentlemen waiting without the street door?" asked Lady Catharine.

"No, your Ladyship. That is to say, before I thought, I allowed the tall one to come within."

"Oh, well then, you see, Mary Connynge," replied Lady Catharine, with the pink flush rising in her cheek, "it were rude to turn them now from our door, since they have already been admitted."

"Yes, we will send to the library for your brother," said Mary Connynge, dimpling at the corners of her mouth.

"No, I think it not needful to do that," replied Lady Catharine, "but we should perhaps learn what this young man brings, and then we'll see to it that we chide him so that he'll no more presume upon our kindness. My brother need not know, and we ourselves will end this forwardness at once, Mary Connynge, you and I. James, you may bring the gentlemen in."

Enter, therefore, John Law and his brother Will, the former seeming thus with ease to have made good his promise to win past the door of the Earl of Banbury.

John Law, as on the morning of the roadside meeting, approached in advance of his more timid brother, though both bowed deeply as they entered. He bowed again respectfully, his eyes not wandering hither and yon upon the splendors of this great room in an ancestral home of England. His gaze was fixed rather upon the beauty of the tall girl before him, whose eyes, now round and startled, were not quite able to be cold nor yet to be quite cast down; whose white throat throbbed a bit under its golden chain; whose bosom rose and fell perceptibly beneath its falls of snowy laces.

"Lady Catharine Knollys," said John Law, his voice deep and even, and showing no false note of embarrassment, "we come, as you may see, to make our respects to yourself and your friend, and to thank you for your kindness to two strangers."

"To two strangers, Mr. Law," said Lady Catharine, pointedly.

"Yes"—and the answering smile was hard to be denied—"to two strangers who are still strangers. I did but bethink me it was sweet to have such kindness. We were advised that London was cruel cold, and that all folk of this city hated their fellow-men. So, since 'twas welcome to be thus kindly entreated, I believed it but the act of courtesy to express our thanks more seeming than we might as that we were two beggars by the wayside. Therefore, I pay the first flower of my perpetual tribute." He bowed and extended, as he spoke, a deep red rose. His eye, though still direct, was as much imploring as it was bold.

Instinctively Mary Connynge and Lady Catharine had drawn together, retreating somewhat from this intrusion. They were now standing, like any school girls, looking timidly over their shoulders, as he advanced. Lady Catharine hesitated, and yet she moved forward a half pace, as though bidden by some unheard voice. "'Twas nothing, what we did for you and your brother," said she. She extended her hand as she spoke. "As for the flower, I think—I think a rose is a sweet-pretty thing."

She bent her cheek above the blossom, and whether the cheek or the petal were the redder, who should say? If there were any ill at ease in that room, it was not Law of Lauriston. He stood calm as though there by right. It was an escapade, an adventure, without doubt, as both these young women saw plainly enough. And now, what to do with this adventure since it had arrived?

"Sir," said Lady Catharine at length, "I am sure you must be wearied with the heavy heats of the town. Your brother must still be weak from his hurt. Pray you, be seated." She placed the rose upon the tabouret as she passed, and presently pulled at the bell cord.

"James," said she, standing very erect and full of dignity, "go to the library and see if Sir Charles be within."

When the butler's solemn cough again gave warning, it was to bring information which may or may not have been news to Lady Catharine. "Your Ladyship," said he, "Sir Charles is said to have taken carriage an hour ago, and left no word."

"Send me Cecile, James," said Lady Catharine, and again the butler vanished.

"Cecile," said she, as the maid at length appeared, "you may serve us with tea."

CHAPTER VIII

CATHARINE KNOLLYS

"You mistake, sir! I am no light o' love, John Law!"

Thus spoke Catharine Knollys. She stood near the door of the great drawing-room of the Knollys mansion, her figure beseeming well its framing of deep hangings and rich tapestries. Her eyes were wide and flashing, her cheeks deeply pink, the sweet bow of her lips half a-quiver in her vehemence. Her surpassing personal beauty, rich, ripe, enticing, gave more than sufficient challenge for the fiery blood of the young man before her.

It was less than two weeks since these two had met. Surely the flood of time had run swiftly in those few days. Not a day had passed that Law had not met Catharine Knollys, nor had yet one meeting been such as the girl in her own conscience dared call better than clandestine, even though they met, as now, under her own roof. Yet, reason as she liked, struggle as she could, Catharine Knollys had not yet been quite able to end this swift voyaging on the flood of fate. It was so strange, so new, so sweet withal, this coming of her suitor, as from the darkness of some unknown star, so bold, so strong, so confident, and yet so humble! All the old song of the ages thrilled within her soul, and each day its compelling melody had accession. That this delirious softening of all her senses meant danger, the Lady Catharine could not deny. Yet could aught of earth be wrong when it spelled such happiness, such sweetness—when the sound of a footfall sent her blood going the faster, when the sight of a tall form, the ring of a vibrant tone, caused her limbs to weaken, her throat to choke?

But ah! whence and why this spell, this sorcery—why this sweetness filling all her being, when, after all, duty and seemliness bade it all to end, as end it must, to-day? Thus had the Lady Catharine reflected but the hour before John Law came; her knight of dreams—tall, yellow-haired, blue-eyed, bold and tender, and surely speaking truth if truth dwelt beneath the stars. Now he would come—now he had come again. Here was his red, red rose once more. Here, burning in her ears, singing in her heart, were his avowing, pleading words. And this must end!

John Law looked at her calmly, but said nothing. One hand, in a gesture customary with him, flicked lightly at the deep cuff of the other wrist, and this nervous movement was the sole betrayal of his uneasiness.

"You come to this house time and again," resumed Catharine Knollys, "as though it were an ancient right on your part, as though you had always been a friend of this family. And yet—"

"And so I have been," broke in her suitor. "My people were friends of yours before we two were born. Why, then, should you advise your servant, as you have, fairly to deny me admission at the door?"

"I have done ill enough to admit you. Had I dreamed of this last presumption on your part I should never have seen your face again."

"'Tis not presumption," said the young man, his voice low and even, though ringing with the feeling to which even he dared not give full expression. "I myself might call this presumption in another, but with myself 'tis otherwise."

"Sir," said Lady Catharine Knollys, "you speak as one not of good mind."

"Not of good mind!" broke out John Law. "Say rather of mind too good to doubt, or dally, or temporize. Why, 'tis plain as the plan of fate! It was in the stars that I should come to you. This face, this form, this heart, this soul—I shall see nothing else so long as I live! Oh, I feel myself unworthy; you have right to think me of no station. Yet some day I shall bring to you all that wealth can buy, all that station can mean. Catharine—dear Lady Kitty—dear Kate—"

"I like not so fast a soothsaying in any suitor of mine," replied Lady Catharine, hotly, "and this shall go no further." Her hand restrained him.

"Then you find me distasteful? You would banish me? I could not learn to endure it!"

Lady Catharine looked at him curiously. "Actually, sir," said she, "you cause me to chill. I could half fear you. What is in your heart? Surely, this is a strange love-making."

"And by that," cried John Law, "know, then the better of the truth. Listen! I know! And this is what I know—that I shall succeed, and that I shall love you always!"

"'Tis what one hears often from men, in one form or

another," said the girl, coolly, seating herself as she spoke.

"Talk not to me of other men—I'll not brook it!" cried he, advancing toward her a few rapid paces. "Think you I have no heart?" His eye gleamed, and he came on yet a step in his strange wooing. "Your face is here, here," he cried, "deep in my heart! I must always look upon it, or I am a lost man!"

"'Tis a face not so fair as that," said the Lady Catharine, demurely.

"'Tis the fairest face in England, or in the world!" cried her lover; and now he was close at her side. Her hand, she knew not how, rested in his own. Something of the honesty and freedom from coquetry of the young woman's nature showed in her next speech, inconsequent, illogical, almost unmaidenly in its swift sincerity and candor.

"'Tis a face but blemished," said she, slowly, the color rising to her cheek. "See! Here is the birth-mark of the house of Knollys. They tell me—my very good friends tell me, that this is the mark of shame, the bar sinister of the hand of justice. You know the story of our house."

"Somewhat of it," said Law.

"My brother is not served of the writ when Parliament is called. This you know. Tell me why?"

"I know the so-called reason," replied John Law. "'Twas brought out in his late case at the King's Bench."

"True. 'Twas said that my grandfather, past eighty, was not the father of those children of his second wife. There is talk that—"

"'Twas three generations ago, this talk of the Knollys shortcoming. I am not eighty. I am twenty-four, and I love you, Catharine Knollys."

"It was three generations ago," said the Lady Catharine, slowly and musingly, as though she had not heard the speech of her suitor. "Three generations ago. Yet never since then hath there been clean name for the Banbury estate. Never yet hath its peer sat in his rightful place in Parliament. And never yet hath eldest daughter of this house failed to show this mark of shame, this unpurged contempt for that which is ordained. Surely it would seem fate holds us in its hands."

"You tell me these things," said John Law, "because you feel it is right to tell them. And I tell you of my future, as you tell me of your past. Why? Because, Lady Catharine Knollys, it has already come to matter of faith between us."

The girl leaned back against the wall near which she had seated herself. The young man bent forward, taking both her hands quietly in his own now, and gazing steadily into her eyes. There was no triumph in his gaze. Perhaps John Law had prescience of the future.

"Oh, sir, I had far liefer I had never seen you," cried Catharine Knollys, bending a head from whose eyes there dropped sudden tears.

"Ah, dear heart, say anything but that!"

"'Tis a hard way a woman must travel at best in this world," murmured the Lady Catharine, with wisdom all unsuited to her youth. "But I can not understand. I had thought that the coming of a lover was a joyous thing, a time of happiness alone."

"Ah, now, in the hour of mist can you not foresee the time of sunshine? All life is before us, my sweet, all life. There is much for us to do, there are so many, many days of love and happiness."

But now the Lady Catharine Knollys veered again, with some sudden change of the inner currents of the feminine soul.

"I have gone far with you, Mr. Law," said she, suddenly disengaging her hand. "Yet I did but give you insight of things which any man coming as you have come should have well within his knowledge. Think not, sir, that I am easy to be won. I must know you equally honest with myself. And if you come to my regard, it must be step by step and stair by stair. This is to be remembered."

"I shall remember."

"Go, then, and leave me for this time," she besought him. But still he could not go, and still the Lady Catharine could not bid him more sternly to depart. Youth—youth, and love, and fate were in that room; and these would have their way.

The beseeching gaze of an eye singular in its power rested on the girl, a gaze filled with all the strange, half mandatory pleading of youth and yearning. Once more there came a shift in the tidal currents of the woman's heart. The Lady Catharine slowly became conscious of a delicious helplessness, of a sinking and yielding which she could not resist. Her head lost power to be erect. It slipped forward on a shoulder waiting as by right. Her breath came in soft measure, and unconsciously a hand was raised to touch the cheek pressed down to hers. John Law kissed her once upon the lips. Suddenly, without plan—in spite of all plan—the seal of a strange fate was set forever on her life!

For a long moment they stood thus, until at length she raised a face pale and sharp, and pushed back against his breast a hand that trembled.

"'Tis wondrous strange," she whispered.

"Ask nothing," said John Law, "fear nothing. Only believe, as I believe."

Neither John Law nor the Lady Catharine Knollys saw what was passing just without the room. They did not see the set face which looked down from the stairway. Through the open door Mary Connynge could see the young man as he stepped out of the door, could see the conduct of the girl now left alone in the drawing-room. She saw the Lady Catharine sink down upon the seat, her head drooped in thought, her hand lying languidly out before her. Pale now and distraught, the Lady Catharine Knollys wist little of what went on before her. She had full concern with the tumult which waged riot in her soul.

Mary Connynge turned, and started back up the stair unseen. She paused, her yellow eyes gone narrow, her little hand clutched tight upon the rail.

CHAPTER IX

IN SEARCH OF THE QUARREL

As Law turned away from the door of the Knollys mansion, he walked with head bent forward, not looking upon the one hand or the other. He raised his eyes only when a passing horseman had called thrice to him.

"What!" cried Sir Arthur Pembroke. "I little looked to see you here, Mr. Law. I thought it more likely you were engaged in other business—"

"Meaning by that—?"

"What should I mean, except that I supposed you preparing for your little affair with Wilson?"

"My little affair?"

"Certainly, with Wilson, as I said. I saw our friend Castleton but now, and he advised me of your promptness. He had searched for you for days, he being chosen by Wilson for his friend—and said he had at last found you in your lodgings. Egad! I have mistook your kidney completely. Never in London was a duel brought on so swift. 'Fight? This afternoon!' said you. Jove! but the young bloods laughed when they heard of it. 'Bloody Scotland' is what they have christened you at the Green Lion. 'He said to me,' said Charlie, 'that he was slow to find a quarrel, but since this quarrel was brought home to him, 'twere meet 'twere soon finished. He thought, forsooth, that four o'clock of the afternoon were late enough.' Gad! But you might have given Wilson time at least for one more dinner."

"What do you mean?" exclaimed Law, mystified still.

"Mean! Why, I mean that I've been scouring London to find you. My faith, man, but thou'rt a sudden actor! Where caught you this unseemly haste?"

"Sir Arthur," said the other, slowly, "you do me too much justice. I have made no arrangement to meet Mr. Wilson, nor have I any wish to do so."

"Pish, man! You must not jest with me in such a case as this. 'Tis no masquerading. Let me tell you, Wilson has a vicious sword, and a temper no less vicious. You have touched him on his very sorest spot. He has gone to meet you this vary hour. His coach will be at Bloomsbury Square this afternoon, and there he will await you. I promise you he is eager as yourself. 'Tis too late now to accommodate this matter, even had you not sent back so prompt and bold an answer."

"I have sent him no answer at all!" cried Law. "I have not seen Castleton at all."

"Oh, come!" expostulated Sir Arthur, his face showing a flush of annoyance.

"Sir Arthur," continued Law, as he raised his head, "I am of the misfortune to be but young in London, and I am in need of your friendship. I find myself pressed for rapid transportation. Pray you, give me your mount, for I must have speed. I shall not need the service of your seconding. Indulge me now by asking no more, and wait until we meet again. Give me the horse, and quickly."

"But you must be seconded!" cried the other. "This is too unusual. Consider!" Yet all the time he was giving a hand at the stirrup of Law, who sprang up and was off before he had time to formulate his own wonder.

"Who and what is he?" muttered the young nobleman to himself as he gazed after the retreating form. "He rides well, at least, as he does everything else well. 'Till I return,' forsooth, 'till I return!' Gad! I half wish you had never come in the first place, my Bloody Scotland!"

As for Law, he rode swiftly, asking at times his way, losing time here, gaining it again there, creating much hatred among foot folk by his tempestuous speed, but giving little heed to aught save his own purpose. In time he reached Bradwell Street and flung himself from his panting horse in front of the dingy door of the lodging house. He rushed up the stairs at speed and threw open the door of the little room. It was empty.

There was no word to show what his brother had done, whither he had gone, when he would return. Around the lodgings in Bradwell Street lay a great and unknown London, with its own secrets, its own hatreds, its own crimes. A strange feeling of on-coming ill seized upon the heart of Law, as he stood in the center of the dull little room, now suddenly grown hateful to him. He dashed his hand upon the table, and stood so, scarce knowing which way to turn. A foot sounded in the hallway, and he went to the door. The ancient landlady confronted him. "Where has my brother gone?" he demanded, fiercely, as she came into view along the ill-lighted passage-way.

"Gone, good sir?" said she, quaveringly. "Why, how should I know where he has gone? More quality has been here this morning than ever I saw in Bradwell Street in all my life. First comes a coach this morning, with four horses as fine as the king's, and a man atop would turn your blood, he was that solemn-like, sir. Then your brother was up here alone, sir, and very still. I will swear he was never out of this room. Then, but an hour ago, here comes another coach, as big as the first, and yellower. And out of it steps another fine lord, and he bows to your brother, and in they get, and off goes the coach. But, God help me, sir! How should I know which way they went, or what should be their errand? Methinks it must be some servant come from the royal palace. Sir, be you two of the nobility? And if you be, why come you here to Bradwell Street? Sir, I am but a poor woman. If you be not of the nobility, then you must be either coiners or smugglers. Sir, I am bethought that you are dangerous guests in my house. I am a poor woman, as you know."

Law flung a coin at her as he sped through the hall and down the stair. "'Twas to Bloomsbury Square," he said, as he sprang into saddle and set heel to the flank of the good horse. "To Bloomsbury Square, then, and fast!"

CHAPTER X

THE RUMOR OF THE QUARREL

Meantime, at the Knollys mansion, there were forthcoming other parts of the drama of the day. The butler announced to Lady Catharine, still sitting dreaming by the window, Sir Arthur Pembroke, now late arrived on foot. Lady Catharine hesitated. "Show the gentleman to this room," she said at length.

Pembroke came forward eagerly as he entered. "Such a day of it, Lady Kitty!" he exclaimed, impulsively. "You will pardon me for coming thus, when I say I have just been robbed of my horse. 'Twas at your very door, and methinks you must know the highwayman. I have come to tell you of the news."

"You don't mean—"

"Yes, but I do! 'Twas no less than Mr. Law, of Scotland. He hath taken my horse and gone off like a whirlwind, leaving me afoot and friendless, save for your good self. I am begging a taste of tea and a little biscuit, for I vow I am half famished."

The Lady Catharine Knollys, in sheer reaction from the

strain, broke out into a peal of laughter.

"Sure, he has strange ways about him, this same Mr. Law," said she. "That young man would have come here direct, and would have made himself quite at home, methinks, had he had but the first encouragement."

"Gad! Lady Catharine, but he has a conceit of himself. Think you of what he has done in his short stay here in town! First, as you know, he sat at cards with two or three of us the other evening—Charlie Castleton, Beau Wilson, myself and one or two besides. And what doth he do but stake a bauble against good gold that he would make *sept et le va*."

"And did it?"

"And did it. Yes, faith, as though he saw it coming. Yet 'twas I who cut and dealt the cards. Nor was that the half of it," he went on. "He let the play run on till 'twas *seize et le va*, then *vingt-un et le va*, then twenty-five. And, strike me! Lady Catharine, if he sat not there cool as my Lord Speaker in the Parliament, and saw the cards run to *trente et le va*, as though 'twere no more to him than the eating of an orange!"

"And showed no anxiety at all?"

"None, as I tell you, and he proved to us plain that he had not two-pence to his name, for that he had been robbed the night before while on his way to town. He staked a diamond, a stone of worth. I must say, his like was never seen at cards."

"He hath strange quality."

"That you may say. Now read me some farther riddles of this same young man. He managed to win from me a little shoe of an American savage, which I had bought at a good price but the day before. It came to idle talk of ladies' shoes, and wagers—well, no matter; and so Mr. Law brought on a sudden quarrel with Beau Wilson. Then, though he seemed not wanting courage, he half declined to face Wilson on the field. Sudden to change as ever, this very morning he sent word to Wilson by Mr. Castleton that he was ready to meet him at four this afternoon. God save us! what a haste was there! And now, to cap it all, he hath taken my horse from me and ridden off to keep an appointment which he says he never made! Gad! These he odd ways enough, and almost too keen for me to credit. Why, 'twould not surprise me to hear that he had been here to make love to the Lady Catharine Knollys, and to offer her the proceeds of his luck at faro. And, strike me! if that same luck holds, he'll have all the money in London in another fortnight! I wish him joy of Wilson."

"He may be hurt!" exclaimed the Lady Catharine, starting up.

"Who? Beau Wilson?" exclaimed Sir Arthur. "Take no fear. He carries a good blade."

"Sir Arthur," said the girl, "is there no way to stop this foolish matter? Is there not yet time?"

"Why, as to that," said Sir Arthur, "it all depends upon the speed of my own horse. I should think myself e'en let off cheaply if he took the horse and rode on out of London, and never turned up again. Yet, I bethink me, he has a way of turning up. If so, then we are too late. Let him go. For me, I'd liefer sit me here with Lady Catharine, who, I perceive, is about now to save my death of hunger, since now I see the tea tray coming. Thank thee prettily."

Lady Catharine poured for him with a hand none too steady.

"Sir Arthur," said she, "you know why I have this concern over such a quarrel. You know well enough what the duello has cost the house of Knollys. Of my uncles, four were killed upon this so-called field of honor. My grandfather met his death in that same way. Another relative, before my time, is reputed to have slain a friend in this same manner. As you know, but three years ago, my brother, the living representative of our family, had the misfortune to slay his kinsman in a duel which sprang out of some little jest. I say to you, Sir Arthur, that this quarrel must be stopped, and we must do thus much for our friends forthwith. It must not go on."

"For our friends! Our friends!" cried Sir Arthur. "Ah, ha! so you mean that the old beau hath hit thee, too, with his ardent eye. Or—hang! What—you mean not that this stranger, this Scotchman, is a friend of yours?"

"I speak but confusedly," said the Lady Catharine. "'Tis my prejudice against such fighting, as you know. Can we not make haste, and so prevent this meeting?"

"Oh, I doubt if there be much need of haste," said Sir Arthur, balancing his cup in his hand judicially. "This matter will fall through at most for the day. They assuredly can not meet until to-morrow. This will be the talk of London, if it goes on in this pell-mell, hurly-burly fashion. As to the stopping of it—well now, the law under William and Mary saith that one who slays another in a duel of premeditation is nothing but a murderer, and may be hanged like any felon; hanged by the neck, till he be dead. Alas, what a fate for this pretty Scotchman!"

Sir Arthur paused. A look of wonder swept across his face. "Open the window, Annie!" he cried suddenly to the servant. "Your mistress is ill."

CHAPTER XI

AS CHANCE DECREED

Mischance delayed the carriage of Beau Wilson in its journeying to Bloomsbury Square. It had not appeared at that moment, far toward evening, when John Law, riding a trembling and dripping steed, came upon one side of this little open common and gazed anxiously across the space. He saw standing across from him a carriage, toward which he dashed. He flung open the carriage door, crying out, even before he saw the face within.

"Will! Will Law, I say, come out!" called he. "What mad trick is this? What—"

He saw indeed the face of Will Law inside the carriage, a face pale, melancholy, and yet firm.

"Get you back into the city!" cried Will Law. "This is no place for you, Jack."

"Boy! Are you mad, entirely mad?" cried Law, pushing his way directly into the carriage and reaching out with an arm of authority for the sword which he saw resting beside his brother against the seat. "No place for me! 'Tis no place for you, for either of us. Turn back. This foolishness must go no further!"

"It must go on now to the end," said Will Law, wearily. "Mr. Wilson's carriage is long past due."

"But you—what do you mean? You've had no hand in this. Even had you—why, boy, you would be spitted in an instant by this fellow."

"And would not that teach you to cease your mad pranks, and use to better purpose the talents God hath given you? Yours is the better chance, Jack."

"Peace!" cried John Law, tears starting to his eyes. "I'll not argue that. Driver, turn back for home!"

The coachman at the box touched his hat with a puzzled air. "I beg pardon, sir," said he, "but I was under orders of the gentleman inside."

"You were sent for Mr. John Law."

"For Mr. Law—"

"But I am John Law, sirrah!"

"You are both Mr. Law? Well, sir, I scarce know which of you is the proper Mr. Law. But I must say that here comes a coach drove fast enough, and perhaps this is the gentleman I was to wait for, according to the first Mr. Law, sir."

"He is coming, then," cried John Law, angrily. "I'll see into this pretty meeting. If this devil's own fool is to have a crossing of steel, I'll fair accommodate him, and we'll look into the reasons for it later. Sit ye down! Be quiet, Will, boy, I say!"

Law was a powerful man, over six feet in height. The sports of the Highlands, combined with much fencing and continuous play in the tennis court, indeed his ardent love for every hardy exercise, had given his form alike solid strength and great activity. "Jessamy Law," they called him at home, in compliment of his slender though full and manly form. Cool and skilful in all the games of his youth, as John Law himself had often calmly stated, in fence he had a knowledge amounting to science, a knowledge based upon the study of first principles. The intricacies of the Italian school were to him an old story. With the single blade he had never yet met his master. Indeed, the thought of successful opposition seemed never to occur to him at all. Certainly at this moment, angered at the impatient insolence of his adversary, the thought of danger was farthest from his mind. Stronger than his brother, he pushed the latter back with one hand, grasping as he did so the small-sword with which the latter was provided. With one leap he sprang from the carriage, leaving Will half dazed and limp within.

Even as he left the carriage step, he found himself confronted with an adversary eager as himself; for at that instant Beau Wilson was hastening from his coach. Vain, weak and pompous in a way, yet lacking not in a certain personal valor, Beau Wilson stopped not for his seconds, tarried not to catch the other's speech, but himself strode madly onward, his point raised slightly, as though he had lost all care and dignity and desired nothing so much as to stab his enemy as swiftly as might be.

It would have mattered nothing now to this Highlander, this fighting Argyll, what had been the reason animating his opponent. It was enough that he saw a weapon bared. Too late, then, to reason with John Law, "Beau" Law of Edinboro', "Jessamy" Law, the best blade and the coolest head in all the schools of arms that taught him fence.

For a moment Law paused and raised his point, whether in query or in salute the onlookers scarce could tell. Sure it was that Wilson was the first to fall into the assault. Scarce pausing in his stride, he came on blindly, and, raising his own point, lunged straight for his opponent's breast. Sad enough was the fate which impelled him to do this thing.

It was over in an instant. It could not be said that there was an actual encounter. The side step of the young Highlander was soft as that of a panther, as quick, and yet as full of savagery. The whipping over of his wrist, the gliding, twining, clinging of his blade against that of his enemy was so swift that eye could scarce have followed it. The eye of Beau Wilson was too slow to catch it or to guard. He never stopped the *riposte*, and indeed was too late to attempt any guard. Pierced through the body, Wilson staggered back, clapping his hands against his chest. Over his face there swept a swift series of changes. Anger faded to chagrin, that to surprise, surprise to fright, and that to gentleness.

"Sir," said he, "you've hit me fair, and very hard. I pray you, some friend, give me an arm."

And so they led him to his carriage, and took him home a corpse. Once more the code of the time had found its victim.

Law turned away from the coach of his smitten opponent, turned away with a face stern and full of trouble. Many things revolved themselves in his mind as he stepped slowly towards the carriage, in which his brother still sat wringing his hands in an agony of perturbation.

"Jack, Jack!" cried Will Law, "Oh, heavens! You have killed him! You have killed a man! What shall we do?"

Law Raised his head and looked his brother in the face, but

seemed scarce to hear him. Half mechanically he was fumbling in the side pocket of his coat. He drew forth from it now a peculiar object, at which he gazed intently and half in curiosity, It was the little beaded shoe of the Indian woman, the very object over which this ill-fated quarrel had arisen, and which now seemed so curiously to intermingle itself with his affairs.

"'Twas a slight shield enough," he said slowly to himself, "yet it served. But for this little piece of hide, methinks there might be two of us going home to-day to take somewhat of rest."

Emerson Hough

CHAPTER XII

FOR FELONY

Late in the afternoon of the day following the encounter in Bloomsbury Square, a little group of excited loiterers filled the entrance and passage way at 59 Bradwell Street, the former lodgings of the two young gentlemen from Scotland. The motley assemblage seemed for the most part to make merry at the expense of a certain messenger boy, who bore a long wicker box, which presently he shifted from his shoulder to a more convenient resting place on the curb.

"Do 'ee but look at un," said one ancient dame. "He! he! Hath a parcel of fine clothes for the tall gentleman was up in third floor! He! he! Clothes for Mr. Law, indeed!"

"Fine clothes, eh?" cried another, a portly dame of certain years. "Much fine clothes he'll need where he'm gone."

"Yes, indeed, that he will na. Bad luck 'twas to Mary Cullen as took un into her house. Now she's no lodging money for her rooms, and her lodgers be both in Newgate; least ways, one of un."

"Ah now, 'tis a pity for Mary Cullen, she do need the money so much—"

"Shut ye all your mouths, the lot o' you," cried Mary Cullen herself, appearing at the door. "'Tis not she is needing the little money, for she has it right here in the corner of her apron. Every stiver Mary Cullen's young men said they'd pay they paid, like the gentlemen they were. I'll warrant the raggle of ye would do well to make out fine as Mary Cullen hath."

"Oh now, is that true, Mary Cullen?" said a voice. "'Twas said that these two were noble folk come here for the sport of it."

"What else but true? Do you never know the look of gentry? My fakes, I'll warrant the young gentleman is back within a fortnight. His brother, the younger one, said to me hisself but this very morn, his brother was hinnocent as a child; that he was obliged to strike the other man for fear of his own life. Now, what can judge do but turn un loose? Four sovereigns he gave me this very morn. What else can judge do but turn un free? Tell me that, now!"

"Let's see the fine clothes," said the first old lady to the apprentice boy, reaching out a hand and pulling at the corner of the box-lid. The youth was nothing loath to show, with professional pride, the quality of his burden, and so raised the lid.

"Land save us! 'Tis gentry sure enough they are," cried the inquisitive one. "Do-a look in there! Such clothes and laces, such a brand new wig, such silken hose! Law o' land! Must have cost all of forty crowns. Mary Cullen, right ye are; 'twas quality ye had with ye, even if 'twas but for little while."

"And them gone to prison, him on trial for his life! I saw un ride out this very yesterday, fast as though the devil was behind un, and a finer body of a man never did I look at in my life. What pity 'tis, what pity 'tis!"

"Well," said the apprentice, with a certain superiority in his air. "I dare wait no longer. My master said the gentleman was to have the clothes this very afternoon. So if to prison he be gone, to prison must I go too." Upon which he set off doggedly, and so removed one of the main causes for the assemblage at the curb.

The apprentice was hungry and weary enough before he reached the somber portals, yet his insistence won past gate-keeper and turnkey, one after another, till at length he reached the jailer who adjudged himself fit to pass upon the stolid demand that the messenger be admitted with the parcel for John Law, Esquire, late of Bradwell Street, marked urgent, and collect fifty sovereigns. The humor of all this appealed to the Jailer mightily.

"Send him along," he said. And the boy came in, much dismayed but still faithful to his trust.

"Please, sir," said the youth, "I would know if ye have John Law, Esquire, in this place; and if so, I would see him. Master said I was not to bring back this parcel till that I had seen John Law, Esquire, and got from him fifty sovereigns. 'Tis for his wedding, sir, and the clothes are of the finest."

The jailer smiled grimly. "Mr. Law gets presents passing soon," said he. "Set down your box. It might be weapons or the like."

"Some clothes," said the apprentice. "Some very fine clothes. They are of our best."

"Ha! ha!" roared the jailer. "Here indeed be a pretty jest. Much need he'll have of fine clothes here. He'll soon take his coat off the rack like the rest, and happen it fits him, very well. Take back your box, boy—or stay, let's have a look in't."

The jailer was a man not devoid of wisdom. Fine clothes sometimes went with a long purse, and a long purge might do wonders to help the comfort of any prisoner in London, as well as the comfort of his keeper. Truly his eyes opened wide as he saw the contents of the box. He felt the lapel of the coat, passing it approvingly between his thumb and finger. "Well, e'en set ye down the box, lad," said he, "and wait till I see where Mr. Law has gone. Hum, hum! What saith the record? Charged that said prisoner did kill—hum, hum! Taken of said John Law six sovereigns, three shillings and sixpence. Item, one snuff-box, gilt. Hour of admission, five o'clock of the afternoon. We shall see, we shall see."

"Sir," said the jailer, approaching the prisoner and his brother, who both remained in the detention room, "a lad hath arrived bearing a parcel for John Law, Esquire. 'Tis not within possibility that you have these goods, but we would know what disposition we shall make of them."

"By my faith!" cried Law, "I had entirely forgot my haberdasher."

The jailer stood on one foot and gave a cough, unnecessarily loud but sufficiently significant. It was enough for the quick wit of Law.

"There was fifty sovereigns on the charge list," said the jailer.

"Sixty sovereigns, I heard you say distinctly," replied Law. "Will, give me thy purse, man!"

Will Law obeyed automatically.

"There," said John Law to the jailer. "I am sure the garments will be very proper. Is it not all very proper?"

The turnkey looked calmly into the face of his prisoner and as calmly replied: "It is, sir, as you say, very proper."

"It would be much relief," said John Law, as the turnkey again appeared, bearing the box in his own hands, "if I might don my new garments. I would liefer make a good showing for thy house, friend, and can not, in this garb."

"Sirrah," said the jailer, "there be rules of this place, as you very well know. Your little chamber was to have been in corridor number four, number twelve of the left aisle. But, sir, as perhaps you know, there be rules which are rules, and rules which are not so much—that is to say—rules, as you might put it, sir. The main thing is that I produce your body on the day of the hearing, which cometh soon. Meantime, since you seem a gentleman, and are in for no common felony, but charged, as I might say, with a light offense, why, sir, in such a case, I might say that a gentleman like yourself, if he cared to wear a bit of good clothes and wear it here in the parlor like, why, sir, I can see no harm in it. And that's competent to prove, as the judge says."

"Very well, then," said Law, "I'll e'en deck out with the gear I should have had to-night had I been free; though I fear my employment this evening will scarce be pleasing as that which I had planned. Will, had I had but one more night at the Green Lion, we'd e'en have needed a special chair to carry home my winnings of their English gold."

Enter then, a few moments later, "Beau" Law, "Jessamy" Law, late of Edinboro', gentleman, and a right gallant figure of a man. Tall he was indeed, and, so clad, making a picture of superb manhood. Ease and grace he showed in every movement. His long fingers closed lightly at top of a lacquered cane which he had found within the box. Deep ruffles of white hung down from his wrists, and a fall of wide lace drooped from the bosom of his ruffled shirt. His wig, deep curled and well whitened, gave a certain austerity to his mien. At his instep sparkled new buckles of brilliants, rising above which sprang a graceful ankle, a straight and well-rounded leg. The long lapels of his rich coat hung deep, and the rich waistcoat of plum-colored satin added slimness to a torso not too bulky in itself. Neat, dainty, fastidious, "Jessamy" Law, late of Edinboro', for some weeks of London, and now of a London prison, scarce seemed a man about to be put on trial for his life.

He advanced from the door of the side room with ease and dignity. Reaching out a snuff-box which he had found in the silken pocket of his new garment, he extended it to the turnkey with an indifferent gesture.

"Kindly have it filled with maccaboy," he said. "See, 'tis quite empty, and as such, 'tis useless."

"Certainly, Captain Law," said the turnkey. "I am a man as knows what a gentleman likes, and many a one I've had here in my day, sir. As it chances, I've a bit of the best in my own quarters, and I'll see that you have what you like."

"Will," said Law to his brother, who had scarce moved during all this, "come, cheer up! One would think 'twas thyself was to be inmate here, and not another."

Will Law burst into tears.

"God knows, 'twere better myself, and not thee, Jack,"

he said.

"Pish! boy, no more of that! 'Twas as chance would have it. I'm never meant for staying here. Come, take this letter, as I said, and make haste to carry it. 'Twill serve nothing to have you moping here. Fare you well, and see that you sleep sound."

Will Law turned, obedient as ever to the commands of the superior mind. He passed out through the heavily-guarded door as the turnkey swung it for him; passed out, turned and looked back. He saw his brother standing there, easy, calm, indifferent, a splendid figure of a man.

CHAPTER XIII

THE MESSAGE

To Will Law, as he turned away from the prison gate upon the errand assigned to him, the vast and shapeless shadows of the night-covered city took the form of appalling monsters, relentless, remorseless, savage of purpose. He passed, as one in some hideous dream, along streets that wound and wound until his brain lost distance and direction. It might have been an hour, two hours, and the clock might have registered after midnight, when at last he discovered himself in front of the dark gray mass of stone which the chairmen assured him was his destination. It was with trepidation that he stepped to the half-lighted door and fumbled for the knocker. The door slowly swung open, and he was confronted by the portly presence of a lackey who stood in silence waiting for his word.

"A message for Lady Catharine Knollys," said Will, with what courage he could summon. "'Tis of importance, I make no doubt." For it was to the Lady Catharine that John Law had first turned. His heart craved one more sight of the face so beloved, one more word from the voice which so late had thrilled his soul. Away from these—ah! that was the prison for him, these were the bars which to him seemed imperatively needful to be broken. Aid he did not think of asking.

Only, across London, in the night, he had sent the cry of his heart: "Come to me!"

"The Lady Catharine is not in at this hour," said the butler, with, some asperity, closing the door again in part.

"But 'tis important. I doubt if 'twill bear the delay of a night." Indeed, Will Law had hitherto hardly paused to reflect how unusual was this message, from such a person, to such address, and at such an hour.

The butler hesitated, and so did the unbidden guest at the door. Neither heard at first the light rustle of garments at the head of the stair, nor saw the face bent over the balustrade in the shadows of the hall.

"What is it, James?" asked a voice from above.

"A message for the Lady Catharine," replied the servant. "Said to be important. What should I do?"

"Lady Catharine Knollys is away," said the soft voice of Mary Connynge, speaking from the stair. Her voice came nearer as she now descended and appeared at the first landing.

"We may crave your pardon, sir," said she, "that we receive you so ill, but the hour is very late. Lady Catharine is away, and Sir Charles is forth also, as usual, at this time. I am left proxy for my entertainers, and perhaps I may serve you in this case. Therefore pray step within."

Reluctantly the butler swung open the door and admitted the visitor. Will Law stood face to face with Mary Connynge, just from her boudoir, and with time for but half care as to the details of her toilet; yet none the less Mary Connynge,

Eve-like, bewitching, endowed with all the ancient wiles of womankind. Will Law gazed, since this was his fate. Unconsciously the sorcery of the sight enfolded the youth as he stood there uncertainly. He saw the round throat, the heavy masses of the dark hair, the full round form. He noted, though he could not define; felt, though he could not classify. He was young. Utterly helpless might have been even an older man in the hands of Mary Connynge at a time like this, Mary Connynge deliberately seeking to ensnare.

"Pardon this robe, but half concealing," said her drooping eye and her half uplifted hands which caught the defining folds yet closer to her bosom. "'Tis in your chivalry I trust. I would not so with others." This to the beholder meant that he was the one man on earth to whom so much could be conceded.

Therefore, following to his own undoing, as though led by some actual command, while but bidden gently by the softest voice in all the kingdom, the young man entered the great drawing-room and waited as the butler lessened the shadows by the aid of candles. He saw the smallest foot in London just peep in and out, suddenly withdrawn as Mary Connynge sat her down.

She held the message now in her hand. In her soul sat burning impatience, in her heart contempt for the callow youth before her. Yet to that youth her attitude seemed to speak naught but deference for himself and doubt for this unusual situation.

"Sir, I am in some hesitation," said Mary Connynge. "There is indeed none in the house except the servants. You say your message is of importance—"

"It has indeed importance," responded Will. "It comes from

my brother."

"Your brother, Mr. Law?"

"From my brother, John Law. He is in trouble. I make no doubt the message will set all plain."

"'Tis most grievous that Lady Catharine return not till to-morrow."

Mary Connynge shifted herself upon her seat, caught once more with swift modesty at the robe which fell from her throat. She raised her eyes and turned them full upon the visitor. Never had the spell of curve and color, never had the language of sex addressed this youth as it did now. Intoxicating enough was this vague, mysterious speech even at this inappropriate time. The girl knew that the mesh had fallen well. She but caught again at her robe, and cast down again her eyes, and voiced again her assumed anxiety. "I scarce know what to do," she murmured.

"My brother did not explain—" said Will.

"In that case," said Mary Connynge, her voice cool, though her soul was hot with impatience, "it might perhaps be well if I took the liberty of reading the message in Lady Catharine's absence. You say your brother is in trouble?"

"Of the worst. Madam, to make plain with you, he is in prison, charged with the crime of murder."

Mary Connynge sank back into her chair. The blood fled from her cheek. Her hands caught each other in a genuine gesture of distress.

"In prison! John Law! Oh heaven! tell me how?" Her voice

was trembling now.

"My brother slew Mr. Wilson in a duel not of his own seeking. It happened yesterday, and so swift I scarce can tell you. He took up a quarrel which I had fixed to settle with Mr. Wilson myself. We all met at Bloomsbury Square, my brother coming in great haste. Of a sudden, after his fashion, he became enraged. He sprang from the carriage and met Mr. Wilson. And so—they passed a time or so, and 'twas done. Mr. Wilson died a few moments later. My brother was taken and lodged in jail. There is said to be bitter feeling at the court over this custom of dueling, and it has long been thought that an example would be made."

"And this letter without doubt bears upon all this? Perhaps it might be well if I made both of us owners of its contents."

"Assuredly, I should say," replied Will, too distracted to take full heed.

The girl tore open the inclosure. She saw but three words, written boldly, firmly, addressed to no one, and signed by no one.

"Come to me!" Thus spoke the message. This was the summons that had crossed black London town that night.

Mary Connynge rose quickly to her feet, forgetting for the time the man who stood before her. The instant demanded all the resources of her soul. She fought to remain mistress of herself. A moment, and she passed Will Law with swift foot, and gained again the stairway in the hall, the letter still fast within her hand. Will Law had not time to ask its contents.

"There is need of haste," said she. "James, have up the calash at once. Mr. Law, I crave your excuse for a time. In a moment I shall be ready to go with you."

In two minutes she was sobbing alone, her face down upon the bed. In five, she was at the door, dressed, cloaked, smiling sweetly and ready for the journey. And thus it was that, of two women who loved John Law, that one fared on to see him for whom he had not sent.

CHAPTER XIV

PRISONERS

The turnkey at the inner door was slothful, sleepy and ill disposed to listen when he heard that certain callers would be admitted to the prisoner John Law.

"Tis late," said he, "and besides, 'tis contrary to the rules. Must not a prison have rules? Tell me that!"

"We have come to arrange for certain matters regarding Mr. Law's defense," said Mary Connynge, as she threw back her cloak and bent upon the turnkey the full glance of her dark eye. "Surely you would not deny us."

The turnkey looked at Will Law with a hesitation in his attitude. "Why, this gentleman I know," he began.

"Yes; let us in," cried Will Law, with sudden energy. "'Tis time that we took steps to set my brother free."

"True, so say they all, young master," replied the turnkey, grinning. "'Tis easy to get ye in, but passing hard to get ye out again. Yet, since the young man ye wish to see is a very decent gentleman, and knoweth well the needs of a poor working body like myself, we will take the matter under advisement, as the court saith, forsooth."

They passed through the heavy gates, down a narrow and heavy-aired passage, and finally into a naked room. It was here, in such somber surroundings, that Mary Connynge saw again the man whose image had been graven on her heart ever since that morn at Sadler's Wells. How her heart coveted him, how her blood leaped for him—these things the Mary Connynges of the world can tell, they who own the primeval heart of womankind.

When John Law himself at length entered the room, he stepped forward at first confidently, eagerly, though with surprise upon his face. Then, with a sudden hesitation, he looked sharply at the figure which he saw awaiting him in the dingy room. His breath came sharp, and ended in a sigh. For a half moment his face flushed, his brow showed question and annoyance. Yet rapidly, after his fashion, he mastered himself.

"Will," said he, calmly, to his brother, "kindly ask the coachman to wait for this lady."

He stood for a moment gazing after the form of his brother as it disappeared in the outer shadows. For this half-moment he took swift counsel of himself. It was a face calm and noncommittal that he turned toward the girl who sat now in the darkest corner of the room, her head cast down, her foot beating a signal of perturbation upon the floor. From the corner of her eye Mary Connynge saw him, a tall and manly man, superbly clad, faultless in physique and raiment from top to toe. He stood as though ready to step into his carriage for some voyage to rout or ball. Youth, vigor, self-reliance, confidence, this was the whole message of the splendid figure. The blood of Mary Connynge, this survival, this half-savage woman, unregulated, unsubdued, leaped high within her bosom, fled to her face, gave color to her cheek and brightness to her eye. Her breath shortened after feline fashion. Deep was calling unto deep, ancient unto ancient, primitive unto primitive. Without the gate of London prison there was one abject prisoner. Within its gates there were two prisoners, and one of them was slave for life!

"Madam," said John Law, in deep and vibrant tone, "you will pardon me if I say that it gives me surprise to see you here."

"Yes; I have come," said the girl, not logically.

"You bring, perhaps, some message?"

"I—I brought a message."

"It is from the Lady Catharine?"

Mary Connynge was silent for a moment. It was necessary that, at least for a moment, the poison of some aeons should distil. There was need of savagery to say what she proposed to say. The voice of training, of civilization, of unselfishness, of friendship raised a protest. Wait then for a moment. Wait until the bitterness of an ambitious and unrounded life could formulate this evil impulse. Wait, till Mary Connynge could summon treachery enough to slay her friend. And yet, wait only until the primitive soul of Mary Connynge should become altogether imperative in its demands! For after all, was not this friend a woman, and is not the earth builded as it is? And hath not God made male and female its inhabitants; and as there is war of male and male, is there not war of female and female, until the end of time?

"I came from the Lady Catharine," said Mary Connynge, slowly, "but I bring no message from her of the sort which perhaps you wished." It was a desperate, reckless lie, a lie almost certain of detection yet it was the only resource of the moment, and a moment later it was too late to recall. One lie must now follow another, and all must make a deadly coil.

"Madam, I am sorry," said John Law, quietly, yet his face twitched sharply at the impact of these cutting words. "Did you know of my letter to her?"

"Am I not here?" said Mary Connynge.

"True, and I thank you deeply. But how, why-pray you, understand that I would be set right. I would not undergo more than is necessary. Will you not explain?"

"There is but little to explain—little, though it may mean much. It must be private. Your brother—he must never know. Promise me not to speak to him of this."

"This means much to me, I doubt not, my dear lady," said John Law. "I trust I may keep my counsel in a matter which comes so close to me."

"Yes, truly," replied Mary Connynge, "if you had set your heart upon a kindly answer."

"What! You mean, then, that she—"

"Do you promise?"

The brows of Law settled deeper and deeper into the frown which marked him when he was perturbed. The blood, settled back, now slowly mounted again into his face, the resentful, fighting blood of the Highlander.

"I promise," he cried. "And now, tell me what answer had the Lady Catharine Knollys."

"She declined to answer," said Mary Connynge, slowly and evenly. "Declined to come. She said that she was ill enough pleased to hear of your brawling. Said that she doubted not the law would punish you, nor doubted that the law was just."

John Law half whirled upon his heel, smote his hands together and laughed loud and bitterly.

"Madam," said he, "I had never thought to say it to a woman, but in very justice I must tell you that I see quite through this shallow falsehood."

"Sir," said Mary Connynge, her hands clutching at the arms of her chair, "this is unusual speech to a lady!"

"But your story, Madam, is most unusual."

"Tell me, then, why should I be here?" burst out the girl. "What is it to me? Why should I care what the Lady Catharine says or does? Why should I risk my own name to come of this errand in the night? Now let me pass, for I shall leave you."

Tho swift jealous rage of Mary Connynge was unpremeditated, yet nothing had better served her real purpose. The stubborn nature of Law was ever ready for a challenge. He caught her arm, and placed her not unkindly upon the chair.

"By heaven, I half believe what you say is true!" said he, as though to himself.

"Yet you just said 'twas false," said the girl, her eyes flashing.

"I meant that what you add is true, and hence the first also must be believed. Then you saw my message?"

"I did, since it so fell out."

"But you did not read the real message. I asked no aid of any one for my escape. I but asked her to come. In sheer truth, I wished but to see her."

"And by what right could you expect that?"

"I asked her as my affianced wife," replied John Law.

Mary Connynge stood an inch taller, as she sprang to her feet in sudden scorn and bitterness.

"Your affianced wife!" cried she. "What! So soon! Oh, rare indeed must be my opinion of this Lady Catharine!"

"It was never my way to waste time on a journey," said John Law, coolly.

"Your wife, your affianced wife?"

"As I said."

"Yes," cried Mary Connynge, bitterly, and again, unconsciously and in sheer anger, falling upon that course which best served her purpose. "And what manner of affianced wife is it would forsake her lover at the first breath of trouble? My God! 'tis then, it seems to me, a woman would most swiftly fly to the man she loved."

John Law turned slowly toward her, his eyes scanning her closely from top to toe, noting the heaving of her bosom, the sparkling of her gold-colored eye, now darkened and half ready to dissolve in tears. He stood as though he were a judge, weighing the evidence before him, calmly, dispassionately.

"Would you do so much as that, Mary Connynge?" asked John Law.

"I, sir?" she replied. "Then why am I here to-night myself? But, God pity me, what have I said? There is nothing but misfortune in all my life!"

It was one rebellious, unsubdued nature speaking to another, and of the two each was now having its own sharp suffering. The instant of doubt is the time of danger. Then comes revulsion, bitterness, despair, folly. John Law trod a step nearer.

"By God! Madam," cried he, "I would I might believe you. I would I might believe that you, that any woman, would come to me at such a time! But tell me—and I bethink me my message was not addressed, was even unsigned—whom then may I trust? If this woman scorns my call at such a time, tell me, whom shall I hold faithful? Who would come to me at any time, in any case, in my trouble? Suppose my message were to you?"

Mary Connynge stirred softly under her deep cloak. Her head was lifted slightly, the curve of cheek and chin showing in the light that fell from the little lamp. The masses of her dark hair lay piled about her face, tumbled by the sweeping of her hood. Her eyes showed tremulously soft and deep now as he looked into them. Her little hands half twitched a trifle from her lap and reached forward and upward. Primitive she might have been, wicked she was, sinfully sweet; and yet she was woman. It was with the voice of tears that she spoke, if one might claim vocalization for her speech.

"Have I not come?" whispered she.

"By God! Mary Connynge, yes, you have come!" cried Law. And though there was heartbreak in his voice, it sounded sweet to the ear of her who heard it, and who now reached up her arms about his neck.

"Ah, John Law," said Mary Connynge, "when a woman loves—when a woman loves, she stops at nothing!"

CHAPTER XV

IF THERE WERE NEED

Time wore on in the ancient capital of England. The tramp of troops echoed in the streets, and the fleets of Britain made ready to carry her sons over seas for wars and for adventures. The intrigues of party against party, of church against church, of Parliament against king; the loves, the hates, the ambitions, the desires of all the city's hurrying thousands went on as ever. Who, then, should remember a single prisoner, waiting within the walls of England's jail? The hours wore on slowly enough for that prisoner. He had faced a jury of his peers and was condemned to face the gallows. Meantime he had said farewell to love and hope and faithfulness, even as he bade farewell to life. "Since she has forsaken me whom I thought faithful," said he to himself, "why, let it end, for life is a mockery I would not live out." And thenceforth, haggard but laughing, pale but with unbroken courage, he trod on his way through his few remaining days, the wonder of those who saw him.

As for Mary Connynge, surely she had matters enough which were best kept secret in her own soul. While Lady Catharine was hoping, and praying, and dreaming and believing, even as the roses left her cheek and the hollows fell beneath her eyes, she saw about her in the daily walks of life Mary Connynge, sleek and rounded as ever. They sat at table together, and neither did the one make sign to the other of her own anxiety, nor did that other give sign of her own treachery. Mary Connynge, false guest, false friend, false woman, deceived so perfectly that she left no indication of deceit. She herself knew, and blindly satisfied herself with the knowledge, that she alone now came close into the life of "Beau" Law, the convict; "Jessamy" Law, the student, the financier, the thinker; John Law, her lord and master. Herein she found the sole compensation possible in her savage nature. She had found the master whom she sought!

Cynically mirthful or irreverently indifferent, yet never did her master's strength forsake him, never did his heart lose its undauntedness. And when he bade Mary Connynge do this or that she obeyed him; when he bade her arise she arose; at his word she came or departed. A dozen nights in the month she was absent from the house of Knollys. A dozen nights Will Law was cozened into frenzy, alternating between a heaven of delight and a hell of despair, and ignorant of her twofold duplicity. A dozen nights John Law knew well enough where Mary Connynge was, though no one else might know. There was feminine triumph now in full in the heart of this Mary Connynge, who had gone white with rage at the sight of a rose offered across her face to another woman. Had she not her master? Was he not hers, all hers, belonging in no wise to any other?

For the future, Mary Connynge did not ponder it. An ephemera, once buried generations deep in the mire and slime of lower conditions, and now craving blindly but the sunlight of the day, she would have sought the deadly caress of life even though at that moment it had sealed her doom. Foolish or wise, she was as she was; since, under our frail society, life is as it is.

Only at night, on those nights when she was sleepless on her own couch beneath the roof of Catharine Knollys, did Mary Connynge allow herself to think. Tell, then, ye who may, whether or not she was a mere survival of some forgotten day of the forest and the glade, as she lay with her hands clasped in brief moments of emotion. Surely she hoped, as all women hope who love, that this might endure for her forever. Yet the next moment there came the thought that inevitably it all must end, and soon. Then her hand clenched, her eyes grew dry and brilliant. She said to herself: "There is no hope. He can not be saved! For this short period of his life he shall be mine, all mine! He shall not be set free! He shall not go away, to belong, at any time, in any part, to any other woman! Though he die, yet shall he love me to the end; me, Mary Connynge, and no other woman!"

Now, under this same roof of Knollys, separated by but a few yards of space, there lay another woman, thinking also of this convict behind the prison bars. But this was a woman of another and a nobler mold. Into the heart of Catharine Knollys there came no mere mad selfishness of desire, yearn though she did in every fiber of her being since that first time she felt the mastering kiss of love. There was born in her soul emotion of a higher sort. The Lady Catharine Knollys prayed, and her prayer was not that her lover should die, but that he might live; that he might be free.

Nor was this hope left to wither unnourished in the mind of the high-bred and courageous English girl. Alone, without confidant to counsel her, with no woman friend to aid her, the Lady Catharine Knollys backed her own hopes and wishes with resource and energy. There came a time, perilously late, when a faint rose showed once more in her cheek, long so worn, a faintly brighter light glowed in her deep eye.

When Sir Arthur Pembroke received a message from the Lady Catharine Knollys advising him that the latter would receive him at her home, it was left for the impulses, the hopes, the imaginings of that modest young nobleman to establish a reason for the message. Puzzling all along his rapid way in answer to the summons, Sir Arthur found the answer which best suited his hopes in the faint flush, the brightened eye of the young woman who received him.

"Lady Catharine," he began, impetuously, "I have come, and let me hope that 'tis at last to have my answer. I have waited—each moment has been a year that I have spent away from you."

"Now, that is very pretty said."

"But I am serious."

"And that is why I do not like you."

"But, Lady Catharine!"

"I should like it better did you but continue as in the past. We have met on the Row, at the routs and drums, in the country; and always I have felt free to ask any favor of Sir Arthur Pembroke. Why could it not be always thus?"

"You might ask my very life, Lady Catharine."

"Ah, there it is! When a man offers his life, 'tis time for a woman to ask nothing."

She turned from the open window, her attitude showing an unwonted weakness and dejection. Sir Arthur still stood near by, his own face frowning and uncertain.

"Lady Catharine," he broke out at length, "for years, as you know, I have sought your favor. I have dared think that sometime the day would come when—my faith! Lady Catharine, the day has come now when I feel it my right to demand the cause of anything which troubles you. And that you are troubled is plain enough. Ever since this man Law—"

"There," cried Lady Catharine, raising her hand. "I beg you to say no more."

"But I will say more! There must be a reason for this."

The face of the young woman flushed in spite of herself, as Pembroke strode closer and gazed at her with sternness.

"Lady Catharine," said he, slowly, "I am a friend of your family. Perhaps now I may be of aid to you. Prove me, and at the last, ask who was indeed your friend."

"We have had misfortunes, we of the family of the Knollys," said Lady Catharine. "This is, perhaps, but the fate of the house of Knollys. It is my fate."

"Your fate!" said Sir Arthur, slowly. "Your fate! Lady Catharine, I thank you. It is at least as well to know the truth."

"Pick out the truth, then, Sir Arthur, as you like it. I am not on the witness stand before you, and you are not my judge. There has been forsworn testimony enough already in this town. Were it not for that, Mr. Law would at this moment be free as you or I."

Sir Arthur struck his hands together in despair, and turning away, strode down the room.

"Oh, I see it all well enough," cried he. "You are mad as any who have hitherto had dealings with this madman from the North."

The girl rose to her full height and stood before him.

"It may be I am mad," said she. "It may be the old Knollys madness. If so, why should I struggle against it? It may be that I am mad. But I venture to say to you that Mr. Law is not born to die in Newgate yards. My life! sir, if I love him, who should say me nay? Now, say to yourself, and to your friends—to all London, if you like, since you have touched me to this point—that Catharine Knollys is friend to Mr. Law, and believes in him, and declares that he shall be freed from his prison, and that within short space! Say that, Sir Arthur; tell them that! And if they argue somewhat from it, why, let them reason it as best they may."

The young man stood, his lips close together, his head still turned away. The girl continued with growing energy.

"I have sent for you to tell you that Mr. Law's life has a value in my eyes. And now, I say to you, Sir Arthur, that you must aid me in his escape."

A beautiful picture she made, tearful, pleading, a lock of her soft red-brown hair falling unnoticed across her tear-wet cheek. It had been ill task, indeed, to make refusal of any sort to a woman so gloriously feminine, so noble, now so beseeching.

"Lady Catharine," said the young man, turning toward her, "this illness, this anxiety—"

"No, I know perfectly well whereof I speak! Listen, and I'll tell you somewhat of news. Montague, chancellor of the exchequer, is my warrant for what I say to you when I tell you that Mr. Law is to be free. Montague himself has said to me, in this very room, that Mr. Law was like to be half the salvation of England in these uncertain times. I could tell you more, but may not. Only look you, Sir Arthur, John Law does not rest in Newgate more than one week from this time!"

Sir Arthur took snuff, his voice at length regaining that composure for which he had sought.

"'Tis very excellent," he said. "For myself, two centuries have been spent in my family to teach me to love like a gentleman, and to deserve you like a man. What does this young man need? A few days of bluster, of assertion! A few weeks of gaming and of roistering, of self-asserted claims! Gad! Lady Catharine, this is passing bitter! And now you ask me to help him."

"I wish you to help him," said Lady Catharine, slowly, "only in that I ask you to help me."

"And if I did?"

"And if you did, you should dwell in a part of my heart forever! Let it be as you like."

"Then," cried the young man, flushing suddenly and hotly as he strode toward her, "do with me as you like! Let me be fool unspeakable!"

"And do you promise?" said Lady Catharine, rising and advancing toward him. Her face was sad and appealing. Her eyes swam in tears, her lips were trembling.

Sir Arthur held out his hand. The Lady Catharine extended

both her own, and he bent and kissed them, tears springing in his eyes. For a time the room was silent. Then the girl turned, her own lashes wet. She stepped at length to a cabinet and took from an inner drawer a paper.

"Sir Arthur, look at this," she Said.

He took it from her and scrutinized it carefully.

"Why, this seems to be a street bill, a placard for posting upon the walls," said he.

"Read it."

"Yes, well—so, so. 'Five hundred pounds reward for information regarding the escaped felon, Captain John Law, convicted of murder and under sentence of death of the King's Bench. The same Law escaped from Newgate prison on the night of'—hum—well—well—'May be known by this description: Is tall, of dark complexion, spare of build, raw-boned, face hath deep pock-marks. Eyes dark; hair dark and scanty. Speaketh broad and loud.' How—how, why my dear Lady Catharine, this is the last proof that thou'rt stark, staring mad! This no more tallies with the true John Law than it does with my hunting horse!"

"And but few would know him by this description?"

"None, absolutely none."

"None could tell 'twas he, even did they meet him full face to face—no one would know it was Mr. Law?"

"Why, assuredly not. 'Tis as unlike him as it could be."

"Then it is well!" said Lady Catharine.

"Well? Very badly done, I should say."

"Oh, my poor Sir Arthur, where are your wits? 'Tis very well because 'tis very ill, this same description."

"Ah, ha!" said he, a sudden light dawning upon him. "Then you mean to tell me that this description was misconceived deliberately?"

"What would you think?"

"Did you do this work yourself?"

"Guess for yourself. Montague, as you know, was once of a pretty imagination, ere he took to finance. If he and the poet Prior could write such conceits as they have created, could not perhaps Montague—or Prior—or some one else—have conceived this description of Mr. Law?"

The young man threw himself into a seat, his head between his hands. "'Tis like a play," said he. "And surely the play of fortune ever runs well enough for Mr. Law."

"Sir Arthur," said Lady Catharine, rising uneasily and standing before him, "I must confess to you that I bear a certain active part in private plans looking to the escape of Mr. Law. I have come to you for aid. Sir Arthur, I pray God that we may be successful."

The young man also rose and began to pace the floor.

"Even did Law escape," he began, "it would mean only his flight from England."

"True," said the Lady Catharine, "that is all planned. The ship even now awaits him in the Pool. He is to take ship at once upon leaving prison, and he sails at once from England. He goes to France."

"But, my dear Lady Catharine, this means that he must part from you."

"Of course, it means our parting."

"Oh, but you said—but I thought—"

"But I said—but you thought—Sir Arthur, do not stand there prating like a little boy!"

"You do not, then, keep your prisoner bound by other fetters after he escapes from Newgate?"

"I do nothing unwomanly, and I do nothing, I trust, ignoble. I go to meet the Knollys fate, whatever it may be."

"Lady Catharine," cried Pembroke, passionately, "I have said I loved you. Never in my life did I love you as I do now!"

"I like to hear your words," said the girl, frankly. "There shall always be your corner in my heart—"

"Yet you will do this thing?"

"I will do this thing. I shall not whimper nor repine. I am sending him away forever, but 'tis needful for his sake. I shall be ready for whatever fate hath for me."

"Tell me, then," said Pembroke, his face haggard and unhappy, "how am I to serve you in this matter."

"In this way: To-morrow night call here with your coach. My household, if they note it, may take your coach for my own, and may perhaps understand that I go to the rout of my Lady Swearingsham. We shall go, instead, to Newgate. For the night, Sir Arthur Pembroke shall serve as coachman. You must drive the carriage to Newgate jail."

"And 'tis there," said Pembroke, slowly, "that the Lady Catharine Knollys, the dearest woman of all England, would take the man who honorably loves her—to Newgate, to feloniously set free a felon? Is it there, then, Lady Catharine, you would go to meet your lover?"

The tall figure of the girl straightened up to its full height. A shade of color came to her cheeks, but her voice was firm, though tears came to her eyes as she answered:

"Aye, sir, I would go to Newgate if there were need!"

CHAPTER XVI

THE ESCAPE

On a certain morning a messenger rode in hot haste up to the prison gate. He bore the livery of Montague. Turnkey after turnkey admitted him, until finally he stood before the cell of John Law and delivered into his hand, as he had been commanded, the message that he bore. That afternoon this same messenger paused at the gate of the house of Knollys. Here, too, he was admitted promptly. He delivered into the hands of the Lady Catharine Knollys a certain message. This was of a Wednesday. On the following Friday it was decreed that the gallows should do its work. Two more days and there would be an end of "Jessamy" Law.

That Wednesday night a covered carriage came to the door of the house of Knollys. Its driver was muffled in such fashion that he could hardly have been known. There stepped from the house the cloaked figure of a woman, who entered the carriage and herself pulled shut the door. The vehicle was soon lost among the darkling streets.

Catharine Knollys had heard the summons of her fate. She now sat trembling in the carriage.

When finally the vehicle stopped at the curb of the walk

which led to the prison gate, a second carriage, as mysterious as the first, came down the street and stopped at a little distance, but close to the curb on the side nearest to the gate. The driver of the first carriage, evidently not liking the close neighborhood at the time, edged a trifle farther down the way. The second carriage thereupon drew up into the spot just vacated, and the two, not easily distinguishable at the hour and in the dark and unlighted street, stood so, each apparently watchful of the other, each seemingly without an occupant.

Lady Catharine had left her carriage before this interchange, and had passed the prison gate alone. Her steps faltered. It was hardly consciously that she finally found her way into the court, through the gate, down the evil-smelling corridors, past the sodden and leering constables, up to the last gate which separated her from him whom she had come to see.

She had been admitted without demur as far as this point, and even now her coming seemed not altogether a matter of surprise. The burly turnkey at the last door stood ready to meet her. With loud commands, he drove out of the corridor the crowd of prison attendants. He approached Lady Catharine, hat in hand and bowing deeply.

"I presume you are the man whom I would see," said she, faintly, almost unequal to the task imposed upon her.

"Aye, Madam, I doubt not, with my best worship for you."

"I was to come"—said Lady Catharine. "I was to speak to you—"

"Aye," replied the turnkey. "You were to come, and you were to speak. And now, what were you to say to me? Was there no given word?"

"There was such a word," she said. "You will understand. It is in the matter of Mr. Law."

"True," said the turnkey. "But I must have the countersign. There are heads to lose in this, yours and mine, if there be mistake."

Lady Catharine raised her head proudly. "It was for Faith," said she, "for Love, and for Hope! These were the words."

Saying which, as though she had called to her aid the last atom of her strength, she staggered back and half fell against the wall near the inner gate. The rude jailer sprang forward to steady her.

"Yes, yes," he whispered, eagerly. "'Tis all proper. Those be the words. Pray you, have courage, lady."

There came into the corridor a murmur of voices, and there was audible also the sound of a man's footfalls approaching along the flags. Catharine Knollys looked through the bars of the gate which the turnkey was already beginning to throw open for her. She looked, and there appeared upon her vision, a sight which caused her heart to stop, which confounded all her reason. From a side door there advanced John Law, magnificently clad, walking now as though he trod the floor of some great hall or banquet room.

The woman waiting without the gate reached out her arms. She would have cried aloud. Then she fell back against the wall, whereat had she not grasped she must have sunk down to the floor.

Upon the arm of John Law, and looking up to him as she walked, there hung the clinging figure of a woman, half-hidden by the flickering shadows of the torches. A deep cloak fell back from her shoulders. It might have been the light fabric of the aborigine. Upon the foot of Mary Connynge, twinkling in and out as she walked, showed the crudely garnished little shoe of the Indian princess over seas, dainty, bizarre, singular, covering the smallest foot in all London town.

"By all the saints!" Law was saying, "you might be the very maker of this little slipper yourself. I have won the forty crowns, I swear! Perforce, I'll leave them to you in my will."

The shock of the light speech made even Mary Connynge wince. For the moment she averted her eyes from the handsome face above her. She looked, and saw what gave her greater shock. Law, too, stared, as her own startled gaze grew fixed. He advanced close to the gate, only to start back in a horror of surprise which racked even his steeled composure.

"Madam!" he cried; and then, "Catharine!"

Catharine Knollys made no answer to him, though she looked straight and calmly into his face, seeming not in the least to see the woman near him. Her eyes were wide and shining. "Sir," said she, "keep fast to Hope! This was for Faith, and for Love!"

The jailer with one quick gesture swung wide the gate. "Haste, haste!" he cried. "Quick and begone! This night may mean my ruin! Get ye gone, all of ye, and give me time to think. Out with ye all, for I must lock the gate!"

John Law passed as one stupefied, the slender form of Mary Connynge still upon his arm. Hands of men hurried them. "Quick! Into the carriage!" one cried.

And now the sounds of feet and voices approaching along the corridor were heard. The jailer swiftly swung the heavy gate to and locked it. Catharine Knollys caught his last gesture, which bade her begone as fast as might be. Her feet were strangely heavy, in spite of her. She reached the curb in time to hear only the whir of wheels as a carriage sped away over the stones of the street. She stood alone, irresolute for half an instant as the crunch of wheels spun up to the curb again. A hand reached out and beckoned; involuntarily she obeyed the summons. Her wrist was seized, and she was half pulled through the door of the carriage.

"What!" cried a voice. "You, Lady Catharine! Why, how is this?"

It was the voice of Will Law, whom she knew, but who certainly was not the one who had brought her hither. The Lady Catharine accepted this last situation as one no longer able to reason. She sank down in the carriage seat, shivering.

"Is all well?" asked Will Law, eagerly.

"He is safe," said Lady Catharine Knollys. "It is done. It is finished."

"What does this mean?" exclaimed Will.

"His carriage—there it is. It goes to the ship—to the Pool. He and Mary Connynge are only just ahead of us. You may hear the wheels. Do you not hear them?" She spoke with leaden voice, and her head sank heavily.

"What! My brother—Mary Connynge—in that carriage— what can you mean? My God! Lady Catharine, tell me, what do you mean?"

"I do not know," said Catharine Knollys. All things now seemed very far away from her. Her head sank gently forward, and she heard not the words of the man who frantically sought to awaken her to speech.

From the prison to London Pool was a journey of some distance across the streets of London. Will Law called out to the driver with savagery in his voice. He shouted, cursed, implored, promised, and betimes held one hand under the soft, heavy tresses of the head now sunk so humbly forward.

The mad ride ended at the quay on Thames side, where the shadows of the tall buildings lay rank and thick upon the earth, where tarry smells and evil odors filled the heavy air, penetrated none the less by the savor of the keen salt air. More than one giant form was outlined in the broad stream, vessels tall and ghost-like in the gloom, shadowy, suggestive, bearing imprint and promise of far lands across the sea.

Here was the initial point of England's greatness. Here on this heavy stream had her captains taken ship. Thence had sailed her admirals to encompass all the world. In these dark massed shadows, how much might there not be of fate and mystery! Whither might not these vessels carry one! To France, to the far-off Indies, to the new-owned islands, to America with its little half-grown ports. Whence and whither? What might not one do, here at this gateway of the world?

"To the brigantine beyond!" cried Will Law to the wherryman who came up. "We want Captain McMasters, of the Polly Perkins. For God's sake, quick! There's that afoot must be caught up within the moment, do you hear!"

The wherryman touched his cap and quickly made ready his

boat. Will Law, understanding naught of this swift coil of events, and not daring to leave Lady Catharine behind him at the carriage, made down the stairway, half carrying the drooping figure which now leaned weakly upon his shoulder.

"Pull now, man! Pull as you never did before!" cried he, and the wherryman bent hard to his oars.

Yet great as was the haste of those who put forth into the foggy Thames, it was more than equalled by that of one who appeared upon the dock, even as the creak of the oars grew fainter in the gloom. There came the rattle of wheels upon the quay, and the sound of a driver lashing his horses. A carriage rolled up, and there sprang from the box a muffled figure which resolved itself into the very embodiment of haste.

"Hold the horses, man!" he cried to the nearest by-stander, and sprang swiftly to the head of the stairs, where a loiterer or two stood idly gazing out into the mist which overhung the water.

"Saw you aught of a man," he demanded hastily, "a man and a woman, a tall young woman—you could not mistake her? 'Twas the Polly Greenway they should have found. Tell me, for God's sake, has any boat put out from this stair?"

"Why, sir," replied one of the wherrymen who stood near by, pipe in mouth and hand in pocket, "since you mention it, there was a boat started but this instant for midstream. They sought McMaster's brigantine, the Polly Perkins, that lies waiting for the tide. 'Twas, as you say, a young gentleman, and with him was a young woman. I misdoubt the lady was ill."

"Get me a boat!" cried the new-comer. "A sovereign, five

sovereigns, ten sovereigns, a hundred—but that ship must not weigh anchor until I board her, do you hear!"

The ring of the imperative voice, and moreover the ring of good English coin, set all the dock astir. Straightway there came up another wherry with two lusty fellows, who laid her at the stair where stood the impatient stranger.

"Hurry, men!" he cried. "'Tis life and death—'tis more than life and death!"

And such fortune attended Sir Arthur Pembroke that forsooth he went over the side of the Polly Perkins, even as the gray dawn began to break over the narrow Thames, and even as the anchor-song of the crew struck up.

CHAPTER XVII

WHITHER

A few hours later a coppery sun slowly dispersed the morning mists above the Thames. The same sun warmed the court-yards of the London jail, which lately had confined John Law, convicted of the murder of Beau Wilson, gentleman. It was discovered that the said John Law had, in some superhuman fashion, climbed the spiked walls of the inner yard. The jailer pointed out the very spot where this act had been done. It was not so plain how he had passed the outer gates of the prison, yet those were not wanting who said that he had overpowered the turnkey at the gate, taken from him his keys, and so forced his way out into London city.

Far and wide went forth the proclamation of reward for the apprehension of this escaped convict. The streets of London were placarded broadcast with bills bearing this description of the escaped prisoner:

"Five hundred pounds reward for information regarding the escaped felon, John Law, convicted in the King's Bench of murder and under sentence of death. The same Law escaped from prison on the night of 20 July. May be known by the following description: Is tall, of dark complexion, spare of build, raw-boned, face hath deep pock-marks. Eyes dark, hair dark and scanty. Speaks broad and loud. Carries his shoulders stooped, and is of mean appearance.

"WESTON, High Sheriff.
Done at Newgate prison, this 21 July."

Yet though the authorities of the law made full search in London, and indeed in other of the principal cities of England, they got no word of the escaped prisoner.

The clouded dawn which broke over the Thames below the Pool might have told its own story. There sat upon the deck of the good ship Polly Greenway, outbound from Thames' mouth, this same John Law. He regarded idly the busy scenes of the shipping about him. His gaze, dull and listless, looked without joy upon the dawn, without inquiry upon the far horizon. For the first time in all his life John Law dropped his head between his hands.

Not so Mary Connynge. "Good sir," cried she, merrily, "'tis morning. Let's break our fast, and so set forth proper on our voyage."

"So now we are free," said Law, dully. "I could swear there were shackles on me."

"Yes, we are free," said Mary Connynge, "and all the world is before us. But saw you ever in all your life a man so dumfounded as was Sir Arthur when he discovered 'twas I, and not the Lady Catharine, had stepped into the carriage? That confusion of the carriages was like to have cost us everything. I know not how your brother made such mistake. He said he would fetch me home the night. Gemini! It sure seems a long way about! And where may be your brother now, or Sir Arthur, or the Lady Catharine—why, 'tis as much confused as though 'twere all in a play!"

"But Sir Arthur cried that my ship was for France. Yet here they tell me that this brigantine is bound for the mouth of the St. Lawrence, in America! What then of this other, and what of my brother—what of us—what of—?"

"Why, I think this," said Mary Connynge, calmly. "That you do very well to be rid of London jail; and for my own part, 'tis a rare appetite the salt air ever gives me!"

Upon the same morning tide there was at this very moment just setting aloft her sails for the first high airs of dawn the ship of McMasters, the Polly Perkins, bound for the port of Brest.

She came down scarce a half-dozen cable lengths behind the craft which bore the fugitives now beginning their journey toward another land. Upon the deck of this ship, even as upon the other, there were those who waited eagerly for the dawn. There were two men here, Will Law and Sir Arthur Pembroke, and whether their conversation had been more eager or more angry, were hard to tell. Will Law, broken and dejected, his heart torn by a thousand doubts and a thousand pains, sat listening, though but half comprehending.

"Every plan gone wrong!" cried Sir Arthur. "Every plan gone wrong, and out of it all we can only say that he has escaped from prison for whom no prison could be enough of hell! Though he be your brother, I tell it to your face, the gallows had been too good for John Law! Look you below. See that girl, pure as an angel, as noble and generous a soul us ever breathed—what hath she done to deserve this fate? You have brought her from her home, and to that home she can not now return unsmirched. And all this for a man who is at this moment fleeing with the woman whom she deemed her friend! What is there left in life for her?"

Will Law groaned and buried his own head deeper in his hands. "What is there left for any of us?" said he. "What is there left for me?"

"For you?" said Sir Arthur, questioningly. "Why, the next ship back from Brest, or from any other port of France. 'Tis somewhat different with a woman."

"You do not understand," said Will Law. "The separation means somewhat for me."

"Surely you do not mean—you have no reference to Mary Connynge?" cried Sir Arthur.

Will bowed his head abjectly and left the other to guess that which sat upon his mind. Sir Arthur drew a long breath and stopped his angry pacing up and down.

"It ran on for weeks," said Will Law. "We were to have been married. I had no thought of this. 'Twas I who took her to and from the prison regularly, and 'twas thus that we met. She told me she was but the messenger of the Lady Catharine."

Sir Arthur drew a long, slow breath. "Then I may say to you," said he, "that your brother, John Law, is a hundred times more traitor and felon than even now I thought him. Yonder he goes"—and he shook his fist into the enveloping mist which hung above the waters. "Yonder he goes, somewhere, I give you warning, where he deems no trail shall be left behind him. But I promise you, whatever be your own wish, I shall follow him into the last corner of the earth, but he shall see me and give account for this! There is none of us he has not deceived, utterly, and like a black-hearted villain. He shall account for it, though it be years from now."

So now, inch by inch, fathom after fathom, cable length after cable length, soon knot after knot, there sped two English ships out into the open seaway. Before long they began to toss restlessly and to pull eagerly at the helm as the scent of the salt seas came in. Yet neither knew fully the destination of the other, and neither knew that upon the deck of that other there was full solution of those questions which now sat so heavily upon these human hearts. Thus, silently, slowly, steadily, the two drew outward and apart, and before that morn was done, both were tossing widely upon the swell of that sea beyond which there lay so much of fate and mystery.

Emerson Hough

BOOK II

AMERICA

CHAPTER I

THE DOOR OF THE WEST

"Nearly a league farther, Du Mesne, and the sun but an hour high. Come, let us hasten!"

"You are right, Monsieur L'as," replied the one addressed, as the first speaker seated himself on the thwart of the boat in whose bow he had been standing. "Bend to it, *mes amis*!"

John Law turned about on the seat, gazing back over the length of the little ship which had brought him and his comrades thus far on the wildest journey he had ever undertaken. Six paddlers there were for this great *canot du Nord*, and steadily enough they sent the thin-shelled craft along over the curling blue waves of the great inland sea. And now their voices in one accord fell into the cadences of an ancient boat-song of New France:

> *"En roulant ma loule, roulant,*
> *Roulant, rouler, ma boule roulant."*

The ictus of the measure marked time for the sweeping paddles, and under the added impetus the paper shell, reinforced as it was by close-laid splints of cedar, and braced by the fiber-fastened thwarts, fairly yielded to the rush of the waves as the stalwart paddlers sent it flying forward. A tiny blur of white showed about the bows, and now and again a splash of spray came inboard, as some little curling white cap was divided by the rush of the swiftly moving prow.

"We shall not arrive too soon, my friend," rejoined the captain of the *voyageurs*, casting an eye back across the great lake, which lay black and ominous under a threatening sky, the sweep and swirl of its white caps ever racing hard after the frail craft, as though eager to break through its paper sides and tear away the human beings who thus fled on so lightly.

This boat, mysteriously appearing as though it were some spirit craft railed from the ancient deeps, was far from the beginning of its wild journey. Wide as the eye might reach, there arose no fleck of snowy canvas, nor showed the dark line of any similar craft propelled by oar or paddle. They were alone, these travelers. Before them, at the entrance of the wide arm of the great lake Michiganon, lay the point even at that early day known as the Door of the West, the beginning of the winding water-way which led on into the interior of that West, then so alluring and unknown. The eyes of all were fixed on the low, white-fronted bluffs, crowned by dark forest growth, which guarded the bay at either hand. This spot, so wild, so remote, so significant—it was home for these *voyageurs* as much as any; as much, too, for Law and the woman who lay back, pale-faced and wide-eyed, among the bales in the great canoe.

In time the graceful craft approached the beach, on which the long waves rolled and curled, now gently, now with imposing force. With the water yet half-leg deep, Du Mesne and two of the paddlers sprang bodily overboard and held the boat back from the pebbles, so that its tender shell might not be damaged. Law himself was as soon as they in the water, and he waded back along the gunwale until he reached the stern, the water nearly up to his hips. Reaching out his arms, he picked up Mary Connynge from her seat and carried her dry-shod ashore, bending down to catch some whispered word. Not so gallant was Du Mesne, the leader of the *voyageurs*. He uttered a few short words of semi-command to the Indian woman, who had been seated on the floor of the canoe, and she, without protest, crawled forward over the thwarts and the heaped bundles until she reached the bow, and then went ankle deep into the creaming flood. The great canoe, left empty and anchored safe from the pebbles of the beach, tossed light as a cork on the incoming waves.

A little open space was quickly found at the edge of the cove in which the disembarkation was made, and here Du Mesne and his followers soon kicked away the twigs and leveled out a smooth place upon the grass. Each man produced from his belt a broad-bladed knife, and for the moment disappeared in the deep fringe of evergreens which lined the shore. Fairly in the twinkling of an eye a rude frame of bent poles was made, above which were spread strips of unrolled birch bark from the cargo of the canoe. Over the spaces left uncovered by the supply of bark sheets there were laid down long mats made by Indian hands from dried reeds and bulrushes, affording no inconsiderable protection against the weather. Inside the lodge, bales of goods and packages of provisions were quickly arranged in comfortable fashion. Gaudy blankets were spread upon layers of soft skins of the buffalo. The Indian woman had meantime struck a fire, whose faint blue smoke curled lakeward in the soft evening air. Quickly, and with the system of experienced campaigners, the evening bivouac had been prepared; and wildly picturesque it must have seemed to a bystander, had there been indeed any possible spectator within many leagues.

Far enough was this from the turmoil of London, which Law

and his companion had left nearly a year before; far enough still from the wild capital of New France, where they had spent the winter, after landing, as much by chance as through any plan, at the port of the St. Lawrence. Ever a demon of unrest drove Law forward; ever there beckoned to him that irresistible West, of which he was one of the earliest to feel the charm. Farther and farther westward, swift and swifter than ever the boats of the fur traders had made the journey before, he and his party, led by Du Mesne, the ex-galley-slave and wanderer whom Law had by chance met again, and gladly, at Montreal, had made the long and dangerous run up the lakes, past Michilimackinac, down the lake of Michiganon, headed toward the interior of a new continent which was then, as for generations after then, the land of wondrous distances, of grand enterprises, of magnificent promises and immense fulfilments. The bales and bundles of this bivouac belonged to John Law, bought by gold from the gaming tables of Montreal and Quebec, and ventured in the one great hazard which appealed to him most irresistibly, the hazard of life and fortune in a far land, where he might live unneighbored, and where he might forget. Gambler in England, gambler again in New France, now trading fur-merchant and *voyageur*, he was, as always, an adventurer. Du Mesne and his hardy crew hailed him already as a new captain of the trails, a new *coureur*, won from the Old World by the savage witchery of the New. He was their brother; and had he indeed owned longer years of training, his keenness of eye, his strength of arm, his tirelessness of limb could hardly have been greater than they seemed in his first voyage to the West.

"*Tous les printemps,
Tant des nouvelles*"

hummed Du Mesne, as he busied himself about the camp, casting the while a cautious eye to note the progress of the threatening storm.

"Tous les amants
Changent des maitresses.
Jamais le bon vin n'endort—
L'amour me reveille!"

"The best is before us now, Monsieur L'as," said Du Mesne, joining Law, at length. "Assuredly the best is always that which is ahead and which is unknown; but in point of fact the hardest of our journey is over, for henceforth we may stretch our legs ashore, and hunt and fish, and make good camps for madame, who, as we both perceive, is much in need of ease and care. We shall make all safe and comfortable for this night, doubt not.

"Meantime," continued he, "let us see that all is well with our men and arms, for henceforth we must put out guards. Attention, comrades! Present your pieces and answer the roll-call! Pierre Berthier!"

"*Ici*! Monsieur," replied the one better known as Pierre Noir, a tall and dark-visaged Canadian, clad in the common costume, half-Indian and half-civilized, which marked his class. A shirt of soft dressed buckskin fell about his thighs; his legs were encased in moose-skin leggings, deeply fringed at the seams. About his middle was a broad sash, once red, and upon his head a scanty cap of similar color was pushed back. At his belt hung the great hunting knife of the *voyageur*, balanced by a keen steel tomahawk such as was in common use among the Indians. In his hand he supported a long-barreled musket, which he now examined carefully in the presence of the captain of the *voyageurs*.

"Robert Challon!" next commanded Du Mesne, and in turn the one addressed looked over his piece, the captain also scrutinizing the flint and priming with careful eye.

"Naturally, *mes enfants*," said he, "your weapons are perfect, as ever. Kataikini, and you, Kabayan, my brothers, let me see," said he to the two Indians, the former a Huron and the latter an Ojibway, both from the shores of Superior. The Indians arose silently, and without protest submitted to the scrutiny which ever seemed to them unnecessary.

"Jean Breboeuf!" called Du Mesne; and in response there arose from the shadows a wiry little Frenchman, who might have been of any age from twenty to forty-five, so sun-burnt and wrinkled, yet so active and vigorous did he seem.

"*Mon ami*," said Du Mesne to him, chidingly, "see now, here is your flint all but out of its engagement. Pray you, have better care of your piece. For this you shall stand the long watch of the night. And now let us all to bed."

One by one the little party was lost to view within the dark interior of the hut which they had arranged for themselves. Du Mesne retired a distance from the fire and seated himself upon a fallen log, his pipe glowing like a coal in the enveloping darkness.

Law himself did not so soon leave the outer air. He remained gazing out at the wild scene about him, at the rolling waves dashing on the shore, their crests whitening in the glare of the lightning, now approaching more closely. He harkened to the roll of the far-off thunder reenforced by the thunder of the waves upon the shore, and noted the sweep of the black forest about, of the black sky overhead, unlit save for one far-off, faint and feeble star.

It was a new world, this that lay around him, a new and savage world. If there were a world behind him, a world

which once held sunlight and flowers, and love and hope—
why then, it was a world lost and gone forever, and it was
very well that this new world should be so different and so
stern.

In the darkness John Law heard a voice, the voice of a
woman in terror. Swiftly he stepped to the door of the rude
lodge.

"Don't let them sing it again—never any more—that song."

"And what, Madam?"

"That one—'*us les amants changent des maitresses!*'"

A moment later she whispered, "I am afraid."

CHAPTER II

THE STORM

Marshaling to the imperious orders of the tempest, and crowding close upon the flaming standards of the lightning, the armies of the clouds came on. The sea-wide surface of the lake went dull, and above it bent a sky appalling in its blackness. The wind at first was light, then fitful and gusty, like the rising choler of a man affronted and nursing his own anger. It gained in volume and swept on across the tops of the forest trees, as though with a hand contemptuous in its strength, forbearing only by reason of its own whimsy. Now and again the cohorts of the clouds just hinted at parting, letting through a pale radiance from the western sky, where lingered the departing day. This light, as did the illuminating glare of the forked flames above, disclosed the while helmets of the trooping waters, rushing on with thunderous unison of tread; and the rattling thunder-shocks, intermittent, though coming steadily nearer, served but to emphasize these foot strokes of the waves. The heavens above and the waters under the earth—these conspired, these marched together, to assail, to overwhelm, to utterly destroy.

To destroy what? Why this wild protest of the wilderness? Was it this wide-blown, scattered fire, whose sparks and ashes were sown broadcast, till but stubborn remnants clung under the sheltering back-log of the bivouac hearth? Was it this frail lodge, built upon pliant, yielding poles, covered cunningly with mats and bark, carpeted with robe of elk and buffalo? Yet why should the elements rage at a tiny fire, and why should they tear at a little house of nomad man, since these things were old upon the earth? Was it somewhat else that incited this elemental rage? This might have been; for surely, builder of this hearth-fire which would not quench, master of this house which would not yield, there was now come up to the door of the wilderness the white man, risen from the sea, heralding the day which the tribes had for generations blindly prophesied! The white man, stern, stubborn, fruitful, had come to despoil the West of its secrets!

Let all the elements therefore join in riotous revolt! Let earth and sea and sky make common cause! Rage, waves, and blaze, ye fiery tongues, and threaten, forests, with all your ominous voices! Smite, destroy, or terrify into swift retreat this little band! Crush out their tenement! Loosen and brush off this feeble finger-grasp at the ancient threshold! With banners of flame, with armies of darkness, with shoutings of the captains of the storms, assail, denude, destroy, if even by the agony of their terrors, these feeble folk now come hither! And by this more especially, since they would set the seal of fruitfulness upon the land, and bring upon the earth a generation yet to follow. Hover about this bed in the frail and swaying lodge of bark and boughs, all ye most terrifying spirits! Let not this thing be!

"Mother of God!" cried Jean Breboeuf, bending low and pulling his tunic tighter by the belt, as he came gasping into the faint circle of light which still remained at the fire log. "'Tis murderous, this storm! Ah, Monsieur du Mesne, we are dead men! But what matter? 'Tis as well now as later. Said I not so to you all the way down Michiganon from the Straits?

A rabbit crossed my path at the last camp before Michilimackinac, and when we took boat to leave the mission at the Straits, three crows flew directly across our way. Did I not beseech you to turn back? Did I not tell you, most of all, that we had no right, honest *voyageurs* that we are, to leave for the woods without confessing to the good father? 'Tis two years now since I have been proper shriven, and two years is too long for a *voyageur* to remain unabsolved. Mother of God! When I see the lightnings and listen to that wind, I bethink me of my sins—my sins! I vow a bale of beaver—"

"Pish! Jean," responded Du Mesne, who had come in from the cover of the wood and was casting about in the darkness as best he might to see that all was made secure. "Thou'lt feel better when the sun shines again. Call Pierre Noir, and hurry, or our canoe will pound to bits upon the beach. Come!"

All three went now knee-deep in the surf, and Du Mesne, clinging to the gunwale as he passed out, was soon waist deep, and time and again lost his footing in the flood.

"Pull!" he cried at last. "Now, *en avant*!" He had flung himself over the stern, and with his knife cut the hide rope of the anchor-stone. Overboard again in an instant, he joined the others in their rush up the beach, and the three bore their ship upon their shoulders above the reach of the waves.

"Myself," said Pierre Noir, "shall sleep beneath the boat to-night, for since she sheds water from below, she may do as well from above."

"Even so, Pierre Noir," said Du Mesne, "but get you the boat farther toward your own camp to-night. Do you not see that Monsieur L'as is not with us?"

"*Eh bien?*"

"And were he not surely with us at such time, unless—?"

"Oh, *assurement!*" replied Pierre Noir. "Jean Breboeuf, aid me in taking the boat back to our camp in the woods."

Now came the rain. Not in steady and even downpour, not with intermittent showers, but in a sidelong, terrifying torrent, drenching, biting, cutting in its violence. The swift weight of the rain gave to the trees more burden than they could bear. As before the storm, when all was still, there had come time and again the warning boom of a falling tree, stricken with mysterious mortal dread of that which was to come, so now, in the riot of that arrived danger, first one and then another wide-armed monarch of the wood crashed down, adding with its downfall to the testimony of the assailing tempest's strength and fury. The lightning now came not only in ragged blazes and long ripping lines of light, but in bursts and shocks, and in bomb-like balls, exploding with elemental detonations. Balls of this tense surcharged essence rolled out over the comb of the bluff, fell upon the shadows of the water, and seemed to bound from crest to white-capped crest, till at last they split and burst asunder like some ominous missiles from engines of wrath and destruction.

And now, suddenly, all grew still again. The sky took on a lighter, livid tone, one of pure venom. There came a whisper, a murmur, a rush as of mighty waters, a sighing as of an army of the condemned, a shrieking as of legions of the lost, a roaring as of all the soul-felt tortures of a world. From the forest rose a continuous rending crash. The whiplash of the tempest cracked the tree trunks as a child beheads a row of daisies. Piled up, falling, riven asunder, torn out by the wind, the giant trees joined the toys which the cynic storm gathered in its hands and bore along until such time as it should please to crush and drop them.

There passed out over the black sea of Michiganon a vast black wraith; a thing horrible, tremendous, titanic in organic power. It howled, execrated, menaced; missed its aim, and passed. The little swaying house still stood! Under the sheltered log some tiny sparks of fire still burned, omen of the unquenchable hearthstones which the land was yet to know!

"Holy God! what was it? What was that which passed?" cried Jean Breboeuf, crawling out from beneath his shelter. "Saint Mary defend us all this night! 'Twas the great Canoe of the Damned, running *au large* across the sky! Mary, Mother of God, hear my vow! Prom this time Jean Breboeuf shall lead a better life!"

The storm, baffled, passed on. The rain, unsatisfied, sullenly ceased in its attack. The waves, hopeless but still vindictive, began to call back their legions from the narrow shore. The lightnings, unsated in their wrath, flared and flickered on and out across the eastward sea. With wild laughter and shrieks and imprecations, the spirit of the tempest wailed on its furious way. The red West had raised its hand to smite, but it had not smitten sure.

In the silence of the night, in the hush following the uproar of the storm, there came a little wailing cry; so faint, so feeble, yet so mighty, so conquering, this sign of the coming generation, the voice of the new-born babe. At this little human voice, born of sorrow and sin, born to suffering and to knowledge, born to life in all its wonders and to death in all its mystery—the elements perchance relented and averted their fury. Not yet was there to be punished sin, or wrong, or doubt, or weakness. Not at once would justice punish the parents of this babe and blot out at once the record of their fault. Storm and lightning, darkness and the night yielded to the voice of the infant and allowed the old story of humanity and sin, and hope and mercy to run on.

The babe wailed faintly in the silence of the night. Under the hearth-log there still endured the fire. And then the red West, seeing itself conquered, smiled and flung wide its arms, and greeted them with the burgeoning dawn, and the voices of birds, with a sky blue and repentant, a sun smiling and not unkind.

CHAPTER III

AU LARGE

It was weeks after the night of the great storm, and the camp of the *voyageurs* still held its place on the shore of the great Green Bay. The wild game and the abundant fishes of the lake gave ample provender for the party, and the little bivouac had been rendered more comfortable in many ways best known to those dwellers of the forest. The light jest, the burst of laughter, the careless ease of attitude showed the light-hearted *voyageurs* content with this, their last abode, nor for the time did any word issue which threatened to end their tarrying.

Law one morning strolled out from the lodge and seated himself on a bit of driftwood at the edge of the forest's fringe of cedars, where, seemingly half forgetting himself in the witchery of the scene, he gazed out idly over the wide prospect which lay before him. He was the same young man as ever. Surely, this increased gauntness was but the result of long hours at the paddle, the hollow cheeks but betokened hard fare and the defining winds of the outdoor air. If the eye were a trace more dim, that could be due but to the reflectiveness induced by the quiet scene and hour. Yet why should John Law, young and refreshed, drop chin in hand and sit there moodily looking ahead of him, comprehending

Emerson Hough

not at all that which he beheld?

Indeed there appeared now to the eye of this young man not the white shores and black crowned bluffs and distant islands, not the sweep of broad-winged birds circling near the waters, nor the shadow of the high-poised eagle drifting far above. He felt not the soft wind upon his cheek, nor noted the warmth of the on-coming sun. In truth, even here, on the very threshold of a new world and a new life, he was going back, pausing uncertainly at the door of that life and of that world which he had left behind. There appeared to him not the rolling undulations of the black-topped forest, not the tossing surface of the inland sea, nor the white-pebbled beach laved by its pulsing waters. He saw instead a white and dusty road, lined by green English hedge-rows. Back, over there, beyond these rolling blue waves, back of the long water trail over which he had come, there were chapel and bell and robed priest, and the word which made all fast forever. But back of the wilderness mission, back of the straggling settlements of Montreal and Quebec, back of the blue waters of the ocean, there, too, were church and minister; and there dwelt a woman whose figure stood now before his eyes, part of this mental picture of the white road lined with the hedges of green.

A hand was laid on his shoulder, and he half started up in sudden surprise. Before him, the sun shining through her hair, her eyes dark in the shadow, stood Mary Connynge. A fair woman indeed, comely, round of form, soft-eyed, and light of touch, she might none the less have been a very savage as she stood there, clad no longer in the dress of civilization, but in the soft native garb of skins, ornamented with the stained quills of the porcupine and the bizarre adornments of the native bead work; in her hair dull metal bands, like any Indian woman, upon her feet little beaded moccasins—the very moccasin, it might have been, which

Law had first seen in ancient London town and which had played so strange a part in his life since then.

"You startled me," said Law, simply. "I was thinking."

A sudden jealous wave of woman's divining intuition came upon the woman at his side. "I doubt not," said she, bitterly, "that I could name the subject of your thought! Why? Why sit here and dream of her, when here am I, who deserve everything that you can give?"

She stood erect, her eyes flashing, her arms outstretched, her bosom panting under the fringed garments, her voice ringing as it might have been with the very essence of truth and passion. Law looked at her steadily. But the shadow did not lift from his brow, though he looked long and pondered.

"Come," said he, at length, gently. "None the less we are as we are. In every game we take our chances, and in every game we pay our debts. Let us go back to the camp."

As they turned back down the beach Law saw standing at a little distance his lieutenant, Du Mesne, who hesitated as though he would speak.

"What is it, Du Mesne?" asked Law, excusing himself with a gesture and joining the *voyageur* where he stood.

"Why, Monsieur L'as," said Du Mesne, "I am making bold to mention it, but in good truth there was some question in my mind as to what might be our plans. The spring, as you know, is now well advanced. It was your first design to go far into the West, and there to set up your station for the trading in furs. Now there have come these little incidents which have occasioned us some delay. While I have not doubted your enterprise, Monsieur, I bethought me perhaps it might be within your plans now to go but little farther on—perhaps, indeed, to turn back—"

"To go back?" said Law.

"Well, yes; that is to say, Monsieur L'as, back again down the Great Lakes."

"Have you then known me so ill as this, Du Mesne?" said Law. "It has not been my custom to set backward foot on any sort of trail."

"Oh, well, to be sure, Monsieur, that I know quite well," replied Du Mesne, apologetically. "I would only say that, if you do go forward, you will do more than most men accomplish on their first voyage *au large* in the wilderness. There comes to many a certain shrinking of the heart which leads them to find excuse for not faring farther on. Yonder, as you know, Monsieur, lie Quebec and Montreal, somewhat better fitted for the abode of monsieur and madame than the tents of the wilderness. Back of that, too, as we both very well know, Monsieur, lie London and old England; and I had been dull of eye indeed did I not recognize the opportunities of a young gallant like yourself. Now, while I know yourself to be a man of spirit, Monsieur L'as, and while I should welcome you gladly as a brother of the trail, I had only thought that perhaps you would pardon me if I did but ask your purpose at this time."

Law bent his head in silence for a moment. "What know you of this forward trail, Du Mesne?" said he. "Have you ever gone beyond this point in your own journeyings?"

"Never beyond this," replied Du Mesne, "and indeed not so far by many hundred miles. For my own part I rely chiefly upon the story of my brother, Greysolon du L'hut, the boldest soul that ever put paddle in the St. Lawrence. My brother Greysolon, by the fire one night, told me that some years before he had been at the mouth of the Green Bay—perhaps near this very spot—and that here he and his brothers found a deserted Indian camp. Near it, lying half in the fire, where he had fallen in exhaustion, was an old, a very old Indian, who had been abandoned by his tribe to die—for that, you must know, Monsieur, is one of the pleasant customs of the wilderness.

"Greysolon and his men revived this savage in some fashion, and meantime had much speech with him about this unknown land at whose edge we have now arrived. The old savage said that he had been many moons north and west of that place. He knew of the river called the Blue Earth, perhaps the same of which Father Hennepin has told. And also of the Divine River, far below and tributary to the Messasebe. He said that his father was once of a war party who went far to the north against the Ojibways, and that his people took from the Ojibways one of their prisoners, who said that he came from some strange country far to the westward, where there was a very wide plain, of no trees. Beyond that there were great mountains, taller than any to be found in all this region hereabout. Beyond these mountains the prisoner did not know what there might be, but these mountains his people took to be the edge of the world, beyond which could live only wicked spirits. This was what the prisoner of the Ojibways said. He, too, was an old man.

"The captive of my brother Greysolon was an Outagamie, and he said that the Outagamies burned this prisoner of the Ojibways, for they knew that he was surely lying to them. Without doubt they did quite right to burn him, for the notion of a great open country without trees or streams is, of course, absurd to any one who knows America. And as for mountains, all men know that the mountains lie to the east of us, not to the westward."

"'Twould seem much hearsay," said Law, "this information which comes at second, third and fourth hand."

"True," said Du Mesne, "but such is the source of the little we know of the valley of the Messasebe, and that which lies beyond it. None the less this idea offers interest."

"Yet you ask me if I would return."

"'Twas but for yourself, Monsieur. It is there, if I may humbly confess to you, that it is my own ambition some day to arrive. Myself—this West, as I said long ago to the gentlemen in London—appeals to me, since it is indeed a land unoccupied, unowned, an empire which we may have all for ourselves. What say you, Monsieur L'as?"

John Law straightened and stiffened as he stood. For an instant his eye flashed with the zeal of youth and of adventure. It was but a transient cloud which crossed his face, yet there was sadness in his tone as he replied.

"My friend," said he, "you ask me for my answer. I have pondered and I now decide. We shall go on. We shall go forward. Let us have this West, my friend. Heaven helping us, let me find somewhere, in some land, a place where I may be utterly lost, and where I may forget!"

CHAPTER IV

THE PATHWAY OF THE WATERS

The news of the intended departure was received with joy by the crew of *voyageurs*, who, on the warning of an instant, fell forthwith to the simple tasks of breaking camp and storing the accustomed bales and bundles in their places in the great *canot du Nord*.

"*La voila!*" said Tete Gris. "Here she sits, this canoe, eager to go on. 'Tis forward again, *mes amis!* Forward once more; and glad enough am I for this day. We shall see new lands ere long."

"For my part," said Jean Breboeuf, "I also am most anxious to be away, for I have eaten this white-fish until I crave no more. I had bethought me how excellent are the pumpkins of the good fathers at the Straits; and indeed I would we had with us more of that excellent fruit, the bean."

"Bah! Jean Breboeuf," retorted Pierre Noir. "'Tis but a poor-hearted *voyageur* would hang about a mission garden with a hoe in his hand instead of a gun. Perhaps the good sisters at the Mountain miss thy skill at pulling weeds."

"Nay, now, I can live as long on fish and flesh as any man," replied Jean Breboeuf, stoutly, "nor do I hold myself, Monsieur Tete Gris, one jot in courage back of any man upon the trail."

"Of course not, save in time of storm," grinned Tete Gris. "Then, it is 'Holy Mary, witness my vow of a bale of beaver!' It is—"

"Well, so be it," said Jean Breboeuf, stoutly. "'Tis sure a bale of beaver will come easily enough in these new lands; and—though I insist again that I have naught of superstition in my soul—when a raven sits on a tree near camp and croaks of a morning before breakfast—as upon my word of honor was the case this morning—there must be some ill fate in store for us, as doth but stand to reason."

"But say you so?" said Tete Gris, pausing at his task, with his face assuming a certain seriousness.

"Assuredly," said Jean Breboeuf. "'Tis as I told you. Moreover, I insist to you, my brothers, that the signs have not been right for this trip at any time. For myself, I look for nothing but disaster."

The humor of Jean Breboeuf's very gravity appealed so strongly to his older comrades that they broke out into laughter, and so all fell again to their tasks, in sheer light-heartedness forgetting the superstitions of their class.

Thus at length the party took ship again, and in time made the head of the great bay within whose arms they had been for some time encamped. They won up over the sullen rapids of the river which came into the bay, toiling sometimes waist-deep at the *cordelle*, yet complaining not at all. So in time they came out on the wide expanse of the shallow lake of the Winnebagoes, which body of water they crossed directly, coming into the quiet channel of the stream which fell in upon its western shore. Up this stream in turn steadily they passed, amid a panorama filled with constant change. Sometimes the gentle river bent away in long curves, with hardly a ripple upon its placid surface, save where now and again some startled fish sprang into the air in fright or sport, or in the rush upon its prey. Then the stream would lead away into vast seas of marsh lands, waving in illimitable reaches of rushes, or fringed with the unspeakably beautiful green of the graceful wild rice plant.

In these wide levels now and again the channel divided, or lost itself in little *cul de sacs*, from which the paddlers were obliged to retrace their way. All about them rose myriads of birds and wild fowl, which made their nests among these marshes, and the babbling chatter of the rail, the high-keyed calling of the coot, or the clamoring of the home-building mallard assailed their ears hour after hour as they passed on between the leafy shores. Then, again, the channel would sweep to one side of the marsh, and give view to wide vistas of high and rolling lands, dotted with groves of hardwood, with here and there a swamp of cedar or of tamarack. Little herds of elk and droves of deer fed on the grass-covered slopes, as fat, as sleek and fearless of mankind as though they dwelt domesticated in some noble park.

It was a land obviously but little known, even to the most adventurous, and as chance would have it, they met not even a wandering party of the native tribes. Clearly now the little boat was climbing, climbing slowly and gently, yet surely, upward from the level of the great Lake Michiganon. In time the little river broadened and flattened out into wide, shallow expanses, the waters known as the Lakes of the Foxes; and beyond that it became yet more shallow and uncertain, winding among quaking bogs and unknown marshes; yet still, whether by patience, or by cheerfulness, or by determination, the craft stood on and on, and so reached that end of the waterway which, in the opinion of the more experienced Du Mesne, must surely be the place known among the Indian tribes as the "Place for the carrying of boats."

Here they paused for a few days, at that mild summit of land which marks the portage between the east bound and the west bound waters; yet, impelled ever by the eager spirit of the adventurer, they made their pause but short. In time they launched their craft on the bright, smooth flood of the river of the Ouisconsins, stained coppery-red by its far-off, unknown course in the north, where it had bathed leagues of the roots of pine and tamarack and cedar. They passed on steadily westward, hour after hour, with the current of this great stream, among little islands covered with timber; passed along bars of white sand and flats of hardwood; beyond forest-covered knolls, in the openings of which one might now and again see great vistas of a scenery now peaceful and now bold, with turreted knolls and sweeping swards of green, as though some noble house of old England were set back secluded within these wide and well-kept grounds. The country now rapidly lost its marshy character, and as they approached the mouth of the great stream, it being now well toward the middle of the summer, they reached, suddenly and without forewarning, that which they long had sought.

The sturdy paddlers were bending to their tasks, each broad back swinging in unison forward and back over the thwart, each brown throat bared to the air, each swart head uncovered to the glare of the midday sun, each narrow-bladed paddle keeping unison with those before and behind, the hand of the paddler never reaching higher than his chin, since each had learned the labor-saving fashion of the Indian canoeman. The day was bright and cheery, the air not too ardent, and across the coppery waters there stretched slants of shadow from the embowering forest trees. They were alone, these travelers; yet for the time at least part of them seemed care-free and quite abandoned to the sheer zest of life. There arose again, after the fashion of the *voyageurs*, the measure of the paddling song, without which indeed the paddler had not been able to perform his labor at the thwart.

"*Dans mon chemin j'ai rencontre—*"

chanted the leader; and voices behind him responded lustily with the next line:

"*Trois cavaliers bien montes—*"
"*Trois cavaliers bien montes—*"

chanted the leader again.

"*L'un a cheval et l'autre a pied—*"

came the response; and then the chorus:

"*Lon, lon laridon daine—*
Lon, lon laridon dai!"

The great boat began to move ahead steadily and more swiftly, and bend after bend of the river was rounded by the rushing prow. None knew this country, nor wist how far the journey might carry him. None knew as of certainty that he would ever in this way reach the great Messasebe; or even if he thought that such would be the case, did any one know how far that Messasebe still might be. Yet there came a time in the afternoon of that day, even as the chant of the *voyageurs* still echoed on the wooded bluffs, and even as the great birch-bark ship still responded swiftly to their gaiety, when, on a sudden turn in the arm of the river, there appeared wide before them a scene for which they had not been prepared. There, rippling and rolling under the breeze, as though itself the arm of some great sea, they saw a majestic flood, whose real nature and whose name each man there knew on the instant and instinctively.

"Messasebe! Messasebe!" broke out the voices of the paddlers.

"Stop the paddles!" cried Du Mesne. "*Voila!*"

John Law rose in the bow of the boat and uncovered his head. It was a noble prospect which lay before him. His was the soul of the adventurer, quick to respond to challenge. There was a fluttering in his throat as he stood and gazed out upon this solemn, mysterious and tremendous flood, coming whence, going whither, none might say. He gazed and gazed, and it was long before the shadow crossed his face and before he drew a sigh.

"Madam," said he, at length, turning until he faced Mary Connynge, "this is the West. We have chosen, and we have arrived!"

CHAPTER V

MESSASEBE

The boat, now lacking its propelling power, drifted on and out into the clear tide of the mighty stream. The paddlers were idle, and silence had fallen upon all. The rush of this majestic flood, steady, mysterious, secret-keeping, created a feeling of awe and wonder. They gazed and gazed again, up the great waterway, across to its farther shore, along its rolling course below, and still each man forgot his paddle, and still the little ship of New France drifted on, just rocking gently in the mimic waves which ruffled the face of the mighty Father of the Waters.

"By our Lady!" cried Du Mesne, at length, and tears stood in his tan-framed eyes as he turned, "'tis true, all that has been said! Here it is, Messasebe, more mighty than any story could have told! Monsieur L'as, 'tis big enough to carry ships."

"'Twill carry fleets of them one day, Du Mesne," replied John Law. "'Tis a roadway fit for a nation. Ah, Du Mesne! our St. Lawrence, our New France—they dwindle when compared to this new land."

"Aye! and 'tis all our own!" cried Du Mesne. "Look; for the

Emerson Hough

last ten days we have scarce seen even the smoke of a wigwam, and, so far as I can tell, there is not in all this valley now the home of a single white man. My friend Du L'hut— he may be far north of the Superior to-day for aught we know, or somewhere among the Sauteur people. If there he any man below us, let some one else tell who that may be. Sir, I promise you, when I see this big water going on so fast and heading so far away from home—well, I admit it causes me to shiver!"

"'Tis much the same," said Law, "where home may be for me."

"Ah, but 'tis different on the Lakes," said Du Mesne, "for there we always knew the way back, and knew that 'twas down stream."

"He says well," broke in Mary Connynge. "There is something in this big river that chills me. I am afraid."

"And what say you, Tete Gris, and you, Pierre Noir?" asked Law.

"Why, myself," replied the former, "I am with the captain. It matters not. There must always be one trail from which one does not return."

"*Oui*," said Pierre Noir. "To be sure, we have passed as good beaver country as heart of man could ask; but never was land so good but there was better just beyond."

"They say well, Du Mesne," spoke John Law, presently; "'tis better on beyond. Suppose we never do return? Did I not say to you that I would leave this other world as far behind me as might be?"

"*Eh bien*, Monsieur L'as, you reply with spirit, as ever," replied Du Mesne, "and it is not for me to stand in the way. My own fortune and family are also with me, and home is where my fire is lit."

"Very well," replied Law. "Let us run the river to its mouth, if need be. 'Tis all one to me. And whether we get back or not, 'tis another tale."

"Oh, I make no doubt we shall win back if need be," replied Du Mesne. "'Tis said the savages know the ways by the Divine River of the Illini to the foot of Michiganon; and that, perhaps, might be our best way back to the Lakes and to the Mountain with our beaver. We shall, provided we reach the Divine River, as I should guess by the stories I have heard, be then below the Illini, the Ottawas and the Miamis, with I know not what tribes from west of the Messasebe. 'Tis for you to say, Monsieur L'as, but for my own part—and 'tis but a hazard at best—I would say remain here, or press on to the river of the Illini."

"'Tis easy of decision, then," replied Law, after a moment of reflection. "We take that course which leads us farther on at least. Again the paddles, my friends! To-night we sup in our own kingdom. Strike up the song, Du Mesne!"

A shout of approval broke from the hardy men along the boat side, and even Jean Breboeuf tossed up his cap upon his paddle shaft.

"Forward, then, *mes amis!*" cried Du Mesne, setting his own paddle-blade deep into the flood. "*En roulant ma boule, roulant—*"

Again the chorus rose, and again the hardy craft leaped onward into the unexplored.

Emerson Hough

Day after day following this the journey was resumed, and day after day the travelers with eager eyes witnessed a prospect of continual change. The bluffs, bolder and more gigantic, towered more precipitous than the banks of the gentler streams which they had left behind. Forests ranged down to the shores, and wide, green-decked islands crept into view, and little timbered valleys of lesser streams came marching down to the imposing flood of Messasebe. Again the serrated bluffs broke back and showed vast vistas of green savannas, covered with tall, waving grasses, broken by little rolling hills, over which crossed herds of elk, and buffalo, and deer.

"'Tis a land of plenty," said Du Mesne one day, breaking the habitual silence into which the party had fallen. "'Tis a great land, and a mighty. And now, Monsieur, I know why the Indians say 'tis guarded by spirits. Sure, I can myself feel something in the air which makes my shoulder-blades to creep."

"'Tis a mighty land, and full of wonders," assented Law, who, in different fashion, had felt the same mysterious spell of this great stream. For himself, he was nearer to reverence than ever yet he had been in all his wild young life.

Now so it happened that at length, after a long though rapid journey down the great river, they came to that stream which they took to be the river of the Illini. This they ascended, and so finally, early in one evening, at the bank of a wide and placid bayou, shaded by willows and birch trees, and by great elms that bore aloft a canopy of clinging vines, they made a landing for the bivouac which was to prove their final tarrying place. The great *canot du Nord* came to rest at the foot of a timbered hill, back of which stretched high, rolling prairies, dotted with little groves and broken with wide swales and winding sloughs. The leaders of the party, with Tete Gris and Pierre Noir, ascended the bluffs and made brief exploration; not more, as was tacitly understood, with view to choosing the spot for the evening encampment than with the purpose of selecting a permanent stopping place. Du Mesne at length turned to Law with questioning gaze. John Law struck the earth with his heel.

"Here!" said he. "Here let us stop. 'Tis as well as any place. There are flowers and trees, and meadows and hedges, like to those of England. Here let us stay!"

"Ah, you say well indeed!" cried Du Mesne, "and may fortune send us happy enterprises."

"But then, for the houses," continued Law. "I presume we must keep close to this little stream which flows from the bluff. And yet we must have a place whence we can obtain good view. Then, with stout walls to protect us, we might— but see! What is that beyond? Look! There is, if I mistake not, a house already builded!"

"'Tis true, as I live!" cried Du Mesne, lowering his voice instinctively, as his quick eye caught the spot where Law was pointing. "But, good God! what can it mean?"

They advanced cautiously into the little open space beyond them, a glade but a few hundred yards across and lined by encircling trees. They saw indeed a habitation erected by human hands, apparently not altogether without skill. There were rude walls of logs, reinforced by stakes planted in the ground. From the four corners of the inclosure projected overhanging beams. There was an opening in the inclosure, as they discovered upon closer approach, and entering at this rude door, the party looked about them curiously.

Du Mesne shut his lips tight together. This was no house

built by the hands of white men. There were here no quarters, no shops, no chapel with its little bell. Instead there stood a few dried and twisted poles, and all around lay the litter of an abandoned camp.

"Iroquois, by the living Mother of God!" cried Pierre Noir.

"Look!" cried Tete Gris, calling them again outside the inclosure. He stood kicking in the ashes of what had been a fire-place. He disclosed, half buried in the charred embers, an iron kettle into which he gazed curiously. He turned away as John Law stepped up beside him.

"There must have been game here in plenty," said Law. "There are bones scattered all about."

Du Mesne and Tete Gris looked at each other in silence, and the former at length replied:

"This is an Iroquois war house, Monsieur L'as," said he. "They lived here for more than a month, and, as you say, they fed well. But these bones you see are not the bones of elk or deer. They are the bones of men, and women, and children."

Law stood taking in each detail of the scene about him.

"Now you have seen what is before us," resumed Du Mesne. "The Iroquois have gone, 'tis true. They have wiped out the villages which were here. There are the little cornfields, but I warrant you they have not seen a tomahawk hoe for a month or more. The Iroquois have gone, yet the fact that they have been here proves they may come again. What say you, Tete Gris; and what is your belief, Pierre?"

Tete Gris remained silent for some moments. "'Tis as

Monsieur says," replied he at length. "'Tis all one to me. I go or stay, as it shall please the others. There is always the one trail over which one does not return."

"And you, Pierre?"

"I stay by my friends," replied Pierre Noir, briefly.

"And you, Monsieur L'as?" asked Du Mesne.

Law raised his head with the old-time determination. "My friends," said he, "we have elected to come into this country and take its conditions as we find them. If we falter, we lose; of that we may rest assured. Let us not turn back because a few savages have been here and have slaughtered a few other savages. For me, there seems but one opinion possible. The lightning has struck, yet it may not strike again at the same tree. The Iroquois have been here, but they have departed, and they have left nothing to invite their return. Now, it is necessary that we make a pause and build some place for our abode. Here is a post already half builded to our hands."

"But if the savages return?" said Du Mesne.

"Then we will fight," said John Law.

"And right you are," replied Du Mesne. "Your reasoning is correct. I vote that we build here our station."

"Myself also," said Tete Gris. And Pierre Noir nodded his assent in silence.

CHAPTER VI

MAIZE

"Ola! Jean Breboeuf," called out Du Mesne to that worthy, who presently appeared, breathing hard from his climb up the river bluff. "Know you what has been concluded?"

"No; how should I guess?" replied Jean Breboeuf. "Or, at least, if I should guess, what else should I guess save that we are to take boat at once and set back to Montreal as fast as we may? But that—what is this? Whose house is that yonder?"

"'Tis our own, *mon enfant*," replied Du Mesne, dryly. "'Twas perhaps the property of the Iroquois a moon ago. A moon before that time the soil it stands on belonged to the Illini. To-day both house and soil belong to us. See; here stood the village. There are the cornfields, cut and trampled by the Iroquois. Here are the kettles of the natives—"

"But, but—why—what is all this? Why do we not hasten away?" broke in Jean Breboeuf.

"Pish! We do not go away. We remain where we are."

"Remain? Stay here, and be eaten by the Iroquois? Nay! not

Jean Breboeuf."

Du Mesne smiled broadly at his terrors, and a dry grin even broke over the features of the impassive old trapper, Tete Gris.

"Not so fast with your going away, Jean, my brother," said Du Mesne. "Thou'rt ever hinting of corn and the bean; now see what can be done in this garden-place of the Iroquois and the Illini. You are appointed head gardener for the post!"

"Messieurs, *me voila*," said Jean Breboeuf, dropping his hands in despair. "Were I not the bravest man in all New France I should leave you at this moment. It is mad, quite mad you are, every one of you! I, Jean Breboeuf, will remain, and, if necessary, will protect. Corn, and perhaps the bean, ye shall have; perhaps oven some of those little roots that the savages dig and eat; but, look you, this is but because you are with one who is brave. *Enfin*, I go. I bend me to the hoe, here in this place, like any peasant."

"An excellent hoe can be made from the blade bone of an elk, as the woman Wabana will perhaps show you if you like," said Pierre Noir, derisively, to his comrade of the paddle.

"Even so," said Jean Breboeuf. "I make me the hoe. Could I have but thee, old Pierre, to sit on a stump and fright the crows away, I make no doubt that all would go well with our husbandry. I had as lief go *censitaire* for Monsieur L'as as for any seignieur on the Richelieu; of that be sure, old Pierre."

"Faith," replied the latter, "when it comes to frightening crows, I'll even agree to sit on a stump with my musket across my knees and watch you work. 'Tis a good place for a sentinel—to keep the crows from picking yet more bones than these which will embarrass you in your hoeing, Jean Breboeuf."

"He says the Richelieu, Du Mesne," broke in John Law, musingly. "Very far away it sounds. I wonder if we shall ever see it again, with its little narrow farms. But here we have our own trails and our own lands, and let us hope that Monsieur Jean shall prosper in his belated farming. And now, for the rest of us, we must look presently to the building of our houses."

Thus began, slowly and in primitive fashion, the building of one of the first cities of the vast valley of the Messasebe; the seeds of civilization taking hold upon the ground of barbarism, the one supplanting the other, yet availing itself of that other. As the white men took over the crude fields of the departed savages, so also they appropriated the imperfect edifice which the conquerors of those savages had left for them. It was in little the story of old England herself, builded upon the races and the ruins of Briton, and Koman, and Saxon, of Dane and Norman.

Under the direction of Law, the walls of the old war house were strengthened with an inner row of palisades, supporting an embankment of earth and stone. The overlap of the gate was extended into a re-entrant angle, and rude battlements were erected at the four corners of the inclosure. The little stream of unfailing water was led through a corner of the fortress. In the center of the inclosure they built the houses; a cabin for Law, one for the men, and a larger one to serve as store room and as trading place, should there be opportunity for trade.

It was in these rude quarters that Law and his companion established that which was the nearest approach to a home that either for the time might claim; and it was thus that both undertook once more that old and bootless human experiment of seeking to escape from one's own self. Silent now, and dutifully obedient enough was this erstwhile English beauty, Mary Connynge; yet often and often Law caught the question of her gaze. And often enough, too, he found his own questioning running back up the water trails, and down the lakes and across the wide ocean, in a demand which, fiercer and fiercer as it grew, he yet remained too bitter and too proud to put to the proof by any means now within his power. Strange enough, savage enough, hopeless enough, was this wild home of his in the wilderness of the Messasebe.

The smoke of the new settlement rose steadily day by day, but it gave signal for no watching enemy. All about stretched the pale green ocean of the grasses, dotted by many wild flowers, nodding and bowing like bits of fragile flotsam on the surface of a continually rolling sea. The little groves of timber, scattered here and there, sheltered from the summer sun the wild cattle of the plains. The shorter grasses hid the coveys of the prairie hens, and on the marsh-grown bayou banks the wild duck led her brood. A great land, a rich, a fruitful one, was this that lay about these adventurers.

A soberness had come over the habit of the master mind of this little colony. His hand took up the ax, and forgot the sword and gun. Day after day he stood looking about him, examining and studying in little all the strange things which he saw; seeking to learn as much as might be of the timorous savages, who in time began to straggle back to their ruined villages; talking, as best he might, through such interpreting as was possible, with savages who came from the west of the Messasebe, and from the South and from the far Southwest; hearing, and learning and wondering of a land which seemed as large as all the earth, and various as all the lands that lay beneath the sun—that West, so glorious, so new, so boundless, which was yet to be the home of countless hearth-fires and the sites of myriad fields of corn. Let others hunt, and fish, and rob the Indians of their furs, after the accepted fashion of the time; as for John Law, he must look about him, and think, and watch this growing of the corn.

He saw it fairly from its beginning, this growth of the maize, this plant which never yet had grown on Scotch or English soil; this tall, beautiful, broad-bladed, tender tree, the very emblem of all fruitfulness. He saw here and there, dropped by the careless hand of some departed Indian woman, the little germinating seeds, just thrusting their pale-green heads up through the soil, half broken by the tomahawk. He saw the clustering green shoots—numerous, in the sign of plenty—all crowding together and clamoring for light, and life, and air, and room. He saw the prevailing of the tall and strong upthrusting stalks, after the way of life; saw the others dwarf and whiten, and yet cling on at the base of the bolder stem, parasites, worthless, yet existing, after the way of life.

He saw the great central stalks spring boldly up, so swiftly that it almost seemed possible to count the successive leaps of progress. He saw the strong-ribbed leaves thrown out, waving a thousand hands of cheerful welcome and assurance—these blades of the corn, so much mightier than any blades of steel. He saw the broad beckoning banners of the pale tassels bursting out atop of the stalk, token of fecundity and of the future. He caught the wide-driven pollen as it whitened upon the earth, borne by the parent West Wind, mother of increase. He saw the thickening of the green leaf at the base, its swelling, its growth and expansion, till the indefinite enlargement showed at length the incipient ear.

He noted the faint brown of the ends of the sweetly-enveloping silk of the ear, pale-green and soft underneath the sheltering and protecting husk, He found the sweet and milk-white tender kernels, row upon row, forming rapidly beneath the husk, Mud saw at length the hardening and darkening of the husk at its free end, which told that man might pluck and eat.

And then he saw the fading of the tassels, the darkening of the silk and the crinkling of the blades; and there, borne on the strong parent stem, he noted now the many full-rowed ears, protected by their husks and heralded by the tassels and the blades. "Come, come ye, all ye people! Enter in, for I will feed ye all!" This was the song of the maize, its invitation, its counsel, its promise.

Under the warped lodge frames which the fires of the Iroquois had spared, there were yet visible clusters of the ears of last year's corn. Here, under his own eye, were growing yet other ears, ripe for the harvesting and ripe for the coming growth. A strange spell fell upon the soul of Law. Visions crossed his mind, born in the soft warm air of these fecundating winds, of this strange yet peaceful scene.

At times he stood and looked out from the door of the palisade, when the prairie mists were rising in the morning at the mandate of the sun, and to his eyes these waving seas of grasses all seemed beckoning fields of corn. These smokes, coming from the broken tepees of the timid tribesmen, surely they arose from the roofs of happy and contented homes! These wreaths and wraiths of the twisting and wide-stalking mists, surely these were the captains of a general husbandry! Ah, John Law, John Law! Had God given thee the right feeling and contented heart, happy indeed had been these days in this new land of thine own, far from ignoble strivings and from fevered dreams, far from aimless struggles and unregulated avarice, far from oppression and from misery, far from bickerings, heart-burnings and envyings! Ah, John Law! Had God but given thee the pure and well-contented heart! For here in the Messasebe, that Mind which made the universe and set man to be one of its little inhabitants— surely that Mind had planned that man should come and grow in this place, tall and strong, and fruitful, useful to all the world, even as this swift, strong growing of the maize.

CHAPTER VII

THE BRINK OF CHANGE

The breath of autumn came into the air. The little flowers which had dotted the grassy robe of the rolling hills had long since faded away under the ardent sun, and now there appeared only the denuded stalks of the mulleins and the flaunting banners of the goldenrod. The wild grouse shrank from the edges of the little fields and joined their numbers into general bands, which night and morn crossed the country on sustained and strong-winged flight. The plumage of the young wild turkeys, stalking in droves among the open groves, began to emulate the iridescent splendors of their elders. The marshes above the village became the home of yet more numerous thousands of clamoring wild fowl, and high up against the blue there passed, on the south-bound journey, the harrow of the wild geese, wending their way from North to South across an unknown empire.

A chill came into the waters of the river, so that the bass and pike sought out the deeper pools. The squirrels busily hoarded up supplies of the nuts now ripening. The antlers of the deer and the elk which emerged from the concealing thickets now showed no longer ragged strips of velvet, and their tips were polished in the preliminary fitting for the fall season of love and combat. There came nights when the white frost hung heavy upon all the bending grasses and the broad-leafed plants, a frost which seared the maize leaves and set aflame the foliage of the maples all along the streams, and decked in a hundred flamboyant tones the leaves of the sumach and all the climbing vines.

As all things now presaged the coming winter, so there approached also the time when the little party, so long companions upon the Western trails, must for the first time know division. Du Mesne, making ready for the return trip over the unknown waterways back to the Lakes, as had been determined to be necessary, spoke of it as though the journey were but an affair of every day.

"Make no doubt, Monsieur L'as," said he, "that I shall ascend this river of the Illini and reach Michiganon well before the snows. Once at the mission of the Miamis, or the village at the river Chicaqua, I shall be quite safe for the winter, if I decide not to go farther on. Then, in the spring, I make no doubt, I shall be able to trade our furs at the Straits, if I like not the long run down to the Mountain. Thus, you see, I may be with you again sometime within the following spring."

"I hope it may be so, my friend," replied Law, "for I shall miss you sadly enough."

"'Tis nothing, Monsieur; you will be well occupied. Suppose I take with me Kataikini and Kabayan, perhaps also Tete Gris. That will give us four paddlers for the big canoe, and you will still have left Pierre Noir and Jean, to say nothing of our friends the Illini hereabout, who will be glad enough to make cause with you in case of need. I will leave Wabana for madame, and trust she may prove of service. See to it, pray you, that she observes the offices of the church; for methinks, unless watched, Wabana is disposed to become careless and un-Christianized."

"This I will look to," said Law, smiling.

"Then all is well," resumed Du Mesne, "and my absence will be but a little thing, as we measure it on the trails. You may find a winter alone in the wilderness a bit dull for you, mayhap duller than were it in London, or even in Quebec. Yet 'twill pass, and in time we shall meet again. Perhaps some good father will be wishing to come back with me to set up a mission among the Illini. These good fathers, they so delight in losing fingers, and ears, and noses for the good of the Church—though where the Church be glorified therein I sometimes can not say. Perhaps some leech—mayhap some artisan—"

"Nay, 'tis too far a spot, Du Mesne, to tempt others than ourselves."

"Upon the contrary rather, Monsieur L'as. It is matter for laughter to see the efforts of Louis and his ministers to keep New France chained to the St. Lawrence! Yet my good lord governor might as well puff out his cheeks against the north wind as to try to keep New France from pouring west into the Messasebe; and as much might be said for those good rulers of the English colonies, who are seeking ever to keep their people east of the Alleghanies."

"'Tis the Old World over again, there in the St. Lawrence," said Law.

"Right you are, Monsieur L'as," exclaimed Du Mesne. "New France is but an extension of the family of Louis. The intendant reports everything to the king. Monsieur So-and-so is married. Very well, the king must know it! Monsieur's eldest daughter is making sheep's eyes at such and such a soldier of the regiment of the king. Very well, this is weighty matter, of which the king must be advised! Monsieur's wife becomes expectant of a son and heir. 'Tis meet that Louis the Great should be advised of this! Mother of God! 'Tis a pretty mess enough back there on the St. Lawrence, where not a hen may cackle over its new-laid egg but the king must know it, and where not a family has meat enough for its children to eat nor clothes enough to cover them. My faith, in that poor medley of little lords and lazy vassals, how can you wonder that the best of us have risen and taken to the woods! Yet 'tis we who catch their beaver for them; and if God and the king be willing, sometime we shall get a certain price for our beaver—provided God and the king furnish currency to pay us; and that the governor, the priest and the intendant ratify the acts of God and the king!"

Law smiled at the sturdy vehemence of the other's speech, yet there was something of soberness in his own reply.

"Sir," said he, "you see here my little crooked rows of maize. Look you, the beaver will pass away, but the roots of the corn will never be torn out. Here is your wealth, Du Mesne."

The sturdy captain scratched his head. "I only know, for my part," said he, "that I do not care for the settlements. Not that I would not be glad to see the king extend his arm farther to the West, for these sullen English are crowding us more and more along our borders. Surely the land belongs to him who finds it."

"Perhaps better to him who can both find and hold it. But this soil will one day raise up a people of its own."

"Yet as to that," rejoined Du Mesne, as the two turned and walked back to the stockade, "we are not here to handle the affairs of either Louis or William. Let us e'en leave that to monsieur the intendant, and monsieur the governor, and our friends, the gray owls and the black crows, the Recollets and the Jesuits. I mind to call this spot home with you, if you like. I shall be back as soon as may be with the things we need, and we shall plant here no starving colony, but one good enough for the home of any man. Monsieur, I wish you very well, and I may congratulate you on your daughter. A heartier infant never was born anywhere on the water trail between the Mountain and the Messasebe. What name have you chosen for the young lady, Monsieur?"

"I have decided," said John Law, "to call her Catharine."

CHAPTER VIII

TOUS SAUVAGES

Had nature indeed intended Law for the wild life of the trail, and had he indeed spent years rather than months among these unusual scenes, he could hardly have been better fitted for the part. Hardy of limb, keen of eye, tireless of foot, with a hand which any weapon fitted, his success as hunter made his companions willing enough to assign to him the chase of the bison or the stag; so that he became not only patron but provider for the camp.

Some weeks after the departure of Du Mesne, Law was returning from the hunt some miles below the station. His tall and powerful figure, hardened by continued outdoor exercise, was scarce bowed by the weight of the wild buck which he bore across his shoulders. His eye, accustomed to the instant readiness demanded in the *voyageur's* life, glanced keenly about, taking in each item of the scene, each movement of the little bird on the tree, the rustling of the grass where a rabbit started from its form, the whisk of the gray squirrel's tail on the limb far overhead.

The touch of autumn was now in the air. The leaves of the wild grapevine were falling. The oaks had donned garments of somber brown, the hickories had lost their leaves, while here and there along the river shores the flaming sentinels of the maples had changed their scarlet uniform for one of duller hue. The wild rice in the marshes had shed its grain upon the mud banks. The acorns were loosening in their cups. Fall in the West, gorgeous, beautiful, had now set in, of all the seasons of the year, that most loved by the huntsman.

This tall, lean man, clad in buckskin like a savage, brown almost as a savage, as active and as alert, seemed to fit not ill with these environments, nor to lack either confidence or contentment. He walked on steadily, following the path along the bayou bank, and at length paused for a moment, throwing down his burden and stooping to drink at the tiny pool made by the little rivulet which trickled down the face of the bluff. Here he bathed his face and hands in the cool stream, for the moment abandoning himself to that rest which the hunter earns. It was when at length he raised his head and turned to resume his burden that his suspicious eye caught a glimpse of something which sent him in a flash below the level of the grasses, and thence to the cover of a tree trunk.

As he gazed from his hiding-place he saw the tawny waters of the bayou broken into a long series of advancing ripples. Passing the fringe of wild rice, swimming down beneath the heavy cordage of the wild grapevines, there came on two canoes, roughly made of elm bark, in fashion which would have shown an older frontiersman full proof of their Western origin.

In the bow of the foremost boat, as Law could now clearly see, sat a slender young man, clad in the uniform, now soiled and faded, of a captain in the British army. His boat was propelled by four dusky paddlers, Indians of the East. Stalwart, powerful, silent, they sent the craft on down stream, their keen eyes glancing swiftly from one point to the other of the ever-changing panorama, yet finding nothing that would seem to warrant pause. Back of the first boat by a short distance came a kindred craft, its crew comprising two white men and two Indian paddlers. Of the white men, one might have been a petty officer, the other perhaps a private soldier.

It was, then, as Du Mesne had said. Every party bound into the West must pass this very point upon the river of the Illini. But why should these be present here? Were they friends or foes? So queried the watcher, tense and eager as a waiting panther, now crouched with straining eye behind the sheltering tree.

As the leading boat swung clear of the shadows, the man in the prow turned his face, scanning closely the shore of the stream. As he did so, Law half started to his feet, and a moment later stepped from his concealment. He gazed again and again, doubting what he saw. Surely those clean-cut, handsome features could belong to no man but his former friend, Sir Arthur Pembroke!

Yet how could Sir Arthur be here? What could be his errand, and how had he been guided hither? These sudden questions might, upon the instant, have confused a brain ready as that of this observer, who paused not to reflect that this meeting, seemingly so impossible, was in fact the most natural thing in the world; indeed, could scarce have been avoided by any one traveling with Indian guides down the waterway to the Messasebe.

The keen eyes of the red paddlers caught sight of the crushed grasses at the little landing on the bayou bank, even as Law rose from his hiding-place. A swift, concerted sweep of the paddles sent the boat circling out into midstream, and before Law knew it he was covered by half a dozen guns. He hardly noticed this. His own gun he left leaning against a tree, and his hand was thrown out high, in front of him as he came on, calling out to those in the stream. He heard the command of the leader in the boat, and a moment later both canoes swung inshore.

"Have down your guns, Sir Arthur," cried Law, loudly and gaily. "We are none but friends here. Come in, and tell me that it is yourself, and not some miracle of mine eyes."

The young man so surprisingly addressed half started from the thwart in his amazement. His face bent into an incredulous frown, scarce carrying comprehension, even as he approached the shore. As he left the boat, for an instant Pembroke's hand was half extended in greeting, yet a swift change came over his countenance, and his body stiffened.

"Is it indeed you, Mr. Law?" he said. "I could not have believed myself so fortunate."

"'Tis myself and no one else," replied Law. "But why this melodrama, Sir Arthur? Why reject my hand?"

"I have sworn to extend to you no hand but that bearing a weapon, Mr. Law!" said Pembroke. "This may be accident, but it seems to me the justice of God. Oh, you have run far, Mr. Law—"

"What mean you, Sir Arthur?" exclaimed Law, his face assuming the dull red of anger. "I have gone where I pleased, and asked no man's leave for it, and I shall live as I please and ask no man's leave for that. I admit that it seems almost a miracle to meet you here, but come you one way or the other, you come best without riddles, and still better without threats."

"You are not armed," said Sir Arthur. He gazed at the bronzed figure before him, clad in fringed tunic and leggings of deer hide; at the belt with little knife and ax, at the gun which now rested in the hollow of his arm. Law himself laughed keenly.

"Why, as to that," said he, "I had thought myself well enough equipped. But as for a sword, 'tis true my hand is more familiar, these days, with the ax and gun."

"The late Jessamy Law shows change in his capacity of renegade," said Pembroke, raspingly. His face displayed a scorn which jumped ill with the nature of the man before him.

"I am what I am, Sir Arthur," said Law, "and what I was. And always I am at any man's service who is in search of what you call God's justice, or what I may call personal satisfaction. I doubt not we shall find my other trinkets in good order not far away. But meantime, before you turn my hospitality into shame, bring on your men and follow me."

His face working with emotion, Law turned away. He caught up the body of the dead buck, and tossing it across his shoulders, strode up the winding pathway.

"Come, Gray, and Ellsworth," said Pembroke. "Get your men together. We shall see what there is to this."

At the summit of the river-bluff Law awaited their arrival. He noted in silence the look of surprise which crossed Pembroke's face as at length they came into view of the little panorama of the stockade and its surroundings.

"This is my home, Sir Arthur," said he simply. "These are my fields. And see, if I mistake not, yonder is some proof of the ability of my people to care for themselves."

He pointed to the gateway, from the loop-holes guarding which there might now be seen protruding two long dark barrels, leveled in the direction of the approaching party. There came a call from within the palisade, and the sound of men running to take their places along the wall. Law raised his hand, and the barrels of the guns were lowered.

"This, then, is your hiding-place!" said Pembroke.

"I call it not such. 'Tis public to the world."

"Tush! You lack not in the least of your old conceit and assurance, Mr. Law!" said Pembroke.

"Nay, I lack not so much in assurance of myself," said Law, "as in my patience, which I find, Sir Arthur, now begins to grow a bit short about its breath. But since the courtesy of the trail demands somewhat, I say to you, there is my home. Enter it as friend if you like, but if not, come as you please. Did you indeed come bearing war, I should be obliged to signify to you, Sir Arthur, that you are my prisoner. You see my people."

"Sir," replied Sir Arthur, blindly, "I have vowed to find you no matter where you should go."

"It would seem that your vow is well fulfilled. But now, since you deal in mysteries, I shall even ask you definitely, Sir Arthur, who and what are you? Why do you come hither, and how shall we regard you?"

"I am, in the first place," said Sir Arthur, "messenger of my Lord Bellomont, governor at Albany of our English colonies. I add my chief errand, which has been to find Mr. Law, whom I would hold to an accounting."

"Oh, granted," replied Law, flicking lightly at the cuff of his tunic, "yet your errand still carries mystery."

"You have at least heard of the Peace of Ryswick, I presume?"

"No; how should I? And why should I care?"

"None the less, the king of England and the king of France are no longer at war, nor are their colonies this side of the water. There are to be no more raids between the colonies of New England and New France. The Hurons are to give back their English prisoners, and the Iroquois are to return all their captives to the French. The Western tribes are to render up their prisoners also, be they French, English, Huron or Iroquois. The errand of carrying this news was offered to me. It agreed well enough with my own private purposes. I had tracked you, Mr. Law, to Montreal, lost you on the Richelieu, and was glad enough to take up this chance of finding you farther to the West. And now, by the justice of heaven, as I have said, I have found you easily."

"And has Sir Arthur gone to sheriffing? Has my friend become constable? Is Sir Arthur a spy? Because, look you, this is not London, nor yet New France, nor Albany. This is Messasebe! This is my valley. I rule here. Now, if kings, or constables, or even spies, wish to find John Law—why, here is John Law. Now watch your people, and go you carefully here, else that may follow which will be ill extinguished."

Pembroke flung down his sword upon the ground in front of him.

"You are lucky, Mr. Law," said he, "lucky as ever. But

surely, never was man so eminently deserving of death as yourself."

"You do me very much honor, Sir Arthur," replied Law. "Here is your sword, sir." Stooping, he picked it up and handed it to the other. "I did but ill if I refused to accord satisfaction to one bringing me such speech as that. 'Tis well you wear your weapons, Sir Arthur, since you come thus as emissary of the Great Peace! I know you for a gentleman, and I shall ask no parole of you to-night; but meantime, let us wait until to-morrow, when I promise you I shall be eager as yourself. Come! We can stand here guessing and talking no longer. I am weary of it."

They came now to the gate of the stockade, and there Pembroke stood for a moment in surprise and perplexity. He was not prepared to meet this dark-haired, wide-eyed girl, clad in native dress of skin, with tinkling metals at wrist and ankle, and on her feet the tiny, beaded shoes. For her part, Mary Connynge, filled with woman's curiosity, was yet less prepared for that which appeared before her—an apparition, as ran her first thought, come to threaten and affright.

"Sir Arthur!" she began, her trembling tongue but half forming the words. Her eyes stared in terror, and beneath her dark skin the blood shrank away and left her pale. She recoiled from him, her left hand carrying behind her instinctively the babe that lay on her arm.

Sir Arthur bowed, but found no word. He could only look questioningly at Law.

"Madam," said the latter, "Sir Arthur Pembroke journeys through as the messenger of Lord Bellomont, governor at Albany, to spread peace among the Western tribes. He has by mere chance blundered upon our valley, and will delay over night. It seemed well you should be advised."

Mary Connynge, gray and pale, haggard and horrified, dreading all things and knowing nothing, found no manner of reply. Without a word she turned and fled back into the cabin.

Sir Arthur once more looked about him. Motioning to the others of the party to remain outside the gate, Law led him within the stockade. On one hand stood Pierre Noir, tall, silent, impassive as a savage, leaning upon his gun and fixing on the red coat of the English uniform an eye none too friendly. Jean Breboeuf, his piece half ready and his voluble tongue half on the point of breaking over restraint, Law quieted with a gesture. Back of these, ranged in a silent yet watchful group, their weapons well in hand, stood numbers of the savage allies of this new war-lord. Pembroke turned to Law again.

"You are strongly stationed, sir; but I do not understand."

"It is my home."

"But yet—why?"

"As well this as any, where one leaves an old life and begins a new," said Law. "'Tis as good a place as any if one would leave all behind, and if he would forget."

"And this—that is to say—madam?"

Sir Arthur stumbled in his speech. John Law looked him straight in the eye, a slow, sad smile upon his face.

"Had we here the plank of poor La Salle his ship," said he,

"we might nail the message of that other renegade above our door—'*Nous sommes tous sauvages*!'"

CHAPTER IX

THE DREAM

That night John Law dreamed as he slept, and it was in some form the same haunting and familiar dream. In his vision he saw not the low roof nor the rude walls about him. To his mind there appeared a little dingy room, smaller than this in which he lay, with walls of stone, with door of iron grating and not of rough-hewn slabs. He saw the door of the prison cell swing open; saw near it the figure of a noble young girl, with large and frightened eyes and lips half tremulous. To this vision he outstretched his hands. He was almost conscious of uttering some word supplicatingly, almost conscious of uttering a name.

Perhaps he slept on. We little know the ways of the land of dreams. It might have been half an instant or half an hour later that he suddenly awoke, finding his hand clapped close against his side, where suddenly there had come a sharp and burning pain. His own hand struck another. He saw something gleaming in the light of the flickering fire which still survived upon the hearth. The dim rays lit up two green, glowing, venomous balls, the eyes of the woman whom he found bending above him. He reached out his hand in the instinct of safety. This which glittered in the firelight was the blade of a knife, and it was in the hand of Mary Connynge!

In a moment Law was master of himself. "Give it to me, Madam, if you please," he said, quietly, and took the knife from fingers which loosened under his grasp. There was no further word spoken. He tossed the knife into a crack of the bunk beyond him. He lay with his right arm doubled under his head, looking up steadily into the low ceiling, upon which the fire made ragged masses of shadows. His left arm, round, full and muscular, lay across the figure of the woman whom he had forced down upon the couch beside him. He could feel her bosom rise and pant in sheer sobs of anger. Once he felt the writhing of the body beneath his arm, but he simply tightened his grasp and spoke no word.

It was not far from morning. In time the gray dawn came creeping in at the window, until at length the chinks between the logs in the little square-cut window and the ill-fitting door were flooded with a sea of sunlight. As this light grew stronger, Law slowly turned and looked at the face beside him. Out of the tangle of dark hair there blazed still two eyes, eyes which looked steadily up at the ceiling, refusing to turn either to the right or to the left. He calmly pulled closer to him, so that it might not stain the garments of the woman beside him, the blood-soaked shirt whose looseness and lack of definition had perhaps saved him from a fatal blow. He paid no attention to his wound, which he knew was nothing serious. So he lay and looked at Mary Connynge, and finally removed his arm.

"Get up," said he, simply, and the woman obeyed him.

"The fire, Madam, if you please, and breakfast."

These had been the duties of the Indian woman, but Mary Connynge obeyed.

"Madam," said Law, calmly, after the morning meal was at

last finished in silence, "I shall be very glad to have your company for a few moments, if you please."

Mary Connynge rose and followed him into the open air, her eyes still fixed upon the dark-crusted stain which had spread upon his tunic. They walked in silence to a point beyond the cabin.

"You would call her Catharine!" burst out Mary Connynge. "Oh! I heard you in your very sleep. You believe every lying word Sir Arthur tells you. You believe—"

John Law looked at her with the simple and direct gaze which the tamer of the wild beast employs when he goes among them, the look of a man not afraid of any living thing.

"Madam," said he, at length, calmly and evenly, as before, "what I have said, sleeping or waking, will not matter. You have tried to kill me. You did not succeed. You will never try again. Now, Madam, I give you the privilege of kneeling here on the ground before me, and asking of me, not my pardon, but the pardon of the woman you have foully stabbed, even as you have me."

The figure before him straightened up, the blazing yellow eyes sought his once, twice, thrice, behind them all the fury of a savage soul. It was of no avail. The cool blue eyes looked straight into her heart. The tall figure stood before her, unyielding. She sought to raise her eyes once more, failed, and so would have sunk down as he had said, actually on her knees before him.

John Law extended a hand and stopped her. "There," said he. "It will suffice. I can not demean you. There is the child."

"You called her Catharine!" broke out the woman once more

in her ungovernable rage. "You would name my child—"

"Madam, get up!" said John Law, sharply and sternly. "Get up on your feet and look me in the face. The child shall be called for her who should have been its mother. Let those forgive who can. That you have ruined my life for me is but perhaps a fair exchange; yet you shall say no word against that woman whose life we have both of us despoiled."

CHAPTER X

BY THE HILT OF THE SWORD

Law passed on out at the gate of the stockade and down to the bivouac, where Pembroke and his men had spent the night.

"Now, Sir Arthur," said he to the latter, when he had found him, "come. I am ready to talk with you. Let us go apart."

Pembroke joined him, and the two walked slowly away toward the encircling wood which swept back of the stockade. Law turned upon him at length squarely.

"Sir Arthur," said he, "I think you would tell me something concerned with the Lady Catharine Knollys. Do you bring any message from her?"

The face of Pembroke flamed scarlet with sudden wrath. "Message!" said he. "Message from Lady Catharine Knollys to you? By God! sir, her only message could be her hope that she might never hear your name again."

"You have still your temper, Sir Arthur, and you speak harsh enough."

"Harsh or not," rejoined Pembroke, "I scarce can endure her name upon your lips. You, who scouted her, who left her, who took up with the lewdest woman in all Great Britain, as it now appears—you who would consort with this creature—"

"In this matter," said John Law, simply, "you are not my prisoner, and I beg you to speak frankly. It shall be man and man between us."

"How you could have stooped to such baseness is what mortal man can never understand," resumed Sir Arthur, bitterly. "Good God! to abandon a woman like that so heartlessly—"

"Sir Arthur," said John Law, his voice trembling, "I do myself the very great pleasure of telling you that you lie!"

For a moment the two stood silent, facing each other, the face of each stony, gone gray with the emotions back of it.

"There is light," said Pembroke, "and abundant space."

They turned and paced back farther toward the open forest glade. Yet now and again their steps faltered and half paused, and neither man cared to go forward or to return. Pembroke's face, stern as it had been, again took on the imprint of a growing hesitation.

"Mr. Law," said he, "there is something in your attitude which I admit puzzles me. I ask you in all honor, I ask you on the hilt of that sword which I know you will never disgrace, why did you thus flout the Lady Catharine Knollys? Why did you scorn her and take up with this woman yonder in her stead?"

"Sir Arthur," said John Law, with trembling lips, "I must be very low indeed in reputation, since you can ask me question such as this."

"But you must answer!" cried Sir Arthur, "and you must swear!"

"If you would have my answer and my oath, then I give you both. I did not do what you suggest, nor can I conceive how any man should think me guilty of it. I loved Lady Catharine Knollys with all my heart. 'Twas my chief bitterness, keener than even the thought of the gallows itself, that she forsook me in my trouble. Then, bitter as any man would be, I persuaded myself that I cared naught. Then came this other woman. Then I—well, I was a man and a fool—a fool, Sir Arthur, a most miserable fool! Every moment of my life since first I saw her, I have loved the Lady Catharine; and, God help me, I do now!"

Sir Arthur struck his hand upon the hilt of his sword. "You were more lucky than myself, as I know," said he, and from his lips broke half a groan.

"Good God!" broke out Law. "Let us not talk of it. I give you my word of honor, there has been no happiness to this. But come! We waste time. Let us cross swords!"

"Wait. Let me explain, since we are in the way of it. You must know that 'twas within the plans of Montague that Lady Catharine Knollys should be the agent of your freedom. I was pledged to the Lady Catharine to assist her, though, as you may perhaps see, sir," and Pembroke gulped in his throat as he spoke, "'twas difficult enough, this part that was assigned to me. It was I, Mr. Law, who drove the coach to the gate, the coach which brought the Lady Catharine. 'Twas she who opened the door of Newgate jail for you. My God!

sir, how could you walk past that woman, coming there as she did, with such a purpose!"

At hearing these words, the tall figure of the man opposed to him drooped and sank, as though under some fearful blow. He staggered to a near-by support and sank weakly to a seat, his head falling between his hands, his whole face convulsed.

"Ah!" said he, "you did right to cross seas in search of me! God hath indeed found me out and given me my punishment. Yet I ask God to bear me witness that I knew not the truth. Come, Sir Arthur! Come, I beseech you! Let us fall to!"

"I shall be no man's executioner for his sentence on himself. I could not fight you now." His eye fell by chance upon the blotch in Law's bloodstained tunic. "And here," he said; "see! You are already wounded."

"'Twas but one woman's way of showing her regard," said Law. "'Twas Mary Connynge stabbed me."

"But why?"

"Nay, I am glad of it; since it proves the truth of all you say, even as it proves me to be the most unworthy man in all the world. Oh, what had it meant to me to know a real love! God! How could I have been so blind?"

"'Tis the ancient puzzle."

"Yes!" cried Law. "And let us make an end of puzzles! Your quarrel, sir, I admit is just. Let us go on."

"And again I tell you, Mr. Law," replied Sir Arthur, "that I will not fight you."

"Then, sir," said Law, dropping his own sword upon the grass and extending his hand with a broken smile, "'tis I who am your prisoner!"

CHAPTER XI

THE IROQUOIS

Even as Sir Arthur and John Law clasped hands, there came a sudden interruption. A half-score yards deeper in the wood there arose a sudden, half-choked cry, followed by a shrill whoop. There was a crashing as of one running, and immediately there pressed into the open space the figure of an Indian, an old man from the village of the Illini. Even as his staggering footsteps brought him within gaze, the two startled observers saw the shaft which had sunk deep within his breast. He had been shot through by an Indian arrow, and upon the instant it was all too plain whose hand had sped the shaft. Following close upon his heels there came a stalwart savage, whose face, hideously painted, appeared fairly demoniacal as he came bounding on with uplifted hatchet, seeking to strike down the victim already impaled by the silent arrow.

"Quick!" cried Law, in a flash catching the meaning of this sudden spectacle. "Into the fort, Sir Arthur, and call the men together!"

Not stopping to relieve the struggles of the victim, who had now fallen forward gasping, Law sprang on with drawn blade to meet the advancing savage. The latter paused for an uncertain moment, and then with a shrill yell of defiance, hurled the keen steel hatchet full at Law's head. It shore away a piece of his hat brim, and sank with edge deep buried in the trunk of a tree beyond. The savage turned, but turned too late. The blade of the swordsman passed through from rib to rib under his arm, and he fell choking, even as he sought again to give vent to his war-cry.

And now there arose in the woods beyond, and in the fields below the hill, and from the villages of the neighboring Indians, a series of sharp, ululating yells. Shots came from within the fortress, where the loop-holes were already manned. There were borne from the nearest wigwams of the Illini the screams of wounded men, the shrieks of terrified women. In an instant the peaceful spot had become the scene of a horrible confusion. Once more the wolves of the woods, the Iroquois, had fallen on their prey!

Swift as had been Law's movements, Pembroke was but a pace behind him as he wrenched free his blade. The two turned back together and started at speed for the palisade. At the gate they met others hurrying in, Pembroke's men joining in the rush of the frightened villagers. Among these the Iroquois pressed with shrill yells, plying knife and bow and hatchet as they ran, and the horrified eyes of those within the palisade saw many a tragedy enacted.

"Watch the gate!" cried Pierre Noir, from his station in the corner tower. As he spoke there came a rush of screaming Iroquois, who sought to gain the entrance.

"Now!" cried Pierre Noir, discharging his piece into the crowded ranks below him; and shot after shot followed his own. The packed brown mass gave back and resolved itself into scattered units, who broke and ran for the nearest cover.

"They will not come on again until dark," said Pierre Noir, calmly leaning his piece against the wall. "Therefore I may attend to certain little matters."

He passed out into the entry-way, where lay the bodies of three Iroquois, abandoned, under the close and deadly fire, by their companions where they had fallen. When Pierre Noir returned and calmly propped up again the door of slabs which he had removed, he carried in his hand three tufts of long black hair, from which dripped heavy gouts of blood.

"Good God, man!" said Pembroke. "You must not be savage as these Indians!"

"Speak for yourself, Monsieur Anglais," replied Pierre, stoutly. "You need not save these head pieces if you do not care for them. For myself, 'tis part of the trade."

"Assuredly," broke in Jean Breboeuf. "We keep these trinkets, we *voyageurs* of the French. Make no doubt that Jean Breboeuf will take back with him full tale of the Indians he has killed. Presently I go out. Zip! goes my knife, and off comes the topknot of Monsieur Indian, him I killed but now as he ran. Then I shall dry the scalp here by the fire, and mount it on a bit of willow, and take it back for a present to my sweetheart, Susanne Duchene, on the seignieury at home."

"Bravo, Jean!" cried out the old Indian fighter, Pierre Noir, the old baresark rage of the fighting man now rising hot in his blood. "And look! Here come more chances for our little ornaments."

Pierre Noir for once had been mistaken and underestimated the courage of the warriors of the Onondagos. Lashing themselves to fury at the thought of their losses, they came on again, now banding and charging in the open close up to the walls of the palisade. Again the little party of whites maintained a steady fire, and again the Iroquois, baffled and enraged, fell back into the wood, whence they poured volley after volley rattling against the walls of the sturdy fortress.

"I am sorry, sir," said Sergeant Gray to Pembroke, "but 'tis all up with me." The poor fellow staggered against the wall, and in a few moments all was indeed over with him. A chance shot had pierced his chest.

"*Peste!* If this keeps up," said Pierre Noir, "there will not be many of us left by morning. I never saw them fight so well. 'Tis a good watch we'll need this night."

In fact, all through the night the Iroquois tried every stratagem of their savage warfare. With ear-splitting yells they came close up to the stockade, and in one such charge two or three of their young men even managed to climb to the tops of the pointed stakes, though but to meet their death at the muzzles of the muskets within. Then there arose curving lines of fire from without the walls, half circles which terminated at last in little jarring thuds, where blazing arrows fell and stood in log, or earth, or unprotected roof. These projectiles, wrapped with lighted birch bark, served as fire brands, and danger enough they carried. Yet, after some fashion, the little garrison kept down these incipient blazes, held together the terrified Illini, repulsed each repeated charge of the Iroquois, and so at last wore through the long and fearful night.

The sun was just rising across the tops of the distant groves when the Iroquois made their next advance. It came not in the form of a concerted attack, but of an appeal for peace. A party of the savages left their cover and approached the fortress, waving their hands above their heads. One of them presently advanced alone.

"What is it, Pierre?" asked Law. "What does the fellow want?"

"I care not what he wants," said Pierre Noir, carefully adjusting the lock of his piece and steadily regarding the savage as he approached; "but I'll wager you a year's pay he never gets alive past yonder stump."

"Stay!" cried Pembroke, catching at the barrel of the leveled gun. "I believe he would talk with us."

"What does he say, Pierre?" asked Law. "Speak to him, if you can."

"He wants to know," said Pierre, as the messenger at length stopped and began a harangue, "whether we are English or French. He says something about there being a big peace between Corlaer and Onontio; by which he means, gentlemen, the governor at New York and the governor at Quebec."

"Tell him," cried Pembroke, with a sudden thought, "that I am an officer of Corlaer, and that Corlaer bids the Iroquois to bring in all the prisoners they have taken. Tell him that the French are going to give up all their prisoners to us, and that the Iroquois must leave the war path, or my Lord Bellomont will take the war trail and wipe their villages off the earth."

Something in this speech as conveyed to the savage seemed to give him a certain concern. He retired, and presently his place was taken by a tall and stately figure, dressed in the full habiliments of an Iroquois chieftain. He came on calmly and proudly, his head erect, and in his extended hand the long-stemmed pipe of peace. Pierre Noir heaved a deep sigh of relief.

"Unless my eyes deceive me," said he, "'tis old Teganisoris himself, one of the head men of the Onondagos. If so, there is some hope, for Teganisoris is wise enough to know when peace is best."

It was, indeed, that noted chieftain of the Iroquois who now advanced close up to the wall. Law and Pembroke stepped out to meet him beyond the palisade, the old *voyageur* still serving as interpreter from the platform at their back.

"He says—listen, Messieurs!—he says he knows there is going to be a big peace; that the Iroquois are tired of fighting and that their hearts are sore. He says—a most manifest lie, I beg you to observe, Messieurs—that he loves the English, and that, although he ought to kill the Frenchmen of our garrison, he will, since some of us are English, and hence his friends, spare us all if we will cease to fight."

Pembroke turned to Law with question in his eye.

"There must be something done," said the latter in a low tone. "We were short enough of ammunition here even before Du Mesne left for the settlements, and your own men have none too much left."

"'Reflect! Bethink yourselves, Englishmen!' he says to us," continued Pierre Noir. "'We came to make war upon the Illini. Our work here is done. 'Tis time now that we went back to our villages. If there is to be a big peace, the Iroquois must be there; for unless the Iroquois demand it, there can be no peace at all.' And, gentlemen, I beg you to remember it is an Iroquois who is talking, and that the truth is not in the tongue of an Iroquois."

"'Tis a desperate chance, Mr. Law," said Pembroke. "Yet if we keep up the fight here, there can be but one end."

"'Tis true," said Law; "and there are others to be considered."

It was hurriedly thus concluded. Law finally advanced toward the tall figure of the Iroquois headman, and looked him straight in the face.

"Tell him," said he to Pierre Noir, "that we are all English, and that we are not afraid; and that if we are harmed, the armies of Corlaer will destroy the Iroquois, even as the Iroquois have the Illini. Tell him that we will go back with him to the settlements because we are willing to go that way upon a journey which we had already planned. We could fight forever if we chose, and he can see for himself by the bodies of his young men how well we are able to make war."

"It is well," replied Teganisoris. "You have the word of an Iroquois that this shall be done, as I have said."

"The word of an Iroquois!" cried Pierre Noir, slamming down the butt of his musket. "The word of a snake, say rather! Jean Breboeuf, harken you to what our leaders have agreed! We are to go as prisoners of the Iroquois! Mary, Mother of God, what folly! And there is madame, and *la pauvre petite*, that infant so young. By God! Were it left to me, Pierre Berthier would stand here, and fight to the end. I know these Iroquois!"

CHAPTER XII

PRISONERS OF THE IROQUOIS

The faith of the Iroquois was worse than Punic, nor was there lacking swift proof of its real nature. Law and Pembroke, the moment they had led their little garrison beyond the gate, found themselves surrounded by a ring of tomahawks and drawn bows. Their weapons were snatched away from them, and on the instant they found themselves beyond all possibility of that resistance whose giving over they now bitterly repented. Teganisoris regarded them with a sardonic smile.

"I see you are all English," said he, "though some of you wear blue coats. These we may perhaps adopt into our tribe, for our boys grow up but slowly, and some of the blue coats are good fighters. These dogs of Illini we shall of course burn. As for your war house, you will no longer need it, since you are now friends of the Iroquois, and are going to their villages. You may say to Corlaer that you well know the Iroquois have no prisoners."

The horrid significance of this threat was all too soon made plain. In an hour the little stockade was but a mass of embers and ashes. In another hour the little valley had become a Gehenna of anguish and lamentations, with whose riot of grief and woe there mingled the savage exultations of a foe whose treachery was but surpassed by his cruelty. Again the planting-ground of the Illini was utterly laid waste, to mark it naught remaining but trampled grain, and heaps of ashes, and remnants of blackened and incinerated bones. By nightfall the party of prisoners had begun a wild journey through the wilderness, whose horrors surpassed any they had supposed to be humanly endurable.

Day after day, week after week, for more than a month, and much of the time in winter weather, they toiled on, part of the way by boat, the remainder of the journey on foot, crossing snow-clogged forest, and tangled thicket and frozen morass, yet daring not to drop out for rest, since to lag might mean to die. It was as though after some frightful nightmare of suffering and despair that at length they reached the villages of the Five Nations, located far to the east, at the foot of the great waterway which Law and his family had ascended more than a year before.

Yet if that which had gone before seemed like some bitter dream, surely the day of awakening promised but little better hope. From village to village, footsore and ill, they were hurried without rest, at each new stopping place the central figures of a barbarous triumph; and nowhere did they meet the representatives of either the French or the English government, whose expected presence had constituted their one ground of hope.

"Where is your big peace?" asked Teganisoris of Pembroke. "Where are the head men of Corlaer? Who brings presents to the Iroquois, and who is to tell us that Onontio has carried the pipe of peace to Corlaer? Here are our villages as when we left them, and here again are we, save for the absent ones who have been killed by your young men. It is no wonder that my people are displeased."

Indeed those of the Iroquois who had remained at home clamored continually that some of the prisoners should be given over to them. Thus, in doubt, uncertainty and terror the party passed through the villages, moving always eastward, until at length they arrived at the fortified town where Teganisoris made his home, a spot toward the foot of Lake Ontario, and not widely removed from that stupendous cataract which, from the beginning of earth, had uplifted its thunderous diapason here in the savage wilderness— Ontoneagrea, object of superstitious awe among all the tribes.

Time hung heavy on the hands of the savages. It was winter, and the parties had all returned from the war trails. The mutterings arose yet more loudly among families who had lost most heavily in these Western expeditions. The shrewd mind of Teganisoris knew that some new thing must be planned. He announced his decision at his own village, after the triumphal progress among the tribes had at length been concluded.

"Since they have sent us no presents," said he, with that daring diplomacy which made him a leader in red states- manship, "let those who stayed at home be given some prisoner in pay for those of their people who have been killed. Moreover, let us offer to the Great Spirit some sacrifice in propitiation; since surely the Great Spirit is offended." Such was the conclusion of this head man of the Onondagos, and fateful enough it was to the prisoners.

The great gorge through which poured the vast waters of the Northern seas was a spot not always visited by those passing up the Great Lakes for the Western stations, nor down the Lakes to the settlements of the St. Lawrence. Yet there was a trail which led around the great cataract, and the occasional *coureurs de bois*, or the passing friars, or the adventurous merchants of the lower settlements now and again left that trail, and came to look upon the tremendous scene of the great falling of the waters. Here where the tumult ascended up to heaven, and where the white-blown wreaths of mist might indeed, even in an imagination better than that of a savage, have been construed into actual forms of spirits, the Indians had, from time immemorial, made their offerings to the genius of the cataract—strips of rude cloth, the skin of the beaver and the otter, baskets woven of sweet grasses, and, after the advent of the white man, pieces of metal or strings of precious beads. Such valued things as these were in rude adoration placed upon rocks or uplifted scaffolds near to the brink of the abyss. This was the spot most commonly chosen by the medicine man in the pursuit of his incantations. It was the church, the wild and savage cathedral of the red men.

Following now the command of their chieftain, the Iroquois left their stationary lodges and moved in a body, pitching a temporary camp at a spot not far from the Falls. Here, in a great council lodge, the older men sat in deliberation for a full day and night. The dull drum sounded continually, the council pipe went round, and the warriors besought the spirits to give them knowledge. The savage hysteria, little by little, yet steadily, arose higher and higher, until at length it reached that point of frenzy where naught could suffice save some terrible, some tremendous thing.

Enforced spectators of these curious and ominous cere-monies, the prisoners looked on, wondering, imagining, hesitating and fearing. "Monsieur," said Pierre Noir, turning at last to Law, "it grieves me to speak, yet 'tis best for you to know the truth. It is to be you or Monsieur Pembroke. They will not have me. They say that it must be one of you two great chiefs, for that you were brave, your hearts were strong, and that hence you would find favor as the adopted child of the Great Spirit who has been offended."

Law looked at Pembroke, and they both regarded Mary Connynge and the babe. "At least," said Law, "they spare the woman and the child. So far very well. Sir Arthur, we are at the last hazard."

"I have asked them to take me," said Pierre Noir, "for I am an old man and have no family. But they will not listen to me."

Pembroke passed his hand wearily across his face. "I have behind me so long a memory of suffering," said he, "and before me so small an amount of promise, that for myself I am content to let it end. It comes to all sooner or later, according to our fate."

"You speak," said Law, "as though it were determined. Yet Pierre says it will not be both of us, but one."

Pembroke smiled sadly. "Why, sir," said he, "do you think me so sorry a fellow as that? Look!" and he pointed to Mary Connynge and the child. "There is your duty."

Law followed his gaze, and his look was returned dumbly by the woman who had played so strange a part in the late passages of his life. Never a word with her had Law spoken regarding his plans or concerning what he had learned from Pembroke. As to this, Mary Connynge had been afraid to ask, nor dare ask even now.

"Besides," went on Pembroke later, as he called Law aside, "there is something to be done—not here, but over there, in England, or in France. Your duty is involved not only with this woman. You must find sometime the other woman. You must see the Lady Catharine Knollys."

Law sunk his head between his hands and groaned bitterly.

"Go you rather," said he, "and spend your life for her. I choose that it should end at once, and here."

"I have not been wont to call Mr. Law a coward," said Pembroke, simply.

"I should be a coward if I should stand aside and allow you to sacrifice yourself; nor shall I do so," replied the other.

"They say," broke in Pierre Noir, who had been listening to the excited harangues of first one warrior and then another, "that both warriors are great chiefs, and that both should go together. Teganisoris insists that only one shall be offered. This last has been almost agreed; but which one of you 'tis to be has not yet been determined."

Dawn came through the narrow door and open roof holes of the lodge. The rising of the sun seemed to bring conviction to the Iroquois. All at once the savage council broke up and scattered into groups, which hurried to different parts of the village. Presently these reappeared at the central lodge. There sounded a concerted savage chant. A ragged column appeared, whose head was faced toward the cataract. There were those who bore strings of beads and strips of fur, even the prized treasures of the tufted scalp locks, whose tresses, combed smooth, were adorned with colored cloth and feathers.

Pierre Noir was silent; yet, as the captives looked, they needed no advice that the sacrificial procession was now forming.

"They said," began Pierre Noir, at length, with trembling voice, turning his eyes aside as he spoke, "that it could not be myself, that it must be one of you, and but one. They are going to cast lots for it. It is Teganisoris who has proposed that the lots shall be thrown by—" Pierre Noir faltered, unwilling to go on.

"And by whom?" asked Law, quietly.

"By—by the woman—by madame!"

CHAPTER XIII

THE SACRIFICE

There was sometimes practised among the Iroquois a game which bore a certain resemblance to the casting of dice, as the latter is known among civilized peoples. The method of the play was simple. Two oblong polished bones, of the bigness of a man's finger, were used as the dice. The ends of these were ground thin and were rudely polished. One of the dice was stained red, the other left white. The players in the game marked out a line on the hard ground, and then each in turn cast up the two dice into the air, throwing them from some receptacle. The game was determined by the falling of the red bone, he who cast this colored bone closer to the line upon the ground being declared the winner. The game was simple, and depended much upon chance. If the red die fell flat upon its face at a point near to the line, it was apt to lie close to the spot where it dropped. On the other hand, did it alight upon either end, it might bound back and fall at some little distance upon one side of the line.

It was this game which, in horrible fashion, Teganisoris now proposed to play. He offered to the clamoring medicine man and his ferocious disciples one of these captives, whose death should appease not only the offended Great Spirit, but also the unsated vengeance of the tribe. He offered, at the same time, the spectacle of a play in which a human life should be the stake. He used as practical executioner the woman who was possessed by one of them, and who, in the crude notions of the savages, was no doubt coveted by both. It must be the hand of this woman that should cast the dice, a white one and a red one for each man, and he whose red die fell closer to the line was winner in the grim game of life and death.

Jean Breboeuf and Pierre Noir stood apart, and tears poured from the eyes of both. They were hardened men, well acquainted with Indian warfare; they had seen the writhings of tortured victims, and more than once had faced such possibilities themselves; yet never had they seen sight like this.

Near the two men stood Mary Connynge, the bright blood burning in her cheeks, her eyes dry and wide open, looking from one to the other. God, who gives to this earth the few Mary Connynges, alone knows the nature of those elements which made her, and the character of the conflict which now went on within her soul. Tell such a woman as Mary Connynge that she has a rival, and she will either love the more madly the man whom she demands as her own, or with equal madness and with greater intensity will hate her lover with a hatred untying and unappeasable.

Mary Connynge stood, her eyes glancing from one to the other of the men before her. She had seen them both proved brave men, strong of arm, undaunted of heart, both gallant gentlemen. God, who makes the Mary Connynges of this earth, only can tell whether or not there arose in the heart of this savage woman, this woman at bay, scorned, rebuked, mastered, this one question: Which? If Mary Connynge hated John Law, or if she loved him—ah! how must have pulsed her heart in agony, or in bitterness, as she took into her hand those lots which were the arbiters of life and death!

Teganisoris looked about him and spoke a few rapid words. He caught Mary Connynge roughly by the shoulder and pulled her forward. The two men stood with faces set and gray in the pitiless light of morn. Their arms were fast bound behind their backs. Eagerly the crowding savages pressed up to them, gesticulating wildly, and peering again and again into their faces to discover any sign of weakness. They failed. The pride of birth, the strength of character, the sheer animal vigor of each man stood him in stead at this ultimate trial. Each had made up his mind to die. Each proposed, not doubting that he would be the one to draw the fatal lot, to die as a man and a gentleman.

Teganisoris would play this game with all possible mystery and importance. It should be told generations hence about the council fires, how he, Teganisoris, devised this game, how he played it, how he drew it out link by link to the last atom of its agony. There was no receptacle at hand in which the dice could be placed. Teganisoris stooped, and without ceremony wrenched from Mary Connynge's foot the moccasin which covered it—the little shoe—beaded, beautiful, and now again fateful. Sir Arthur smiled as though in actual joy.

"My friend," said he, "I have won! This might be the very slipper for which we played at the Green Lion long ago."

Law turned upon him a face pale and solemn. "Sir," said he, "I pray God that the issue may not be as when we last played. I pray God that the dice may elect me and not yourself."

"You were ever lucky in the games of chance," replied Pembroke.

"Too lucky," said Law. "But the winner here is the loser, if it be myself."

Teganisoris roughly took from Mary Connynge's hand the little bits of bone. He cast them into the hollow of the moccasin and shook them dramatically together, holding them high above his head. Then he lowered them and took out from the receptacle two of the dice. He placed his hand on Law's shoulder, signifying that his was to be the first cast. Then he handed back the moccasin to the woman.

Mary Connynge took the shoe in her hand and stepped forward to the line which had been drawn upon the ground. The red spots still burned upon her cheeks; her eyes, amber, feline, still flamed hard and dry. She still glanced rapidly from one to the other, her eye as lightly quick and as brilliant as that of the crouched cat about to spring.

Which? Which would it be? Could she control this game? Could she elect which man should live and which should die—this woman, scorned, abased, mastered? Neither of these sought to read the riddle of her set face and blazing eyes. Each as he might offered his soul to his Creator.

The hand of Mary Connynge was raised above her head. Her face was turned once more to John Law, her master, her commander, her repudiator. Slowly she turned the moccasin over in her hand. The white bone fell first, the red for a moment hanging in the soft folds of the buckskin. She shook it out. It fell with its face nearly parallel to the ground and alighted not more than a foot from the line, rebounding scarce more than an inch or so. Low exclamations arose from all around the thickened circle.

"As I said, my friend," cried Sir Arthur, "I have won! The throw is passing close for you."

Teganisoris again caught Mary Connynge by the shoulder, and dragged her a step or so farther along the line, the two dice being left on the ground as they had fallen. Once more, her hand arose, once more it turned, once more the dice were cast.

The goddess of fortune still stood faithful to this bold young man who had so often confidently assumed her friendship. His life, later to be so intimately concerned with this same new savage country, was to be preserved for an ultimate opportunity.

The white and the red bone fell together from the moccasin. Had it been the white that counted, Sir Arthur had been saved, for the white bone lay actually upon the line. The red fell almost as close, but alighted on its end. As though impelled by some spirit of evil, it dropped upon some little pebble or hard bit of earth, bounded into the air, fell, and rolled quite away from the mark!

Even on that crowd of cruel savages there came a silence. Of the whites, one scarce dared look at the other. Slowly the faces of Pembroke and Law turned one toward the other.

"Would God I could shake you by the hand," said Pembroke. "Good by."

"As for you, dogs and worse than dogs," he cried, turning toward the red faces about him, "mark you! where I stand the feet of the white man shall stand forever, and crush your faces into the dirt!"

Whether or not the Iroquois understood his defiance could not be determined. With a wild shout they pressed upon him. Borne struggling and stumbling by the impulse of a dozen hands, Pembroke half walked and half was carried over the distance between the village and the brink of the chasm of Niagara.

Until then it had not been apparent what was to be the nature of his fate, but when he looked upon the sliding floor of waters below him, and heard beyond the thunderous voices of the cataract, Pembroke knew what was to be his final portion.

There was, at some distance above the great falls, a spot where descent was possible to the edge of the water. Pembroke's feet were loosened and he was compelled to descend the narrow path. A canoe was tethered at the shore, and the face of the young Englishman went pale as he realized what was to be the use assigned it. Bound again hand and foot, helpless, he was cast into this canoe. A strong arm sent the tiny craft out toward midstream.

The hands of the great waters grasped the frail cockleshell, twisted it about, tossed it, played with it, and claimed it irrevocably for their own. For a few moments it was visible as it passed on down, with the resistless current of the mighty stream. Almost at the verge of the plunge, the eyes watching from the shore saw at a distance the struggle made by the victim. He half raised himself in the boat and threw himself against its side. It was overset. For one instant the cold sun shone glistening on the wet bark of the upturned craft. It was but a moment, and then there was no dot upon the solemn flood.

CHAPTER XIV

THE EMBASSY

"Monsieur! Madame! Pierre Noir! Listen to me! I have saved you! I, Jean Breboeuf, I have rescued you!"

So spoke Jean Breboeuf, thrusting his head within the door of the lodge in which were the remaining prisoners of the Iroquois.

It was indeed Jean Breboeuf who, strolling beyond the outer edge of the village, had been among the first to espy an approaching party of visitors. Of any travelers possible, none could have been more important to the prisoners. Too late, yet welcome even now, the embassy from New France among the Iroquois had arrived. In an instant the village was in an uproar.

The leader of this embassy from Quebec was one Captain Joncaire, at that time of the French settlements, but in former years a prisoner among the Onondagos, where he was adopted into the tribe and much respected. Joncaire was accompanied by a priest of the Jesuit brotherhood, by a young officer late of the regiment Carignan, and by two or three petty Canadian officials, as well as a struggling retinue of savages picked up on the way between Lake George and the Indian villages. He advanced now at the head of his little party, bearing in his hand a wampum belt. He pushed aside the young men, and demanded that he be brought to the chief of the village. Teganisoris himself presently advanced to meet him, and of him Joncaire demanded that there should at once be called a full council of the tribe; with which request the chief of the Onondagos hastened to comply.

Fully accustomed to such ceremonies, Joncaire sat in the council calmly listening to the speeches of its orators, and at length arose for his own reply. "Brothers," said he, "I have here"—and he drew from his tunic a copy of the decree of Louis XIV declaring peace between the French and the English colonies—"a talking paper. This is the will of Onontio, whom you love and fear, and it is the will of the great father across the water, whom Onontio loves and fears. This talking paper says that our young men of the French colonies are no longer to go to war against Corlaer. The hatchet has been buried by the two great fathers. Brothers, I have come to tell you that it is time for the Iroquois also to bury the hatchet, and to place upon it heavy stones, so that it never again can be dug up.

"Brothers, as you know, the great canoes from across the sea are bringing more and more white men. Look about you, and tell me where are your fathers and your brothers and your sons? Half your fighting men are gone; and if you turn to the West to seek out strong young men from the other tribes, which of them will come to sit by your fires and be your brothers? The war trails of the Nations have gone to the West as far as the Great River. All the country has been at war. The friends of Onontio beyond Michilimackinac have been so busy fighting that they have forgotten to take the beaver, or if they have taken it, they have been afraid to bring it down the water trail to us, lest the Iroquois or the English should rob them.

"Brothers, a great peace is now declared. Onontio, the father of all the red men, has taken the promises of his children, the Hurons, the Algonquins, the Miamis, the Illini, the Outagamies, the Ojibways, all those peoples who live to the west, that they will follow the war trail no more. Next summer there will be a great council. Onontio and Corlaer have agreed to call the tribes to meet at the Mountain in the St. Lawrence. Onontio says to you that he will give you back your prisoners, and now he demands that you in return give back those whom you may have with you. This is his will; and if you fail him, you know how heavy is his hand.

"Brothers, I see that you have prisoners here, white prisoners. These must be given up to us. I will take them with me when I return. For your Indian captives, it is the will of Onontio that you bring them all to the Great Peace in the summer, and that you then, all of you, help to dig the great hill under which the hatchet is going to be buried. Then once more our rivers will not be red, and will look more like water. The sun will not shine red, but will look as the sun should look. The sky will again be blue. Our women and our children will no longer be afraid, and you Iroquois can go to sleep in your houses and not dread the arms of the French. Brothers, I have spoken. Peace is good."

Teganisoris replied in the same strain as that chosen by Joncaire, assuring him that he was his brother; that his heart went out to him; that the Iroquois loved the French; and that if they had gone to war with them, it was but because the young men of Corlaer had closed their eyes so that they could not see the truth. "As to these prisoners," said he, "take them with you. We do not want them with us, for we fear they may bring us harm. Our medicine man counseled us to offer up one of these prisoners as a sacrifice to the Great Spirit. We did so. Now our medicine man has a bad dream. He says that the white men are going to come and tear down our houses and trample our fields. When the time comes for the peace, the Iroquois will be at the Mountain. Brother, we will bury the hatchet, and bury it so deep that henceforth none may ever again dig it up."

"It is well," said Joncaire, abruptly. "My brothers are wise. Now let the council end, for my path is long and I must travel back to Onontio at once."

Joncaire knew well enough the fickle nature of these savages, who might upon the morrow demand another council and perhaps arrive at different conclusions. Hearing there were no white prisoners in the villages farther to the west, he resolved to set forth at once upon the return with those now at hand. Hurrying, therefore, as soon as might be, to their leader, he urged him to make ready forthwith for the journey back to the St. Lawrence.

"Unless I much mistake, Monsieur," said he to Law, "you are that same gentleman who so set all Quebec by the ears last winter. My faith! The regiment Carignan had cause to rejoice when you left for up river, even though you took with you half the ready coin of the settlement. Yet come you once more to meet the gentlemen of France, and I doubt not they will be glad as ever to stake you high, as may be in this poverty-stricken region. You have been far to the westward, I doubt not. You were, perhaps, made prisoner somewhere below the Straits."

"Far below; among the tribe of the Illini, in the valley of the Messasebe."

"You tell me so! I had thought no white man left in that valley for this season. And madame—this child—surely 'twas the first white infant born in the great valley."

"And the most unfortunate."

"Nay, how can you say that, since you have come more than half a thousand miles and are all safe and sound to-day? Glad enough we shall be to have you and madame with us for the winter, if, indeed, it be not for longer dwelling. I can not take you now to the English settlements, since I must back to the governor with the news. Yet dull enough you would find these Dutch of the Hudson, and worse yet the blue-nosed psalmodists of New England. Much better for you and your good lady are the gayer capitals of New France, or *la belle France* itself, that older France. Monsieur, how infinitely more fit for a gentleman of spirit is France than your dull England and its Dutch king! Either New France or Old France, let me advise you; and as to that new West, let me counsel that you wait until after the Big Peace. And, in speaking, your friend, Du Mesne, your lieutenant, the *coureur*—his fate, I suppose, one need not ask. He was killed—where?"

Law recounted the division of his party just previous to the Iroquois attack, and added his concern lest Du Mesne should return to the former station during the spring and find but its ruins, with no news of the fate of his friends.

"Oh, as to that—'twould be but the old story of the *voyageurs*," said Joncaire. "They are used enough to journeying a thousand miles or so, to find the trail end in a heap of ashes, and to the tune of a scalp dance. Fear not for your lieutenant, for, believe me, he has fended for himself if there has been need. Yet I would warrant you, now that this word for the peace has gone out, we shall see your friend Du Mesne as big as life at the Mountain next summer, knowing as much of your history as you yourself do, and quite counting upon meeting you with us on the St. Lawrence, and madame as well. As to that, methinks madame will be better with us on the St. Lawrence than on the savage Messasebe. We have none too many dames among us, and I need not state, what monsieur's eyes have told him every morning— that a fairer never set foot from ship from over seas. Witness my lieutenant yonder, Raoul de Ligny! He is thus soon all devotion! Mother of God! but we are well met here, in this wilderness, among the savages. *Voila*, Monsieur! We take you again captive, and 'tis madame enslaves us all!"

There had indeed ensued conversation between the young French officer above named and Mary Connynge; yet prompt as might have been the former with gallant attentions to so fair a captive, it could not have been said that he was allowed the first advances. Mary Connynge, even after a month of starving foot travel and another month of anxiety at the Iroquois villages, had lost neither her rounded body, her brilliance of eye and color, nor her subtle magnetism of personality. It had taken stronger head than that of Raoul de Ligny to withstand even her slight request. How, then, as to Mary Connynge supplicating, entreating, craving of him protection?

"Ah, you brave Frenchmen," said she to De Ligny, advancing to him as he stood apart, twisting his mustaches and not unmindful of this very possibility of a conversation with the captive. "You brave Frenchmen, how can we thank you for our salvation? It was all so horrible!"

"It is our duty to save all, Madame," rejoined De Ligny; "our happiness unspeakable to save such as Madame. I swear by my sword, I had as soon expected to find an angel with the Iroquois as to meet there Madame! Quebec—all Quebec has told me who Madame was and is. And I am your slave."

"Oh, sir, could you but mean that!" and there was turned upon him the full power of a gaze which few men had ever been able to withstand. The blood of De Ligny tingled as he bowed and replied.

"If Madame could but demand one proof."

Mary Connynge stepped closer to him. "Hush!" she said. "Speak low! Do not let it seem that we are interested. Keep your own counsel. Can you do this?"

The eyes of the young officer gleamed. He was bold enough to respond. This his temptress noted.

He nodded.

"You see that man—the tall one, John Law? Listen! It is from him I ask you to save me. Oh, sir, there is my captivity!"

"What! Your husband?"

"He is not my husband."

"*Mais*—a thousand pardons. The child—your pardon."

"Pish! 'Tis the child of an Indian woman."

"Oh!" The blood again came to the young gallant's forehead.

"Listen, I tell you! I have been scarce better than a prisoner in this man's hands. He has abused me, threatened me, would have beaten me—"

"Madame—Mademoiselle!"

"'Tis true. We have been far in the West, and I could not escape. Good Providence has now brought my rescue—and you, Monsieur! Oh! tell me that it has brought me safety, and also a friend—that it has brought me you!"

With every pulse a-tingle, every vein afire, what could the young gallant do? What but yield, but promise, but swear, but rage?

"Hush!" said Mary Connynge, her own eyes gleaming. "Wait! The time will come. So soon as we reach the settlements, I leave him, and forever! Then—" Their hands met swiftly. "He has abandoned me," murmured Mary Connynge. "He has not spoken to me for weeks, other than words of 'Yes,' or 'No,' 'Do this,' or 'Do that!' Wait! Wait! How soon shall we be at Montreal?"

"Less than a month. 'Twill seem an age, I swear!"

"Madam," interrupted Law, "pardon, but Monsieur Joncaire bids us be ready. Come, help me arrange the packs for our journey. Perhaps Lieutenant de Ligny—for so I think they name you, sir—will pardon us, and will consent to resume his conversation later."

"Assuredly," said De Ligny. "I shall wait, Monsieur."

"So, Madam," said Law to Mary Connynge, as they at last found themselves alone in the lodge, arranging their few belongings for transport, "we are at last to regain the settlements, and for a time, at least, must forego our home in the farther West. In time—"

"Oh, in time! What mean you?"

"Why, we may return."

"Never! I have had my fill of savaging. That we are left alive is mighty merciful. To go thither again—never!"

"And if I go?"

"As you like."

"Meaning, Madam—?"

"What you like."

Law seated himself on the corded pack, bringing the tips of his fingers together.

"Then my late sweetheart has somewhat changed her fancy?"

"I have no fancy left. What I was once to you I shall not recall more than I can avoid in my own mind. As to what you heard from that lying man, Sir Arthur—"

"Listen! Stop! Neither must you insult the dead nor the absent. I have never told you what I learned from Sir Arthur, though it was enough to set me well distraught."

"I doubt not that he told you 'twas I who befooled Lady Catharine; that 'twas I who took the letter which you sent—"

"Stay! No. He told me not so much as that. But he and you together have told me enough to show me that I was the basest wretch on earth, the most gullible, the most unspeakably false and cruel. How could I have doubted the faith of Lady Catharine—how, but for you? Oh, Mary Connynge, Mary Connynge! Would God a man were so fashioned he might better withstand the argument of soft flesh and shining eyes! I admit, I believed the disloyal one, and doubted her who was loyalty itself."

"And you would go back into the wilderness with one who was as false as you say."

"Never!" replied John Law, swiftly. "'Tis as you yourself say. 'Tis all over. Hell itself hath followed me. Now let it all go, one with the other, little with big. I did not forget, nor should I though I tried again. Back to Europe, back to the gaming tables, to the wheels and cards I go again, and plunge into it madder than ever did man before. Let us see if chance can bring John Law anything worse than what he has already known. But, Madam, doubt not. So long as you claim my protection, here or anywhere on earth—in the West, in France, in England—it is yours; for I pay for my folly like a man, be assured of that. The child is ours, and it must be considered. But once let me find you in unfaithfulness—once let me know that you resign me—then John Law is free! I shall sometime see Catharine Knollys again. I shall give her my heart's anguish, and I shall have her heart's scorn in return. And then, Mary Connynge, the cards, dice, perhaps drink—perhaps gold, and the end. Madam, remember! And now come!"

CHAPTER XV

THE GREAT PEACE

Of the long and bitter journey from the Iroquois towns to Lake St. George, down the Richelieu and thence through the deep snows of the Canadian winter, it boots little to make mention; neither to tell of that devotion of Raoul de Ligny to the newly-rescued lady, already reputed in camp rumor to be of noble English family.

"That *sous-lieutenant*; he is *tete montee* regarding madame," said Pierre Noir one evening to Jean Breboeuf. "As to that—well, you know Monsieur L'as. Pouf! So much for yon monkey, *par comparaison*."

"He is a great *capitaine*, Monsieur L'as," said Jean Breboeuf. "Never a better went beyond the Straits."

"But very sad of late."

"Oh, *oui*, since the death of his friend, Monsieur *le Capitaine* Pembroke—may Mary aid his spirit!"

"Monsieur L'as goes not on the trail again," said Pierre Noir. "At least not while this look is in his eye."

"The more the loss, Pierre Noir; but some day the woods will call to him again. I know not how long it may be, yet some day Mother Messasebe will raise her finger and beckon to Monsieur L'as, and say: 'Come, my son!' 'Tis thus, as you know, Pierre Noir."

Yet at length the straggling settlements at Montreal were reached, and here, after the fashion of the frontier, some sort of *menage* was inaugurated for Law and his party. Here they lived through the rest of the winter and through the long, slow spring.

And then set on again the heats of summer, and there came apace the time agreed upon, in the month of August, for the widely heralded assembling of the tribes for the Great Peace; one of the most picturesque, as it was one of the most remarkable and significant meetings of widely diverse human beings, that ever took place within the ken of history.

They came, these savages, now first owning the strength of the invading white men, from all the far and unknown corners of the Western wilderness. They came afoot, and with little trains of dogs, in single canoes, in little groups and growing flotillas and vast fleets of canoes, pushing on and on, down stream, following the tide of the furs down this pathway of more than a thousand miles. The Iroquois, for once mindful of a promise, came in a compact fleet, a hundred canoes strong, and they stalked about the island for days, naked, stark, gigantic, contemptuous of white and red men, of friend and foe alike. The scattered Algonquins, whose villages had been razed by these same savage warriors, came down by scores out of the Northern woods, along little, unknown streams, and over paths with which none but themselves were acquainted. From the North, group joined group, and village added itself to village, until a vast body of people had assembled, whose numbers would have been hard to estimate, and who proved difficult enough to accommodate. Yet from the farther West, adding their numbers to those already gathered, came the fleets of the driven Hurons, and the Ojibways, and the Miamis, and the Outagamies, and the Ottawas, the Menominies and the Mascoutins—even the Illini, late objects of the wrath of the Five Nations. The whole Western wilderness poured forth its savage population, till all the shores of the St. Lawrence seemed one vast aboriginal encampment. These massed at the rendezvous about the puny settlement of Montreal in such numbers that, in comparison, the white population seemed insignificant. Then, had there been a Pontiac or a Tecumseh, had there been one leader of the tribes able to teach the strength of unity, the white settlements of upper America had indeed been utterly destroyed. Naught but ancient tribal jealousies held the savages apart.

With these tribesmen were many prisoners, captives taken in raids all along the thin and straggling frontier; farmers and artisans, peasants and soldiers, women raped from the farms of the Richelieu *censitaires*, and wood-rangers now grown savage as their captors and loth to leave the wild life into which they had so naturally grown. It was the first reflex of the wave, and even now the bits of flotsam and jetsam of wild life were fain to cling to the Western shore whither they had been carried by the advancing flood. This was the meeting of the ebb with the sea that sent it forward, the meeting of civilized and savage; and strange enough was the nature of those confluent tides. Whether the red men were yielding to civilization, or the whites all turning savage—this question might well have arisen to an observer of this tremendous spectacle. The wigwams of the different tribes and clans and families were grouped apart, scattered along all the narrow shore back of the great hill, and over the Convent gardens; and among these stalked the native French, clad in coarse cloth of blue, with gaudy belt and buckskins, and cap of fur and moccasins of hide, mingling fraternally with their tufted and bepainted visitors, as well as with those rangers, both envied and hated, the savage *coureurs de bois* of the far Northern fur trade; men bearded, silent, stern, clad in breech-clout and leggings like any savage, as silent, as stoical, as hardy on the trail as on the narrow thwart of the canoe.

Savage feastings, riotings and drunkenness, and long debaucheries came with the Great Peace, when once the word had gone out that the fur trade was to be resumed. Henceforth there was to be peace. The French were no longer to raid the little cabins along the Kennebec and the Penobscot. The river Richelieu was to be no longer a red war trail. The English were no longer to offer arms and blankets for the beaver, belonging by right of prior discovery to those who offered French brandy and French beads. The Iroquois were no longer to pursue a timid foe across the great prairies of the valley of the Messasebe. The Ojibways were not to ambush the scattered parties of the Iroquois. The unambitious colonists of New England and New York were to be left to till their stony farms in quiet. Meantime, the fur trade, wasteful, licentious, unprofitable, was to extend onward and outward in all the marches of the West. From one end of the Great River of the West to the other the insignia of France and of France's king were to be erected, and France's posts were to hold all the ancient trails. Even at the mouth of the Great River, forestalling these sullen English and these sluggish English colonists, far to the south in the somber forests and miasmatic marshes, there was to be established one more ruling point for the arms of Louis the Grand. It was a great game this, for which the continent of America was in preparation. It was a mighty thing, this gathering of the Great Peace, this time when colonists and their king were seeing the first breaking of the wave on the shore of an empire alluring, wonderful, unparalleled.

Into this wild rabble of savages and citizens, of priest and soldier and *coureur*, Law's friends, Pierre Noir and Jean Breboeuf, swiftly disappeared, naturally, fitly and unavoidably. "The West is calling to us, Monsieur," said Pierre Noir one morning, as he stood looking out across the river. "I hear once more the spirits of the Messasebe. Monsieur, will you come?"

Law shook his head. Yet two days later, as he stood at that very point, there came to him the silent feet of two *coureurs* instead of one. Once more he heard in his ear the question: "Monsieur L'as, will you come?"

At this voice he started. In an instant his arms were about the neck of Du Mesne, and tears were falling from the eyes of both in the welcome of that brotherhood which is admitted only by those who have known together arms and danger and hardship, the touch of the hard ground and the sight of the wide blue sky.

"Du Mesne, my friend!"

"Monsieur L'as!"

"It is as though you came from the depths of the sea, Du Mesne!" said Law.

"And as though you yourself arose from the grave, Monsieur!"

"How did you know—?"

"Why, easily. You do not yet understand the ways of the wilderness, where news travels as fast as in the cities. You were hardly below the foot of Michiganon before runners from the Illini had spread the news along the Chicaqua, where I was then in camp. For the rest, the runners brought also news of the Big Peace. I reasoned that the Iroquois would not dare to destroy their captives, that in time the agents of the Government would receive the captives of the Iroquois—that these captives would naturally come to the settlements on the St. Lawrence, since it was the French against whom the Iroquois had been at war; that having come to Montreal, you would naturally remain here for a time. The rest was easy. I fared on to the Straits this spring, and then on down the Lakes. I have sold our furs, and am now ready to account to you with a sum quite as much as we should have expected.

"Now, Monsieur," and Du Mesne stretched out his arm again, pointing to the down-coming flood of the St. Lawrence, "Monsieur, will you come? I see not the St. Lawrence, but the Messasebe. I can hear the voices calling!"

Law dashed his hand across his eyes and turned his head away. "Not yet, Du Mesne," said he. "I do not know. Not yet. I must first go across the waters. Perhaps sometime—I can not tell. But this, my comrades, my brothers, I do know; that never, until the last sod lies on my grave, will I forget the Messasebe, or forget you. Go back, if you will, my brothers; but at night, when you sit by your fireside, think of me, as I shall think of you, there in the great valley. My friends, it is the heart of the world!"

"But, Monsieur—"

"There, Du Mesne—I would not talk to-day. At another time. Brothers, adieu!"

"Adieu, my brother," said the *coureur*, his own emotion showing in his eyes; and their hands met again.

"Monsieur is cast down," said Du Mesne to Pierre Noir later, as they reached the beach. "Now, what think you?

"Usually, as you know, Pierre, it is a question of some woman. It reminds me, Wabana was remiss enough when I left her among the Illini with you. Now, God bless my heart, I find her—how think you? With her crucifix lost, cooking for a dirty Ojibway!"

"Mary Mother!" said Pierre Noir, "if it be a matter of a woman—well, God help us all! At least 'tis something that will take Monsieur L'as over seas again."

"'Tis mostly a woman," mused Du Mesne; "but this passeth my wit."

"True, they pass the wit of all. Now, did I ever tell thee about the mission girl at Michilimackinac—but stay! That for another time. They tell me that our comrade, Greysolon du L'hut, is expected in to-morrow with a party from the far end of Superior. Come, let us have the news."

"*Tous les printemps,
Tant des nouvelles*,"

hummed Du Mesne, as he flung his arm above the shoulder of the other; and the two so disappeared adown the beach.

Dully, apathetically, Law lived on his life here at Montreal for yet a time, at the edge of that wilderness which had proved all else but Eden. Near to him, though in these guarded times guest by necessity of the good sisters of the Convent, dwelt Mary Connynge. And as for these two, it might be said that each but bided the time. To her Law might as well have been one of the corded Sulpician priests; and she to him, for all he liked, one of the nuns of the Convent garden. What did it all mean; where was it all to end? he asked himself a thousand times; and a thousand times his mind failed him of any answer. He waited, watching the great encampment disappear, first slowly, then swiftly and suddenly, so that in a night the last of the lodges had gone and the last canoe had left the shore. There remained only the hurrying flood of the St. Lawrence, coming from the West.

The autumn came on. Early in November the ships would leave for France. Yet before the beginning of November there came swiftly and sharply the settlement of the questions which racked Law's mind. One morning Mary Connynge was missing from the Convent, nor could any of the sisters, nor the mother superior, explain how or when she had departed!

Yet, had there been close observers, there might have been seen a boat dropping down the river on the early morning of that day. And at Quebec there was later reported in the books of the intendant the shipping, upon the good bark Dauphine, of Lieutenant Raoul de Ligny, sometime officer of the regiment Carignan, formerly stationed in New France; with him a lady recently from Montreal, known very well to Lieutenant de Ligny and his family; and to be in his care *en voyage* to France; the name of said lady illegible upon the records, the spelling apparently not having suited the clerk who wrote it, and then forgot it in the press of other things.

Certain of the governor's household, as well as two or three *habitants* from the lower town, witnessed the arrival of this lady, who came down from Montreal. They saw her take boat for the bark Dauphine, one of the last ships to go down the river that fall. Yes, it was easily to be established. Dark, with singular, brown eyes, *petite*, yet not over small, of good figure—assuredly so much could be said; for obviously the king, kindly as he might feel toward the colony of New France, could not send out, among the young women supplied to the colonists as wives, very many such demoiselles as this; otherwise assuredly all France would have followed the king's ships to the St. Lawrence.

John Law, a grave and saddened man, yet one now no longer lacking in decision, stood alone one day at the parapet of the great rock of Quebec, gazing down the broad expanse of the stream below. He was alone except for a little child, a child too young to know her mother, had death or disaster at that time removed the mother. Law took the little one up in his arms and gazed hard upon the upturned face.

"Catharine!" he said to himself. "Catharine! Catharine!"

"Pardon, Monsieur," said a voice at his elbow. "Surely I have seen you before this?"

Law turned. Joncaire, the ambassador of peace, stood by, smiling and extending his hand.

"Naturally, I could never forget you," said Law.

"Monsieur looks at the shipping," said Joncaire, smiling. "Surely he would not be leaving New France, after so luckily escaping the worst of her dangers?"

"Life might be the same for me over there as here," replied Law. "As for my luck, I must declare myself the most unfortunate man on earth."

"Your wife, perhaps, is ill?"

"Pardon, I have none."

"Pardon, in turn, Monsieur—but, you see—the child?"

"It is the child of a savage woman," said Law.

Joncaire pulled aside the infant's hood. He gave no sign, and a nice indifference sat in his query: "*Une belle sauvage?*"

"*Belle sauvage!*"

BOOK III

FRANCE

CHAPTER I

THE GRAND MONARQUE

On a great bed of state, satin draped, flanked with ancient tapestries, piled sickeningly soft with heaps of pillows, there lay a thin, withered little man—old, old and very feeble. His face was shrunken and drawn with pain; his eyes, once bright, were dulled; his brow, formerly imperious, had lost its arrogance. Under the coverings which, in the unrest of illness, he now pulled high about his face, now tossed restlessly aside, his figure lay, an elongated, shapeless blot, scarce showing beneath the silks. One limb, twitched and drawn up convulsively, told of a definite seat of pain. The hands, thin and wasted, lay out upon the coverlets; and the thumbs were creeping, creeping ever more insistently, under the cover of the fingers, telling that the battle for life was lost, that the surrender had been made.

It was a death-bed, this great bed of state; a death-bed situated in the heart of the greatest temple of desire ever built in all the world. He who had been master there, who had set in order those miles of stately columns, those seas of glittering gilt and crystal, he who had been magician, builder, creator, perverter, debaser—he, Louis of France, the Grand Monarque, now lay suffering like any ordinary human being, like any common man.

Last night the four and twenty violins, under the king's command, had shrilled their chorus, as had been their wont for years while the master dined. This morning the cordon of drums and hautboys had pealed their high and martial music. Useless. The one or the other music fell upon ears too dull to hear. The formal tribute to the central soul for a time continued of its own inertia; for a time royalty had still its worship; yet the custom was but a lagging one. The musicians grimaced and made what discord they liked, openly, insolently, scorning this weak and withered figure on the silken bed. The cordon of the white and blue guards of the Household still swept about the vast pleasure grounds of this fairy temple; yet the officers left their posts and conversed one with the other. Musicians and guards, spectators and populace, all were waiting, waiting until the end should come. Farther out and beyond, where the peaked roofs of Paris rose, back of that line which this imperious mind had decreed should not be passed by the dwellings of Paris, which must not come too near this temple of luxury, nor disturb the king while he enjoyed himself—back of the perfunctorily loyal guards of the Household, there reached the ragged, shapeless masses of the people of Paris and of France, waiting, smiling, as some animal licking its chops in expectation of some satisfying thing. They were waiting for news of the death of this shrunken man, this creature once so full of arrogant lust, then so full of somber repentance, now so full of the very taste of death.

On the great tapestry that hung above the head of the curtained bed shone the double sun of Louis the Grand, which had meant death and devastation to so much of Europe. It blazed, mimicking the glory that was gone; but toward it there was raised no sword nor scepter more in vow or exaltation. The race was run, the sun was sinking to its setting. Nothing but a man—a weary, worn-out, dying man—was Louis, the Grand Monarque, king for seventy-two years of France, almost king of Europe. This death-bed lay in the center of a land oppressed, ground down, impoverished. The hearts and lives of thousands were in these colonnades. The people had paid for their king. They had fed him fat and kept him full of loves. In return, he had trampled the people into the very dust. He had robbed even their ancient nobles of honors and consideration. Blackened, ruined, a vast graveyard, a monumental starving-ground, France lay about his death-bed, and its people were but waiting with grim impatience for their king to die. What France might do in the future was unknown; yet it was unthinkable that aught could be worse than this glorious reign of Louis, the Grand Monarque, this crumbling clod, this resolving excrescence, this phosphorescent, disintegrating fungus of a diseased life and time.

Seventy-two years a king; thirty years a libertine; twenty years a repentant. Son, grandson, great-grandson, all gone, as though to leave not one of that once haughty breed. For France no hope at all; and for the house of Bourbon, all the hope there might be in the life of a little boy, sullen, tiny, timid. Far over in Paris, busy about his games and his loves, a jesting, long-curled gallant, the Duke of Orleans, nephew of this king, was holding a court of his own. And from this court which might be, back to the court which was, but which might not be long, swung back and forth the fawning creatures of the former court. This was the central picture of France, and Paris, and of the New World on this day of the year 1715.

In the room about the bed of state, uncertain groups of watchers whispered noisily. The five physicians, who had tried first one remedy and then another; the rustic physician whose nostrum had kept life within the king for some unexpected days; the ladies who had waited upon the relatives of the king; some of the relatives themselves;

Villeroy, guardian of the young king soon to be; the bastard, and the wife of that bastard, who hoped for the king's shoes; the mistress of his earlier years, for many years his wife—Maintenon, that peerless hypocrite of all the years—all these passed, and hesitated, and looked, waiting, as did the hungry crowds in Paris toward the Seine, until the double sun should set, and the crawling thumbs at last should find their shelter. The Grand Monarque was losing the only time in all his life when he might have learned human wisdom.

"Madame!" whispered the dry lips, faintly.

She who was addressed as madame, this woman Maintenon, pious murderer, unrivaled hypocrite, unspeakably self-contained dissembler, the woman who lost for France an empire greater than all France, stepped now to the bed-side of the dying monarch, inclining her head to hear what he might have to say. Was Maintenon, the outcast, the widow, the wife of the king, at last to be made ruler of the Church in France? Was she to govern in the household of the king even after the king had departed? The woman bent over the dying man, the covetousness of her soul showing in her eyes, struggle as she might to retain her habitual and unparalleled self-control.

The dying man muttered uneasily. His mind was clouded, his eyes saw other things. He turned back to earlier days, when life was bright, when he, Louis, as a young man, had lived and loved as any other.

"Louise," he murmured. "Louise! Forgive! Meet me—Louise—dear one. Meet me yonder—"

An icy pallor swept across the face of the arch hypocrite who bent over him. Into her soul there sank like a knife this consciousness of the undying power of a real love. La

Valliere, the love of the youth of Louis, La Valliere, the beautiful, and sweet, and womanly, dead and gone these long years since, but still loved and now triumphant—she it was whom Louis now remembered.

Maintenon turned from the bed-side. She stood, an aged and unhappy woman, old, gray and haggard, not success but failure written upon every lineament. For one instant she stood, her hands clenched, slow anger breaking through the mask which, for a quarter of a century, she had so successfully worn.

"Bah!" she cried. "Bah! 'Tis a pretty rendezvous this king would set for me!" And then she swept from the room, raged for a time apart, and so took leave of life and of ambition.

At length even the last energies of the once stubborn will gave way. The last gasp of the failing breath was drawn. The herald at the window announced to the waiting multitude that Louis the Fourteenth was no more.

"Long live the king!" exclaimed the multitude. They hailed the new monarch with mockery; but laughter, and sincere joy and feasting were the testimonials of their emotions at the death of the king but now departed.

On the next day a cheap, tawdry and unimposing procession wended its way through the back streets of Paris, its leader seeking to escape even the edges of the mob, lest the people should fall upon the somber little pageant and rend it into fragments. This was the funeral cortege of Louis, the Grand Monarque, Louis the lustful, Louis the bigot, Louis the ignorant, Louis the unhappy. They hurried him to his resting-place, these last servitors, and then hastened back to the palaces to join their hearts and voices to the rising wave of joy which swept across all France at the death of this beloved ruler.

Now it happened that, as the funeral procession of the king was hurrying through the side streets near the confines of the old city of Paris, there encountered it, entering from the great highway which led from the east up to the city gates, the carriage of a gentleman who might, apparently with justice, have laid some claim to consequence. It had its guards and coachmen, and was attended by two riders in livery, who kept it company along the narrow streets. This equipage met the head of the hurrying funeral cortege, and found occasion for a moment to pause. Thus there passed, the one going to his grave, the other to his goal, the two men with whom the France of that day was most intimately concerned.

There came from the window of the coach the voice of one inquiring the reason of the halt, and there might have been seen through the upper portion of the vehicle's door the face of the owner of the carriage. He seemed a man of imposing presence, with face open and handsome, and an eye bright, bold and full of intelligence. His garb was rich and elegant, his air well contained and dignified.

"Guillaume," he called out, "what is it that detains us?"

"It is nothing, Monsieur L'as," was the reply, "They tell me it is but the funeral of the king."

"*Eh bien!*" replied Law, turning to one who sat beside him in the coach. "Nothing! 'Tis nothing but the funeral of the king!"

CHAPTER II

EVER SAID SHE NAY

The coach proceeded steadily on its way, passing in toward that quarter where the high-piled, peaked roofs and jagged spires betokened ancient Paris. On every hand arose confused sounds from the streets, now filled with a populace merry as though some pleasant carnival were just beginning. Shopkeeper called across to his neighbor, tradesman gossiped with gallant. Even the stolid faces of the plodding peasants, fresh past the gate-tax and bound for the markets to seek what little there remained after giving to the king, bore an unwonted look, as though hope might yet succeed to their surprise.

"Ohe! Marie," called one stout dame to another, who stood smiling in her doorway near by. "See the fine coach coming. That is the sort you and I shall have one of these days, now that the king is dead. God bless the new king, and may he die young! A plague to all kings, Marie. And now come and sit with my man and me, for we've a bottle left, and while it lasts we drink freedom from all kings!"

"You speak words of gold, Suzanne," was the reply. "Surely I will drink with you, and wish a pleasant and speedy death to kings."

"But now, Marie," said the other, argumentatively, "as to my good duke regent, that is otherwise. It goes about that he will change all things. One is to amuse one's self now and then, and not to work forever for the taxes and the conscription. Long live the regent, then, say I!"

"Yes, and let us hope that regents never turn to kings. There are to be new days here in France. We people, aye, my faith! We people, so they say, are to be considered. True, we shall have carriages one day, Marie, like that of my Lord who passes."

John Law and his companions heard broken bits of such speech as this as they passed on.

"Ah, they talk," replied he at last, turning toward his companions, "and this is talk which means something. Within the year we shall see Paris upside down. These people are ready for any new thing. But"—and his face lost some of its gravity—"the streets are none too safe to-day, my Lady. Therefore you must forgive me if I do not set you down, but keep you prisoner until you reach your own gates. 'Tis not your fault that your carriage broke down on the road from Marly; and as for my brother Will and myself, we can not forego a good fortune which enables us at last to destroy a certain long-standing debt of a carriage ride given us, once upon a time, by the Lady Catharine Knollys."

"At least, then, we shall be well acquit on both sides," replied the soft voice of the woman. "I may, perhaps, be an unwilling prisoner for so short a time."

"Madam, I would God it might be forever!"

It was the same John Law of old who made this impetuous reply, and indeed he seemed scarce changed by the passing of these few years of time. It was the audacious youth of the English highway who now looked at her with grave face, yet with eyes that shone.

Some years had indeed passed since Law, turning his back upon the appeal of the wide New World, had again set foot upon the shores of England, from which his departure had been so singular. Driven by the goads of remorse, it had been his first thought to seek out the Lady Catharine Knollys; and so intent had he been on this quest, that he learned almost without emotion of the king's pardon which had been entered, discharging him of further penalty of the law of England. Meeting Lady Catharine, he learned, as have others since and before him, that a human soul may have laws inflexible; that the iron bars of a woman's resolve may bar one out, even as prison doors may bar him in. He found the Lady Catharine unshakeable in her resolve not to see him or speak with him. Whereat he raged, expostulated by post, waited, waylaid, and so at length gained an interview, which taught him many things.

He found the Lady Catharine Knollys changed from a light-hearted girl to a maiden tall, grave, reserved and sad, offering no reproaches, listening to no protestations. Told of Sir Arthur Pembroke's horrible death, she wept with tears which his survivor envied. Told at length of the little child, she sat wide-eyed and silent. Approached with words of remorse, with expostulations, promises, she shrank back in absolute horror, trembling, so that in very pity the wretched young man left her and found his way out into a world suddenly grown old and gray.

After this dismissal, Law for many months saw nothing, heard nothing of this woman whom he had wronged, even as he received no sign from the woman who had forsaken him over seas. He remained away as long as might be, until his violent nature, geyser-like, gathered inner storm and fury by repression, and broke away in wild eruption.

Once more he sought the presence of the woman whose face haunted his soul, and once more he met ice and adamant stronger than his own fires. Beaten, he fled from London and from England, seeking still, after the ancient and ineffective fashion of man, to forget, though he himself had confessed the lesson that man can not escape himself, but takes his own hell with him wherever he goes.

Rejected, as he was now, by the new ministry of England, none the less every capital of Europe came presently to know John Law, gambler, student and financier. Before every ruler on the continent he laid his system of financial revolution, and one by one they smiled, or shrugged, or scoffed at him. Baffled once more in his dearest purpose, he took again to play, play in such colossal and audacious form as never yet had been seen even in the gayest courts of a time when gaming was a vice to be called national. No hazard was too great for him, no success and no reverse sufficiently keen to cause him any apparent concern. There was no risk sharp enough to deaden the gnawing in his soul, no excitement strong enough to wipe away from his mind the black panorama of his past.

He won princely fortunes and cast them away again. With the figure and the air of a prince, he gained greater reputation than any prince of Europe. Upon him were spent the blandishments of the fairest women of his time. Yet not this, not all this, served to steady his energies, now unbalanced, speeding without guidance. The gold, heaped high on the tables, was not enough to stupefy his mind, not enough though he doubled and trebled it, though he cast great golden markers to spare him trouble in the counting of his winnings. Still student, still mathematician, he sought at Amsterdam, at

Paris, at Vienna, all new theories which offered in the science of banking and finance, even as at the same time he delved still further into the mysteries of recurrences and chance.

In this latter such was his success that losers made complaint, unjust but effectual, to the king, so that Law was obliged to leave Paris for a time. He had dwelt long enough in Paris, this double-natured man, this student and creator, this gambler and gallant, to win the friendship of Philippe of Orleans, later to be regent of France; and gay enough had been the life they two had led—so gay, so intimate, that Philippe gave promise that, should he ever hold in his own hands the Government of France, he would end Law's banishment and give to him the opportunity he sought, of proving those theories of finance which constituted the absorbing ambition of his life.

Meantime Law, ever restless, had passed from one capital of Europe to another, dragging with him from hotel to hotel the young child whose life had been cast in such feverish and unnatural surroundings. He continued to challenge every hazard, fearless, reckless, contemptuous, and withal wretched, as one must be who, after years of effort, found that he could not banish from his mind the pictures of a dark-floored prison, and of a knife-stab in the dark, and of raging, awful waters, and of a girl beautiful, though with sealed lips and heart of ice. From time to time, as was well known, Law returned to England. He heard of the Lady Catharine Knollys, as might easily be done in London; heard of her as a young woman kind of heart, soft of speech, with tenderness for every little suffering thing; a beautiful young woman, whose admirers listed scores; but who never yet, even according to the eagerest gossip of the capital, had found a suitor to whom she gave word or thought of love.

So now at last the arrogant selfishness of his heart began to yield. His heart was broken before it might soften, but soften at last it did. And so he built up in his soul the image of a grave, sweet saint, kindly and gentle-voiced, unapproachable, not to be profaned. To this image—ah, which of us has not had such a shrine!—he brought in secret the homage of his life, his confessions, his despairs, his hopes, his resolutions; guiding thereby all his life, as well as poor mortal man may do, failing ever of his own standards, as all men do, yet harking ever back to that secret sibyl, reckoning all things from her, for her, by her.

There came at length one chastened hour when they met in calmness, when there was no longer talk of love between them, when he stood before her as though indeed at the altar of some marble deity. Always her answer had been that the past had been a mistake; that she had professed to love a man, not knowing what that man was; that she had suffered, but that it was better so, since it had brought understanding. Now, in this calmer time, she begged of him knowledge of this child, regretting the wandering life which had been its portion, saying that for Mary Connynge she no longer felt horror and hatred. Thus it was that in a hasty moment Law had impulsively begged her to assume some sort of tutelage over that unfortunate child. It was to his own amazement that he heard Lady Catharine Knollys consent, stipulating that the child should be placed in a Paris convent for two years, and that for two years John Law should see neither his daughter nor herself. Obedient as a child himself he had promised.

"Now, go away," she then had said to him. "Go your own way. Drink, dice, game, and waste the talents God hath given you. You have made ruin enough for all of us. I would only that it may not run so far as to another generation."

So both had kept their promises; and now the two years were

done, years spent by Law more manfully than any of his life. His fortune he had gathered together, amounting to more than a million livres. He had sent once more for his brother Will, and thus the two had lived for some time in company in lower Europe, the elder brother still curious as ever in his abstruse theories of banking and finance—theories then new, now outlived in great part, though fit to be called a portion of the great foundation of the commercial system of the world. It was a wiser and soberer and riper John Law, this man who had but recently received a summons from Philippe of Orleans to be present in Paris, for that the king was dying, and that all France, France the bankrupt and distracted, was on the brink of sudden and perhaps fateful change.

With a quick revival of all his Highland superstition, Law hailed now as happy harbinger the fact that, upon his entry into Paris, the city once more of his hopes, he had met in such fashion this lady of his dreams, even at such time as the seal of silence was lifted from his lips. It was no wonder that his eye gleamed, that his voice took on the old vibrant tone, that every gesture, in thought or in spite of thought, assumed the tender deference of the lover.

It was a fair woman, this chance guest of the highway whom he now accosted—bronze-haired, blue-eyed, soft of voice, queenly of mien, gentle, calm and truly lovable. Oh, what waste that those arms should hold nothing, that lips such as those should know no kisses, that eyes like those should never swim in love! What robbery! What crime! And this man, thief of this woman's life, felt his heart pinch again in the old, sharp anguish of remorse, bitterest because unavailing.

For the Lady Catharine herself there had been also many changes. The death of her brother, the Earl of Banbury, had wrought many shifts in the circumstances of a house apparently pursued by unkind fate. Left practically alone and caring little for the life of London, even after there had worn away the chill of suspicion which followed upon the popular knowledge of her connection with the escape of Law from London, Lady Catharine Knollys turned to a life and world suddenly grown vague and empty. Travel upon the continent with friends, occasional visits to the old family house in England, long sojourns in this or the other city—such had been her life, quiet, sweet, reproachless and unreproaching. For the present she had taken an hotel in the older part of Paris, in connection with her friend, the Countess of Warrington, sometime connected with the embassy of that Lord Stair who was later to act as spy for England in Paris, now so soon to know tumultuous scenes. With these scenes, as time was soon to prove, there was to be most intimately connected this very man who, now bending forward attentively, now listening respectfully, and ever gazing directly and ardently, heard naught of plots or plans, cared naught for the Paris which lay about, saw naught but the beautiful face before him, felt naught but some deep, compelling thrill in every heart-string which now reaching sweet accord in spite of fate, in spite of the past, in spite of all, went singing on in a deep melody of joy. This was she, the idol, the deity. Let the world wag. It was a moment yet ere paradise must end!

"Madam, I would God it might be forever!" said Law again. The old stubborn nature was showing once more, but under it something deeper, softer, tenderer.

A sudden panic fear called at the heart of her to whom he spoke. Two rosy spots shone in her cheeks, and as she gazed, her eyes showed the veiled softening of woman's gentleness. There fell a silence.

"Madam, I could feel that this were Sadler's Wells over again," said Law a moment later.

But now the carriage had arrived at the destination named by Lady Catharine. Law sprang out, hat in hand, and assisted Lady Catharine to the curb. A passing flower girl, gaily offering her wares, paused as the carriage drew up. Law turned quickly and caught from her as many roses as his hand could grasp, handing her in return half as much coin as her smaller palm could hold. He turned to the Lady Catharine, and bowed with that grace which was the talk of a world of gallants. In his hand he extended a flower.

"Madam, as before!" he said.

There was a sob in his voice. Their eyes met fairly, unmasked as they had not been for years. Tears came into the man's eyes, the first that had ever sat there; tears for the past, tears for that sweetness which once might have been.

"'Tis for the king! They weep for the king!" sang out the hard voice of the flower girl, ironically, as she skipped away. "Ohe, for the king, for the king!"

"Nay, for the queen!" said John Law, as he gazed into the eyes of Catharine Knollys.

CHAPTER III

SEARCH THOU MY HEART

"Only believe me, Lady Catharine, and I shall do everything I promised years ago—I shall lay all France at your feet. But if you deny me thus always, I shall make all France a mockery."

"Monsieur is fresh from the South of France," replied the Lady Catharine Knollys. "Has Gascon wine perhaps put Gascon speech into his mouth?"

"Oh, laugh if you like," exclaimed Law, rising and pacing across the great room in which these two had met. "Laugh and mock, but we shall see!"

"Granted that Mr. Law is well within his customary modesty," replied Lady Catharine, "and granted even that Mr. Law has all France in the hollow of his hand to-day, to do with as he likes, I must confess I see not why France should suffer because I myself have found it difficult to endorse Mr. Law's personal code of morals."

It was the third day after Law's entry into Paris, and the first time for more than two long years that he found himself alone with the Lady Catharine Knollys. His eagerness might have excused his impetuous and boastful speech.

As for the Lady Catharine, that one swift, electric moment at the street curb had well-nigh undone more than two years of resolve. She had heard herself, as it were in a dream, promising that this man might come. She had found herself later in her own apartments, panting, wide-eyed, afraid. Some great hand, unseen, uninvited, mysterious, had swept ruthlessly across each chord of womanly reserve and resolution which so long she had held well-ordered and absolutely under control. It was self-distrust, fear, which now compelled her to take refuge in this woman's fence of speech with him. "Surely," argued she with herself, "if love once dies, then it is dead forever, and can never be revived. Surely," she insisted to herself, "my love is dead. Then—ah, but then was it dead? Can my heart grow again?" asked the Lady Catharine of herself, tremblingly. This was that which gave her pause. It was this also which gave to her cheek its brighter color, to her eye a softer gleam; and to her speech this covering shield of badinage.

Yet all her defenses were in a way to be fairly beaten down by the intentness of the other. All things he put aside or overrode, and would speak but of himself and herself, of his plans, his opportunities, and of how these were concerned with himself and with her.

"There are those who judge not so harshly as yourself, Madam," resumed Law. "His Grace the regent is good enough to believe that my studies have gone deeper than the green cloth of the gaming table. Now, I tell you, my time has come—my day at last is here. I tell you that I shall prove to you everything which I said to you long ago, back there in old England. I shall prove to you that I have not been altogether an idler and a trifler. I shall bring to you, as I promised you long ago, all the wealth, all the distinction—"

"But such speech is needless, Mr. Law," came the reply. "I have all the wealth I need, nor do I crave distinction, save of my own selection."

"But you do not dream! This is a day unparalleled. There will be such changes here as never yet were known. Within a week you shall hear of my name in Paris. Within a month you shall hear of it beyond the gates of Paris. Within a year you shall hear nothing else in Europe!"

"As I hear nothing else here now, Monsieur?"

Like a horse restless under the snaffle, the man shook his head, but went on. "If you should be offered wealth more than any woman of Paris, if you had precedence over the proudest peers of France—would these things have no weight with you?"

"You know they would not."

Law cast himself restlessly upon a seat across the room from her. "I think I do," said he, dejectedly. "At times you drive me to my wit's end. What then, Madam, would avail?"

"Why, nothing, so far as the past is to be reviewed for you and me. Yet, I should say that, if there were two here speaking as you and I, and if they two had no such past as we—then I could fancy that woman saying to her friend, 'Have you indeed done all that lay within you to do?'"

"Is it not enough—?"

"There is nothing, sir, that is enough for a woman, but all!"

"I have given you all."

"All that you have left—after yourself."

"Sharp, sharp indeed are your words, my Lady. And they are most sharp because they come with justice."

"Oh," broke out the woman, "one may use sharp words who has been scorned for her own false friend! You would give me all, Mr. Law, but you must remember that it is only what remains after that—that—"

"But would you, could you, have cared had there been no 'that'? Had I done all that lay in me to do, could you then have given me your confidence, and could you have thought me worthy of it?"

"Oh, 'if!'"

"Yes, 'if!' 'If,' and 'as though,' and 'in that case'—these are all we have to console us in this life. But, sweet one—"

"Sir, such words I have forbidden," said Lady Catharine, the blood for one cause or another mounting again into her cheek.

"You torture me!" broke out Law.

"As much as you have me? Is it so much as that, Mr. Law?"

He rose and stood apart, his head falling in despair. "As I have done this thing, so may God punish me!" said he. "I was not fit, and am not. Yet I was bold enough to hope that there could be some atonement, some thing—if my suffering—"

"There are things, Mr. Law, for which no suffering atones. But why cause suffering longer for us both? You come again and again. Could you not leave me for a time untroubled?"

"How can I?" blazed the man, his forehead furrowed up into a frown, the moist beads on his brow proving his own intentness. "I can not! I can not! That is all I know. Ask me not why. I can not; that is all."

"Sir," said Lady Catharine, "this seems to me no less than terrible."

"It is indeed no less than terrible. Yet I must come and come again, bound some day to be heard, not for what I am, but for what I might be. 'Tis not justice I would have, dear heart, but mercy, a woman's mercy!"

"And you would bully me to agree with you, as I said, in regard to your own excellent code of morals, Mr. Law?"

"You evade, like any woman, but if you will, even have it so. At least there is to be this battle between us all our lives. I will be loved, Lady Catharine! I must be loved by you! Look in my heart. Search beneath this man that you and others see. Find me my own fellow, that other self better than I, who cries out always thus. Look! 'Tis not for me as I am. No man deserves aught for himself. But find in my heart, Lady Catharine, that other self, the man I might have been! Dear heart, I beseech you, look!"

Impulsively, he even tore apart the front of his coat, as though indeed to invite such scrutiny. He stood before her, trembling, choking. The passion of his speech caused the color again to rush to the Lady Catharine's face. For a moment her bosom rose and fell tumultuously, deep answering as of old unto deep, in the ancient, wondrous way.

"Is it the part of manhood to persecute a woman, Mr. Law?"

she asked, her own uncertitude now showing in her tone.

"I do not know," he answered.

Lady Catharine looked at him curiously.

"Do you love me, Mr. Law?" she asked, directly.

"I have no answer."

"Did you love that other woman?"

It took all his courage to reply. "I am not fit to answer," said he.

"And you would love me, too, for a time and in a way?"

"I will not answer. I will not trifle."

"And I am to think Mr. Law better than himself, better than other men; since you say no man dare ask actual justice?"

"Worse than other men, and yet a man. A man—my God! Lady Catharine—a man unworthy, yet a man seized fatally of that love which neither life nor death can alter!"

As one fascinated, Lady Catharine sat looking at him. "Then," said she, "any man may say to any woman—Mr. Law says to me—'I have cared for such, and so many other women to the extent, let us say, of so many pounds sterling. But I love you to the extent of twice as many pounds, shillings and pence?' Is that the dole we women may expect, Mr. Law?"

"Have back your own words!" he cried. "Nothing is enough but all! And as God witnesseth in this hour, I have loved you with all my heart-beats, with all my prayers. I call upon you now, in the name of that love I know you once bore me—"

Upon the face of the Lady Catharine there blazed the red mark of the shame of Knollys. Covering her face with her hands, she suddenly bent forward, and from her lips there broke a sob of pain.

In a flash Law was at her side, kneeling, seeking to draw away her fingers with hands that trembled as much as her own.

"Do not! Do not!" he cried. "I am not worth it! It shall be as you like. Let me go away forever. This I can not endure!"

"Ah, John Law, John Law!" murmured Catharine Knollys, "why did you break my heart!"

CHAPTER IV

THE REGENT'S PROMISE

"Tell me, then, Monsieur L'as, of this new America. I would fain have some information at first hand. There was rumor, I know not how exact, that you once traveled in those regions."

Thus spake his Grace Philippe, Duke of Orleans, regent of France, now, in effect, ruler of France. It was the audience which had been arranged for John Law, that opportunity for which he had waited all his life. Before him now, as he stood in the great council chamber, facing this man whose ambitions ended where his own began—at the convivial board and at the gaming table—he saw the path which led to the success that he had craved so long. He, Law of Lauriston, sometime adventurer and gambler, was now playing his last and greatest game.

"Your Grace," said he, "there be many who might better than I tell you of that America."

"There are many who should be able, and many who do," replied the regent. "By the body of the Lord! we get nothing but information regarding these provinces of New France, and each advice is worse than the one preceding it. The gist of it all is that my Lord Governor and my very good intendant can never agree, save upon one point or so. They want more money, and they want more soldiers—ah, yes, to be sure, they also want more women, though we sent them out a ship load of choice beauties not more than a six-month ago. But tell me, Monsieur L'as, is it indeed true that you have traveled in America?"

"For a short time."

"I have heard nothing regarding you from the intendant at Quebec."

"Your Grace was not at that time caring for intendants. 'Twas many years ago, and I was not well known at Quebec by my own name."

"*Eh bien*? Some adventure, then, perhaps? A woman at the bottom of it, I warrant."

"Your Grace is right."

"'Twas like you, for a fellow of good zest. May God bless all fair dames. And as to what you found in thus following—or was it in fleeing—your divinity?"

"I found many things. For one, that this America is the greatest country of the world. Neither England nor France is to be compared with it."

The regent fell back in his chair and laughed heartily.

"Monsieur, you are indeed, as I have ever found you, of most excellent wit. You please me enormously."

"But, your Grace, I am entirely serious."

"Oh, come, spoil not so good a jest by qualifying, I beseech you! England or France, indeed—ah, Monsieur L'as, Monsieur L'as!"

"Your own city of New Orleans, Sire, will lie at the gate of a realm greater than all France. Your Grace will hand to the young king, when he shall come of age, a realm excellently worth the ownership of any king."

"You say rich. In what way?" asked the regent. "We have not had so much of returns after all. Look at Crozat? Look at—"

"Oh fie, Crozat! Your Grace, he solved not the first problem of real commerce. He never dreamed the real richness of America."

Philippe sat thoughtful, his finger tips together. "Why have we not heard of these things?" said he.

"Because of men like Crozat, of men like your governors and intendants at Quebec. Because, your Grace, as you know very well, of the same reason which sent me once from Paris, and kept me so long from laying before you these very plans of which I now would speak."

"And that cause?"

"Maintenon."

"Oh, ah! Indeed—that is to say—"

"Louis would hear naught of me, of course. Maintenon took care that he should find I was but heretic."

"As for myself," said Philippe the regent, "heretic or not heretic makes but small figure. 'Twill take France a century to overcome her late surfeit of religion. For us, 'tis most a question of how to keep the king in the saddle and France underneath."

"Precisely, your Grace."

"Frankly, Monsieur L'as, I take it fittest now not so much to ponder over new worlds as over how to keep in touch with this Old World yet awhile. France has danced, though for years she danced to the tune of Louis clad in black. Now France must pay for the music. My faith, I like not the look of things. This joyful France to-day is a hideous thing. These people laugh! I had sooner see a lion grin. Now to govern those given us by Providence to govern," and the regent smiled grimly at the ancient fiction, "it is most meet that the governed should produce somewhat of funds in order that they may be governed."

"Yes, and the error has been in going too far," said Law. "These people have been taxed beyond the taxation point. Now they laugh."

"Yes; and by God, Monsieur L'as, when France laughs, beware!"

"Your Grace admits that France has no further resources."

"Assuredly."

"Then tax New France!" cried Law, his hand coming down hard upon the table, his eyes shining. "Mortgage where the security doubles every year, where the soil itself is security for wealth greater than all Europe ever owned."

"Oh, very well, Monsieur; though later I must ask you to explain."

"You admit that no more money can be forced from the people of France."

"Ask the farmers of the taxes. Ask Chamillard of the Treasury. My faith, look out of the window! Listen! Do I not tell you that France is laughing?"

"Very well. Let us also laugh. Let us all laugh together. There is money in France, more money in Europe. I assure you these people can be brought to give you cheerfully all they have."

"It sounds well, Monsieur L'as, but let me ask you how?"

"France is bankrupt—this is brutal, but none the less true. France must repudiate her obligations unless something be swiftly done. It is not noble to repudiate, your Grace. Yet, if we cancel and not repudiate, if we can obtain the gold of France, of Europe—"

"Body of God! but you speak large, my friend."

"Not so large. All subjects shrink as we come close to them by study. 'Tis easy to see that France has not money enough for her own business. If we had more money in France, we should have more production, and if we had more production, we might have taxes. Thereby we might have somewhat in our treasury wherewith to keep the king in the saddle, and not under foot."

"Then, if I follow you," said Philippe, leaning slightly forward and again placing his finger tips judicially together, "you would coin greater amounts of money. Then, I would ask you, where would you get your gold for the coinage?"

"It is not gold I would coin," said Law, "but credit."

"The kingdom hath been run on credit for these many years."

"No, 'tis not that kind of credit that I mean. I mean the credit which comes of confidence. It is fate, necessity, which demands a new system. The world has grown too much for every man to put his sixpence into the other man's hand, and carry away in a basket what he buys. We are no longer savages, to barter beads for hides. Yet we were as savages, did we not come to realize that this insufficient coin must be replaced, in the evolution of affairs, just as barter has long ago been, replaced."

"And by what?"

"As I said, by credit."

"Do not annoy me by things too deep, but rather suggest some definite plan, if that may be."

"First of all, then, as I said to you years ago, we need a bank, a bank in which all the people of France shall have absolute confidence."

"You would, then, wish a charter of some sort?"

"Only provided your Grace shall please. I have of my own funds a half million livres or more. This I would put into a bank of general nature, if your Grace shall please. That should be some small guarantee of my good faith in these plans."

"Monsieur L'as would seem to have followed play to his good fortune."

"Never to so good fortune as when first I met your Grace," replied Law. "I have given to games of chance the severest thought and study. Just as much more have I given thought and study to this enterprise which I propose now to lay before you."

"And you ask the patent of the Crown for your bank?"

"It were better if the institution received that open endorsement."

A slow frown settled upon the face of the other. "That is, at the beginning, impossible, Monsieur L'as," said the regent. "It is you who must prove these things which you propose."

"Let it be so, then," said Law, with conviction. "I make no doubt I shall obtain subscriptions for the shares. Remember my words. Within a few months you shall see trebled the energies of France. Money is the only thing which we have not in France. Why, your Grace, suppose the collectors of taxes in the South of France succeed in raising the king's levies. That specie must come by wheeled vehicle all the way to Paris. Consider what loss of time is there, and consider what hindrance to the trade of the provinces from which so much specie is taken bodily, and to which it can return later only a little at a time. Is it any wonder that usury is eating up France? There is not money enough—it is the one priceless thing; by which I mean only that there is not belief, not confidence, not credit enough in France. Now, given a bank which holds the confidence of the people, and I promise the king his taxes, even as I promise to abolish usury. You shall see money at work, money begetting money, and that begetting trade, and that producing comfort, and comfort making easier the collection of the king's taxes."

"By heaven! you begin to make it somewhat more plain to me."

"One thing I beg you to observe most carefully, your Grace," said Law, "nor must it ever be forgotten in our understanding. The shares of this bank must have a fixed value in regard to the coin of the realm. There must be no altering of the value of our coin. Grant that the coin does not fluctuate, and I promise you that my bank *actions*, notes of the chief bank of Paris, shall soon be found better than gold or silver in the eyes of France. Moreover, given a greater safety to foreign gold, and I promise you that too shall pour into Paris in such fashion as has never yet been seen. Moreover, the people will follow their coin. Paris will be the greatest capital of Europe. This I promise you I can do."

"In effect," said the regent, smiling, "you promise me that you can build a new Paris, a new world! Yet much of this I can in part believe and understand. Let that be as it may. The immediate truth is that something must be done, and done at once."

"Obviously."

"Our public debt is twenty-six hundred millions of livres. Its annual interest is eighty millions of livres. We can not pay this interest alone, not to speak of the principal. Obviously, as you say, the matter admits of no delay. Your bank—why, by heaven, let us have your bank! What can we do without your bank? Lastly, how quickly can we have it?"

"Sire, you make me the happiest man in all the world!"

"The advantage is quite otherwise, sir. But my head already swims with figures. Now let us set the rest aside until tomorrow. Meantime, I must confess to you, my dear friend, there is somewhat else that sits upon my mind."

A change came upon the demeanor of his Grace the regent.

Laying aside the dignity of the ruler with the questions of state, he became again more nearly that Philippe of Orleans, known by his friends as gay, care free and full of *camaraderie.*

"Your Grace, could I be of the least personal service, I should be too happy," said Law.

"Well, then, I must admit to you that this is a question of a diamond."

"Oh, a diamond?"

"The greatest diamond in the world. Indeed, there is none other like it, and never will be. This Jew hounds me to death, holding up the thing before mine eyes. Even Saint Simon, that priggish little duke of ours, tells me that France should have this stone, that it is a dignity which should not be allowed to pass away from her. But how can France, bankrupt as she is, afford a little trifle which costs three million francs? Three million francs, when we can not pay eighty millions annual interest on our debts!"

"'Tis as you say, somewhat expensive," said Law.

"Naturally, for I say to you that this stone had never parallel in the history of the world. It seems that this overseer in the Golconda mines got possession of it in some fashion, and escaped to Europe, hiding the stone about his person. It has been shown in different parts of Europe, but no one yet has been able to meet the price of this extortioner who owns it."

"And yet, as Saint Simon says, there is no dignity too great for the throne of France."

"Yet, meantime, the king will have no use for it for several years to come. There is the Sancy stone—"

"And, as your Grace remembers, this new stone would look excellent well upon a woman?" said Law. He gazed, calm and unsmiling, directly into the eyes of Philippe of Orleans.

"Monsieur L'as, you have the second sight!" cried the latter, unblushingly. "You have genius. May God strike me blind if ever I have seen a keener mind than thine!"

"All warm blood is akin," replied John Law. "This stone is perhaps for your Grace's best beloved?"

"Eh—ah—which? As you know—"

"Ah! Perhaps for La Parabere. Richly enough she deserves it."

"Ah, Monsieur L'as, even your mind is at fault now," cried the regent, shaking his finger exultingly. "I covet this new stone, not for Parabere nor for any one of those dear friends whom you might name, and whom you may upon occasion have met at some of my little suppers. It is for another, whose name or nature you can not guess."

"Not that mysterious beauty of whom rumor goes about this week, the woman rated surpassing fair, who has lately come into the acquaintance of your Grace, and whom your Grace has concealed as jealously as though he feared to lose her by some highway robbery?"

"It is the same, I must admit!"

Law remained thoughtful for a time. "I make no doubt that the Hebrew would take two million francs for this stone," said he.

"Perhaps, but two millions is the same as three millions," said Philippe. "The question is, where to get two millions."

"As your Grace has said, I have been somewhat fortunate at play," replied Law, "but I must say that this sum is beyond me, and that both the diamond and the bank I can not compass. Yet, your Grace has at disposal the crown jewels of France. Now, beauty is the sovereign of all sovereigns, as Philippe of Orleans must own. To beauty belongs the use of these crown jewels. Place them as security, and borrow the two millions. For myself, I shall take pride in advancing the interest on the sum for a certain time, until such occasion as the treasury may afford the price of this trinket. In a short time it will be able to do so, I promise your Grace; indeed able to buy a dozen such stones, and take no thought of the matter."

"Monsieur L'as, do you actually believe these things?"

"I know them."

"And you can secure for me this gem?"

"Assuredly. We shall have it. Let it be called the 'Regent's Diamond,' after your Grace of Orleans. And when the king shall one day wear it, let us hope that he will place it as fitly as I am sure your Grace will do, on the brow of beauty— even though it be beauty unknown, and kept concealed under princely prerogative!"

"Ah! You are too keen, Monsieur L'as, too keen to see my new discovery. Not for a little time shall I take the risk of introducing this fair friend to one so dangerous as yourself; but one of these times, my very good friend, if you can secure for me this diamond, you shall come to a very little supper, and see where for a time I shall place this gem, as you say, on the brow of beauty. For the sake of Monsieur L'as, head magician of France my mysterious alien shall then unmask."

"And then I am to have my bank?"

"Good God, yes, a thousand banks!"

"It is agreed?"

"It is agreed."

CHAPTER V

A DAY OF MIRACLES

The regent of France kept his promise to Law, and the latter in turn fulfilled his prophecy to the regent. Moreover, he swiftly went far toward verifying his boast to the Lady Catharine Knollys; for in less than a month his name was indeed on every tongue in Paris. The Banque Generale de L'as et Compagnie was seized upon by the public, debtor and creditor alike, as the one new thing, and hence as the only salvation. As ever, it pleased Paris to be mystified. In some way the rumor spread about that Monsieur L'as was *philosophique*; that the Banque Generale was founded upon "philosophy." It was catch-word sufficient for the time.

"*Vive* Jean L'as, *le philosophe*—Monsieur L'as, he who has saved France!" So rang the cry of the shallow-witted people of an age splendid even in its contradictions. And meantime the new bank, crudely experimental as it was, flourished as though its master spirit had indeed in his possession the philosopher's stone, turning all things to gold.

One day, shortly after the beginning of that brilliantly spectacular series of events destined so soon to make Paris the Mecca of the world, there sat at table, in a little, obscure *cabaret* of the gay city, a group of persons who seemed to have chosen that spot for purposes of privacy. Yet privacy was difficult where all the curious passers-by stared in amaze at the great coach near the door, half filling the narrow and unclean street—a vehicle bearing the arms of no less a person than that august and unscrupulous representative of the French nobility, the Prince de Conti. No less a person than the prince himself, thin-faced, aquiline and haughty, sat at this table, looking about him like any common criminal to note whether his speech might be overheard. Next to him sat a hook-nosed Jew from Austria, Fraslin by name, one of many of his kind gathered so quickly within the last few weeks in Paris, even as the scent of carrion fetches ravens to the feast. Another of the party was a man of middle age, of handsome, calm, patrician features and an unruffled mien—that De la Chaise, nephew of the confessor of Louis the Grand, who Was later to represent the young king in the provinces of Louisiana.

Near by the latter, and indeed the central figure of this gathering, was one less distinguished than either of the above, evidently neither of churchly ancestry nor civic distinction—Henri Varenne, sometime clerk for the noted Paris Freres, farmers of the national revenues. Varenne, now serving but as clerk in the new bank of L'as et Compagnie, could have been called a man of no great standing; yet it was he whose presence had called hither these others to this unusual meeting. In point of fact, Varenne was a spy, a spy chosen by the jealous Paris Freres, to learn what he might of the internal mechanism of this new and startling institution which had sprung into such sudden prominence.

"As to the bank of these brothers L'as," said the Prince de Conti, rapping out emphasis with his sword hilt on the table, "it surely has much to commend it. Here is one of its notes, and witness what it says. 'The bank promises to pay to the bearer at sight the sum of fifty livres in coin of the weight and standard of this day.' That is to say, of this date which it bears. Following these, are the words 'value received.' Now, my notary tells me that these words make this absolutely safe, so that I know what it means in coin to me at this day, or a year from now. Is it not so, Monsieur Fraslin?"

The Jew reached out his hand, took the note, and peered over it in close scrutiny.

"'Tis no wonder, Monsieur le Prince," said he, presently, "that orders have been given by the Government to receive this note without discount for the payment of the general taxes. Upon my reputation, I must say to you that these notes will pass current better than your uncertain coin. The specie of the king has been changed twice in value by the king's orders. Yet this bases itself upon a specie value which is not subject to any change. Therein lies its own value."

"It is indeed true," broke in Varenne. "Not a day goes by at this new bank but persons come to us and demand our notes rather than coin of the realm of France."

"Yes, yes," broke in the prince, "we are agreed as to all this, but there is much talk about further plans of this Monsieur L'as. He has the ear of his Grace the regent, surely. Now, sir, tell us what you know of these future affairs."

"The rumor is, as I understand it," answered Varenne, "that he is to take over control of the Company of the West—to succeed, in short, to the shoes of Anthony Crozat. There come curious stories of this province of Louisiana."

"Of course," resumed the prince, with easy wisdom, "we all of us know of the voyage of L'Huillier, who, with his four ships, went up this great river Messasebe, and who, as is well known, found that river of Blue Earth, described by early writers as abounding in gold and gems."

"Aye, and there comes the strange part of it, and this is what I would lay before your Lordships, as bearing upon the value of the shares of this new bank, since it is taking over the charter of the Company of the West. It is news not yet known upon the street. The story goes that the half has not been told of the wealth of these provinces.

"Now, as you say, L'Huillier had with him four ships, and it is well known that his gentlemen had with them certain ladies of distinction, among these a mysterious dame reported to have earlier traveled in portions of New France. The name of this mysterious female is not known, save that she is reported to have been a good friend of a *sous-lieutenant* of the regiment Carignan, sometime dweller at Quebec and Montreal, and who later became a lieutenant under L'Huillier. It is said that this same mysterious fair, having returned from America and having cast aside her lieutenant, has come under protection of no less a person than his Grace Philippe of Orleans, the regent. Now, as you know, the bank is the best friend of the regent, and this mysterious dame, as we are advised by servants of his Grace's household, hath told his Grace such stories of the wealth of the Messasebe that he has secretly and quickly made over the control of the trade of those provinces to this new bank. There is story also that his Grace himself will not lack profit in this movement!"

The hand of Conti smote hard upon the table. "By heaven! it were strange thing," said he, "if this foreign traveler should prove the same mysterious beauty Philippe is reported to have kept in hiding. My faith, is it indeed true that we are come upon a time of miracles?"

"Listen!" broke in again Varenne, his ardor overcoming his

obsequiousness. "These are some of the tales brought back—and reported privately, I can assure you, gentlemen, now for the first time and to yourselves. The people of this country are said to be clad in beauteous raiment, made of skins, of grasses, and of the barks of trees. Their ornaments are made of pure, yellow gold, and of precious gems which they pick up from the banks of the streams, as common as pebbles here in France. The climate is such that all things grow in the most unrivaled fruitfulness. There is neither too much sun nor too much rain. The lakes and rivers are vast and beautiful, and the forests are filled with myriads of strange and sweet-voiced birds. 'Tis said that the dream of Ponce de Leon hath been realized, and that not only one, but scores of fountains of youth have been discovered in this great valley. The people are said never to grow old. Their personal beauty is of surpassing nature, and their disposition easy and complaisant to the last degree—"

"My faith, say on!" broke in De la Chaise. "'Tis surely a story of paradise which you recount."

"But, listen, gentlemen! The story goes yet farther. As to mines of gold and silver, 'twas matter of report that such mines are common in all the valley of the Messasebe. Indeed the whole surface of the earth, in some parts, is covered with lumps of gold, so that the natives care nothing for it. The bottoms of the streams, the beaches of the lakes, carry as many particles of gold as they have pebbles and little stones. As for silver, none take note of it. 'Tis used as building stone."

"In the name of Jehovah, is there support for these wonders you have spoken?" broke in Fraslin the Jew, his eyes shining with suppressed excitement.

"Assuredly. Yet I am telling not half of the news which came to my knowledge this very morning—the story is said to have emanated from the Palais Royal itself, and therefore, no doubt, is to be traced to this game unknown queen of the Messasebe. She reports, so it is said, that beyond the country where L'Huillier secured his cargo of blue earth, there is a land where grows a most peculiar plant. The meadows and fields are covered with it, and it is said that the dews of night, which gather within the petals of these flowers, become, in the course of a single day, nothing less than a solid diamond stone! From this in time the leaves drop down, leaving the diamond exposed there, shining and radiant."

"Ah, bah!" broke in Fraslin the Jew. "Why believe such babblings? We all know that the diamond is a product not of the vegetable but of the mineral world!"

"So have we known many things," stoutly replied Varenne, "only to find ourselves frequently mistaken. Now for my part, a diamond is a diamond, be it born in a flower or broken from a rock. And as for the excellence of these stones, 'tis rumored that the lady hath abundant proof. 'Tis no wonder that the natives of the valley of the Messasebe robe themselves in silks, and that they deck themselves carelessly with precious stones, as would a peasant of ours with a chain of daisy blossoms. Now, if there be such wealth as this, is it not easy to see the profit of a bank which controls the trade with such a province? True, there have been some discoveries in this valley, but nothing thorough. 'Tis but recent the thing hath been done thorough."

The Prince de Conti sat back in his chair and drew a long breath. "If these things be true," said he, "then this Monsieur L'as is not so bad a leader to follow."

"But listen!" exclaimed Varenne once more. "I have not even yet told you the most important thing, and this is rumor which perhaps your Grace has caught. 'Tis whispered that the bank of the brothers L'as is within a fortnight to be changed."

"What is that?" queried Fraslin quickly. "'Tis not to be abandoned?"

"By no means. Abandoned would be quite the improper word. 'Tis to be improved, expanded, increased, magnified! My Lords, there is the opportunity of a life-time for every one of us here!"

"Say on, man, say on!" commanded the prince, the covetousness of his soul shining in his eyes as he leaned forward.

"I mean to say this," and the spy lowered his voice as he looked anxiously about. "The regent hath taken a fancy to be chief owner himself of an enterprise so profitable. In fine, the Banque Generale is to become the Banque Royale. His Majesty of France, represented by his Grace the regent, is to become the head banker of France and Europe! Monsieur L'as is to be retained as director-general of this Banque Royale. There are to be branches fixed in different cities of the realm, at Lyons, at Tours, at Amiens, at Rochelle, at Orleans—in fact, all France is to go upon a different footing."

The glances of the Prince de Conti and the Austrian met each other. The Jew drew a long breath as he sat back in his chair, his hands grasping at the edge of the table. Try as he might, he scarce could keep his chin from trembling. He licked out his tongue to moisten his lips.

"There is so much," resumed Varenne, "that 'tis hard to tell it all. But you must know that this Banque Royale will be still more powerful than the old one. There will be incorporated with it, not only the Company of the West, but also the General Company of the Indies, as you know, the most considerable mercantile enterprise of France. Now listen! Within the first year the Banque Royale will issue one thousand million livres in notes. This embodiment of the Compagnie Generale of the Indies will warrant, as I know by the secret plans of the bank, the issue of notes amounting to two billion livres. Therefore, as Monsieur de la Chaise signifies, he who is lucky enough to-day to own a few *actions* of the Banque Royale, or even the old *actions* of Monsieur L'as' bank, which will be redeemed by its successor, is in a way to gain greater sums than were ever seen on the face of any investment from the beginning of the world until to-day! Now, as I was about to ask of you, Monsieur Fraslin—"

The speaker turned in his chair to where Fraslin had been but a moment before. The chair was empty.

"Our friend stepped to the door but on the instant," said De la Chaise. "He is perhaps—"

"That he has," cried Varenne. "He is the first of us to profit! Monsieur le Prince, in virtue of what I have said to you, if you could favor me with an advance of a few hundred louis, I could assure my family of independence. Monsieur le Prince! Monsieur le Prince—"

Monsieur le Prince, however, was not so far behind the Austrian! Varenne followed him, tugging at his coat, but Conti shook him off, sprang into his carriage and was away.

"To the Place Vendome!" he cried to his coachman, "and hasten!"

De la Chaise, aristocratic, handsome and thick-witted,

remained alone at the table, wondering what was the cause of this sudden commotion. Varenne re-appeared at the door wringing his hands.

"What is it, my friend?" asked De la Chaise. "Why all this haste? Why this confusion?"

"Nothing!" exclaimed Varenne, bitterly, "except that every minute of this day is worth a million francs. Man, do you know?"—and in his frenzy he caught De la Chaise by the collar and half shook him out of his usual calm—"man, can you not see that Jean L'as has brought revolution into Paris? Oh! This L'as, this devil of a L'as! A thousand louis, my friend, a hundred, ten—give me but ten louis, and I will make you rich! A day of miracles is here!"

CHAPTER VI

THE GREATEST NEED

There sprang now with incredible swiftness upward and outward an Aladdin edifice of illusion. It was as though indeed this genius who had waved his wand and bidden this fairy palace of chimera to arise, had used for his material the intangible, iridescent film of bubbles, light as air. Wider and wider spread the balloon of phantasm. Higher and higher it floated, on it fixed the eyes of France. And France laughed, and asked that yet other bubbles should be blown.

All France was mad, and to its madness there was joined that of all Europe. The population of Paris doubled. The prices of labor and commodities trebled in a day. There was now none willing to be called artisan. Every man was broker in stocks. Bubbles, bubbles, dreams, fantasies—these were the things all carried in their hands and in their hearts. These made the object of their desire, of their pursuit unimaginably passionate and frenzied.

With a leap from the somberness of the reign of Louis, all France went to the extreme of levity. Costumes changed. Manners, but late devout, grew debonair. Morals, once lax, now grew yet more lax. The blaze and tinsel, the music and the rouge, the wine, the flowing, uncounted gold—all Paris might have been called a golden brothel of delirious delight, tenanted by a people utterly gone mad.

It was a house made of bubbles. Its domes were of bubbles. Its roof was of bubbles, and its walls. Its windows were of that nacreous film. Even its foundations had naught in them more substantial than an evanescent dream of gauze-like web, frail as the spider's house upon the dew-hung grasses.

Yet as to this latter, there should be somewhat of qualification. The wizard who created this fairy structure saw it swiftly grow beyond its original plan, saw unforeseen results spring from those causes which were first well within his comprehension.

Berated by later generations as an adventurer, a schemer, a charlatan, Law originally deserved anything but such a verdict of his public. Dishonest he was not, insincere he never was; and as a student of fundamentals, he was in advance of his age, which is ever to be accursed. His method was but the forerunner of the modern commercial system, which is of itself to-day but a tougher faith bubble, as may be seen in all the changing cycles of finance and trade. His bank was but a portion of a nobler dream. His system was but one vast belief, one glorious hope.

The Company of the West—this it was that made John Law's heart throb. America—its trade—its future! John Law, dead now and gone—he was the colossal pioneer! He saw in his dreams what we see to-day in reality; and no bubble of all the frenzied Paris streets equaled this splendid dream of a renewed and revived humanity that is a fact to-day.

But there came to this dreamer and doer, at the very door of his success, that which arrested him even upon his entering in. There came the preliminary blow which in a flash his far-seeing mind knew was to mean ultimate ruin. In a word, the loose principles of a dissolute man were to ruin France, and with it one who had once saved France from ruin.

Philippe of Orleans found it ever difficult to say no to a friend, and more so if that friend were a woman; and of the latter sort, none had more than he. Men and women alike, these could all see only this abundance of money made of paper. What, then, was to prevent the regent, all powerful, from printing more and yet more of it, and giving it to his friends? The regent did so. Never were mistresses better paid than those of Philippe of Orleans, receiving in effect faithlessness in return for insincerity.

Philippe of Orleans could not see why, since credit based on specie made possible a great volume of accepted notes, a credit based on all France might not warrant an indefinite issue of such notes. He offered his director-general all the concessions which the crown could give, all the revenue-producing elements of France—in effect, all France itself, as security. In return he asked but the small privilege of printing for himself as much money as he chose and whenever he saw fit!

The notes of the private bank of Law were an absolute promise to pay a certain and definite sum, not a changeable or indefinite sum; and Law made it a part of his published creed that any banker was worthy of death who issued notes without having the specie wherewith to pay them. He insisted that the payment should mean specie in the value of the day on which the note was issued. This item the regent liked little, as being too irksome for his temper. Was it not of record how Louis, the Grand Monarque, had twice made certain millions for himself by the simple process of changing the value of the coin? Dicing, drinking, amorous Philippe, easy-going, shallow-thinking, truly wert thou better

Emerson Hough

fitted for a throne than for a banker's chair!

The royal bank, which the regent himself hastened to foster when he saw the profits of the first private bank of circulation and discount France had ever known, issued notes against which Law entered immediately his firm protest. He saw that their tenor spelled ruin for the whole system of finance which, at such labor, he had erected. These notes promised to pay, for instance, fifty livres "in silver coin," not "in coin of the weight and standard of this day," as had the honester notes of Law's bank. That is to say, the notes meant nothing sure and nothing definite. They might be money for a time, but not forever; and this the director-general was too shrewd a man not to know.

"But under this issue you shall have all France," said the regent to him one day, as they renewed their discussion yet again upon this scheme. "You shall have the farming of the taxes. I will give you all the foreign trade as monopoly, if you like—will give you the mint—will give you, in effect, as I have said, all France. But, Monsieur my director-general, I must have money. It is for that purpose that I appoint you director-general—because I find you the most remarkable man in all the world."

"Your Grace," said Law, "print your notes thus, and print them to such extent as you wish, and France is again worse than bankrupt! Then, indeed, you have worse than repudiated the debts of France."

"Ah bah! *mon drole*! You are ill to-day. You have a *migraine*, perhaps? What folly for you to speak thus. France hath swiftly grown so strong that she can never again be ruined. What ails my magician, my Prince of Golconda, this morning? France bankrupt! Even were it so, does that relieve me of this begging of De Prie, of Parabere, and all the others? My God, Monsieur L'as, they are like leeches! They think me made of money."

"And your Grace thinks France made of money."

"Nay; I only think my director-general is made of money, or can make it as he likes."

And this was ever the end of Law's reproaches and his expostulations. This, then, was to be the end of his glorious enterprises, thought he, as he sat one morning, staring out of the window when left alone. This sordid love for money for its own sake—this was to be the limit of an ambition which dealt in theories, in men, in nations, and not in livres and louis d'or! Law smiled bitterly. For an instant he was not the confident man of action and of affairs, not the man claiming with assurance the perpetual protection of good fortune. He sat there, alone, feeling nothing but the great human craving for sympathy and trust. A line of carriages swept back across the street at his window, and streams of nobles besought entrance at his door. And the man who had called out all these, the man for whose friendship all Europe clamored—that man sat with aching heart, longing, craving, begging now of fortune only the one thing—a friend!

At last he arose, his face showing lean and haggard. He passed into another room.

"Will," said he, "I am at a place where I am dizzy and need a hand. You know what hand it means for me. Can you go—will you take her, as you did once before for me, a message? I can not go. I can not venture into her presence. Will you go? Tell her it is the last time! Tell her it is the last!"

CHAPTER VII

THE MIRACLE UNWROUGHT

"You do not know my brother, Lady Catharine."

Thus spoke Will Law, who had been admitted but a half hour since at the great door of the private hotel where dwelt the Lady Catharine Knollys.

"'Twould seem, then, 'tis by no fault of his," replied Lady Catharine, hotly.

"And is that not well? There are many in Paris who would fain change places with you, Lady Catharine."

"Would heaven they might!" exclaimed she. "Would that my various friends, or the prefect of police, or heaven knows who that may have spread the news of my acquaintance with your brother, would take me out of that acquaintance!"

"They might hold his friendship a high honor," said Will.

"Oh, an honor! Excellent well comes this distinguished honor. Sirrah, carriages block my street, filled with those who beseech my introduction to John Law. I am waylaid if I step abroad, by women—persons of quality, ladies of the realm, God knoweth what—and they beg of me the favor of an introduction to John Law! There seems spread, I know not how, a silly rumor of the child Kate. And though I did scarce more than name a convent for her attendance, there are now out all manner of reports of Monsieur John Law's child, and—what do I say—'tis monstrous! I protest that I have come closer than I care into the public thoughts with this prodigy, this John Law, whose favor is sought by every one. Honor!—'tis not less than outrage!"

"'Tis but argument that my brother is a person not without note."

"But granted. 'We have seen his carriage at your curb,' they say. I insist that it is a mistake. 'But we saw him come from your door at such and such an hour.' If he came, 'twas but for meeting such answer as I have always given him. Will they never believe—will your brother himself never believe that, though did he have, as he himself says, all France in the hollow of his hand, he could be nothing to me? Now I will make an end to this. I will leave Paris."

"Madam, you might not be allowed to go."

"What! I not allowed to go! And what would hinder a Knollys of Banbury from going when the hour shall arrive?"

"The regent."

"And why the regent?"

"Because of my brother."

"Your brother!"

"Assuredly. My brother is to-day king of Paris. If he liked he could keep you prisoner in Paris. My brother does as he chooses. He could abolish Parliament to-morrow if he chose. My brother can do all things—except to win from you, Lady Catharine, one word of kindness, of respect. Now, then, he has come to the end. He told me to come to you and bear his word. He told me to say to you that this is the last time he will importune, the last time that he will implore. Oh, Lady Catharine! Once before I carried to you a message from John Law—from John Law, not in distress then more than he is now, even in this hour of his success."

Lady Catharine paled as she sank back into her seat. Her white hand caught at the lace at her throat. Her eyes grew dark in their emotion.

"Yes, Madam," went on Will Law, tears shining in his own eyes, "'twas I, an unfaithful messenger, who, by an error, wrought ruin for my brother and for yourself, even as I did for myself. Madam, hear me! I would be a better messenger to-day."

Lady Catharine sat still silent, her bosom heaving, her eyes gone wide and straining.

"I have seen my brother weep," said Will, going on impulsively. "I have seen him walk the floor at night, have heard him cry out to himself. They call him crazed. Indeed he is crazed. Yet 'tis but for one word from you."

"Sir," said Lady Catharine, struggling to gain self-control, and in spite of herself softened by this appeal, "you speak well."

"If I do, 'tis but because I am the mouth-piece of a man who all his life has sought to speak the truth; who has sought—yes, I say to you even now, Lady Catharine—who has sought always to live the truth. This I say in spite of all that we both know."

There came no reply from the woman, who sat still looking at him, not yet moved by the voice of the proxy as she might then have been by the voice of that proxy's principal. Vehemently the young man, ordinarily so timid and diffident, approached her.

"Look you!" exclaimed he. "If my brother said he could lay France at your feet, by heaven! he can well-nigh do so now. See! Here are some of the properties he has lately purchased in the realm of France. The Marquisat d'Effiat—'tis worth eight hundred thousand livres; the estate of Riviere—worth nine hundred thousand livres; the estate of Roissy—worth six hundred and fifty thousand livres; the estates of Berville, of Fontaine, of Yville, of Gerponville, of Tancarville, of Guermande—the tale runs near a score! Lately my brother has purchased the Hotel Mazarin, and the property at Rue Vivienne, paying for them one million two hundred thousand livres. He has other city properties, houses in Paris, estates here and there, running not into the hundreds of thousands, but into the millions of livres in actual value. Among these are some of the estates of the greatest nobles of France. Their value is more than any man can compute. Is this not something? Moreover, there goes with it all the dignity of the most stupendous personal success ever made by a single man since the world began. 'Tis all yours, Lady Catharine. And unless you share it, it has no value to my brother. I know myself that he will fling it all away, calling it worthless, since he can not have that greatest fortune which he craves!"

"Sirrah, I have entertained much speech of both yourself and your brother, because I would not seem ungracious nor forgetful. Yet this paying of court by means of figures, by virtue of lists of estates—do you not know how ineffectual this must seem?"

"If you could but understand!" cried Will. "If you could but believe that there is none on earth values these less than my brother. Under all this he has yet greater dreams. His ambition is to awaken an old world and to build a new one. By heaven! Lady Catharine, I am asked to speak for my brother, and so I shall! These are his ambitions. First of all, Lady Catharine, you. Second, America. Third, a people for America—a people who may hope! Oh, I admit all the folly of his life. He played deep, yet 'twas but to forget you. He drank, but 'twas to forget you. Foolish he was, as are all men. Now he succeeds, and finds he can not forget you. I have told you his ambitions, Madam, and though others may never know nor acknowledge them, you, at least, must do so. And I beg you to remember, Madam, that of all his ambitions, 'twas you, Lady Catharine, your favor, your kindness, your mercy, that made his first and chief desire."

"As for that," said the woman, somewhat scornfully, "if you please, I had rather I received my protestations direct; and your brother knows I forbid him further protestations. He has, it is true, raised some considerable noise by way of enterprises. That I might know, even did I not see this horde of dukes and duchesses and princes of the blood, clamoring for the recognition of even his remotest friends. I know, too, that he is accepted as a hero by the people."

"And well he may be. Coachmen and valets have liveries of their own these days. Servants now eat from plate, and clerks have their own coaches. Paris is packed with people, and, look you, they are people no longer clamoring for bread. Who has done this? Why, my brother, John Law of Lauriston, Lady Catharine, who loves you, and loves you dearly."

The old wrinkle of perplexity gathered between the brows of the woman before him. Her face was clouded, the changeful eyes now deep covered by their lids.

Lacking the precise word for that crucial moment, Will Law broke further on into material details. "To be explicit, as I have said," resumed he, "everything seems to center about my brother, the director-general of finance. He took the old notes of the government, worth not half their face, and in a week made them treble their face value. The king owes him over one hundred million livres to-day. My brother has taken over the farming of the royal taxes. And now he forms a little Company of the Indies; and to this he adds the charter of the Senegal Company. Not content, he adds the entire trade of the Indies, of China and the South Seas. He has been given the privilege of the royal farming of tobacco, for which he pays the king the little trifle of two hundred million livres, and assures to the king certain interest moneys, which, I need not say, the king will actually obtain. In addition to these things, he has lately been given the mint of France. The whole coinage of the realm has been made over to this Company of the Indies. My brother pays the king fifty million livres for this privilege, and this he will do within fifteen months. All France is indeed in the hands of my brother. Now, call John Law an adventurer, a gambler, if you will, and if you can; but at least admit that he has given life and hope to the poor of France, that he has given back to the king a people which was despoiled and ruined by the former king. He has trebled the trade of France, he has saved her honor, and opened to her the avenues of a new world. Are these things nothing? They have all been done by my brother, this man whom you believe incapable of faith and constancy. Good God! It surely seems that he has at least been constant to himself!"

"Oh, I hear talk of it all. I hear that a share in the new

company promises dividends of two hundred livres. I hear talk of shares and 'sub-shares,' called 'mothers,' and 'daughters,' and 'granddaughters,' and I know not what. It seems as though half the coin were divided into centimes, and as though each centime had been planted by your brother and had grown to be worth a thousand pounds. I admit somewhat of knowledge of these miracles."

"True, Lady Catharine. Can there not be one miracle more?"

Lady Catharine Knollys bent her face forward upon her hands, unhappiness in every gesture.

"Sir," said she, "it grieves my heart to say it; yet this answer you must take to your brother, John Law. That miracle hath not yet been wrought which can give us back the past again."

"This," said Will Law, sadly, "is this all the message I may take?"

"It is all."

"Though it is the last?"

"It is the last."

CHAPTER VIII

THE LITTLE SUPPER OF THE REGENT

Paris, city of delights, Paris drunk with gold, mad with the delirium of excesses, Paris with no aim except joy, no method but extravagance, held within her gilded gates one citadel of sensuality which remained ever an object of mystery, a source of curiosity even in that dissipated and pleasure-sated city. In the Palais Royal, back of the regally beautiful gardens, back of the noble rows of trees, beyond the gates of iron and the guards in uniform, lived France's regent, in a city of libertines the prince of libertines. In a city where there were more mistresses than wives, he it was who led the list of the licentious. In a city of unregulated vice and yet of exquisitely ordered taste, he it was who accorded to himself daily pleasures which were admittedly beyond approach. How unspeakably unbridled, how delightfully wicked, how temptingly ingenious in their features the little suppers of the regent might be—these were matters of curious interest to all, of intimate knowledge to but few.

It was to one of these famous yet mysterious gatherings that the regent of France had invited the master of that great and glittering bubble house, wherein dwelt so insecurely the affairs of France. John Law, director-general of the finances, controller of the Company of the Indies, was chosen by

Philippe of Orleans for a position not granted to the crafty Dubois or to the shrewd D'Argenson, the last of that strange trinity who made his council. John Law, gallant, graceful, owner of a reputation as wit and beau scarce behind that of his sudden fame as financier, was admitted not only to the business affairs of the gay duke, but to his pleasures as well. To him and his brother Will, still associated in large measure in the stupendous operations of the director-general, there came the invitation of the regent, practically the command of the king, to join the regent after the opera for a little supper at the Palais Royal.

Law would have excused himself from this unsought honor. "Your Grace will observe," said he, "that my time is occupied to the full. The people scarcely suffer me to rest at night. Perhaps your Grace might not care for company so dull as mine."

"Fie! my friend, my very good friend," replied Philippe. "Have you become *devot*? Whence this sudden change? Consider; 'tis no hardship to meet such ladies as Madame de Sabran, or Madame de Prie—designer though I fear De Prie is for the domestic felicity of the youthful king—nor indeed my good friend, La Parabere, somewhat pale and pensive though she groweth. And what shall I say for Madame de Tencin, the *spirituelle*, who is to be with us; or Madame de Caylus, niece of Maintenon, but the very opposite of Maintenon in every possible way? Moreover, we are promised the attendance of Mademoiselle Aisse. She hath become devout of late, and thinks it a sin even to powder her hair, but Aisse devout is none the less Aisse the beautiful."

"Surely your Grace hath never lacked in excellent taste, and that is the talk of Paris," replied Law.

"Oh, well, long training bringeth perfection in due time,"

replied Philippe of Orleans, composedly, it having no ill effect with him to call attention to his numerous intrigues. "It should hardly be called a poor privilege, after all, to witness the results of that highly cultivated taste, as it shall be displayed this evening, not to mention the privilege you will have of meeting one or two other gentlemen; and lastly, of course, myself, if you be not tired of such company."

"Your Grace," replied Law, "you both honor and flatter me."

"Why, sir, you speak as if this were a new experience for you. Now, in the days—"

"'Tis true; but of late years I have grown grave in the cares of state, as your Grace may know."

"And most efficiently," replied the regent. "But stay! I have kept until the last my main attraction. You shall witness there, I give you my word, the making public of the secret of the fair unknown who is reputed to have been especially kind to Philippe of Orleans for these some months past. Join us at the little enterprise, my friend, and you shall see, I promise you, the most beautiful woman in Paris, crowned with the greatest gem of all the world. The regent's diamond, that great gem which you have made possible for France, shall, for the first time, and for one evening at least, adorn the forehead of the regent's queen of beauty!"

As the gay words of the regent fell upon his ears, there came into Law's heart a curious tension, a presentiment, a feeling as though some great and curious thing were about to happen. Yet ever the challenge of danger was one to draw him forward, not to hold him back. If for a moment he had hesitated, his mind was now suddenly resolved.

"Your Grace," said he, "your wish is for me command, and

certainly in this instance is peculiarly agreeable."

"As I thought," replied the regent. "Had you hesitated, I should have called your attention to the fact that the table of the Palais Royal is considered to possess somewhat of character. The Vicomte de Bechamel is at the very zenith of his genius, and he daily produces dishes such as all Paris has not ever dreamed. Moreover, we have been fortunate in some recent additions of most excellent *vin d'Ai*. I make no doubt, upon the whole, we shall find somewhat with which to occupy ourselves."

Thus it came about that, upon that evening, there gathered at the entrance of the Palais Royal, after an evening with Lecouvreur at the Theatre Francais, some scattered groups of persons evidently possessing consequence. The chairs of others, from more distant locations, threading their way through the narrow, dark and unlighted streets of the old, crude capital of France, brought their passengers in time to a scene far different from that of the gloomy streets.

The little supper of the regent, arranged in the private *salle*, whose decorations had been devised for the special purpose, was more entrancing than even the glitter of the mimic world of the Theatre Francais. There extended down the center of the room, though filling but a small portion of its vast extent, the grand table provided for the banquet, a reach of snowy linen, broken at the upper end by the arm of an abbreviated cross. At each end of this cross-arm stood magnificent candelabra, repeated at intervals along the greater extension of the board. Noble epergnes, filled with the choicest plants, found their reflections in plates of glass cunningly inlaid here and there upon the surface of the table. Vast mirrors, framed in wreaths of roses and surmounted by little laughing cupids, gleamed in the walls of the room, and in the faces of these mirrors were reflected the beams of the many-colored tapers, carried in brackets of engraved gold and silver and many-colored glasses. The ceiling of the room was a soft mass of silken draperies, depending edgewise from above, thousands of yards of the most expensive fabrics of the world. From these, as they were gently swayed by the breath of invisible fans, there floated delicious, languorous perfumes, intoxicating to the senses. On any hand within the great room, removed at some distance from the table, were rich, luxurious couches and divans.

As one trod within the door of this temple of the senses, surely it must have seemed to him that he had come into another world, which at first glance might have appeared to be one of an unrighteous ease, an unprincipled enjoyment and an unmanly abandonment to embowered vice. Yet here it was that Philippe of Orleans, ruler of France, spent those hours most dear to him. If he gave thought to affairs of state during the day it was but that these affairs of state might give to him the means to indulge fancies of his own. Alike shrewd and easy, alike haughty and sensuous, here it was that Philippe held his real court.

These young gentlemen of France, these *roues* who have come to meet Philippe at his little supper—how different from the same beings under the rule of the Grand Monarque. Their coats are no longer dark in hue. Their silks and velvets have blossomed out, even as Paris has blossomed since the death of Louis the Grand. Jabots of lace are shown in full abundance, and so far from the abolishment of jewels from their garb, rubies, sapphires, diamonds sparkle everywhere, from the clasp of the high ruffles of the neck to the buckles of the red-heeled shoes. Powder sparkles on the head coverings of these new gallants of France. They step daintily, yet not ungracefully, into this brilliantly-lighted room, these creatures, gracious and resplendent, sparkling, painted, ephemeral, not unsuited to the place and hour.

For the ladies, witness the attire, for instance, of that Madame de Tencin, the wonder of the wits of Paris. A full blue costume, with pannier more than five yards in circumference, under a skirt of silver gauze, trimmed with golden gauze and pink crape, and a train lying six yards upon the floor, showing silver embroideries with white roses. The sleeves are half-draped, as is the skirt, and each caught up with diamonds, showing folds lying above and below the silk underneath. Madame wears a necklace of rubies and of diamonds, and above the pannier a belt of diamonds and rubies. Her hair is dressed, following the mental habit of madame, in the Greek style, and abundantly trimmed with roses and gems and bits of silver gauze. There is a little crown upon the top of madame's coiffure. Her bodice, cut sufficiently low, is seen to be of light silken weave. From her hair depends a veil of light gauze covered with gold spangles, and it is secured upon the left side by a hand's grasp of pink and white feathers, surmounted by a magnificent heron plume of long and silken whiteness. The gloves of madame are white silk, and so also, as she is not reluctant to advise, are her stockings, picked out with pink and silver clocks. Her shoes, made by the celebrated *cordonnier*, Raveneau, show heels three inches in height. As madame enters she casts aside the camlet coat which has covered her costume. She sweeps back the veil, endangering its confining clasp of plumes. Madame makes a deliberate and open inspection of her face in her little looking-glass to discover whether her *mouches* are well placed. She carefully arranges the patch upon the middle of her cheek. She would be "gallant" to-night, would lay aside things *spirituelle*. She twirls carelessly her fan, a creation of ivory and mother of pearl, elaborately carved, tipped with gold and silver and set with precious stones.

Close at the elbow of Madame de Tencin steps a figure of different type, a woman not accustomed to please by brilliance of mind or vivacity of speech, but by sheer femininity of face and form. Tall, slender, yet with figure divinely proportioned, this beautiful girl, Haidee, or Mademoiselle Aisse, reputed to be of Turkish or Circassian birth, and possessed of a history as strange as her own personality is attractive, would seem certainly as pure as angel of the skies. Not so would say the gossips of Paris, who whisper that mademoiselle is not happy from her *chevalier*—who speak of a certain visit to England, and a little child born across seas and not acknowledged by its parent. Aisse, the devout, the beautiful, is no better than others of her sex in this gay city. True, she has abandoned all artificial aids to the complexion and appears distinct among her flattering rivals, the clear olive of her skin showing in strange contrast to the heightened colors of her sisters. Yet Aisse, the toast of Europe and the text of poets, proves herself not behind the others in the loose gaiety of this occasion.

And there came others: Madame de Prie, later to hold such intimate relations with the fortunes of France in the selection of a future queen for the boy king; De Sabran, plain, gracious and good-natured; Parabere, of delicately oval face, of tiny mouth, of thin high nose and large expressive eyes, her soft hair twined with a deep flushed rose, and over her corsage drooping a continuous garland of magnificent flowers. Also Caylus the wit, Caylus the friend of Peter the Great, by duty and by devotion a *religieuse*, but by thought and training a gay woman of the world—all these butterflies of the bubble house of Paris came swimming in as by right upon this exotic air.

And all of these, as they advanced into the room, paused as they met, coming from the head of the apartment, the imposing figure of their host. Philippe of Orleans, his powdered wig drawn closely into a half-bag at the nape of the neck, his full eye shining with merriment and good nature, his soft, yet not unmanly figure appearing to good advantage in his well-chosen garments, advances with a certain dignity to meet his guests. He is garbed in a coat made of watered silk, its straight collar faced with dark-green material edged with gold. A green and gold shoulder knot sets off the garment, which is provided with large opal buttons set in brilliants, this same adornment appearing on the hilt of his sword, which he lays aside as he approaches. From the sides of his wig depend two carefully-arranged locks, dusted with a tan-colored powder. His small-clothes, of lighter hue than the coat, display fitly the proportions of his lower limbs. The high-heeled shoes blaze with the glare of reflected lights as the diamonds change their angles during the calm advance down the room.

"Welcome, my very dear ladies," exclaimed Philippe, advancing to the head of the board and at once setting all at ease, if any there needed such encouragement, by the grace and good feeling of his air. "You do me much honor, ladies. If I be not careful, the fair Adrienne will become jealous, since I fear you have deserted the pomp of the play full early for the table of Philippe. Ladies, as you know, I am your devoted slave. Myself and the Vicomte de Bechamel have labored, seriously labored, for your welfare this day. I promise you something of the results of those painstaking efforts, which we both hope will not disappoint you. Mean-time, that the moments may not lag, let me recommend, if I am allowed, this new vintage of Ai, which Bechamel advises me we have never yet surpassed in all our efforts. Madame de Tencin, let me beg of you to be seated close to my arm. Not upon this side, Mademoiselle Haidee, if you please, for I have been wheedled into promising that station this night to another. Who is it to be, my dear Caylus? Ah, that is my secret! Presently we shall see. Have I not promised you an occasion this evening? And did Philippe ever fail in his endeavors to please? At least, did he ever cease to strive to please his angels? Now, my children, accept the blessing of your father Philippe, your friend, who, though years may multiply upon him, retains in his heart, none the less, for each and all of you, those sentiments of passion and of admiration which constitute for him his dearest memories! Ladies, I pray you be seated. I pray you tarry not too long before proving the judgment of Bechamel in regard to this new vintage of Ai."

"Ah, your Grace," exclaimed De Tencin, "were it not Philippe of Orleans, we women might not be apt to sit in peace together. Yet, as we have earlier proved your hospitality, we may perhaps not scruple to continue."

Philippe smiled blandly. The remark was not ill-fitted to the actual case. Though the regent counted his sweethearts by scores, he dismissed the one with the same air of interest as he welcomed the other, and indeed ended by retaining all as his friends.

"Madame de Tencin, in admiration there can be no degrees," said he. "In love there can be no rank."

"Why, then, do you place as your chief guest this other, this unknown?" pouted Mademoiselle Aisse, as she seated herself, turning upon her host the radiance of her large, dark eyes. "Is this stranger, then, so passing fair?"

"Not so fair as you, my lovely Haidee, that I may swear, and safely, since she is not yet present. Yet I announce to you that she is *tres interessante*, my unknown queen of beauty, my *belle sauvage* from America. But see! Here she comes. 'Tis time for her to appear, and not keep our guests in waiting."

There sounded at the back of the great hall the tinkle of a little bell of some soft metal. It approached, and with it the sweeping stir of heavy silken garb. The door opened, admitting a still greater blaze of light, and there swept into the hall, as though swimming upon the flood of this added brilliance, a figure striking enough to arouse attention even at that time and place, even among the beauties of the court of France. There advanced, calm and stately, with the gliding ease of a perfect carriage, the figure of a woman, slender, with full bright eyes and somber hair—so much might be seen at a glance. Yet the newcomer left somewhat of query in the mind of womankind accustomed to view in detail any costume.

The stranger was enveloped in a wide and undefining garment, a sweeping robe fit for any duchess of the realm, whose flowing folds showed a magnificent tissue of silver embroidery covered with golden flowers, below the plum-color and green. The high corsage of the white robe covered the bosom fully, and was caught at the throat with a bunch of blazing jewels. Under these soft draperies, tinkling in time with the movements of an otherwise noiseless tread, there sounded ever the faint note of the little bell. At the toe of shoes otherwise silent, there peeped in and out the flash of diamonds, and in the dark masses of her hair, shifting as she trod beneath each new sconce in turn, and catching more and more brilliance as she advanced, there smoldered the flame of a mass of scintillating gems. A queen's raiment was that of this unknown beauty, and she herself might have been a queen as she swept down the great hall, scornfully careless of the eyes of those other beauties.

She stepped to the place at the regent's right hand, with head high and eyes undrooping. For a dramatic instant she paused, as though in the rehearsal of a part—a part of which it might be said that the regent was not alone the author. This triumph of woman over other women, this triumph of vice over other vice, of effrontery over effrontery akin—this could not have been so planned and executed by any but a woman. One another these beauties might tolerate, knowing one another's frailties as they did; yet the elegance, the disdain, the indifference of this newcomer—this they could not support. Hatred sat in the bosom of each woman there as she swept her courtesy to the new guest of the regent, who took her place as of right at the head of the board and near the regent's arm.

"Our gentlemen are somewhat late this evening," exclaimed Philippe. "'Tis too bad the Abbe Dubois could not be with us to-night to administer clerical consolation."

"Ah! *le drole* Dubois!" exclaimed Madame de Tencin.

"And that vagabond, the Due de Richelieu—but we may not wait. Again ladies, the glasses, or Bechamel will be aggrieved. And finally, though I perceive most of you have graciously unmasked, let me say that the moment has now arrived when we make plain all secrets."

He turned his gaze upon the woman at his right. As though at a signal, she half rose, unclasped the circlet of gems at her throat, and swept back across the arm of her chair the soft garment which enveloped her.

A sigh, a long breath of amazement broke from those other dames of Paris. Not one of them but was sated with the blaze of diamonds, the rich, red light of rubies and the fathomless radiance of sapphires. Silks and satins and cloth of gold and silver had few novelties for them. The costumers of Paris, center of the world of art, even in those times of unrivaled extravagance and unbridled self-gratification, held no new surprise for these beauties, possessed so long of all that their imagination required or that princely liberality could supply. Yet here indeed was a surprise.

As she stood at the regent's right, calmly and composedly looking down the long board as she arranged her drapery before reseating herself, this new favorite of the regent appeared in the full costume of the American native! A long soft tunic of exquisitely dressed white leather fell below her hips, intricately embroidered in the native bead work of America, and stained with great blotches of colors done in the quills of the porcupine—heavy reds, sprightly yellows, and deep blues. Down the seams of this loose-fitting tunic depended little waving fringes. The belt which caught it at the waist was wrought likewise in beads. Beneath the level of the table, as she stood, the inquiring eyes might not so clearly see; yet the white leggings, fringed and beaded, and covered by a sweeping blanket of snowy buckskin, might have been seen to finish at the ankle and blend in texture and ornamentation with tiny shoes, which covered the smallest foot yet seen in Paris—shoes at the side of which there dangled the little bells of metal whose tones had told her coming.

Here and there upon the bead work of the native artist, who had made this attire at the expense of so much patient effort, there blazed the changing rays of real gems, diamonds, rubies, emeralds—every stone known as precious. As the full bosom of the scornful beauty rose and fell there were cast about in sprays of light the reflections of these gems. Bracelets of dull, beaten metal hung about her wrists. In her hair were ornaments of some dull blue stone. Barbaric, beautiful, fascinating, savage she surely seemed as she met unruffled the startled gaze of these beautiful women of the court, who never, at even the most fanciful *bal masque* in all Paris, had seen costume like to this.

"Ladies, *la voila!*" spoke the regent. "*Ma belle sauvage!*"

The newcomer swept a careless courtesy as she took her seat. As yet she had spoken no word. The door at the lower end of the hall opened.

"His Grace le Duc de Richelieu," announced the attendant, who stood beneath the board.

There advanced into the room, with slouchy, ill-bred carriage, a young man whose sole reputation was that of being the greatest rake in Paris, the Duc de Richelieu, half-gamin, half-nobleman, who counted more victims among titled ladies than he had fingers on his hands, whose sole concern of living was to plan some new impassioned avowal, some new and pitiless abandonment. This creature, meeting the salute of the regent, and catching at the same moment a view of the regent's guest, found eyes for nothing else, and stood boldly gazing at the face of her whom Paris knew for the first time and under no more definite title than that of "*Belle Sauvage.*"

"Pray you, be seated, Monsieur le Duc," said the regent, calmly, and the latter was wise enough to comply.

"Your Grace," said Madame de Sabran, "was it not understood that we were to meet to-night none less than the wizard, Monsieur L'as?"

"Monsieur L'as will be with us, and his brother," replied Philippe. "But now I ask you to bear witness to the shrewdness of your friend Philippe in entertainment. I bethought me that, as we were to have with us the master of the Messasebe, it were well to have with us also the typified genius of that same Messasebe. 'Twas but a little conceit of my own. And why—*mon enfant*, what is it to you? What do you know of our controller of finance?"

The face of the woman at his right had suddenly gone white with a pallor visible even beneath its rouge and patches. She half turned, as though to push back her chair from the board, would have arisen, would have spoken perhaps; yet act and gesture were at the time unnoticed.

"His Excellency, Monsieur Jean L'as, *le controleur-general,*" came the soft tones of the attendant near the door. "Monsieur Guillaume L'as, brother of the *controleur-general.*"

The eyes of all were turned toward the door.. Every petted bolle of Paris there assembled shifted bodily in her seat, turning her gaze upon that man whose reputation was the talk of all the realm of France.

There appeared now the tall, erect and vigorous form of a man owning a superb physical beauty. Powerful, yet not too heavy for ease, his figure retained that elasticity and grace which had won him favor in more than one court of Europe. He himself might have been king as he advanced steadily up the brilliantly-illuminated room. His costume, simply made, yet of the richest materials of the time; his wig, highly powdered though of modest proportions; his every item of apparel appeared alike of great simplicity and barren of pretentiousness. As much might be said for the garb of his brother, who stepped close behind him, a figure less self-contained than that of the man who now occupied the absorbed attention of the public mind, even as he now filled the eager eyes of those who turned to greet his entrance.

"Ah, Monsieur L'as, Monsieur L'as!" exclaimed Philippe of Orleans, stepping forward to welcome him and taking the hand of Law in both his own. "You are welcome, you are very welcome indeed. The soup will be with us presently, and the wine of Ai is with us now. You and your brother are with us; so all at last is well. These ladies are, as I believe, all within your acquaintance. You have been present at the *salon* of Madame de Tencin. You know her Grace the Duchesse de Falari, recently Madame d'Artague? Mademoiselle de Caylus you know very well, and of course also Mademoiselle Aisse, *la belle Circassienne*—But what? *Diable!* Have you too gone mad? Come, is the sight of my guest too much for you also, Monsieur L'as?"

There was irritation in the tone with which the regent uttered this protest, yet he continued.

"Monsieur L'as, 'tis but a little surprise I had planned for you. Mademoiselle, my princess of the Messasebe, let me present Monsieur Jean L'as, king of the Messasebe, and hence your sovereign! This is my fair unknown, whose face I have promised you should see to-night—this, Monsieur L'as, is my princess, the one whom I have seen fit to honor this evening by the wearing of the chief gem of France."

The regent fumbled for an instant at his fob. He stepped to the side of the faltering figure which stood arrayed in all its savage finery. One movement, and upon the dark locks which fell about her brow there blazed the unspeakable fires of a stone whose magnificence brought forth exclamations of awe from every person present.

"See!" cried Philippe of Orleans. "'Twas on the advice and by the aid of Monsieur L'as that I secured the gem, whose like is not known in all the world. 'Tis chief of the crown jewels of the realm of France, this stone, now to be known as the regent's diamond. And now, as regent of France and master for a day of her jewels, I place this gem upon the brow of her who for this night is to be your queen of beauty!"

Emerson Hough

The wine of Ai had already done part of its work. There were brightened eyes, easy gestures and ready compliance as the guests arose to quaff the toast to this new queen.

As for the queen herself, she stood faltering, her eyes averted, her limbs trembling. John Law, tall, calm, self-possessed, did not take his seat, but stood with set, fixed face, gazing at the woman who held the place of honor at the table of the regent.

"Come! Come!" cried the latter, testily, his wine working in his brain. "Why stand you there, Monsieur L'as, gazing as though spellbound? Salute, sir, as I do, the chief gem of France, and her who is most fit to wear it!"

John Law stood, as though he had not heard him speak. There swept through the softly brilliant air, over the flash and glitter of the great banquet board, across the little group which stood about it, a sudden sense of a strange, tense, unfamiliar situation. There came to all a presentiment of some unusual thing about to happen. Instinctively the hands paused, even as they raised the bright and brimming glasses. The eyes of all turned from one to the other, from the stern-faced man to the woman decked in barbaric finery, who now stood trembling, drooping, at the head of the table.

Law for a moment removed his gaze from the face of the regent's guest. He flicked lightly at the deep cuff of lace which hung about his hands. "Your Grace is not far wrong," said he. "I regret that you do not have your way in planning for me a surprise. Yet I must say to you, that I have already met this lady."

"What?" cried the regent. "You have met her? Impossible! Incredible! How, Monsieur L'as? We will admit you wizard enough, and owner of the philosopher's stone—owner of anything you like, except this secret of mine own. According to mademoiselle's own words, it would have been impossible."

"None the less, what I have said is true," said John Law, calmly, his voice even and well-modulated, vibrating a little, yet showing no trace of anger nor of emotional uncontrol.

"But I tell you it could not be!" again exclaimed the regent.

"No, it is impossible," broke in the young Duc de Richelieu. "I would swear that had such beauty ever set foot in Paris before now, the news would so have spread that all France had been at her feet."

Law looked at the impudent youth with a gaze that seemed to pass through him, seeing him not. Then suddenly this scene and its significance, its ultimate meaning seemed to take instant hold upon him. He could feel rising within his soul a flood of irresistible emotions. All at once his anger, heritage of an impetuous youth, blazed up hot and furious. He trod a step farther forward, after his fashion advancing close to that which threatened him.

"This lady, your Grace," said he, "has been known to me for years. Mary Connynge, what do you masquerading here?"

A sudden silence fell, a silence broken at length by the voice of the regent himself.

"Surely, Monsieur L'as," said Philippe, "surely we must accept your statements. But Monsieur must remember that this is the table of the regent, that these are the friends of the regent. We bring no recollections here which shall cut short the joy of any person. Sir, I would not reprimand you, but I must beg that you be seated and be calm!"

Yet the imperious nature of the other brooked not even so pointed a rebuke. As though he had not heard, Law stepped yet a pace nearer to the woman, upon whom he now bent the blaze of his angered eyes. He looked neither to right nor left, but visually commanded the woman until in turn her eyes sought his own.

"This woman, your Grace," said Law, at length, "was for some time in effect my wife. This I do not offer as matter of interest. What I would say to your Grace is this—she was also my slave!"

"Sirrah!" cried the regent.

"Ah, Dame!" exclaimed the Duc de Richelieu. And even from the women about there came little murmurs of expostulation. Indeed there might have been pity, even in this assemblage, for the agony now visible upon the brow of Mary Connynge.

"Monsieur, the wine has turned your head," said the regent scornfully. "You boast!"

"I boast of nothing," cried Law, savagely, his voice now ringing with a tone none present had ever known it to assume. "I say to you again, this woman was my slave, and that she will again do as I shall choose. Your Grace, she would come and wipe the dust from my shoes if I should command it! She would kneel at my feet, and beg of me, if I should command it! Shall I prove this, your Grace?"

"Oh, assuredly!" replied the regent, with a sarcasm which now seemed his only relief. "Assuredly, if Monsieur L'as should please. We here in Paris are quite his humble servants."

Law said nothing. He stood with his biting blue eyes still fixed upon Mary Connynge, whose own eyes faltered, trying their utmost to escape from his; whose fingers, resting just lightly on the snowy Hollands of the table cloth, moved tremulously; whose limbs appeared ready to sink beneath her.

"Come, then, Mary Connynge!" cried Law at last, his teeth setting savagely together. "Come, then, traitress and slave, and kneel before me, as you did once before!"

Then there ensued a strange and horrible spectacle. A hush as of death fell upon the group. Mary Connynge, trembling, halting, yet always advancing, did indeed as her master had bidden! She passed from the head of the table, back of the chair of the regent, who stood gazing with horror in his eyes; she passed the chair of Aisse, near which Law now stood; she paused in front of him, and stood as though in a dream. Her knees would have indeed sunk beneath her. She drew from her bosom a silken kerchief, as though she would indeed have performed the ignoble service which had been threatened for her. There came neither voice nor motion to those who saw this thing. The sheer force of one strong nature, terrible in the intensity of one supreme moment—this might have been the spell which commanded at the table of the regent. Yet this did occur.

There came a sound which broke the silence, which caused all to start as with swift relief. A sob, short, dry, hard, as from one whose heart is broken, came from beyond the place where Law stood facing the trembling woman. The eyes of all turned upon Will Law, from whom had burst this irrepressible exclamation of agony. Will Law, as one grown swiftly old, haggard, broken-down, stood gazing in wide-eyed horror at this woman, so humiliated in the presence of all in this brilliantly-lighted hall; before the blazing mirrors which should have reflected back naught but beauty and joy; under the twining roses, which should have been the signs manual of undying love; under the smiling cherubs, which should have typified the deities of happy love. Will Law, too, had loved. Perhaps still he loved.

This sharp sound served to break also the spell under which Law himself seemed held. He cast aloft his arms, as in remorse or in despair. Then he extended a hand to the woman who would have sunk before him.

"God forgive me! Madam," he cried. "I had forgot. Savage indeed you are and have been, but 'tis not for me to treat you brutally."

"Your Grace," said he, turning toward the regent, "I crave your pardon. Our explanations shall reach you on the morrow."

He turned, and taking his brother by the arm, advanced toward the door at which he had recently entered, pausing not to look behind him. Had his eye been more curious as he and his half-fainting brother bowed before passing through the door, it might have seen that which he must long have borne in memory.

Mary Connynge, trembling, pallid, utterly broken, never found her way back to the right hand of the regent. She half stumbled into a chair near the foot of the table. Her bosom fluttered at the base of the throat. Half blindly she reached out her hand toward a glass of wine which stood near by, foaming and sparkling, its gem-like drops of keen pungency swimming continuously up to the surface. Her hand caught at the slender stem of the glass. Leaning upon her left arm, she half rose as though to put it to her lips. Her head moved, as though she would follow the retreating figure of the man who had thus scornfully used her. All at once, slowly, and then with a sudden crash, she sank down upon her seat and fell forward across the table. The fragile glass snapped in her fingers. The amber wine rushed in swift flood across the linen. In the broadening stain there fell and lay blazing the great gem of France.

CHAPTER IX

THE NEWS

"Lady Kitty! Lady Kitty! Have you heard the news?"

Thus, breathless, the Countess of Warrington, Lady Catharine's English neighbor in exile, who burst into the drawing-room early in the morning, not waiting for announcement of her presence.

"Nay, not yet, my dear," said Lady Catharine, advancing and embracing her. "What is it, pray? Has the poodle swallowed a bone, or the baby perhaps cut another tooth? And, forsooth, how is the little one?"

Lady Emily Warrington, slender, elegant, well clad, and for the most part languorously calm, was in a state of excitement quite without her customary *aplomb*. She sank into a seat, fanning herself with a vigor which threatened ruin to the precious slats of a fan which bore the handiwork of Watteau.

"The streets are full of it," said she. "Have you not heard, really?"

"I must say, not yet. But what is it?"

"Why, the quarrel between the regent and his director-general, Mr. Law."

"No, I have not heard of it." Lady Catharine sought refuge behind her own fan. "But tell me" she continued.

"But that is not all. 'Twas the reason for the quarrel. Paris is all agog. 'Twas about a woman!"

"You mean—there was—a woman?"

"Yes, it all happened last night, at the Palais Royal. The woman is dead—died last night. 'Tis said she fell in a fit at the very table—'twas at a little supper given by the regent—and that when they came to her she was quite dead."

"But Mr. Law—"

"'Twas he that killed her!"

"Good God! What mean you?" cried Lady Catharine, her own face blanching behind her protecting fan. The blood swept back upon her heart, leaving her cold as a statue.

"Why," continued the caller, in her own excitement to tell the news scarce noting what went on before her, "it seems that this mysterious beauty of the regent's, of whom there has been so much talk, proved to be none other than a former mistress of this same Mr. Law, who is reputed to have been somewhat given to that sort of thing, though of late monstrous virtuous, for some cause or other. Mr. Law came suddenly upon her at the table of the regent, arrayed in some kind of savage finery—for 'twas in fashion a mask that evening, as you must know. And what doth my director-general do, so high and mighty? Why, in spite of the regent and in spite of all those present, he upbraids her, taunts her, reviles her, demanding that she fall on her knees before him, as it seems indeed she would have done—as, forsooth, half the dames of Paris would do to-day! Then, all of a sudden, my Lord Director changes, and he craves pardon of the woman and of the regent, and so stalks off and leaves the room! And now then the poor creature walks to the table, would lift a glass of wine, and so—'tis over! 'Twas like a play! Indeed all Paris is like a play nowadays. Of course you know the rest."

A gesture of negative came from the hand that lay in Lady Catharine's lap. The busy gossip went on.

"The regent, be sure, was angry enough at this cheapening of his own wares before all, and perhaps 'tis true he had a fancy for the woman. At any rate, 'tis said that this very morning he quarreled hotly with Mr. Law. The latter gave back words hot as he received, and so they had it violent enough. 'Tis stated on the Quinquempoix that another must take Mr. Law's place. But if Mr. Law goes, what will become of the System? And what would the System be without Mr. Law? And what would Paris be without the System? Why, listen, Lady Catharine! I gained fifty thousand livres yesterday, and my coachman, the rascal, in some manner seems to have done quite as well for himself. I doubt not he will yet build a mansion of his own, and perhaps my husband may drive for him! These be strange days indeed. I only hope they may continue, in spite of what my husband says."

"And what says he?" asked Lady Catharine, her own voice sounding to her unfamiliar and far away.

"Why, that the city is mad, and that this soon must end—this Mississippi bubble, as my Lord Stair calls it at the embassy."

"Yet I have heard all France is prosperous."

"Oh, yes indeed. 'Tis said that but yesterday the kingdom paid four millions of its debt to Bavaria, three millions of its debt to Sweden—yet these are not the most pressing debts of France."

"Meaning—"

"Why, the debts of the regent to his friends—those are the important things. But the other day he gave eighty thousand livres to Madame Chateauthiers, as a little present. He gave two hundred thousand livres to the Abbe Something-or-other, who asked for it, and another thousand livres to that rat Dubois. The thief D'Argenson ever counsels him to give in abundance now that he hath abundance, and the regent is ready with a vengeance with his compliance. Saint Simon, that priggish duke, has had a million given him to repay a debt his father took on for the king a generation ago. To the captain of the guard the regent gives six hundred thousand livres, for carrying the fan of the regent's forgotten wife; to the Prince Courtenay, two hundred thousand, most like because the prince said he had need of it; a pension of two hundred thousand annually to the Marquise de Bellefonte, the second such sum, because perhaps she once made eyes at him; a pension of sixty thousand livres to a three-year-old relative to the Prince de Conti, because Conti cried for it; one hundred thousand livres to Mademoiselle Haidee, because she has a consumption; and as much more to the Duchesse de Falari, because she has not a consumption. Bah! The credit of France might indeed, as my husband says, be called leaking through the slats of fans."

"But, look you!" she went on, "how Mr. Law feathers his own nest. He bought lately, for a half million livres, the house of the Comte de Tesse; and on the same day, as you know, the Hotel Mazarin. There is no limit to his buying of estates. This, so says my husband, is the great proof of his honesty. He puts his money here in France, and does not send it over seas. He seems to have no doubt, and indeed no fear, of anything."

Lady Warrington paused, half for want of breath. Silence fell in the great room. A big and busy fly, deep down in the crystal *cylindre* which sheltered a taper on a near-by table, buzzed out a droning protest. The face of Lady Catharine was averted.

"You did not tell me, Lady Emily," said she, with woman's feigned indifference, "what was the name of this poor woman of the other evening."

"Why, so I had forgot—and 'tis said that Mr. Law, after all, comported himself something of the gentleman. No one knows how far back the affair runs, nor how serious it was. And indeed I have seen no one who ever heard of the woman before."

"And the name?"

"'Twas said Mr. Law called her Mary Connynge."

The big fly, deep down in the crystal cage, buzzed on audibly; and to one who heard it, the drone of the lazy wings seemed like the roars of a thousand tempests.

CHAPTER X

MASTER AND MAN

John Law, idle, preoccupied, sat gazing out at the busy scenes of the street before him. The room in which he found himself was one of a suite in that magnificent Hotel de Soisson, bought but recently of the Prince de Carignan for the sum of one million four hundred thousand livres, which had of late been chosen as the temple of Fortuna. The great gardens of this distinguished site were now filled with hundreds of tents and kiosks, which offered quarters for the wild mob of speculators which surged and swirled and fought throughout the narrow avenues, contending for the privilege of buying the latest issue of the priceless shares of the Company of the Indies.

The System was at its height. The bubble was blown to its last limit. The popular delirium had grown to its last possible degree.

From the window these mad mobs of infuriated human beings might have seemed so many little ants, running about as though their home had been destroyed above their heads. They hastened as though fleeing from the breath of some devouring flame. Surely the point of flame was there, at that focus of Paris, this focus of all Europe; and thrice refined was the quality of this heat, burning out the hearts of those distracted ones.

Yet it was a scene not altogether without its fascinations. Hither came titled beauties of Paris, peers of the realm, statesmen, high officials, princes of the blood; all these animated but by one purpose—to bid and outbid for these bits of paper, which for the moment meant wealth, luxury, ease, every imaginable desire. It seemed indeed that the world was mad. Tradesmen, artisans, laborers, peasants, jostled the princes and nobility, nor met reproof. Rank was forgotten. Democracy, for the first time on earth, had arrived. All were equal who held equal numbers of these shares. The mind of each was blank to all but one absorbing theme.

Law looked over this familiar scene, indifferent, calm, almost moody, his cheek against his hand, his elbow on his chair. "What was the call, Henri," asked he, at length, of the old Swiss who had, during these stormy times, been so long his faithful attendant. "What was the last quotation that you heard?"

"Your Honor, there are no quotations," replied the attendant. "'Tis only as one is able to buy. The *actions* of the last issue, three hundred thousand in all, were swept away at a breath at fifteen thousand livres the share."

"Ninety times what their face demands," said Law, impassively.

"True, some ninety times," said the Swiss. "'Tis said that of this issue the regent has taken over one-third, or one hundred thousand, himself. 'Tis this that makes the price of the other two-thirds run the higher, since 'tis all that the public has to buy."

"Lucky regent," said Law, sententiously. "Plenty would seem to have been his fortune!"

He grimly turned again to his study of the crowds which swarmed among the pavilions before his window. Outside his door he heard knockings and cries, and impatient footfalls, but neither he nor the impassive Swiss paid to these the least attention. It was to them an old experience.

"Your Honor, the Prince de Conti is in the antechamber and would see you," at length ventured the attendant, after listening for some time with his ear at an aperture in the door.

"Let the Prince de Conti wait," said Law, "and a plague take him for a grasping miser! He has gained enough. Time was when I waited at his door."

"The Abbe Dubois—here is his message pushed beneath the door."

"My dearest enemy," replied Law, calmly. "The old rat may seek another burrow."

"The Duchesse de la Rochefoucauld."

"Ah, then, she hath overcome her husband's righteousness of resolution, and would beg a share or so? Let her wait. I find these duchesses the most tiresome animals in the world."

"The Madame de Tencin."

"I can not see the Madame de Tencin."

"A score of dukes and foreign princes. My faith! master, we have never had so large a line of guests as come this morning." The stolid impassiveness of the Swiss seemed on the point of giving way.

"Let them wait," replied Law, evenly as before. "Not one of them would listen to me five years ago. Now I shall listen to them—shall listen to them knocking at my door, as I have knocked at theirs. To-day I am aweary, and not of mind to see any one. Let them wait."

"But what shall I say? What shall I tell them, my master?"

"Tell them nothing. Let them wait."

Thus the crowd of notables packed into the anterooms waited at the door, fuming and execrating, yet not departing. They all awaited the magician, each with the same plea—some hope of favor, of advancement, or of gain.

At last there arose yet a greater tumult in the hall which led to the door. A squad of guardsmen pushed through the packed ranks with the cry: "For the king!" The regent of France stood at the closed door of the man who was still the real ruler of France.

"Open, open, in the name of the king!" cried one, as he beat loudly on the panels.

Law turned languidly toward the attendant. "Henri," said he, "tell them to be more quiet."

"My master, 'tis the regent!" expostulated the other, with somewhat of anxiety in his tones.

"Let him wait," replied Law, coolly. "I have waited for him."

"But, my master, they protest, they clamor—"

"Very well. Let them do so—but stay. If it is indeed the regent, I may as well meet him now and say that which is in my mind. Open the door."

The door swung open and there entered the form of Philippe of Orleans, preceded by his halberdiers and followed close by a rush of humanity which the guards and the Swiss together had much pains to force back into the anteroom.

"How now, Monsieur L'as, how now?" fumed the regent, his heavy face glowing a dull red, his prominent eyes still more protruding, his forehead bent into a heavy frown. "You deny entrance to our person, who are next to the body of his Majesty?"

"Did you have delay?" asked Law, sweetly. "'Twas unfortunate."

"'Twas execrable!"

"True. I myself find these crowds execrable."

"Nay, execrable to suffer this annoyance of delay!"

"Your Grace's pardon," said Law, coolly. "You should have made an appointment a few days in advance."

"What! The regent of France need to arrange a day when he would see a servant!"

"Your Grace is unfortunate in his choice of words," replied Law, blandly. "I am not your servant. I am your master."

The regent sank back into a chair, gasping, his hand clutching at the hilt of his sword.

"Seize him! Seize him! To the Bastille with him! The presumer! The impostor!"

Yet even the guards hesitated before the commanding presence of that man whom all had been so long accustomed to obey. With hand upraised, Law gazed at them for one instant, and then gave them no further attention.

"Yet these words I must hasten to qualify," resumed he. "True, I am at this moment your master, your Grace, but two minutes hence, and for all time thereafter, I shall no longer be your master. Your Grace was once so good as to make me head of certain financial matters, and to give me control of them. The fabric of this Messasebe, which you see without, was all my own. It was this which made me master of Paris, and of every man within the gates of Paris. So far, very well. My plans were honest, and the growth of France—nay, let us say the resurrection of France—the new life of France—shows how my own plans were made and how well I knew that which was to happen. I made you rich, your Grace. I gave you funds to pay off millions of your private debts, millions to gratify your fancies. I gave you more millions to pay the debts of France. France and her regent have again taken a position of honor in the eyes of the world. You may well call me master of your fate, who have been able to accomplish these things. So long as you knew your master, you did well. Now your Grace has seen fit to change masters. He would be his own master again. There can not be two in control of a concern like this. Sir, the two minutes hare elapsed. I am your very humble servant!"

The regent still sat staring from his chair, and speech was yet denied him.

"There are your people. There is your France," said Law, beckoning as he turned toward the window and pointing to the crowd without. "There is your France. Now handle it, my master! Here are the reins! Now drive; but see that you be careful how you drive. Come, your Grace," said he, mockingly, over his shoulder. "Come, and see your France!"

The audacity of John Law was a thing without parallel, as had been proved a hundred times in his strange life and in a hundred places. His sheer contemptuous daring brought Philippe of Orleans to his senses. He relaxed now in his purpose, changeable as was his wont, and advanced towards Law with hand outstretched.

"There, there, Monsieur L'as, I did you wrong, perhaps," said he. "But as to these hasty words, pray reconsider them at once. 'Twill have a bad effect should a breath of this get afloat. Indeed, 'twas because of some such thing that I came to see you this morning. A most unspeakable, a most incredible thing hath occurred. It comes to me with certain confirmation that there have been shares sold upon the street at twelve thousand livres to the *action*, whereas, as you very well know, fifteen thousand should be the lowest price to-day."

"And what of that, your Grace?" said Law, calmly. "Is it not what you planned? Is it not what you have been expecting?"

"How, sirrah! What do you mean?"

"Why, I mean this, your Grace," said Law, calmly, "that since you have taken the reins, it is you who must drive the chariot. I shall suggest no plans, shall offer no remedy. But, if you still lack ability to see how and why this thing has attained this situation, I will take so much trouble as to make it plain."

"Go on, then, sir," said the regent. "Is not all well? Is there any danger?"

"As to danger," said Law, "we can not call it a time of danger after the worst has happened."

"What do you mean?"

"Why, that the worst has happened. But, as I was about to say, I shall tell you how it happened."

The gaze of the regent fell. His hand trembled as he fumbled at his sword hilt.

"Your Grace," said Law, calmly, "will do me the kindness to remember that when I first asked of you the charter of the Banque Generale, to be taken privately in the name of myself and my brother, I told you that any banker merited the punishment of death if he issued notes or bills of exchange without having their effective value safe in his own strong boxes."

"Well, what of that?" queried the regent, weakly.

"Nothing, your Grace, except that your Grace deserves the punishment of death."

"How, sir! Good God!"

"If the truth of this matter should ever become known, those people out there, that France yonder, would tear your Grace limb from limb, and trample you in the dust!"

The livid face of the regent went paler as the other spoke. There was conviction in those tones which could not fail to reach even his heavy wits.

"Let me explain," went on Law. "I beg your Grace to remember again, that when your Grace was good enough to take out of the hands of my brother and myself our little bank—which we had run honorably and successfully—you changed at one sweep the whole principle of honest banking. You promised to pay something which was unstipulated. You issued a note back of which there was no value, no fixed limit of measurement. Twice you have changed the coinage of the realm, and twice assigned a new value to your specie. No one can tell what one of your shares in the stock of the Indies means in actual coin. It means nothing, stands for nothing, is good for nothing. Now, think you, when these people, when this France shall discover these facts, that they will be lenient with those who have thus deceived them?"

"Yet your theory always was that we had too great a scarcity of money here in France," expostulated the regent.

"True, so I did. We had not enough of good money. We can not have too little of false money, of money such as your Grace—as you thought without my knowledge—has been so eager to issue from the presses of our Company. It had been an easy thing for the regent of France to pay off all the debts of the world from now until the verge of eternity, had not his presses given out. Money of that sort, your Grace, is such as any man could print for himself, did he but have the linen and the ink."

The regent again dropped to his chair, his head falling forward upon his breast.

"But what does it all mean? What shall be done? What will be the result?" he asked, his voice showing well enough the anxiety which had swiftly fallen upon his soul.

"As to that," replied Law, laconically, "I am no longer master here. I am not controller of finance. Appoint Dubois, appoint D'Argenson. Send for the Brothers Paris. Take them to this window, your Grace, and show them your people, show them your France, and then ask them to tell you what shall be done. Cry out to all the world, as I know you will, that this was the fault of an unknown adventurer, of a Scotch gambler, of one John Law, who brought forth some pretentious schemes to the detriment of the realm. Saddle upon me the blame for all this ruin which is coming. Malign me, misrepresent me, imprison me, exile me, behead me if you like, and blame John Law for the discomfiture of France! But when you come to seek your remedies, why, ask no more of John Law. Ask of Dubois, ask of D'Argenson, ask of the Paris Freres; or, since your Grace has seen fit to override me and to take these matters in his own hands, let your Grace ask of himself! Tell me, as regent of France, as master of Paris, as guardian of the rights of this young king, as controller of the finances of France, as savior or destroyer of the welfare of these people of France and of that America which is greater than this France—tell me, what will you do, your Grace? What do you suggest as remedy?"

"You devil! you arch fiend!" exclaimed the regent, starting up and laying his hand on his sword. "There is no punishment you do not deserve! You will leave me in this plight—you—you, who have supplanted me at every turn; you who made that horrible scene but last night at my own table, within the very gates of the Palais Royal; you, the murderer of the woman I adored! And now, you mocker and flouter of what may be my bitterest misfortune—why, sir, no punishment is sharp enough for you! Why do you stand there, sir? Do you dare to mock me—to mock us, the person of the king?"

"I mock not in the least, your Grace," said John Law, "nor do aught else that ill beseems a gentleman. I should have been proud to be known as the friend of Philippe of Orleans, yet I stand before that Philippe of Orleans and tell him that that man doth not live, nor that set of terrors exist, which can frighten John Law, nor cause him to depart from that stand which he once has taken. Sir, if you seek to frighten me, you fail."

"But, look you—consider," said the regent. "Something must be done."

"As I said," replied Law.

"But what is going to happen? What will the people do?"

"First," said Law, judicially, flicking at the deep lace of his cuff as though he were taking into consideration the price of a wig or cane, "first, the price of a share having gone to twelve thousand livres this morning, by two o'clock will be so low as ten thousand. By three o'clock this afternoon it will be six thousand. Then, your Grace, there will be panic. Then the spell will be broken. France will rub her eyes and begin to awaken. Then, since the king can do no wrong, and since the regent is the king, your Grace can do one of two things. He can send a body-guard to watch my door, or he can see John Law torn into fragments, as these people would tear the real author of their undoing, did they but recognize him."

"But can nothing be done to stop this? Can it not be accommodated?"

"Ask yourself. But I must go on to say what these people will do. All at once they will demand specie for their notes. The Prince de Conti will drive his coaches to the door of your bank, and demand that they be loaded with gold. Jacques and Raoul and Pierre, and every peasant and pavior in Paris will come with boxes and panniers, and each of them will also demand his gold. Make edicts, your Grace. Publish broadcast and force out into publicity, on every highway of France, your decree that gold and silver are not so good as your bank notes; that no one must have gold or silver; that no one must send his gold and silver out of France, but that all must bring it to the king and take for it in exchange these notes of yours. Try that. It ought to succeed, ought it not, your Grace?" His bantering tone sank into one of half plausibility.

"Why, surely. That would be the solution."

"Oh, think you so? Your Grace is wondrous keen as a financier! Now take the counsel of Dubois, of D'Argenson, my very good friends. This is what they will counsel you to do. And I will counsel you at the same time to avail yourself of their advice. Tell all France to bring in its gold, to enable you to put something essential under the value of all this paper money which you have been sending out so lavishly, so unthinkingly, so without stint or measure."

"Yes. And then?"

"Why, then, your Grace," said Law, "then we shall see what we shall see!"

The regent again choked with anger. Law continued. "Go on. Smooth down the back of this animal. Continue to reduce these taxes. The specie of the realm of France, as I am banker enough to know, is not more than thirteen hundred millions of livres, allowing sixty-five livres to the marc. Yet long before this your Grace has crowded the issue of our *actions* until there are out not less than twenty-six hundred millions of livres in the stock of our Company. Your Brothers Paris, your D'Argenson, your Dubois will tell you how you can make the people of France continue to believe that twice two is not four, that twice thirteen is not twenty-six!"

"But this they are doing," broke in the regent, with a ray of hope in his face. "This they are doing. We have provided for that. In the council not an hour ago the Abbe Dubois and Monsieur d'Argenson decided that the time had come to make some fixed proportion between the specie and these notes. We have to-day framed an edict, which the Parliament will register, stating that the interests of the subjects of the king require that the price of these bank notes should be lessened, so that there may be some sort of accommodation between them and the coin of the realm. We have ordered that the shares shall, within thirty days, drop to seventy-five hundred livres, in another thirty days to seven thousand livres, and so on, at five hundred livres a month, until at last they shall have a value of one-half what they were to-day. Then, tell me, my wise Monsieur L'as, would not the issue of our notes and the total of our specie be equal, one with the other? The only wrong thing is this insulting presumption of these people, who have sold *actions* at a price lower than we have decreed."

Law smiled as he replied. "You say excellently well, my master. These plans surely show that you and your able counselors have studied deeply the questions of finance! I have told you what would happen to-day without any decree of the king. Now go you on, and make your decrees. You will find that the people are much more eager for values which are going up than values which are going down. Start your shares down hill, and you will see all France scramble for such coin, such plate, such jewels as may be within the ability of France to lay her hands upon. Tell me, your Grace, did Monsieur d'Argenson advise you this morning as to the total issue of the *actions* of this Company?"

"Surely he did, and here I have it in memorandum, for I was

to have taken it up with yourself," replied the regent.

"So," exclaimed Law, a look of surprise passing over his countenance, until now rigidly controlled, as he gazed at the little slip of paper. "Your Grace advises me that there are issued at this time in the shares of the Company no less than two billion, two hundred and thirty-five million, eighty-five thousand, five hundred and ninety livres in notes! Against this, as your Grace is good enough to agree with me, we have thirteen hundred millions of specie. Your Grace, yourself and I have seen some pretty games in our day. Look you, the merriest game of all your life is now but just before you!"

"And you would go and leave me at this time?"

"Never in my life have I forsaken a friend at the time of distress," replied Law. "But your Grace absolved me when you forsook me, when you doubted and hesitated regarding me, and believed the protestations of those not so able as myself to judge of what was best. And now it is too late. Will your Grace allow me to suggest that a place behind stout gates and barred doors, deep within the interior of the Palais Royal, will be the best residence for him to-night—perhaps for several nights to come?"

"And yourself?"

"As for myself, it does not matter," replied Law, slowly and deliberately. "I have lived, and I thought I had succeeded. Indeed, success was mine for some short months, though now I must meet failure. I have this to console me—that 'twas failure not of my own fault. As for France, I loved her. As for America, I believe in her to-day, this very hour. As for your Grace in person, I was your friend, nor was I ever disloyal to you. But it sometimes doth seem that, no matter how sincere be one in one's endeavors, no matter how cherished, no matter how successful for a time may be his ambitions, there is ever some little blight to eat the face of the full fruit of his happiness. To-morrow I shall perhaps not be alive. It is very well. There is nothing I could desire, and it is as well to-morrow as at any time."

"But surely, Monsieur L'as," interrupted the regent, with a trace of his old generosity, "if there should be outbreak, as you fear, I shall, of course, give you a guard. I shall indeed see you safe out of the city, if you so prefer, though I had much liefer you would remain and try to help us undo this coil, wherein I much misdoubt myself."

"Your Grace, I am a disappointed man, a man with nothing in the world to comfort him. I have said that I would not help you, since 'twas yourself brought ruin on my plans, and cast down that work which I had labored all my life to finish. Yet I will advise this, as being your most immediate plan. Smooth down this France as best you may. Remit more taxes, as I said. Depreciate the value of these shares gently, but rapidly as you can. Institute great numbers of perpetual annuities. Juggle, temporize, postpone, get for yourself all the time you can. Trade for the people's shares all you have that they will take. You can never strike a balance, and can never atone for the egregious error of this over-issue of stock which has no intrinsic value. Eventually you may have to declare void many of these shares and withdraw from the currency these *actions* for which so recently the people have been clamoring."

"That means repudiation!" broke in the regent.

"Certainly, your Grace, and in so far your Grace has my extremest sympathy. I know it was your resolve not to repudiate the debts of France, as those debts stood when I first met you some years ago. That was honorable. Yet now the debts of France are immeasurably greater, rich as France thinks herself to be. Not all France, were the people and the produce of the commerce counted in the coin, could pay the debt of France as it now exists. Hence, honorable or not, there is nothing else—it is repudiation which now confronts you. France is worse than bankrupt. And now it would seem wise if your Grace took immediate steps, not only for the safety of his person, but for the safety of the Government."

"Sir, do you mean that the people would dare, that they would presume—"

"The people are not what they were. There hath come into Europe the leaven of the New World. I had looked there to see a nobler and a better France. It is too late for that, and surely it is too late for the old ways of this France which we see about us. You can not presume now upon the temper of these folk as you might have done fifty years ago. The Messasebe, that noble stream, it hath swept its purifying flood throughout the world! Look you, at this moment there is tumbling this house which we have built of bubbles, one bubble upon another, blowing each bubble bigger and thinner than the last. Mine is not the only fault, nor yet the greatest fault. I was sincere, where others cared naught for sincerity. Another day, another people, may yet say the world was better for my effort, and that therefore at the last I have not failed."

CHAPTER XI

THE BREAKING OF THE BUBBLE

It was the evening of the day following that on which John Law and the regent of France had met in their stormy interview. During the morning but little had transpired regarding the significant events of the previous day. In these vast and excited crowds, divided into groups and cliques and factions, aided by no bulletins, counseled by no printed page, there was but little cohesion of purpose, since there was little unity of understanding. The price of shares at one kiosk might be certain thousands of livres, whereas a square away, the price might vary by half as many livres; so impetuous was the advance of these continually rising prices, and so frenzied and careless the temper of those who bargained for them.

Yet before noon of the day following the decree of the regent, which fixed the value of *actions* upon a descending scale, the news, after a fashion of its own, spread rapidly abroad, and all too swiftly the truth was generally known. The story started in a rumor that shares had been offered and declined at a price which had been current but a few moments before. This was something which had not been known in all these feverish months of the Messasebe. Then came the story that shares could not be counted upon to realize over eight thousand livres. At that the price of all the *actions* dropped in a flash, as Law had prophesied. A sudden wave of sanity, a panic chill of sober understanding swept over this vast multitude of still unreasoning souls who had traded so long upon this impossible supposition of an ever-advancing market. Reason still lacked among them, yet fear and sudden suspicion were not wanting. Man after man hastened swiftly away to sell privately his shares before greater drop in the price might come. He met others upon the same errand.

Precisely the reverse of the old situation now obtained. As all Paris had fought to buy, so now all Paris fought to sell. The streets were filled with clamoring mobs. If earlier there had been confusion, now there was pandemonium. Never was such a scene witnessed. Never was there chronicled so swift and utter reversion of emotion in the minds of a great concourse of people. Bitter indeed was the wave of agony that swept over Paris. It began at the Messasebe, in the gardens of the Hotel de Soisson, at that focus hard by the temple of Fortuna. It spread and spread, edging out into all the remoter portions of the walled city. It reached ultimately the extreme confines of Paris. Into the crowded square which had been decreed as the trading-place of the Messasebe System, there crowded from the outer purlieus yet other thousands of excited human beings. The end had come. The bubble had burst. There was no longer any System of the Messasebe!

It was late in the day, in fact well on toward might, when the knowledge of the crash came into the neighborhood where dwelt the Lady Catharine Knolls. To her the news was brought by a servant, who excitedly burst unannounced into her mistress's presence.

"Madame! Madame!" she cried. "Prepare! 'Tis horrible! 'Tis

impossible! All is at an end!"

"What mean you, girl!" cried Lady Catharine, displeased at the disrespect. "What is happening? Is there fire? And even if there were, could you not remember your duty more seemly than this?"

"Worse, worse than fire, Madame! Worse than anything! The bank has failed! The shares of the System are going down! 'Tis said that we can get but three thousand livres the share, perhaps less—perhaps they will go down to nothing. I am ruined, ruined! We are all ruined! And within the month I was to have been married to the footman of the Marquis d'Allouez, who has bought himself a title this very week!"

"And if it has fallen so ill," said Lady Catharine, "since I have not speculated in these things like most folk, I shall be none the worse for it, and shall still have money to pay your wages. So perhaps you can marry your marquis after all."

"But we shall not be rich, Madame! We are ruined, ruined! *Mon Dieu*! we poor folk! We had the hope to be persons of quality. 'Tis all the work of this villain Jean L'as. May the Bastille get him, or the people, and make him pay for this!"

"Stop! Enough of this, Marie!" said the Lady Catharine, sternly. "After this have better wisdom, and do not meddle in things which you do not understand."

Yet scarce had the girl departed before there appeared again the sound of running steps, and presently there broke, equally unannounced, into the presence of his mistress, the coachman, fresh from his stables and none too careful of his garb. Tears ran down his cheeks. He flung out his hands with gestures as of one demented.

"The news!" cried he. "The news, my Lady! The horrible news! The System has vanished, the shares are going down!"

"Fellow, what do you here?" said Lady Catharine. "Why do you come with this same story which Marie has just brought to me? Can you not learn your place?"

"But, my Lady, you do not understand!" reiterated the man, blankly. "'Tis all over. There is no Messasebe; there is no longer any System, no longer any Company of the Indies. There is no longer wealth for the stretching out of the hand. 'Tis all over. I must go back to horses—I, Madame, who should presently have associated with the nobility!"

"Well, and if so," replied his mistress, "I can say to you, as I have to Marie, that there will still be money for your wages."

"Wages! My faith, what trifles, my Lady! This Monsieur L'as, the director-general, he it is who has ruined us! Well enough it is that the square in front of his hotel is filled with people! Presently they will break down his doors. And then, pray God they punish him for this that he has done!"

The cheek of Lady Catharine paled and a sudden flood of contending emotions crossed her mind. "You do not tellme that Monsieur L'as is in danger, Pierre?" said she.

"Assuredly. Perhaps within the very hour they will tear down his doors and rend him limb from limb. There is no punishment which can serve him right—him who has ruined our pretty, pretty System. *Mon Dieu*! It was so beautiful!"

"Is this news certain?"

"Assuredly, most certain. Why should it not be? The entire square in front of the Hotel de Soisson is packed. Unless my

Lady needs me, I myself must hasten thither to aid in the punishment of this Jean L'as!"

"You will stay here," said Lady Catharine. "Wait! There may be need! For the present, go!"

Left alone, Lady Catharine stood for a moment pale and motionless, in the center of the room. She strode then to the window and stood looking fixedly out. Her whole figure was tense, rigid. Yonder, over there, across the gabled roofs of Paris, they were clamoring at the door of him who had given back Paris to the king, and Franceagain to its people. They were assailing him—this man so long unfaltering, so insistent on his ambitions, so—so steadfast! Could she call him steadfast? And they would seize him in spite of the courage which she knew would never fail. They would kill, they would rend, they would trample him! They would crush that glorious body, abase the lips that had spoke so well of love!

The clenched fingers of Lady Catharine broke apart, her arms were flung wide in a gesture of resolution. She turned from the window, looking here and there about the room. Unconsciously she stopped before the great cheval-glass that hung against the wall. She stood there, looking at her own image, keenly, deeply.

She saw indeed a woman fit for sweet usages of love, comely and rounded, deep-bosomed, her oval face framed in the piled masses of glorious red-brown hair. But her wide, blue eyes, scarce seeing this outward form, stared into the soul of that other whom she witnessed.

It was as though the Lady Catharine Knollys at last saw another self and recognized it! A quick, hard sob broke from her throat. In haste she flew, now to one part of the room, now to another, picking up first this article and then that which seemed of need. And so at last she hurried to the bell-cord.

"Quick," cried she, as the servant at length appeared. "Quick! Do not delay an instant! My carriage at once!"

CHAPTER XII

THAT WHICH REMAINED

As for John Law, all through that fatal day which meant for him the ruin of his ambitions, he continued in the icy calm which, for days past, had distinguished him. He discontinued his ordinary employments, and spent some hours in sorting and destroying numbers of papers and documents. His faithful servant, the Swiss, Henri, he commanded to make ready his apparel for a journey.

"At six this evening," said he, "Henri, we shall be ready to depart. Let us be quite ready well before that time."

"Monsieur is leaving Paris?" asked the Swiss, respectfully.

"Quite so."

"Perhaps for a stay of some duration?"

"Quite so, indeed, Henri."

"Then, sir," expostulated the Swiss, "it would require a day or so for me to properly arrange your luggage."

"Not at all," replied Law. "Two valises will suffice, not

Emerson Hough

more, and I shall perhaps not need even these."

"Not all the apparel, the many coats, the jewels—"

"Do not trouble over them."

"But what disposition shall I make—?"

"None at all. Leave all these things as they are. But stay—this package which I shall prepare for you—take it to the regent, and have it marked in his care and for the Parliament of France."

Law raised in his hands a bundle of parchments, which one by one he tore across, throwing the fragments into a basket as he did so.

"The seat of Tancarville," he said. "The estate of Berville; the Hotel Mazarin; the lands of Bourget; the Marquisat of Charleville; the lands of Orcher; the estate of Roissy—Gad! what a number of them I find."

"But, Monsieur," expostulated the Swiss, "what is that you do? Are these not your possessions?"

"Not so, *mon ami*," replied Law. "They once were mine. They are estates in France. Take back these deeds. Dead Sully may have his own again, and each of these late owners of the lands. I wished them for a purpose. That purpose is no longer possible, and now I wish them no more. Take back your deeds, my friends, and bear in your minds that John Law tore them in two, and thus canceled the obligation."

"But the moneys you have paid—they are enormous. Surely you will exact restitution?"

"Sirrah, could I not afford these moneys?"

"Admirably at the time," replied the Swiss, with the freedom of long service. "But for the future, what do we know? Besides, it is a matter of right and justice."

"Ah, *mon ami*" said Law, "right and justice are no more. But since you speak of money, let us take precautions as to that. We shall need some money for our journey. See, Henri! Take this note and get the money which it calls for. But no! The crowd may be too great. Look in the drawer of my desk yonder, and take out what you find."

The Swiss did as he was bidden, but at length returned with troubled face.

"Monsieur," said he, "I can find but a hundred louis."

"Put half of it back," said Law. "We shall not need so much."

"But, Monsieur, I do not understand."

"We shall not need more than fifty louis. That is enough. Leave the rest," said Law. "Leave it where you found it"

"But for whom? Does Monsieur soon return?"

"No. Leave it for him who may be first to find it. These dear people without, these same people whom I have enriched, and who now will claim that I have impoverished them— these people will demand of me everything that I have. As a man of honor I can not deny them. They shall have every Jot and stiver of the property of John Law, even the million or so of good coin which he brought here to Paris with him. The coat on my back, the wheels beneath me, gold enough to pay for the charges of the inns through France—that is all that

John Law will take away with him."

The arms of the old servant fell helpless at his side. "Sir, this is madness," he expostulated.

"Not so, Henri," replied Law, leniently. "Madness enough there has been in Paris, it is true, but madness not mine nor of my making. For madness, look you yonder."

He pointed a finger through the window where the stately edifice of the Palais Royal rose.

"My good friend the regent—it is he who hath been mad," continued Law. "He, holding France in trust, has ruined France forever."

"Monsieur, I grieve for you," said the Swiss. "I have seen your success in these years and, as you may imagine, have understood something of your affairs as time went on."

"And have you not profited by your knowledge in these times?"

"I have had the salary your Honor has agreed to pay me," replied the Swiss.

"And no more?"

"No more."

"Why, there are serving folk in France by the hundreds who have grown millionaires by the knowledge of their employers' affairs these last two years in Paris. Never was such a time in all the world for making money. Have you been more blind than they? Why did you not tell me? Why did you not ask?"

"I was content with your employment. Monsieur L'as. I would ask no better master."

"It is not so with certain others. They think me a hard master enough, and having displaced me, will do all they can to punish me. But now, Henri, you will perhaps need to look elsewhere for a master. I am going far away—perhaps across the seas. It may he—but I know not where and care not where my foot may wander hereafter, nor will I seek now to plan for it. As for you, Henri, since you admit you have been thus blind to your own interests, let us look to that. Go to the desk again. Take out the drawer—that one on the left hand. So—bring it to me."

The servant obeyed. Law took from his hand the receptacle, and with a sweep of his hand poured out on the table its contents. A mass of glittering gems, diamonds, sapphires, pearls, emeralds, fell and spread over the table top. The light cast out by their thousand facets lit up the surroundings with shimmering, many-colored gleams. The wealth of a kingdom might have been here in the careless possession of this man, whose resources had been absolutely without measure.

"Help yourself, Henri," said Law, calmly, and turned about to his employment among the papers. A moment later he turned again to see his servant still standing motionless.

"Well?" said Law.

"I do not understand," said the Swiss.

"Take what you like," said Law. "I have said it, and I mean it. It is for your pay, because you have been honest, because I understand you as a faithful man."

"But, Monsieur, these things have very great value," said the

Swiss. "Let me ask how is it that you yourself take so little gold along? Does Monsieur purpose to take with him his fortune in gems and jewels instead?"

"By no means. I purpose taking but fifty louis, as I have said."

"Monsieur would have me replace the drawer?"

"How do you mean?"

"Why, I want none of them."

"Why?"

"Because Monsieur wants none of them."

"Fie! Your case is quite different from mine."

"Perhaps, but I want none of them."

"Are you afraid?"

"Monsieur!"

"Do you not think them genuine stones?"

"Assuredly," said the Swiss, "else why should we have cared for them among our gems?"

"Well, then, I command you as your master, to take forth some of these jewels and keep them for your own."

"But no," replied the Swiss. "It is only after Monsieur."

"What? Myself?"

"Assuredly."

"Then, for the sake of precedent," said Law, "let me see. Well, then, I will take one gem, only one. Here, Henri, is the diamond which I brought with me when I came to Paris years ago. It was the sole jewel owned then by my brother and myself, though we had somewhat of gold between us, thanks to this same diamond. It was once my sole capital, in years gone by. Perhaps we may need a carriage through France, and this may serve to pay the hire of a vehicle from one of my late dukes or marquises. Or perhaps at best I may send this same stone across the channel to my brother Will, who has wisely gone to Scotland, or should have departed before this. So, very well, Henri, to oblige you I will take this single stone. Now, do you help yourself."

"Since Monsieur limits himself to so little," said the Swiss, sturdily, "I shall not want more. This little pin will serve me, and I shall wear it long in memory of your many kindnesses."

Law rose to his feet and caught the good fellow by the hand.

"By heaven, I find you of good blood!" said he. "My friend, I thank you. And now put up the box. I shall not counsel you to take more than this. We shall leave the rest for those who will presently come to claim it."

For some time silence reigned in the great room, as Law, deeply engaged in the affairs before him, buried himself in the mass of scattered books and papers. Hour after hour wore on, and at last he turned from his employment. His face showed calm, pale, and furrowed with a sadness which till now had been foreign to it. He arose at last, and with a sweep of his arm pushed back the papers which lay before him.

"There," said he. "This should conclude it all. It should all be plain enough now to those who follow."

"Monsieur is weary," mentioned the faithful attendant. "He would have some refreshment."

"Presently, but I think not here, Henri. My household is not all so faithful as yourself, and I question if we could find cook or servants for the table below. No, we are to leave Paris to-night, Henri, and it is well the journey should begin. Get you down to the stables, and, if you can, have my best coach brought to the front door."

"It may not be quite safe, if Monsieur will permit me to suggest."

"Perhaps not. These fools are so deep in their folly that they do not know their friends. But safe or not, that is the way I shall go. We might slip out through the back door, but 'tis not thus John Law will go from Paris."

The servant departed, and Law, left alone, sat silent and motionless, buried in thought. Now and again his head sank forward, like that of one who has received a deep hurt. But again he drew himself up sternly, and so remained, not leaving his seat nor turning toward the window, beyond which could now be heard the sound of shouting, and cries whose confused and threatening tones might have given ground for the gravest apprehension. At length the Swiss again reported, much agitated and shaken from his ordinary self-control.

"Monsieur," said he, "come. I have at last the coach at the door. Hasten, Monsieur; a crowd is gathering. Indeed, we may meet violence."

Law seemed not to hear him, but sat for a time, his head still bowed, his eyes gazing straight before him.

"But, Monsieur," again broke in the Swiss, anxiously, "if I may interrupt, there is need to hasten. There will be a mob. Our guard is gone."

"So," said Law. "They were afraid?"

"Surely. They fled forthwith when they heard the people below crying out at the house. They are indeed threatening death to yourself. They cry that they will burn the house— that should you appear, they will have your blood at once."

"And are you not afraid?" asked Law.

"I am here. Does not Monsieur fear for himself?"

Law shrugged his shoulders. "There are many of them, and we are but two," said he. "For yourself, go you down the back way and care for your own safety. I will go out the front and meet these good people. Are we quite ready for the journey?"

"Quite ready, as you have directed."

"Have you the two valises, with the one change of clothing?"

"They are here."

"And have you the fifty louis, as I stated?"

"Here in the purse."

"And I think you have also the single diamond."

"It is here."

"Then," said Law, "let us go."

He rose, and scarce looking behind him, even to see that his orders to the servant had been obeyed, he strode down the vast stairway of the great hotel, past many precious works of art, between walls hung with richest tapestries and noble paintings. The click of his heel on a chance bit of exposed marble here and there echoed hollow, as though indeed the master of the palace had been abandoned by all his people. The great building was silent, empty.

"What! Are you, then, here?" he said, seeing the servant had disobeyed his instructions and was following close behind him. He alone out of those scores of servants, those hundreds of fawning nobles, those thousands of sycophant souls who had but lately cringed before him, now accompanied the late master of France as he turned to leave the house in which he no longer held authority.

Without, but the door's thickness from where he stood, there arose a tumult of sound, shouts, cries, imprecations, entreaties, as though the walls of some asylum for the unfortunate had broken away and allowed its inmates to escape unrestrained, irreclaimable, impossible to control.

"Down with Jean L'as! Down with Jean L'as!" rose a cadenced, rhythmic shout, the accord of a mob of Paris beating into its tones. And this steady burden was broken by the cries of "Enter! Enter! Break down the door! Kill the monster! Assassin! Thief! Traitor!" No word of the vocabulary of scorn and loathing was wanting in their cries.

Hearing these cries, the face of this fighting man now grew hot with anger, and now it paled with grief and sorrow. Yet he faltered not, but stepped on, confidently. The Swiss opened the door and stood at the head of the flight of stairs. Tall, calm, pale, fearless, John Law stood facing the angry mob, his eyes shining brightly. He laid his hand for an instant upon his sword, yet it was but to unbuckle the belt. The weapon he left leaning against the wall, and so stepped on down toward the crowd.

He was met by a rush of excited men and women, screaming, cursing, giving vent to inarticulate and indistinguishable speech. A man laid his hand upon his shoulder. Law caught the hand, and with a swift wrench of the wrist, threw the owner of it to the ground. At this the others gave back, and for half a moment silence ensued. The mob lacked just the touch of rage to hurl themselves upon him. He raised his hand and motioned them aside.

"Are you not Jean L'as?" cried one dame, excitedly, waving in his face a handful of the paper shares of the latest issue in the Company of the Indies. "Are you not Jean L'as? Tell me, then, where is my money for these things? What shall I get for this rotten paper?"

"You are Jean L'as, the director-general!" cried a man, pushing up to his side. "'Twas you that ruined the Company. See! Here is all that I have!" He wept as he shook his bunch of paper in John Law's face. "Last week I was worth half a million!" He wept, and tore across, with impotent rage, the bundle of worthless paper.

"Down with Jean L'as! Down with Jean L'as!" came the recurrent cry. A rush followed. The carriage, towering above the ring of the surrounding crowd, showed its coat of arms, and thus was recognized. A paving-stone crashed through its heavy window. A knife ripped up the velvets of the cushions.

The coachman was pulled from his box. The horses, plunging with terror, were cut loose from the pole and led away. With shouts and cries of rage and busy zeal, one madman vied with another in tearing, cutting and destroying the vehicle, until it stood there ruined, without means of locomotion, defaced and useless. And still the ring of desperate humanity closed around him who had late been master of all France.

"What do you want, my friends?" asked he, calmly, as for an instant there came a lull in the tumult. He stood looking at them curiously now, his dulling eyes regarding them as though they presented some new and interesting study. "What is it that you desire?" he repeated.

"We want our money," cried a score of voices. "We want back that which you have stolen."

"You are not exact," replied Law, calmly. "I have not your money, nor yet have I stolen it. If you have suffered by this foolish panic, you do not mend matters by thus treating me. By heaven, you go the wrong way to get anything from me! Out of the way, you *canaille*! Do you think to frighten me? I made your city. I made you all Now, do you think to frighten me, John Law?"

"Oh! You would go away, you want to escape!" cried the voices of those near at hand. "We will see as to that!"

Again they fell upon the carriage, and still they hemmed him in the closer.

"True, I am going away," said Law. "But you can not say that I tried to steal away without your knowing it. There, up the stairs, are my papers. You will see in time that I have concealed nothing. Now I am going to leave Paris, it is true;

but not because I am afraid to stay here. 'Tis for other reason, and reason of mine own."

"'Twas you who ruined Paris—this city which you now seek to leave!" shrieked the dame who had spoken before, still shaking her useless bank-notes in her hand. .

"Oh, very well, my friend. For the argument, let us agree upon that," said Law.

"You ruined our Company, our beautiful Company!" cried another.

"Certainly. Since I was the originator of it, that follows as matter of reason," replied Law.

"Ah, he admits it! He admits it!" cried yet another. "Don't let him escape. Kill him! Down with Jean L'as!"

"We are going to kill you precisely here!" cried a huge fellow, brandishing a paving-stone before his eyes. "You are not fit to live."

"As to that," said Law, "I agree with you perfectly. My hand upon it; I am not fit to live. I have found that I made mistakes. I have found that there is nothing left to desire. I have found out that all this money is not worth the having. I have found out so many things, my very dear friends, that I quite agree with you. For if one must want to live before he is fit to live, then indeed I am not fit. But what then?"

"Kill him! Kill him! Strike him down!" cried out a voice back of the giant with the menacing paving-stone.

"Oh, very well, my friends," resumed the object of their fury, flicking again with his old, careless gesture at the deep cuff of his wrist. "As you like in regard to that. More than one man has offered me that happiness in the past, yet it was many a long year since, any man could trouble me by announcing that he was about to kill me."

Something in the attitude of the man stayed the hands of the most dangerous members of the mob. Yet ever there came the cry from back of them. "Down with Jean L'as! He has ruined everything!"

"Friends," responded Law to this cry, bitterly, "you little know how true you speak. It was indeed John Law who brought ruin to everything. It was indeed he who threw away what was worth more than all the gold in France. It is indeed he who has failed, and failed most utterly. You can not frighten John Law, but you may do as you like with him, for surely he has failed!"

The bitterness of despair was in his tones. Then, perhaps, the sullen, savage crowd had wrought their last act of anger and revenge on him, had it not been for a sudden change in that tide of ill fortune that now seemed to carry him forward to his doom. There came a sound of far-off cries, a distant clacking of hoofs, the clatter of steel, many shouts, entreaties and commands. The close-packed crowd which filled the open space in front of the hotel writhed, twisted, turned and would have sought to resolve itself into groups and individuals. Some cried out that the troops were coming. A detachment of the king's household, sent out to disperse these dangerous gatherings, came full front down the street, as had so often come the arm of the military in this turbulent old city of Paris. Remorselessly they rode over and through the mob, driving them, dispersing them. A moment later, and Law stood almost alone at the steps of his own house. The squadron wheeled, headed by an officer, who rode upon him with sword uplifted as though to cut him down. Law raised his hand at this new menace.

"Stop!" he cried. "I am the cause of this rioting. I am John Law."

"What! Monsieur L'as?" cried the lieutenant. "So the people have found you, have they?"

"It would so seem. They have destroyed my carriage, and they would have killed me," replied Law. "But I perceive it is Captain Mirabec. 'Twas I who got you your commission, as you may remember."

"Is it so?" replied the other, with a grin. "I have no recollection. Since you are Jean L'as, the late director-general, the pity is I did not let the people kill you. You are the cause of the ruin of us all, the cause of my own ruin. Three days more, and I had been a major-general. I had nearly the sum in *actions* ready to pay over at the right place. By our Lady of Grace, I am minded to run you through myself, for a greater villain never set foot in France!"

"Monsieur, I am about to leave France," said Law.

"Oh, you would leave us? You would run away?"

"As you like. But most of all, I am now very weary. I would not remain here longer talking. Henri, where are you?"

The faithful Swiss, who had remained close to his employer all the time, and who had been not far from his side during the scenes just concluded, was in a moment at his side. He hardly reached his master too soon, for as he passed his arm about him, the head of Law sank wearily forward. He might, perhaps, have sunk to the ground had he lacked a supporting arm.

At this moment there came again the sound of hoofs upon the pavement. There was the rush of a mounted outrider, and hard after him sped the horses of a carriage, whose driver pulled up close at the curb and scarce clear of the little group gathered there. The door of the coach was opened, and at it appeared the figure of a woman, who quickly descended from the step.

"What is it?" she cried. "Is not this the residence of Monsieur Law?" The officer saluted, and the few loiterers gave back and made room, as she stepped fully into the street and advanced with decision towards those whom she saw.

"Madam," replied the Swiss, "this is the residence of Monsieur L'as, and this is Monsieur L'as himself. I fear he is taken suddenly ill."

The lady stepped quickly to his side. As she did so, Law, as one not fully hearing, half raised his head. He looked full into her face, and releasing himself from the arms of his servant, stood thus, staring directly at the visitor, his face haggard, his fixed eyes bearing no sign of actual recognition.

"Catharine! Catharine!" he exclaimed. "Oh God, how cruel of you too to mock me! Catharine!"

The unspeakable yearning of the cry went to the heart of her who heard it. She put out a hand and laid it on his forehead. The Swiss motioned toward the house. And even as the officer wheeled his troop to depart, these two again ascended the steps, half carrying between them a stumbling man, who but repeated mumblingly to himself the same words:

"Mockery! Mockery!"

CHAPTER XIII

THE QUALITY OF MERCY

Within the great house there was silence, for the vistas of the wide interior led far back from the street and its tumult; nor did there arise within the walls any sound of voice or footfall. Of the entire household there was but one left to do the master service.

They entered the great hall, passed the foot of the wide stairway, and turned at the first *entresol*, where were seats and couches. The servant paused for a moment and looked inquiringly at the lady with whom he now found himself in company.

"The times are serious," he began. "I would not intrude, Madame, yet perhaps you are aware—"

"I am a friend of monsieur," replied Lady Catharine. "He is ill. See, he is not himself. Tell me, what is this illness?"

"Madame," said the Swiss, gravely, "his illness is that of grief. Monsieur's failure sits heavily upon him."

"How long is it since he slept?" asked the lady, for she noted the drooping head of the man now reclining upon the couch.

"Not for many days and nights," replied the Swiss. "He has for the last few days been under much strain. But shall I not assist you, Madame? You are, perhaps—pardon me, since I do not know your relationship with monsieur—"

"A friend of years ago. I knew Mr. Law when he lived in England."

"I perceive. Perhaps Madame would be alone for a time? If you please, I will seek aid."

They approached the side of the couch. Law's head lay back upon the cushions. His breath came deeply and slowly, not stertorously nor labored.

"How strange," whispered the Swiss, "he sleeps!"

Such was indeed the truth. The iron nature, so long overwrought, now utterly unstrung, had yielded for the first time to the stress of nature and of events. The relief from what he had taken to be death had come swiftly, and the reaction brought a lethal calm of its own. If he had indeed recognized the face of the woman who had touched him with her hand, it was as though he had witnessed her in a vision, a dream bitter and troubled, since it was a dream impossible to be true.

The Swiss looked still hesitatingly at the lady who had thus strangely come upon the scene, noticing her sweet and tender mouth, her cheeks just faintly tinged with pink, her eyes shining with a soft, mysterious radiance. She approached the couch and laid both her hands upon the face of the unconscious man. Tears sprang within her eyes and fell from her dark lashes. The old servant looked up at her, simply.

"Madame would be alone with monsieur?" asked he. "It will

be better."

Lady Catharine Knollys, left alone, gazed upon the sleeper. John Law, the failure, lay there, supine, abased, cast-down, undone, shorn utterly of his old arrogance of mind and mien. Fortune, wealth, even the boon of physical well-being—all had fled from him. The pride of a superb manhood had departed from the lines of this limp figure. The cheeks were lined and sunken, the eye, even had the lid not covered it, lacked the late convincing fire. No longer commanding, no longer strong, no longer gay and debonair, he lay, a man whose fate was failure, as he himself had said.

The woman who stood with clasped hands, gazing at him, tears welling in her eyes—she, so closely linked to his every thought for these many years—well enough she knew the story of his boundless ambitions, now so swiftly ended. Well enough, too, she knew the shortcomings of this mortal man before her. Even as she had in her mirror looked into her own soul, so now she saw deep into his heart as he lay there, helpless, making no further plea for himself, urging no claim, making no explanations nor denials, no asseverations, no promises. Did she indeed see and recognize again, as sometimes gloriously happens in this poor life of ours, that other and inner man, the only one fit to touch a woman's hand—the man who might have been? Did she see this, and greet again the friend of long ago? God, who hath given mercy, remedy alone sufficing for the ill that men may do, He alone may know these things.

Could John Law failing be John Law succeeding, and in his most sublime success? Upon the wreck and ruin of the old nature could there grow another and a better man? Mayhap the answer to this was what the eye of woman saw. How else could there have come into this great room, so late the scene of turbulent activities, this vast and soothing calm? How else could this man's breath come now so deep and regular and content? The angels of God may know, they who drop down the gentle dew of heaven.

An hour passed by. A soft tread came to the door, but Henri heard no sound, and saw only the prone figure of the sleeper, and beside it the form of the woman, who still held his hand in her own. Still the hours wore on, and still the watch continued, there under the mysteries of Life and of Love, of Mercy and of Forgiveness. And so at last the gray dawn broke again. The panes of the high mullioned windows were tinged with splashes of color. The pale light crept into the room, slowly revealing and lighting up its splendors.

With the dawn there came into the heart of Catharine Knollys a flood of light and joy. Why, she knew not; how, she cared not; yet she knew that the shadows were gone. The same tide of peace and calm might have swept into the bosom of the man before her. He stirred, moved. His eyes opened wide, in their gaze wonder and disbelief, yet hope and longing.

"Catharine," he murmured, "Catharine! Is it you? Catharine! Dear Kate!"

She bent over and softly kissed his face. "Dear heart," she whispered, "I have loved you always. Awake. The day has come. There is another world before us. See, I have come to you, dear heart, for Faith, and for Love, and for Hope!"

ABOUT THE AUTHOR

Emerson Hough (1857-1923) was an American author, best known for writing western stories.

Hough was born in Newton, Iowa, and graduated from the University of Iowa with a law degree. He moved to White Oaks, New Mexico, and practiced law there but eventually turned to literary work by taking camping trips and writing about them for publication.

He is best known as a novelist, writing The Mississippi Bubble as well as The Covered Wagon, about Oregon Trail pioneers, which later became successful as a movie, running 59 weeks at the Criterion Theater in New York City, passing the record set by Birth of a Nation. Other notable works included Story of the Cowboy, Way of the West, Singing Mouse Stories, and Passing of the Frontier, and writing the "Out-of-Doors" column for the Saturday Evening Post.

Hough was also a conservationist, and was the catalyst behind a law passed by the U.S. Congress to protect the buffalo in Yellowstone National Park. He married Charlotte Chesebro of Chicago in 1897 and made that city his home.

Choose from Thousands of 1stWorldLibrary Classics By

A. M. Barnard
Ada Leverson
Adolphus William Ward
Aesop
Agatha Christie
Alexander Aaronsohn
Alexander Kielland
Alexandre Dumas
Alfred Gatty
Alfred Ollivant
Alice Duer Miller
Alice Turner Curtis
Alice Dunbar
Allen Chapman
Alleyne Ireland
Ambrose Bierce
Amelia E. Barr
Amory H. Bradford
Andrew Lang
Andrew McFarland Davis
Andy Adams
Angela Brazil
Anna Alice Chapin
Anna Sewell
Annie Besant
Annie Hamilton Donnell
Annie Payson Call
Annie Roe Carr
Annonaymous
Anton Chekhov
Archibald Lee Fletcher
Arnold Bennett
Arthur C. Benson
Arthur Conan Doyle
Arthur M. Winfield
Arthur Ransome
Arthur Schnitzler
Arthur Train
Atticus
B.H. Baden-Powell
B. M. Bower
B. C. Chatterjee
Baroness Emmuska Orczy
Baroness Orczy
Basil King
Bayard Taylor
Ben Macomber
Bertha Muzzy Bower
Bjornstjerne Bjornson

Booth Tarkington
Boyd Cable
Bram Stoker
C. Collodi
C. E. Orr
C. M. Ingleby
Carolyn Wells
Catherine Parr Traill
Charles A. Eastman
Charles Amory Beach
Charles Dickens
Charles Dudley Warner
Charles Farrar Browne
Charles Ives
Charles Kingsley
Charles Klein
Charles Hanson Towne
Charles Lathrop Pack
Charles Romyn Dake
Charles Whibley
Charles Willing Beale
Charlotte M. Braeme
Charlotte M. Yonge
Charlotte Perkins Stetson
Clair W. Hayes
Clarence Day Jr.
Clarence E. Mulford
Clemence Housman
Confucius
Coningsby Dawson
Cornelis DeWitt Wilcox
Cyril Burleigh
D. H. Lawrence
Daniel Defoe
David Garnett
Dinah Craik
Don Carlos Janes
Donald Keyhoe
Dorothy Kilner
Dougan Clark
Douglas Fairbanks
E. Nesbit
E. P. Roe
E. Phillips Oppenheim
E. S. Brooks
Earl Barnes
Edgar Rice Burroughs
Edith Van Dyne
Edith Wharton

Edward Everett Hale
Edward J. O'Biren
Edward S. Ellis
Edwin L. Arnold
Eleanor Atkins
Eleanor Hallowell Abbott
Eliot Gregory
Elizabeth Gaskell
Elizabeth McCracken
Elizabeth Von Arnim
Ellem Key
Emerson Hough
Emilie F. Carlen
Emily Bronte
Emily Dickinson
Enid Bagnold
Enilor Macartney Lane
Erasmus W. Jones
Ernie Howard Pie
Ethel May Dell
Ethel Turner
Ethel Watts Mumford
Eugene Sue
Eugenie Foa
Eugene Wood
Eustace Hale Ball
Evelyn Everett-green
Everard Cotes
F. H. Cheley
F. J. Cross
F. Marion Crawford
Fannie E. Newberry
Federick Austin Ogg
Ferdinand Ossendowski
Fergus Hume
Florence A. Kilpatrick
Fremont B. Deering
Francis Bacon
Francis Darwin
Frances Hodgson Burnett
Frances Parkinson Keyes
Frank Gee Patchin
Frank Harris
Frank Jewett Mather
Frank L. Packard
Frank V. Webster
Frederic Stewart Isham
Frederick Trevor Hill
Frederick Winslow Taylor

Friedrich Kerst
Friedrich Nietzsche
Fyodor Dostoyevsky
G.A. Henty
G.K. Chesterton
Gabrielle E. Jackson
Garrett P. Serviss
Gaston Leroux
George A. Warren
George Ade
Geroge Bernard Shaw
George Cary Eggleston
George Durston
George Ebers
George Eliot
George Gissing
George MacDonald
George Meredith
George Orwell
George Sylvester Viereck
George Tucker
George W. Cable
George Wharton James
Gertrude Atherton
Gordon Casserly
Grace E. King
Grace Gallatin
Grace Greenwood
Grant Allen
Guillermo A. Sherwell
Gulielma Zollinger
Gustav Flaubert
H. A. Cody
H. B. Irving
H.C. Bailey
H. G. Wells
H. H. Munro
H. Irving Hancock
H. R. Naylor
H. Rider Haggard
H. W. C. Davis
Haldeman Julius
Hall Caine
Hamilton Wright Mabie
Hans Christian Andersen
Harold Avery
Harold McGrath
Harriet Beecher Stowe
Harry Castlemon
Harry Coghill
Harry Houidini

Hayden Carruth
Helent Hunt Jackson
Helen Nicolay
Hendrik Conscience
Hendy David Thoreau
Henri Barbusse
Henrik Ibsen
Henry Adams
Henry Ford
Henry Frost
Henry James
Henry Jones Ford
Henry Seton Merriman
Henry W Longfellow
Herbert A. Giles
Herbert Carter
Herbert N. Casson
Herman Hesse
Hildegard G. Frey
Homer
Honore De Balzac
Horace B. Day
Horace Walpole
Horatio Alger Jr.
Howard Pyle
Howard R. Garis
Hugh Lofting
Hugh Walpole
Humphry Ward
Ian Maclaren
Inez Haynes Gillmore
Irving Bacheller
Isabel Cecilia Williams
Isabel Hornibrook
Israel Abrahams
Ivan Turgenev
J.G.Austin
J. Henri Fabre
J. M. Barrie
J. M. Walsh
J. Macdonald Oxley
J. R. Miller
J. S. Fletcher
J. S. Knowles
J. Storer Clouston
J. W. Duffield
Jack London
Jacob Abbott
James Allen
James Andrews
James Baldwin

James Branch Cabell
James DeMille
James Joyce
James Lane Allen
James Lane Allen
James Oliver Curwood
James Oppenheim
James Otis
James R. Driscoll
Jane Abbott
Jane Austen
Jane L. Stewart
Janet Aldridge
Jens Peter Jacobsen
Jerome K. Jerome
Jessie Graham Flower
John Buchan
John Burroughs
John Cournos
John F. Kennedy
John Gay
John Glasgworthy
John Habberton
John Joy Bell
John Kendrick Bangs
John Milton
John Philip Sousa
John Taintor Foote
Jonas Lauritz Idemil Lie
Jonathan Swift
Joseph A. Altsheler
Joseph Carey
Joseph Conrad
Joseph E. Badger Jr
Joseph Hergesheimer
Joseph Jacobs
Jules Vernes
Julian Hawthrone
Julie A Lippmann
Justin Huntly McCarthy
Kakuzo Okakura
Karle Wilson Baker
Kate Chopin
Kenneth Grahame
Kenneth McGaffey
Kate Langley Bosher
Kate Langley Bosher
Katherine Cecil Thurston
Katherine Stokes
L. A. Abbot
L. T. Meade

L. Frank Baum
Latta Griswold
Laura Dent Crane
Laura Lee Hope
Laurence Housman
Lawrence Beasley
Leo Tolstoy
Leonid Andreyev
Lewis Carroll
Lewis Sperry Chafer
Lilian Bell
Lloyd Osbourne
Louis Hughes
Louis Joseph Vance
Louis Tracy
Louisa May Alcott
Lucy Fitch Perkins
Lucy Maud Montgomery
Luther Benson
Lydia Miller Middleton
Lyndon Orr
M. Corvus
M. H. Adams
Margaret E. Sangster
Margret Howth
Margaret Vandercook
Margaret W. Hungerford
Margret Penrose
Maria Edgeworth
Maria Thompson Daviess
Mariano Azuela
Marion Polk Angellotti
Mark Overton
Mark Twain
Mary Austin
Mary Catherine Crowley
Mary Cole
Mary Hastings Bradley
Mary Roberts Rinehart
Mary Rowlandson
M. Wollstonecraft Shelley
Maud Lindsay
Max Beerbohm
Myra Kelly
Nathaniel Hawthrone
Nicolo Machiavelli
O. F. Walton
Oscar Wilde

Owen Johnson
P.G. Wodehouse
Paul and Mabel Thorne
Paul G. Tomlinson
Paul Severing
Percy Brebner
Percy Keese Fitzhugh
Peter B. Kyne
Plato
Quincy Allen
R. Derby Holmes
R. L. Stevenson
R. S. Ball
Rabindranath Tagore
Rahul Alvares
Ralph Bonehill
Ralph Henry Barbour
Ralph Victor
Ralph Waldo Emmerson
Rene Descartes
Ray Cummings
Rex Beach
Rex E. Beach
Richard Harding Davis
Richard Jefferies
Richard Le Gallienne
Robert Barr
Robert Frost
Robert Gordon Anderson
Robert L. Drake
Robert Lansing
Robert Lynd
Robert Michael Ballantyne
Robert W. Chambers
Rosa Nouchette Carey
Rudyard Kipling
Saint Augustine
Samuel B. Allison
Samuel Hopkins Adams
Sarah Bernhardt
Sarah C. Hallowell
Selma Lagerlof
Sherwood Anderson
Sigmund Freud
Standish O'Grady
Stanley Weyman
Stella Benson
Stella M. Francis

Stephen Crane
Stewart Edward White
Stijn Streuvels
Swami Abhedananda
Swami Parmananda
T. S. Ackland
T. S. Arthur
The Princess Der Ling
Thomas A. Janvier
Thomas A Kempis
Thomas Anderton
Thomas Bailey Aldrich
Thomas Bulfinch
Thomas De Quincey
Thomas Dixon
Thomas H. Huxley
Thomas Hardy
Thomas More
Thornton W. Burgess
U. S. Grant
Upton Sinclair
Valentine Williams
Various Authors
Vaughan Kester
Victor Appleton
Victor G. Durham
Victoria Cross
Virginia Woolf
Wadsworth Camp
Walter Camp
Walter Scott
Washington Irving
Wilbur Lawton
Wilkie Collins
Willa Cather
Willard F. Baker
William Dean Howells
William le Queux
W. Makepeace Thackeray
William W. Walter
William Shakespeare
Winston Churchill
Yei Theodora Ozaki
Yogi Ramacharaka
Young E. Allison
Zane Grey

www.ingramcontent.com/pod-product-compliance
Lightning Source LLC
Chambersburg PA
CBHW032136270626
47172CB00008B/84